THE HEMINGWAY DECEPTION

Tj O'CONNOR

SUSPENSE PUBLISHING

THE HEMINGWAY DECEPTION
by
Tj O'Connor

PAPERBACK EDITION
* * * * *
PUBLISHED BY:
Suspense Publishing

COPYRIGHT
2023 Tj O'Connor

PUBLISHING HISTORY:
Suspense Publishing, Paperback and Digital Copy, March 2023

ISBN: 979-8-218-10332-3

Cover Design: Shannon Raab
Cover Photographer: shutterstock/ Borka Kiss
Cover Photographer: shutterstock/ Lucky-photographer

For Jan O.
Friend, Critic, and Sort-of Stepmom
One of the Strongest, Finest Ladies I Ever Knew.

PRAISE FOR
THE HEMINGWAY DECEPTION

"Great characters, non-stop action, a twisted plot, and exotic locations—*The Hemingway Deception* is exactly what an international thriller should be. Couldn't put it down."
—DP Lyle, Award-Winning Author of the *Jake Longly* and *Cain/Harper* Thriller Series

"*A* rollercoaster ride of international intrigue, governmental deception and the meaning of family. Tj O'Connor's real-life knowledge of geopolitical affairs shines through on every quick-turning page. Bravo!"
—Matt Coyle, Author of the Bestselling *Rick Cahill* Crime Series

"There are no wimps in this fast-paced thriller, male or female. The relentless action will have you flying through the pages, eager to know what happens next."
—Terry Shames, Author of the Award-Winning *Samuel Craddock* Series

"A riveting 'ripped from the headlines' international thriller: Two women fighting for what they believe; a horrifying assassination plot; deadly enemies, including some in our own government; and a mysterious operative named Hemingway who must be found. O'Connor, a real life anti-terrorism expert, takes us on a roller coaster ride of action, intrigue, betrayal and stunning twists in *The Hemingway Deception*. Read it!"
—R.G. Belsky, Award-Winning Author of the *Clare Carlson* Series

"Tj O'Connor does it again in *The Hemingway Deception*. His action-packed writing is founded in real-world experience with anti-terrorism and threat analysis consulting. This time, he adds kick-ass women to the mix, building in multiple layers of complexity often overlooked in thrillers."
—Dawn Brotherton, Author of the *Jackie Austin Mysteries* and *Eastover Treasures*

"O'Connor brings together his background as an intelligence officer and consultant with deep experience in the field of counterterrorism for a riveting story that takes the reader on a trip through the urban ghettos and steaming jungles of Latin America—not to mention those in Washington, D.C.—that have become the playing fields of modern terrorism, narco-trafficking, and nasty geopolitics. O'Connor has a feel for the impact and challenges this work can have for those who inhabit this world, not only on their lives but also on those they love, a human dimension that is often lacking in other portrayals. Definitely recommended reading."
—Bill Rapp, CIA Veteran and Author of the *Cold War* Thriller Series with Coffeetown Press

"*The Hemingway Deception* is a fast paced political thriller that grabs the reader early and won't let go…a masterfully written political thriller the reader will devour."
—Larry Enmon, U.S. Secret Service (Ret.) and Author of *Worst Case Scenario*

"Subterfuge reigns supreme in Tj O'Connor's latest page-turning thriller, *The Hemingway Deception*. With government operatives and assassins at every turn the stakes literally couldn't be higher. Highly recommended!"
— Bruce Robert Coffin, Award-Winning Author of the *Detective Byron Mysteries*

"From the plush offices of Washington, D.C. to the steaming jungles of Central America; from Havana to the U.S. border, Tj

O'Connor proves he is an author with a clear handle on his terrain, and the expertise to craft a first-class spy thriller. O'Connor deftly weaves a plot that pits powerful domestic political alliances against Latin American ideologies that erupt in sudden and unexpected violence as both factions compete in the hunt for a nearly-mythical covert operative code-named 'Hemingway.' *The Hemingway Deception* is a genuine spy novel with all the trimmings: there is treachery, intrigue and violence aplenty…and of course, deceit. It has a plot that's whiplash-quick, and moves faster than the speed of deception itself."
—Baron R. Birtcher, Award-Winning Author of *Reckoning*

"*The Hemingway Deception* is a thriller for any reader wanting to be that fly on the wall. O'Connor never leaves the reader behind. And the denouement, beyond superb."
—Thomas Sloan, Retired Secret Service Agent and Author of
Bratva's Rose Tattoo and *Guardians of Democracy*

"A wildly imaginative non-stop twisting thrill ride. Tj O'Connor's *The Hemingway Deception* reels you in from the start. Full of suspense and surprises right to the end, this is a page turner you won't be able to put down. O'Connor nails it!"
—David Sears, Retired USN, Former SEAL and Author of
Smarter Not Harder

"Tj O'Connor takes the reader on a fast-paced journey of international intrigue, laced with the dangers of criminal cartels and hostile intelligence operatives, overlayed with the even more despicable actions of American politicians. Tj spins a story that twists and turns and navigates through the jungles of Central and South America, as well as the halls of government agencies in Washington, DC. A well-written and suspenseful book by a master author with years of personal experience navigating the very agencies and situations that he writes about."
—Gregory Olmstead, Retired U.S. Military Intelligence Officer,
Federal Law Enforcement Officer, and Former USG Senior
Advisor on Anti-terrorism

Ana Karras is running from her past.
Catalina Reyes is running toward hers.
Two deadly women—one treacherous mission.
A Cuba-America war is at stake.
Why does everyone want them both dead?
The answer is simple...Hemingway.

THE HEMINGWAY DECEPTION

Tj O'CONNOR

1

June 1, Midday–Central Park, Manhattan, New York

Deception is the sword of the cunning. A tool. A weapon. It's the strategy of a provocateur—a method to cause one's opponent to wreak havoc upon themselves while concealing one's true endgame. Other times, it's a mask used by the desperate for simple survival. It's an escape.

Ana Karras knew about deception and provocation. She knew about strategy and survival, too. She was a student of both with mixed results. Her entire life up to this moment had been about survival, often as a result of deception. Other times, she'd survived by sheer will and, most importantly, luck.

Pain.

A sharp, phantom-finger began a slow, agonizing trek along Ana's left side and across her belly. It followed the path—lines of ugly scars—just as the blade had weeks before. She cringed and reflexively caressed her stomach to ease the discomfort—subconscious spasms reminding her of her near-death at the hands of a predator.

In a moment it passed. It always did.

She sighed and gazed over Central Park, focusing on children playing in the distance, willing the pain into exile. It came less each day—some days, only once or twice—and then, only for brief moments. A sign both the body and the mind were healing.

Now, if only her memory would heal.

Ana was thirty but had experienced a great deal for her years—an adventurer by heart, a fighter by trade, and a survivor by choice. Her flowing auburn hair and big, dark Latina eyes favored her Cuban father. Her figure—curvaceous and full—was a gift from her mother's Greek heritage, with skin a rich almond that blended her dual heritage into an exotic, sensual tone.

It had been only a week since she'd begun to feel pretty again. Her ordeal in the jungle had nearly taken her life and left her thin and withered. Slowly, she'd regained enough weight to fill out her jeans and cotton blouse so they weren't too baggy. Her cheekbones and legs had lost their gaunt appearance. Only recently had she rekindled normalcy.

For the past few weeks, she had convalesced along Central Park's paths and greens. Without the love of a small, abandoned child and her stray dog, she wasn't sure she would have even returned to New York. Still, she had, and every day had made her stronger, less afraid, more ready to begin life again. It took nearly a month after waking in a nearby private hangar—bandaged and strapped to a gurney—to regain pieces of her former self. As she healed, haunting memories began to drift into her thoughts. Confused memories at first. Nightmares now—wispy vignettes of pain and danger.

Mamá and Pappa. The jungle camps. Colombia…*Cabrera.*

Despite all that had happened to her, she wouldn't give up. As soon as her memories were clear and her body capable, she would return to Colombia and find her parents. She'd bring them home and help them rebuild their lives away from the jungle camps. Most importantly, bring them home to escape their past. All their pasts.

Start life again. A simpler life. A saner life.

"I'll find you, Mamá and Pappa," she whispered to herself. "Both of you."

A ball nearly too big for the thin dog's mouth rolled into the tall grass near a stand of Hemlock trees beside the walking path. The scruffy-faced, mix-breed tried desperately to follow it, but the leash reigned him back until his master released the brake and allowed a few more feet of the line.

"Lobo's doing so good, isn't he?" the little light-skinned, reddish-haired Latina called, struggling to control the three-legged dog now rutting in the grass for his ball. "Don't you think, Aunty Ana?"

"Aunty" was a faux title—a ruse to deflect unwanted questions. There was no blood between Sarah and her. No lineage. No history. They'd met at a dusty roadside gas station two months ago. Days later, they'd survived the horrific attack that left Lobo and Ana close to death. In their short time together, they'd formed a bond that Ana refused to relinquish. Sarah was alone in the world. So was Ana—nearly. Neither would be alone again.

Not after Cabrera.

"Yes, Sarah. Lobo is doing very well." Ana caressed the scar along her belly, soothing the lingering discomfort. The knife attack had proven vicious and painful, but many of the wounds had been superficial. One was not. Luck and a stranger—just a faint image logged in her memory—had saved their lives. Now, each time her finger traced the thin, red lines across her body, she prayed the scars would heed her caress and fade to nothing, forever.

In time. Soon. One day.

She looked down at Sarah and gripped the seven-year-old's hand to keep her from being yanked into the weeds by Lobo. "You must control him."

"I'm trying. He's so strong."

Sarah tugged on the leash and Lobo appeared from the tall weeds, ball in mouth. He hobbled back onto the walking path, virtually immune to his handicap, wagging wildly. As Sarah beckoned him, he scampered on his remaining legs and wheezed a bit from the exertion. A dark scar, all but hidden in his fur, adorned his shoulder where his front left leg should be. A bullet had shattered the leg as he protected Sarah from Ana's assailant. A second bullet had glanced off his chest and left only torn muscle and flesh. The dog was saved by a hasty aim. Like Ana, he had survived for two reasons: Sarah and the stranger. Before they had found the dog wandering Cabrera's streets, he'd survived alone for who knew how long. Sarah instantly adopted him, just as Ana had her. His love for the girl had carried him through the attack and his recovery.

Now, like Ana walking the park, Lobo was once again playing ball.

Ana giggled as Lobo refused to return the ball to Sarah. Who had saved them in Colombia, she didn't know. She couldn't remember. Just a dark silhouette standing above her. A soft, kind voice. A gentle hand on hers. The compassion to save Lobo.

"Ana?" A voice shook her from her thoughts.

She turned to see a gray-haired, stunning woman approaching along the path. Her maternal grandmother—Yiayia Poppi—was still beautiful at seventy-five. Her thoughtful, strong character was as young as a woman half her age. Poppi was a 'Yiayia'—a grandmother—a Greek badge of honor.

"You were somewhere else just then. Remember something?" Poppi asked. "Anything new?"

"Not really, Yiayia. Now and then a flash of memory. Nothing else." The voids unnerved her still. "I wish there was more. I have so many questions."

"You should never have gone there." Poppi faced her squarely. "He is not worth it. You were nearly killed—*again*."

"Stop it. I was there searching for Mamá *and* Pappa."

"Your father is trouble."

"And Mamá?"

"Yes, Irena. Time will tell, I suppose." Sadness filled Poppi's face. "Your father took her from me years ago. She made her choices then. I pray things will be different for you. That is why your grandfather took care of you before he died, Ana. He wanted you to be different."

"And I'm disappointing him." Ana looked away as regret washed over her. She'd never met Theo Karras—a successful New York restauranteur. He'd died a year before Ana made her first trip to Queens to meet him and Poppi. But Theo had loved her, nonetheless. He'd left her a sizable trust that paid her travel to and from Queens in the summers, and for her college education. Even after graduating, there was still enough principle remaining to live on for the next few years. She would soon find employment and save some for Sarah's future education.

"Your grandfather would love you no matter what. As I have. Just as I love Irena no matter what."

"I have to find them, Yiayia Poppi." It troubled her how much hate Poppi held toward her father. "If I hadn't gone looking for them, I never would have found Sarah. Who would have rescued her? Who would be her family now?"

Poppi raised a finger to make a point, but lowered it quickly. "Yes, Sarah is a godsend. I wish I could thank whoever saved you all."

Ana agreed.

"If you remember anything more, you will tell me, won't you?"

"Of course. Even with your scolding."

Poppi changed the subject and looked down at Sarah trying to pry the ball from Lobo's mouth. "Sarah, what would you like to do now?"

"Ice cream." She gave up the ball with a big, spreading smile. "Lobo needs some, too. Can we?"

"Lobo needs ice cream?" Ana knelt and pulled Sarah to her, kissing her cheeks until she giggled and pulled away. "Are you trying to bribe him for his ball?"

Sarah shrugged. "Maybe."

"I need ice cream, too," Poppi said. "Ice cream is therapeutic."

Sarah beamed. "Lobo's hot, Aunty Ana. Running on three legs makes him need ice cream. Ice cream is *temapewdic*."

"Yes, ice cream it is, Koúkla." Ana released her to Poppi. "There's a nice stand just over the hill."

"I like when you call me Koúkla, Aunty Ana." Sarah giggled. "I never had a nickname before." Then, her eyes softened; her voice fell to a whisper. "But I want a real last name, too."

Ana pulled her close again. "You are a Karras now, Sarah. And I am your aunty."

"Thank you, Aunty Ana." Sarah clutched her tightly with one arm, squeezing Poppi's hand with the other. "I love you both."

Ana basked in the child's affection. If only she'd shared this love with her own mamá even once, perhaps her life would be different somehow. Instead, she'd only had bitter memories and wishes. But she had Sarah now, and that was worth the pain she'd endured.

"Giving you our name is a sign of love, Sarah. As is giving you the nickname, Koúkla mou,"—my doll, Poppi said. "All the women in my family had nicknames."

Sarah turned her eyes up to Ana. "What was yours, Aunty Ana?"

"I don't recall."

"*Paidí Diávolos*," Poppi said, winking. "It means the 'Devil Child.'"

"Because she was bad a lot, Yiayia Poppi?" Sarah asked. "When she was young like me?"

The happiness drained from Poppi's face. "I did not see Aunty Ana very much when she was your age, Sarah. Not very much at all."

"I was bad sometimes." Ana shot a cautionary glance at Poppi, but said to Sarah, "Maybe a lot."

Sarah's face scrunched up. "Koúkla is Greece?"

"It is Greek, Sarah," Poppi said. "We are all Greek in this family."

"But I'm, ah…" Sarah wrinkled her nose. "Latin, ah…"

"Latina," Ana said. "You are part Colombian and part American—I think. I am part Latina, too. My mamá is Greek-American. My pappa is Cuban."

"Greek? Cuban?" Sarah's face showed concern. "Aunty Ana, where are your mamá and pappa?"

"I don't know." Ana knelt to answer her. "They got lost in Colombia, Sarah. I went looking for them. That is how I found you."

"I wish my mamá and pappa were just lost." Sarah's face saddened and her eyes glistened with sudden tears. "Not dead."

The words brought tears to Ana's eyes, too, and for a long moment, she hugged Sarah tightly. "I know, little one. Perhaps, just perhaps, that is why I found you. Because we are the same. Now we are together."

Sarah pulled back from Ana and a big, warm smile blossomed on her face. "I'm so glad you found me, Aunty Ana. I love you."

"I love you, too."

"Enough of the sad talk," Poppi said. "Greek, Cuban, Colombian…we are all Americans."

Ana took Lobo's leash. "I'll take the beast. Get your ice cream."

"Ice cream, ice cream," Sarah chanted. "Let's go."

As they walked off, Sarah chanted some Greek rhyme Poppi was teaching her. A few steps later, she turned, smiled, and waved back at Ana. Then she skipped out of sight over a knoll on the path a hundred feet away.

Ana had many happy memories of skipping and singing in the park alongside Poppi. Each summer, after her ninth birthday, she'd returned from Colombia to Queens every year to visit. Poppi crammed nine months of absence into each summer. There were picnics in the park, trips to museums, theater—everything completely opposite of the hot, dangerous life she had in the Colombian jungle. Those few weeks each year fused them together, stronger than any other traditional family life could.

"Come, Lobo." Ana tried to pull him from the tall grass, but he wouldn't budge. "Lobo, come here. Sarah will be back soon, I promise."

The dog went rigid. His tail lowered and his teeth bared. This was not the angst from Sarah leaving. It was something else.

Someone else.

Three men crested the knoll where Sarah and Poppi had just passed. They stopped, and for a few moments, looked behind them down the path toward Sarah and Poppi. Finally, they turned and continued her way.

The three walked in a staggered line. Two square-framed Latinos walked front and rear, both wearing suits and dark sunglasses. Between them was a heavier Latino—a robust man—in khaki slacks, a dark, button-down dress shirt, and a wide-brimmed Panama hat.

That man? Her belly scars tingled.

Panama Hat wore large aviator sunglasses that, along with the hat sitting low on his brow, helped obscure part of his face. He stopped abruptly at a path intersection a few yards from where she sat, glanced around, and spoke quietly to the man ahead of him. His escorts stopped in unison, holding their position as though fixed in place by some unseen barricade surrounding them. Panama Hat looked at Ana, spoke again to his cohorts, laughed, and continued forward.

A shiver unsettled her. Icy fingers gripped her spine and began the climb upward, chilling her body and snagging her breath.

What was it about him? Something familiar. Disturbing. Her scars suddenly burned and sent hot needles deep inside her soul.

These men…what is it, Ana?

They grew closer.

Lobo moved beside Ana and lowered into a protective crouch. He snarled through bared teeth. He quivered, readying for battle.

"No, Lobo. It's all right." *Was it?*

The dog trembled, rose and crouched—stepped forward and retreated—refusing to obey her commands. His eyes locked on the large man.

"What a silly dog," Panama Hat said to her as they came closer. "He manages on three legs?"

"He does quite fine." Heat raced through her as the man's voice sent alarms off. "Do I know you?"

"I don't know." He cocked his head. "Do you?"

"I…I'm unsure." Something about him was too familiar—something threatening and dark. A voice and image that hovered just beyond her memory, taunting her. "You're familiar. Yes, I think…."

"You are mistaken." He gestured to his men and they moved on.

As they passed on the far side of the path, Panama Hat turned and glared at Lobo. He gave Ana a thin, cynical grin as he removed his sunglasses and looked squarely at her.

Their eyes met.

Fire. Pain. No. No. No.

A storm exploded and a wave of memories were unleashed. Lightning erupted in her thoughts. Images swirled and combined, like a tornado touching down. A recollection…a man standing over her as she lay on her back, her body enveloped in pain. The searing stab of steel penetrated her side. Punches. Kicks. She felt life draining from her belly. Darkness tried to claim her as the cold enveloped her. Voices and shapes whirled and settled into firm memories. The man standing over her spoke her name—*he knew her.* He ordered someone to "finish her" as he watched her cut and beaten. That man…

Panama Hat.

No, Ana. Could it be?

He was here, watching her from the walking path twenty feet away.

Here?

Alarm bells clanged as the past collided with the present. She started to rise from the bench but stopped, dizzy and uncertain. She pulled Lobo close against her legs and held his collar. Her breath refused to come. Her scars turned into trails of fire.

No. Not him. Not here...how?

Panama Hat continued to stare, wearing a thin, taunting grin. He spoke to his men; they turned and stared, as well.

She focused on only him, trying to find something to prove he was not her nightmare. Another wave of nausea gripped her.

Nine, nine, nine.

A cluster of dark reddish scars—the pattern of the number nine—disfigured his right cheek. A grotesque blemish that sent black spots across her eyes and weakened her to a near-faint.

Nine, nine, nine.

Colonel Vergara. He was here.

Nine, nine, nine.

Her scars burned so hot now that she grabbed her side, bent forward, and muffled a cry. Like dawn breaking, the dark shroud that'd cloaked her thoughts lifted and floated away. Another rush of thoughts commenced. Faces and words. Deeds and misdeeds. Angst and terror.

Colombia. Cabrera. Colonel Vergara—the man that nearly killed her.

Nine, nine, nine.

2

TWO MONTHS EARLIER

April 4, Late Afternoon–Cabrera Village, Antioquia Department, Northeastern Colombia Near the Panama Border

Ana stood in the swirling dust among dozens of other Cabrera villagers gathered in the square. They had been herded like cattle by soldiers in black uniforms. All around them, military trucks rolled through the streets. Masked soldiers searched homes and shops. They gathered up occupants and added them to the pack. No one dared challenge the men—no one Ana heard, at least.

She dared not. If these men discovered her secret—her true identity—two things were certain: She would never find her parents, and she would never leave Colombia again. Both outcomes would be because she was dead.

Though Ana Karras was not known in Colombia, Ana Montilla was—notoriously. Ana Karras and Ana Montilla were two sides to the same coin. She was born in Colombia and raised in jungle guerrilla camps—a beautiful, intelligent girl honed by tough comrades and dangerous surroundings. Raised as one of them, Ana Montilla was a jungle fighter. A strong, daring woman whose fearlessness had often invited more danger than necessary. She was often impulsive, reckless, and tenacious. Traits feared in the camp's men. Traits unexpected in her.

Ana Montilla was the woman Ana Karras loathed to become again. She had left that life—and her alter ego—behind eight years ago. Recently, Ana Karras had returned to South America to find her parents, and wherever she went, Ana Montilla followed.

That was the one fact about her former life that gave Ana the most angst—that Ana Montilla constantly simmered just below her skin, waiting for the right time, the right situation to take control of her life once again. The opportunity to pull her back into a life of chaos and violence. For years, she'd kept *that Ana* locked and hidden away—a demon remanded to the underworld, tethered to the past.

Looking around Cabrera now, she feared those bonds might be broken and the demon would be released.

Beside her, seven-year-old Sarah—an orphaned child found wandering alone and afraid—clutched her leg with one hand and held tightly to a scruffy dog's leash with the other. The dog stood rock-still in front of them both, teeth bared, growling a warning.

"No, Lobo," Ana whispered. "Easy, boy."

Sarah threw her arms around his neck. "Lobo, stay with me. Miss Ana will protect us."

"Sarah," Ana whispered, "it will be all right."

"Yes, Miss Ana." Sarah wiped tears away, nearly dropping Lobo's leash. "Me and Lobo aren't afraid."

"Good." Ana pulled the child tighter against her. "Stay close."

A short, lumpy, unshaven man turned from a group of soldiers standing near one of the trucks. He adjusted the gun belt riding low on his hip like a television gunslinger and smoothed his black combat uniform. With a casual, almost Hollywood-like gesture, he adjusted his dark sunglasses and strode toward her. He stopped an arm's length away and took his time looking her over—slow and probing—leaving her feeling dirty and violated.

Lobo strained against his leash and snapped at him, but the man kicked a boot of sand at him. The dog growled again, and the man took a cautious step back.

"I am Major Alberto Gonzales Nicasio," he said in Spanish.

"Who are you and why are you in my town?"

Do not make things worse, Ana. Keep to your cover story.

"Major Nicasio, I am Ana Karras." She dropped her eyes and played innocent. "I am here to—"

"Wait." Major Nicasio snapped a finger at one of his men. "Tomãs, could she be the one?"

"Un minuto, Major." Tomãs, a large, bulky soldier hiding behind sunglasses, pulled out a cell phone from his uniform pocket. He tapped on the screen, pincered his fingers, and brought up a photograph. He handed the phone to the major. "She resembles her, yes. But I am unsure."

Ana glanced at Tomãs. His Spanish was different than the others. Different than Major Nicasio's. She knew the varied Colombian accents and dialects. Tomãs's was not Colombian; it was…Cubano. As she listened to the other soldiers speaking nearby, it struck her they were Cuban, too.

What were Cuban soldiers doing in Colombia?

Major Nicasio studied her, then the photo on the cell phone, and studied her again. He made the comparison several times before shaking his head.

"No, Tomãs, she is not the one." He turned the phone toward Ana. "Have you seen this woman, señorita?"

The picture was of a young, pretty Latina in a military uniform—a Cuban military uniform. The woman bore some resemblance to her—pretty, dark haired, with a slender face. She appeared a little older than Ana, but shared the dark, Cuban accents in her eyes.

"No," she said. "I have not."

"Pity." Major Nicasio turned to Tomãs. "Search her."

Tomãs stepped forward and gestured for her to raise her hands. The moment he reached for her, Lobo lunged at him and sent him back-stepping to the merriment of the other soldiers looking on. He instantly pulled a long-bladed knife from his gun belt.

Sarah cried, "Stop it. Leave my dog alone."

"Forgive me, Major," Ana said, pulling Lobo back, closer to Sarah. "The little dog is afraid. We are all afraid."

Major Nicasio waved to one of his men who snatched the leash and dragged Lobo aside.

"No, he's my dog," Sarah cried. "Give him back."

Ana touched her shoulder. "It is all right, Sarah. They will not hurt him."

"As long as he minds himself." Tomãs sheathed his knife and stepped close again, nudging Ana's arms into the air. When she slowly complied, he grinned. His hands moved from her shoulders, down each arm in a slithering trail. At her wrists, they ventured to her hips and began a slower, deeper probe of her body. They moved around her back to her buttocks and returned to her round, full bosom where he kneaded and grabbed, all the while mumbling his admiration.

The other soldiers murmured and cajoled one another.

Ana was thankful she couldn't see Tomãs's eyes behind his dark sunglasses. She knew he was staring and lusting as he groped her. She knew if she saw those eyes, her control might wane, and Ana Montilla might strike out.

"I have no weapons." Ana stepped back. "Por favor, the child. This is not necessary."

"Don't move." Tomãs grabbed her arms and pulled her back into position. He continued his probing down each leg and up her thighs, rubbing her in a violation that made her ill. When he was through, he dug his hands into her jeans pockets and probed further, closing on something there.

"Please, no."

He withdrew an old, faded photograph from her front pocket, unfolded it, and handed it to the major. "She has this, Major."

Major Nicasio glanced at the picture; his eyes snapped up and locked on hers. "You seek this man?"

Ana nodded. "Yes. I…"

"I see." Major Nicasio's mouth transformed into a snide grin. "How curious."

"I don't understand."

"Oh, I think you do." He stepped forward and grabbed her arm, lifting her up onto her tiptoes and against him. "You come to my town to find el doctor? Something you wish to tell me, señorita?"

3

April 4, Late Afternoon–Cabrera Village, Antioquia Department, Northeastern Colombia Near the Panama Border

"Leave Miss Ana, alone!" Sarah kicked Major Nicasio's leg. "She hasn't done nothin.'"

"Away, brat." He nodded toward Tomãs, who grabbed Sarah and stripped her from Ana's side. Major Nicasio glanced down at the photograph once again. "Tell me, señorita. Why do you seek el doctor?"

El doctor—Doctor Manuel Montilla—was a middle-aged man worn down by life and work in Colombia. Born and trained in Cuba, he came to Colombia as a young man seeking adventure and a place to use his new skills as a medical man. There, he'd met Ana's mother, Irena—a young, New York free spirit on a mission trip to the jungles. In no time, the two married and, soon after, conceived her. Since then, their lives revolved around a dangerous Colombian life in the jungle camps. Just a few years ago, Ana returned to New York to attend school. Eight months ago, her parents' disappearance from the camps brought her back from Queens to search for them.

Now, it appeared she was not the only one searching for her

pappa. She knew her reasons. Major Nicasio's reasons worried her.

"Major, I came to Colombia with Doctors of the World," she delivered the opening of her cover story. "Several of us came north to El Parque Nacional at Los Katíos looking for Doctor Montilla. He worked with us in the past. We came to find him. I got separated from the group and—"

"Lies, señorita."

Her story was fragile—partly true, mostly deception. In Medellin, she'd received a tip from a *real* doctor working with Doctors of the World—an international consortium of medical professionals dedicated to bringing care and medicine to every corner of the world—that her pappa might be in Antioquia. Having no other leads, she headed north. Along her journey, she'd rescued Sarah and had taken her here, to Cabrera. That had been three days ago.

"I have told you the truth. Dr. Montilla was giving aid—"

"He was not," Major Nicasio said dryly. "El doctor is a Cuban terrorist working with the FARC swine against my country. Since you seek el doctor, you must be FARC, too."

FARC—The People's Revolutionary Armed Forces of Colombia—was Colombia's most lethal and long-standing terrorist army. They'd operated with near impunity since the early 1960s in Colombia's jungles and cities, often taking control of villages and communities across the country. Their goals are like those of many leftist terrorists—defeat the government, more for the people, down with the wealthy. They claim to defend the countryside from government overreach and its violence against the Colombian people; although, more often, their methods are far more brutal than any government overreach. Oddly enough for a terrorist group, the FARC often put its money where its mouth was by providing more than just protection to the people beneath its umbrella. It often provided food, shelter, education, medical needs, and jobs—albeit directed toward its own cause—to villagers, farmers, and others who supported them. It also offered pain and suffering for any who chose to cross them. Of course, all this took money and resources, so FARC undertook campaigns to finance its needs—kidnapping, robbery, extortion, etc. Oh, and drugs. Lots and lots of drugs.

Cocaine, mostly. That was a billion-dollar business that helped the group take hold of Colombia and never let go. Even members of the government, military, and foreign businesses fell under FARC's boots. Often, the policía were paid off or were FARC guerrillas themselves, as were many in the Colombian military ranks.

The mention of FARC had Ana Montilla awakening just below her skin.

"No, Major." A chill ran through her. "I know nothing of FARC. He's a doctor who goes where he's needed the most."

Major Nicasio's face broke into a grin. "Lies."

Ana glanced at Sarah who began crying quietly—tears and sniffles arrived as fear etched her face. She held Lobo—her arms wrapped tightly around him for comfort. Tomãs stood behind them, a knife menacingly carving the air above them.

"Por favor." Ana grabbed Nicasio's arm. "She has done nothing."

He pulled away. "Then tell me the truth."

"I have, Major."

A black Hummer rolled into the square and skidded to a stop. From the open vehicle window, someone called out, "Major, is this her?"

"No, Colonel Vergara." Major Nicasio didn't take his eyes off Ana. "She may still be important. She searches for Montilla. It seems el doctor is popular in my country, no? First, you come from Havana looking for him. Now, this chica arrives."

Ana strained to see this person addressed as Colonel Vergara. Cuban military in Colombia was extraordinary—the two countries were bitter enemies brought about by Havana's support of FARC. After being partially disbanded in 2016, its recent resurgence was once again focused on the destruction of the Colombian government, to which Havana was keen to assist. Yet here, there seemed to be a truce.

Something bizarre had apparently happened to allow the Cubans onto Colombian soil.

Ana stole glances at the Hummer as Major Nicasio and Colonel Vergara discussed their search for the mysterious woman in Tomãs's cell phone photograph. Whoever she was, they were desperate to find her—and desperate to find el doctor…her pappa.

But why?

Vergara exited the Hummer and walked toward her, with Nicasio following. He was a tall, robust man with a wrestler's physique. His eyes were deep set and cold. He had little hair but for thick, gray patches on the sides and a well-trimmed gray mustache. He wore dark slacks and a white cotton shirt. He looked like a big-city businessman, strangely out of place among the brooding camouflaged gunmen and cowering townspeople. There was one thing, however, one deformity that mesmerized her—a mat of dark red scars along his upper right cheek. The scars, perhaps the remnants of childhood acne, stenciled the number nine on his face, stretching from the corner of his mouth to his right eye.

She fixated on the scar. Why, she didn't know, but the disfigurement worried her. Was nine a bad omen?

Vergara reached out and took her chin, breaking her focus. He moved her face from side to side and studied her. "Yes, a very pretty woman. I may have to bring her back with us for further, eh…interrogation. Regrettably, though, this is not…."

"Hemingway," Major Nicasio sputtered. After he spoke, his face twisted, as if suddenly realizing his announcement was out loud. "It is not her."

"Major." Vergara faced him, and glared. "You will forget that name."

"Si, Colonel." Major Nicasio flushed. "My apologies."

Ana looked at Sarah and put on a brave face. She tried to reach for her, but Tomãs aimed his knife and warned her back. Lobo snarled and twisted away from Sarah, causing another soldier to grab his leash and yank him back again.

The soldiers laughed and kicked at him. Only a couple glancing blows hit his hindquarters as he dodged and twisted, each time gnashing his teeth to warn them away.

"No, no." Sarah escaped Tomãs's grip and confronted the soldier holding Lobo. "Leave him alone."

"Shut up, brat." He shoved her backward into Tomãs. "Get away or I'll kill him."

Tomãs grabbed Sarah's hair and yanked her off balance. He lifted his knife and touched her cheek, allowing the blade to barely nick her flesh. "*Puta*, I'll cut you if you do that again."

Sarah cried, "Miss Ana."

In a sudden swell of anger, Ana Montilla broke free and took control.

"Leave her." Ana spun away from Vergara and leapt at Tomãs. She landed a heel-kick into his knee that buckled him. Her palm shot out, drove deep into his solar plexus, and knocked him backward onto the ground. He released Sarah. "Do not touch this child again."

Ana, what have you done? Stop.

Tomãs erupted off the ground and onto his feet and slashed out with his knife at Sarah. "I kill you both."

Ana spun on the ball of her foot and snapped a kick into his side, knocking him off balance. As she landed, she struck two fast, hard punches into his face.

He was down again.

Two soldiers rushed forward and grabbed her arms, pulling them behind her tightly.

"*Puta*, you pay for this." Rage consumed Tomãs's face as he returned to his feet and punched her powerfully in her belly. He grabbed her by the throat with one hand and lifted her onto her toes. With his other hand, he slashed at her with his knife. "Bleed, chica."

The blade stabbed her—sliced her; the pain was instant and intense.

She hung in his grip, both arms still held tightly behind her. The blade sliced her side but did not penetrate deeply; instead, it cut and maimed, opening her skin to bleed. As blood soaked her blouse, she tried to cry out, but Tomãs' grip on her throat muted her.

"Stop," Vergara barked. "Release her."

"*Puta*." Tomãs slashed her twice more, leaving trails of blood across her body. "I will…"

"You will not," Vergara ordered. "I said, stop."

Tomãs squeezed her throat again before he tossed her to the ground and kicked viciously at her head.

Sarah cried out but was instantly silenced in a muffled struggle.

Ana rolled away, trying to soften the impact, but his boot landed solidly against her head and black spots exploded across her vision. Her thoughts slowed and waned. The pain consumed her. The blackness began to win.

Hold on, Ana. Hold on for Sarah.

"Get back, I said," Vergara growled. "What have you done?"

Tomãs kicked her twice more.

The darkness swelled around her. Her eyes blinked open as Vergara stood above her. The light and dark battled for control over her, like a dangerous dance in and out. Fighting to stay awake, she fixed her eyes on Vergara's face. Each time she opened her eyes, she tried to focus on something…anything…to keep herself in the light.

The scar.

Focus, Ana, focus. Nine…nine…nine.

Somewhere, Sarah cried out again and snapped silent. Lobo barked and growled—struggling against something or someone.

Her eyes slowly opened again. Vergara still stood over her, concern in his eyes.

"This is not good, Tomãs," he growled. "Look what you have done."

"But Colonel—"

"Shut up." Vergara was angry. "I knew of this pretty one. I had my orders to look for her."

"You knew of her?" It was Major Nicasio's voice. "I know nothing of this one, Colonel."

"No one need know but me," Vergara snapped. "She was to help me find el doctor. Now, she is finished. If I cannot find the other woman, Havana will be furious."

"Colonel, I didn't know," Major Nicasio whined. "What shall I do?"

Vergara began issuing orders, but Ana couldn't find meaning in his words. Everything around her faded away, leaving her alone and empty. The humid air filled her nostrils and choked her. She tried to push the darkness away, but it was heavy and cold. Pain drummed her ears. The sun singed her wounds with stinging fingers. Yet, for a fleeting moment, that warmth comforted her as the cold enveloped her once more and led her toward the darkness.

"Help me…por favor…the little one…Sarah…help…"

Muffled voices, their meaning obscure, surrounded her. Shuffling feet.

Lobo barked. Sarah cried in terror.

Fight, Ana. Fight. She had to stay awake. *Sarah...Sarah... Sarah....* Her eyes were seeing and unseeing—intermittent flashes of light and shadows. Shock concealed the world until she forced her eyes open and saw the blade hovering above her again. Her mind was fading—shutting down—losing the fight.

Ana Montilla, save me.

She was spent, lost somewhere, unable to find the path back. She opened her eyes and saw only the glint of Tomãs's knife taunting her. She fixated on it.

Vergara came into view again. "She is done."

"No, please...." Her eyes closed on Vergara's scar. *Nine...nine... nine....* "Please, no...."

Somewhere Sarah cried, "No, no, Miss Ana."

Lobo barked rabidly, snarled, and barked again.

"No, not Lobo," Sarah yelled in panic.

A shot.

Silence.

"Miss Ana...help me...." Sarah's voice was lost as a second shot split the air.

Ana tried to move—tried to turn and find the little girl. Somewhere, Lobo whimpered, and Sarah consoled him. A few eye flutters later, Sarah sat beside her, holding Lobo limply in her lap, the flow of red life oozing across her torso and down her legs and arms.

Was the blood Sarah's or Lobo's?

"Sarah...run...hide...."

Another kick to her ribs, but there was no pain. Her senses were spent.

"Finish her, Tomãs," Vergara commanded. "Let the wild dogs take the rest."

Ana reached for Sarah but couldn't find her. Tears cascaded down her cheeks as her body chilled. With the last of her breath, she raised her voice and managed, "I will come for you. All...of... you. I will come...."

It wasn't your fault, Ana. It wasn't your fault.

4

PRESENT DAY

June 1, Early Evening–Queens, New York

"Cuban military in Colombia?" Poppi looked over at a thin, handsome, silver-haired man across the room. "What do you think, William?"

William Tillson was Poppi's lifelong friend and an ever-present fixture in Ana's life since she returned from Colombia to attend college eight years ago. He was a wealthy, firebrand entrepreneur who'd made and lost fortunes in dozens of enterprises since his youth. His latest successful enterprise was an international information brokerage, gathering and selling business intelligence for wealthy clients. He was a man of worldly intellect, careful thought, and steadfast reason.

"Cuban military in Colombia?" William's doubt was thick in his voice. "That would be very odd, given the political climate between them. Are you sure, Ana?"

"His name is Colonel Vergara." She closed her eyes and captured his face—that vision sent shivers through her. "He had Cuban soldiers with him. There was a Colombian officer, too. They were working together to find Pappa."

"Your father?" Poppi asked. "Nonsense. Why would they want him?"

"It's true, Poppi."

"You remember this now?" Poppi said. "You haven't been good with memories, Ana. Perhaps you're mistaken."

No, she was not mistaken. For two months those memories were a void. Vergara's appearance returned them to her. Their faces. Their voices. Their misdeeds—the pain. "It was him, Yiayia. It was Vergara and his men in the park. One was named Tomás—he was the one who hurt me. They nearly killed me and left me for dead."

"Why?" Poppi asked. "Why did they do that?"

Because Ana Montilla defended little Sarah.

"Why rarely matters in Colombia," she said. "It just happened."

"It was those men in the park who attacked you?" Poppi went to the bar in the corner of the living room. She pulled the cork from a half-full bottle of wine, filled a glass, and turned to Ana. "You have not remembered who brought you home from Colombia, have you?"

Who indeed? "No. I don't remember any of that. Not yet."

"If you are right—and I do not think you are—these are dangerous men." Poppi's face tightened. "You must stay far away and forget them."

"That's good advice, Ana," William said. "You're lucky you got out of Colombia. Don't make things worse."

"And you promised me that you would leave that life behind you." Poppi stabbed a finger at her. "What if the government learned about you? You know what that might mean."

She did but she wasn't sure she could stop any of it. She'd felt sick and weak since Colonel Vergara spoke to her in the park. If he was here—for any reason—then her fate was intertwined with his. Whatever that meant escaped her now. But that very thought chilled her.

She glanced from William to Poppi. "When I saw Vergara, it started coming back. I remember more about Cabrera—I remember him. I think he recognized me, too."

"Oh?" William asked. "Did he say something?"

"He commented about Lobo. When I asked if I knew him, he

denied it. When he left, he turned back to me. He grinned like he knew me and was trying to intimidate me. It was terrifying."

Poppi stared at her for the longest time before lifting her glass and downing the wine in one long, steady gulp. "You could be wrong, Ana."

"I'm not wrong. I remember. In Cabrera, Vergara had a strange scar across his cheek—it looked like the number nine. The man in the park had the same scar." She breathed a long sigh and explained everything she now recalled from Cabrera.

William and Poppi exchanged uneasy glances.

Poppi said, "It could be your imagination tricking you into believing they are one and the same, Ana."

"Trauma will do that," William added. "You can't be sure."

"I know what I saw."

"No, you don't." Poppi's voice was sharp. "Scar or not, it doesn't matter. You cannot fight a man like him. What can you do?"

If you only knew all I can do, perhaps you might hate me as much as you hate Pappa. "I don't know. I need to come to terms with it all. Then—"

"Then nothing, Ana," William interrupted. "I know about these things. You can do nothing. But I can."

If there was anyone Ana knew who could handle problems like Vergara, it was William. His business intelligence company served high-net worth captains of industry and the occasional government client. It was hugely successful. He was known as the man who could reach anything—*anyone*—broker meetings, deals, or provide the means for others to do so themselves. Over the years, he'd connected titans of industry, world leaders, and even the occasional crime bosses. Those successes had amassed him more money than he could ever spend—or his family and children and their children could spend, if he'd ever had any family. He did not. He had also amassed a significant reputation as a cunning, powerful problem solver.

"You stay clear of this," William said. "I'll find Vergara and check him out."

"No." Ana was firm. "I need to remember the rest, first. You can't dig around on him, William."

"Why not? It's what I do," he said matter-of-factly. "I'm good at it, too. Think of my firm as a private CIA of sorts, but no skullduggery, of course. Let me help. If I find something, I'll handle the police for you."

"The police? And tell them what?" Ana's face grew hot. "That a Cuban butcher mysteriously appeared in Central Park right in front of me? That he tried to kill me once and he may be back to finish me? No. No police."

William glanced between Ana and Poppi. "I don't understand. If this is Vergara, he's dangerous. Why not bring in the police?"

"She's right, William. No police." Poppi stood and set her wine on the fireplace mantel. "Years ago Ana, well...she was with her parents in Colombia, as you know. But she was not who she is today. You know what I've told you about Manuel and Irena. If you go to the police, they may ask too many questions about Ana. Questions we are not prepared to answer."

"Like why I was in Cabrera. I might have to explain who Mamá and Pappa are, where they've been, and what they have done. What I have done, too." Her eyes locked onto William with a mixture of fear and sadness. "Do you know what will happen? To me?"

"Yes, I guess I do." William exchanged glances with Poppi. "I don't understand it all, but I won't do anything without your blessing."

"Thank you." Ana forced a smile that fooled no one. "William, I hope you know I appreciate you wanting to help. I do."

After Poppi became a widow some twenty-plus years ago, William returned to Manhattan after decades away. Once home, he reconnected with Poppi—they'd been lifelong friends from the old neighborhood. Since then, he'd become her intimate companion. With that role, came his surrogacy as Ana's grandfather—an ear to listen, a shoulder to cry on, a guiding hand on her missteps.

"Good." William's cell vibrated and he slipped it from his pocket. Before tapping on the call, he said, "But I think you should consider Sarah in all this. After all, she was in Cabrera, too."

Sarah. Dear God, she hadn't thought of Sarah.

Ana had found the green-eyed seven-year-old at that rundown roadside gas station in Colombia's Antioquia mountains. She had noticed the pretty, young child playing in a dirty alcove of the station where a few sundry household items were sold. Sarah had politely asked her to play a game, first in Spanish, then in English when Ana hadn't responded quickly enough. The station owner, an elderly man barely able to care for himself, found her wandering around his station one day—filthy, starving, and dehydrated. He took her in and kept her in a back room, waiting for someone to claim her. The next day, he learned from a local farmer that her parents were dead—an American missionary who'd married a local girl. They were killed in an accident and Sarah must have wandered from the crash. She had no other family. Despite several attempts, the authorities hadn't responded to take her into government care. Cabrera was the closest town—an hour's drive away—so Ana took her there, hoping to find someone to take her in. She'd also hoped to find Mamá and Pappa there, too.

Of course, what she found in Cabrera nearly killed them both.

"My little Sarah." Ana thought about what might happen to her. "I have to protect her."

"Don't worry about Sarah." Poppi went to her and held her in a long embrace. "Never worry about her."

"I worry about you both." A shiver ran through her. Was Vergara there for her? What if somehow he had tracked her to New York to ensure her silence? Could Poppi raise a seven-year-old? For how long? And what would happen to Poppi? Was she in danger, too?

There was only one way to find and defeat Vergara. To do that, she knew she would have to break a promise—one simple promise—that she would never be Ana Montilla again.

After leaving Colombia to live with Poppi and attend college, she'd promised Poppi—and herself—she'd never, ever, become *that* Ana again. Yet in Cabrera, she had failed. Her demon escaped. Had she not, perhaps things would have been different.

But did different mean better?

"Ana?" William said. "Why would Vergara come here if he thought you were dead?"

"I don't know." And she didn't. "But he *is* here. It has to be for Sarah and me."

"Nonsense." Poppi's face showed frustration. "I think you

simply imagined the man in the park was this Cuban colonel. He is probably someone else. Let it go, child."

No. The memories Vergara returned to her were real. He was real. The danger was real.

"I can't let it go, Poppi."

"Why? This is silly to think this man came all the way from Colombia—even Cuba—just for you."

Something stabbed at her. "No, Poppi, not for me."

"No, of course not." Poppi finished her glass of wine. "If you had stayed out of Colombia, none of this would have happened."

"What about Mamá and Pappa? Am I supposed to stop looking for them? Abandon them?"

"Let me worry about them."

"What does that mean?" Ana stared at her. "Do you know something?"

"Of course not. How could I?" Poppi poured herself more wine. "Leave this be, Ana. I beg you."

William walked to Poppi. "Alas, I'm afraid I must go, my dear."

"Now?" Poppi was surprised. "You only got in this afternoon?"

"That call was my office." He kissed Poppi's cheek. "I have to get back. If all goes well, I'll return the day after tomorrow."

"What about our plans?" Poppi frowned. "All right. Off with you."

William turned to Ana. "You have my number, Ana. Call me if you need anything. Don't hesitate. I can take care of all this for you—quietly."

"Thank you, William. I appreciate it."

After another kiss on Poppi's cheek, he walked to the front door and was gone.

Ana stared at nothing as worry consumed her. She could never allow anyone—William included—to probe her past. Even given the threat Vergara might mean, she had to deal with it on her own. William's offer to help was admirable under normal circumstances, but her life did not revolve around normal circumstances. Neither he nor Poppi understood the true magnitude of her past life. Her other life. Ana Montilla's life. Neither could fathom the peril she would be in should the authorities learn her truths. While Poppi knew she had secrets buried deep, she didn't know their depth. The real truth. The ugly truth.

Ana prayed she never would.

5

June 1, Early Evening–Queens, New York

"William means well, Ana," Poppi said, opening another bottle of wine. "He is worried about you."

"I know." 'Meaning well' could still destroy her. "He's a good man."

"He is. At some point, we should consider his help." Poppi poured two glasses from the bottle and handed one to her. "He does work for other governments, you know. Not always ours."

"Really?"

"Oh, he's no spy. It's all aboveboard. Perhaps in a few days we should—"

"No." Ana's tone was harsher than she'd planned, so she lightened it with, "I would not look good in an orange jumpsuit, Yiayia."

"Ana," Poppi's eyes flared. "That's not funny."

"I'm sorry." She tried to smile but couldn't. "You have to consider that if they found out about my past, they will also find out about Sarah. They'd take her."

"Oh my, yes." Poppi's face paled. "A mother must protect her children—and their children. I will not allow anything to harm either of you."

"But…"

"There is no 'but.'" Poppi took Ana's hand and pulled it close. "No one will harm my family again. Not as your father did."

"Enough about Pappa." Ana pulled her hand away. "Why can't you forgive them as you have me?"

"Because he took Irena from me." Poppi took Ana's shoulders and squared off on her. "Because he kept you from me for so long. Because of the many things he has done. Because...."

"Because of what I did."

"No." Poppi's eyes glistened. "Because of what he made you do. What he created in you."

"I am no better than he." Ana pulled away from her again. "Am I? The things I—"

"Stop. I don't want to know."

No, you don't. If you did, you would hate me, too.

"You are better than them both. You came home. My Irena never did. Perhaps she cannot."

After high school, Irena Karras became a missionary looking for God and adventure. Mostly, it was to escape Queens. On an extended mission trip to Colombia, Irena met young Manuel Montilla. In no time, they married and continued their life there. Poppi never met her son-in-law, and Irena never returned to New York. The young couple spent their lives in Central and South America, where Manuel practiced medicine—or so Poppi believed—and Irena worked as a nurse in his clinic. In the mid-1990s, Poppi received a telephone call from Colombia—one of only two yearly calls from Irena. Ana Penelope Montilla had been born. But she would not meet her granddaughter for many more years.

"You returned to me, Ana." Poppi smiled. "You became the Ana I always wished you to be."

"I know, Yiayia. I know. But I fear for Mamá and Pappa."

"Why do you say that?"

"They left the camps—first Pappa, then Mamá after him." A tingle of memories popped open. "Vergara was looking for him in Cabrera. And...he was looking for someone other than Pappa... it scares me."

"Hemmy-way," a meek voice came from the hall, and Sarah walked into the living room. "Those bad men said Hemmy-way,

Aunty. Remember?"

Hemmy-way? Yes…Hemingway.

Ana turned as Sarah climbed onto the couch carrying two coloring books and a plastic tub of crayons. Lobo was on her heels, hobbling into place to curl up at her feet.

"Sarah?" Ana sat beside her and kissed her forehead. "Do you remember what else they said that day?"

"Yes." Sarah's face scrunched into a pout. "Those men hurt you, Aunty. They hurt, Lobo, too."

"Yes, they did." Ana pulled Sarah close, hugging her tightly. "Lobo and I are fine now. Everything is better. We're all safe."

"Because that man helped us, Aunty."

"That man?" Ana thought back. "Yes…I remember. He came soon after they hurt me."

"He gave me candy and fixed up you and Lobo. He was nice."

Yes, that man. Ana pictured the faint silhouette of a man leaning over her. He had spoken sweetly to Sarah, calming her tears and promising that everything would be all right. He kept Sarah close as he tended her injuries and worked feverishly on Lobo's wounds. Just a hazy image, still fleeting from her memory.

Who was he and where had he come from?

"Aunty Ana," Sarah said, "who's Hemmy-way?"

"I don't know, Sarah. Someone important, though." Another memory opened like a book in her thoughts. "Wait…one of them said something. He thought Pappa was with this Hemingway person or knew him. And something about a woman—a female Cuban soldier. They thought I looked like her."

"They were bad men, Aunty." Sarah held up a fist full of crayons. "They should get beat up and policemen should put them in jail."

"Now, we can't beat people up," Poppi said. Then, she changed the subject. "Done with your cartoons, Sarah?"

"No." Sarah was not easily distracted. "Aunty, are you going to find the man in the park?"

Sarah had seen Vergara in the park.

Ana hugged her. "Don't worry about him. You're safe here."

While Ana had suffered physical injuries in Cabrera, Sarah had suffered others—night terrors and stress, fears of abandonment.

Those fears manifested at the most unusual times. Shopping in the mall and losing sight of Ana for just a second. Playing in Poppi's yard when a loud vehicle rolled by in the alley. Too many sleepless nights. Too many untamed fears. While Ana could only comfort her and wish the horrible fears away, Lobo had always been her salvation. Her unshakable protector slept in her arms, walked at her side, and stayed close when those terrors found her. Once he was in her embrace, the demons fled.

Seemingly on cue, Lobo looked up from the floor, checked that she was safe, and fell back asleep.

"I know, Aunty Ana." Sarah stood on the couch and wrapped her arms around Ana's neck, squeezing so hard the crayons fell from her grasp. "I love you."

"I love you, too. Very, very much." Ana kissed her cheeks. "What do you want to do? Cartoons? Coloring?"

"The magic trick?" Sarah asked, grinning. "Can I do it, Aunty? Make the lights go on and off? Just once?"

"All right," Ana said. "Do the magic."

First, Sarah ran through the living room pulling down the window shades to wash the room in total darkness. Then, her eyes flashed wide and she clapped her hands together twice. Instantly, the living room and hallway lights flashed off. The house was in total darkness. She giggled wildly and clapped her hands twice again. The lights came on.

"That's so funny, Aunty Ana. I clapped the lights."

"It's magic, isn't it?" Ana slid her back against the couch cushions. "What next, Sarah? How about we—"

"What about the man in the park, Aunty?"

"He's gone, Sarah. Don't worry about him," Poppi said.

"No, he's not. That's why I didn't finish my cartoons." Sarah pointed down the hall toward the kitchen. "He's in our backyard."

6

June 1, Early Evening–Queens, New York

Colonel Vergara is in our backyard?

"Take Sarah upstairs, Yiayia." Ana scooped Sarah up and passed her to Poppi. "I'll go see this man."

"What? No," Poppi said. "Surely it's her imagination or just a neighbor walking by."

Perhaps. "Are you sure it's the man from the park, Sarah?"

"Uh-huh. I saw him by the ice cream shop and when we were walking in the park."

"Okay, Sarah." Ana forced a smile that felt as fake as it must have looked. "Go with Yiayia Poppi."

"Ana, let me go look," Poppi said. "If it's Vergara, he won't know me."

"No. Take her upstairs."

"Ana, you're overreacting."

Ana shook her head. "Go, please."

"Fine. Do not do anything stupid." Poppi carried Sarah to the stairs. "You were right earlier."

"About the police?"

"No. That you will not look good in orange."

As soon as they disappeared up the stairs, Ana went to the

44

bookshelf near the basement door. She had to stop, close her eyes, and get control. Fear and uncontrolled action were dangerous. She knew better. She'd trained better.

A cool head and control could not only save her life, but others, too.

When she was ten, she'd been waiting for a Medellin bus near her parent's camp. Outside the bus stop, guerrillas and the National Police collided. She'd been terrified and tried to run from the bus stop, but panic had carried her into the middle of the melee. If not for a quick-minded old man who ran from cover and tackled her to the ground, she would have been cut to pieces in the gunfire. After the shootout, she stood to thank him but he was dead—bullets that would have killed her had taken him instead.

Easy, Ana. Calm. It was probably nothing.

Lobo barked at the rear of the house. Once. Twice. A howl.

It was *something*.

From behind the bookshelf, she pulled the nine-millimeter semiautomatic pistol from its hiding place. She snapped back the Beretta's slide to chamber a round, leveled it tight to her chest, and the two moved as one toward the kitchen.

Lobo stood at the back door with his front foot propped up on the window ledge, barking. Of all the security precautions she'd put in place at Poppi's house, Lobo was the best.

She stood beside him at the rear door and peered out—nothing but the narrow, fenced-in rear yard bathed in the coming night met her gaze. The sun was nearly down, and the darkness had begun to take over the sky, casting the yard in deep shadows. Along the left side of the yard was a narrow, single-car garage where Poppi kept her car, a lawnmower, and gardening supplies—a passion that consumed her far too much for the few square yards of earth she owned. A new barbecue grill sat in the opposite corner near the gate, covered by a black plastic cover that now, in this dim light, looked like a crouching figure. That, and the four-chair patio set sitting atop the fieldstone patio were the only dangers in sight.

It was hard to see clearly in the dusk. The spotlight above the rear door was out—a faulty switch she swore a hundred times to replace. She jiggled the switch beside the door anyway, but the light refused to cooperate. She cursed. Her palms grew sweaty, and she changed gun hands to wipe each on her jeans. As she did, guilt crept over her.

Guilt?

All she had learned in Colombia failed her in Queens. There had been a threat in the park—a threat near Sarah—and she hadn't acted; instead, she'd been withered by panic. Vergara was here in New York, at one point within arm's reach of her family. He might be lurking outside her home now. So far, she'd done nothing to defend herself or Sarah. She'd fallen victim to a false belief—that the dangers of the camps could never reach her in New York. What good were her training and skills if she was defeated so easily by apathy and complacency?

A cold, heavy knot formed in her stomach. Had she already failed Sarah?

She thought back to Central Park. Sarah must have seen him on the footpath as she went with Poppi for ice cream. How long had he been there? How much had Vergara learned about them? Enough that he was outside, right now, preparing an attack?

Ana Karras had failed. Should Ana Montilla fix this?

Lobo barked again and shot a look at Ana, wagging his tail.

"What do you think, boy?" Ana looked around the rear yard again. "Is he gone?"

Woof.

As silently as she could, she unlocked the door and slipped outside onto the stoop with her pistol ready. The moment she closed the door behind her, self-loathing stabbed her.

Dammit, Ana. What are you thinking?

She was visible. Vulnerable. With her back to the door, the inside kitchen light—she'd failed to turn it off—silhouetted her to anyone watching from the dark. If there was a killer stalking her house, she was an easy target.

A silly mistake. A fool's mistake. A deadly mistake.

Were her skills that diminished? She'd failed to react to Vergara in the park—she should have followed him and learned where he stayed. She had the necessary skills. What she'd learned in the camps and practiced in the Colombian towns and cities was significant—

combat skills, surveillance, all manner of dirty tricks and tactics. She had become a skilled, lethal fighter who many had feared. She could defeat him.

Really, Ana? Where are your skills now? You just stepped out into the field of fire, backlit and vulnerable.

"Field of fire, Ana?" She allowed a nervous laugh. "This is Queens, not Bogota. Come on, girl, get it together."

The figure in the yard might be no more than a little girl's whimsical imagination. Perhaps Sarah mistook a passing neighbor for the man in the park. Perhaps she'd overheard her and Poppi talking and it had ignited a youthful illusion.

Perhaps.

The gate banged in the breeze and sent needles through her. Her eyes and the green glow of the Beretta's tritium sights searched the yard. The gate was always locked—always. A rule she and Poppi followed religiously for Sarah's safety.

Someone *had* been there.

She pulled her pistol into a retention position and moved along the side fence, keeping low and using the dim shadows to conceal her progress. The fence was six feet high; the gate was locked with a padlock and hasp. The key was hanging on a hook inside the kitchen door. Now, however, the gate was open and the lock dangled innocently on its hasp.

She eased through the gate, pistol out. Once in the alley, she pivoted in a quick circle and swept the area in smooth, freeze-frame movements.

Nothing.

Wait…there, at the end of her circle.

A figure of average height and square shoulders moved through the fading light. He was no more than a dark silhouette a hundred feet from her and moving quickly away.

"You, stop!" She lifted her pistol to firing position. "Stop."

Nothing.

"Stop."

The man quickened his pace. When he reached the end of the alley, he turned right onto the side street and disappeared.

The man in the alley was not Colonel Vergara. Their physiques were easily different, even in the dark. Their height and girth. The way they moved. Nothing was the same. Of course, that meant nothing. Vergara would have minions to do his bidding as he had in Cabrera. He could have sent one of his bodyguards for her and Sarah. If there were two, there could be more.

Calm, Ana. Reason…think. The danger has passed.

But for how long?

Subconsciously, she rubbed the scar along her side as it tingled beneath her fingers.

Stop this, Ana. Take control.

She would not be anyone's prey. She had fallen victim to Vergara and his thugs once. She vowed that no one, especially Vergara, would ever hurt her or Sarah again. No one.

She'd promised Poppi—promised herself—not to ever be Ana Montilla again.

That promise would now have to be broken.

7

June 1, Evening–The Mall, Washington, DC

The runner glided through the darkness, appearing and disappearing through the cones of streetlamp lights like a wraith, unnoticed by passersby. Alex McLaren felt at home jogging in the darkness along the National Mall—more at home than in most big cities in the middle of the day. Dressed in an expensive European running suit and high-tech cross-trainers, he sipped on a bottle of water he pulled from his nylon runner's pack and scanned the shadows around him for anyone wishing him ill will.

He checked his watch as he did each quarter mile. He was thirty seconds off his pace, so he increased his speed. He tapped the control on his earbuds and moved down his playlist—Iron Maiden's "Loneliness of the Long-Distance Runner." The surge of endorphins tingled as he pressed on harder. Crushing his next two laps, he skirted the Reflecting Pool and ended his two-hour run at the Lincoln Memorial. As he removed his earbuds, he walked off heated limbs and focused on regaining a normal breath and pulse.

He stretched his legs and back, cooled down, and took in the night air. He was tall and trim with a face that often got mistaken for the actor Paul Walker—or vice versa as he often claimed. He had many years ahead of him in Washington, and he wanted to keep fit and ready for each one. It would take strength, endurance, and guile to maneuver up the ranks of DC's elite. Forever impatient, he was a young man to have the position he held already. It came partially from his connections and partially from the success that perseverance paid. Some thought it was pure luck. Luck played no part. His successes were more about his well-endowed self-assuredness and hefty ruthlessness.

Luck was a fool's ambition.

Something tickled his nerves and he dodged into the shadows of a tree just off the sidewalk. He scanned Constitution Avenue ahead of him.

The black Hummer was back.

Since beginning his run, the SUV had been parked adjacent to the Lincoln Memorial. That was two hours ago. Later, it had moved along Seventeenth Street across the Mall behind him. Now, it sat a hundred yards ahead of him on Constitution.

Any common observation—a person, a vehicle, anything—separated by time, distance, or place could be surveillance. To McLaren, all surveillance was hostile.

He reached into his pack's side pouch and checked that the compact .22-caliber semiautomatic pistol was properly positioned for easy access. Then, he sprinted among the trees and maneuvered, unseen, to within ten yards of the vehicle.

Caution and training stilled him.

In the nation's capital, large, black, expensive automobiles were not uncommon—especially SUVs. Most were operated by the government—someone's government—or private services for the more wealthy or prestigious. Fewer were owned by Joe Citizen, but there were some. Observing one around the National Mall was commonplace, even at this late hour. What was unusual about this one, other than the frequency with which he'd observed it being close to being a coincidence, was that not so coincidentally, he'd seen this same vehicle in McLean earlier in the evening. That was before his run, when he was sitting outside The Greek Taverna—his favorite restaurant in the Metro area. It had made the block three times before parking across the street until he'd finished his meal.

Coincidences were common thought for the average man—

most often a fabrication of the imagination or simple happenstance. For an intelligence operative seasoned in the bowels of Kabul and Baghdad, however, they were danger signs. The prelude to threats.

McLaren didn't believe in coincidence. It's why he had survived as long as he had. It's why he planned to survive a long, long time. It's why he now slipped his pistol out of his backpack and eased from the trees toward the vehicle.

He stayed below the occupant's line of sight and reached the passenger side of the Hummer without being detected. There, he rose and placed the barrel of his .22 against the front passenger window and tapped lightly—a Hollywood play he'd always loved.

The window descended; the man inside stared above the pistol sights, unfazed.

"McLaren," the man said, "get in."

"Roll down the rear window."

The man started to open his door when McLaren touched the pistol barrel to his cheek—another Hollywood play.

"Bad idea." McLaren stepped away from the Hummer so the door wouldn't hit him should the man try to knock him away. "Rear window. I want to see who's so shy."

"For Christ's sake, McLaren," a familiar voice growled from the back seat, "get in. It's important."

"Can you guys be more cliché?" He returned the pistol to his backpack and opened the rear door. "Nighttime pickup with goons in a black SUV? At least you're not wearing trench coats and fedoras."

The rear cabin light flipped on and the man inside, dressed in a dark suit and expensive tie, leaned toward the open door. He was an older man in his late sixties, with gray hair and a clean-shaven face that showed the weathering that came from years of hard experience and bad habits. He was stout with a large, barrel chest.

"Just get in," the man said. "We're going to talk and drive."

"Only if you stop for coffee, Danny."

"Danny?" The older man frowned. "My, my, you're getting full of yourself."

"Why not call and set up an appointment? You've been tailing me all night."

"Screw appointments. I don't trust other people's phones; I don't trust yours for sure. Frankly, I sure as hell don't trust you."

"The feeling is mutual, *Danny*." McLaren slid into the rear seat and pushed on the front passenger headrest to get his aide's attention. "You guys need training. I spotted you following me all over town. You should have just come inside earlier for some souvlaki and retsina."

The security man grunted and refused to look back.

"Drive," Danny ordered.

A few seconds later, they were lost in the ribbon of DC traffic lights.

"There's a good coffee shop on Vermont." McLaren settled his backpack between his knees. "I don't suppose this is a social call."

"I don't do social calls," Danny said. "For a CIA man, you're not very intuitive, are you?"

"Intuitive enough to sneak up on you. What do you want?"

"Special assignment."

"I don't do special assignments at this hour."

Danny forced a laugh. "You do what I tell you."

Thirty minutes later, they reached the corner of 35th Street Northwest and Reservoir Road, just outside Georgetown University. The conversation had been direct and concise—no room for pleasantries. By the time they pulled to the curb, McLaren knew he'd only gotten part of the story.

"What's so important about Raul Anibal Vacarro?" McLaren asked.

"Just find him and see what he's got."

"Got?"

Danny's face tightened. "Dammit, McLaren, do I have to spell it out?"

"Yes."

"He has information for me—me, alone. Find out what he's got—all of it—and hold him until I decide what to do."

McLaren knew where this was going. "You mean hold him until you want him dead."

Danny lifted his chin but remained silent.

"Say it, Danny, the whole truth. Or I walk."

Danny fumed. "What the hell difference does it make? You won't be doing it. You'll give orders to that Trane guy and he'll do it."

"If that's what has to happen."

"It might. But not until I say so."

"Why not send your own people to do your dirty work? You know, the mercenaries I know you have on speed dial? They won't ask questions like I will about what you're asking."

"I'm not asking," Danny said. "The boss is picking his winners and losers for this next job. Your exploits in Afghanistan came to his attention. You can thank me later. He thinks you're a good addition to the team. Or shall we call it a 'relationship.'"

"We don't have a relationship, Danny. We have an understanding."

"Yeah, we do." Danny grinned. "As long as that understanding is clear."

"Oh, sure. We're pals."

"No, we're not. But since I don't mind you enjoying the added profits from your previous assignment in Afghanistan, I believe you're perfect for our upcoming needs."

"Why don't I feel lucky?"

There was silence for the longest time.

"Take him home," Danny finally said to the driver. "We'll save him the cab fare."

"No." McLaren slapped the back of the front seat. "I'm an Uber kind of guy. The company is better. Leave me here."

"Whatever." Danny reached into a compartment on his door and retrieved a file. He opened it, scanned the first few pages beneath the overhead light, and then handed it to him. "You'll need this."

McLaren didn't have to read much before he knew why the meeting resembled a Bogart movie. By the middle of the second page, he stopped reading. He folded the file and tucked it into his runner's pack. "This is novel. A little murky, but novel."

"Do you understand your assignment?"

"Yeah, sure. I snatch up Vacarro and, well…have a conversation with him."

Danny nodded.

"Then, you order me to kill him."

"Knock that off." Danny's face contorted. "Whatever he gives you stays between him, you, and me. No one else. Got it?"

"I'll have Trane—"

"Fine. Trane. He's expendable, too." Danny turned off the overhead light. "Simple enough now?"

"Besides Trane, I'll need help from official channels. You know, to find Señor Vacarro."

"No." Danny pointed to the runner's pack and the file he'd given McLaren. "That's all you'll need. No official support. Just you and Trane."

"Tell me why."

"Because I want it done."

Heat rose in McLaren's face as he slid out of the SUV onto the sidewalk. "I haven't agreed yet."

The window rolled up as the Hummer drove away.

8

June 1, Evening–Cartago, Costa Rica

The Americans would never see her coming.

Catalina Reyes was on a mission. It was not her first mission. That had been twenty years ago when she was just fifteen. But it was her most important mission. A life-changing one. Perhaps a life-ending one as well. Whether success or failure, it would also be her last. First, she had to overcome her past. Overcome her fears. Then, Cat had to survive the pursuit. Finally, she would have to reach her target and execute the plan. In the end, there would come the escape.

Her entire adult life had been about that one focus: her target. This target. Washington.

She lay on the bedroll, sleepless and unsettled. It had been nearly three months since she'd left Cuba. Three months hiding and maneuvering. Waiting on el doctor to leave the breadcrumb trail north to America, one town, one safe house at a time. North to her target. Much of that time, she'd gone to ground in one safe house or another. A moving target was sometimes easier to find than a stationary one. Movement drew attention. Movement brought the hunters. So she hid. Waited. Prayed she still had the skills that she'd once mastered as one of Havana's best *Dirección de Inteligencia—*

Cuban Intelligence—operatives. Prayed she could outplay those operatives who were Havana's spy masters now.

It had been many years since her last mission. Before that, she'd operated throughout Central and South America. Many missions. Dangerous missions. As a pretty Latina, men were quick to engage her and slow to recognize the threat. Her looks gave her access to her targets; her skills conquered them.

That all changed fifteen years ago. Her previous mission. The life-changing mission that had both failed and succeeded. It had cost her the love of her life. And, nearly dying, she buried her strength and confidence alongside him. Since then, life revolved around her son, Mateo. He was the reason she went on. The reason she had endured so much loss and pain. So much grief and failure.

Until last year.

"Mateo," she whispered to no one, "I will come for you. What I must do, I do for you. Be brave."

One sunny, hot morning when she and Mateo had been hunting shells on a Havana beach, Ñico appeared. He came to destroy her. He came for Mateo. When she later awoke in the wet sand, bruised and bloodied, her husband and son were gone.

For the second time, her life was snatched away by a madman. A different madman, perhaps, but a madman all the same.

This current mission was going to save Mateo.

Did she still have it? Was she still a skilled, dangerous operative? Did she have the confidence, the instincts and willingness, to do what it would take to evade her enemies and reach her target?

Do I? That single doubt haunted her. It brought tremors to her hands. It forced her eyes to the ground and caused her to question every step she'd taken forward. Every little inch. Every hope.

Not any longer. You can do this, Cat—a familiar voice whispered—*I am with you.*

"Reynaldo?" She sat upright and searched the darkness. There was no one there—just the empty, dark flat secured by a man she hadn't seen in fifteen years. "Please, Reynaldo, don't leave me. I do this for us. For Mateo."

She'd been in this backstreet apartment waiting for el doctor's next signal. It had been weeks. His next message promised to be the next steps in a circuitous route leading northwest into Nicaragua, through Honduras, and on to Mexico. Once in Mexico, el doctor would arrange her crossing into America and onward to her target.

Always ahead was Operation Perro.

Always ahead was her target. Always behind was Mateo. But soon, with luck and perseverance, they would be united again. Mother and son.

"Reynaldo, I need you. I cannot do this alone. Please...."

Her fingers closed around the crucifix hanging around her neck—a gift so important that its promises were more than simply faith and sacrifice. It was her life. Her mission. Her future. It was the difference between success and failure. Failing would mean more than just a death sentence. It might mean many death sentences. It would perhaps even mean Mateo's.

Sweet, innocent Mateo. So young to be such a significant piece in a dangerous game.

Chancing a flicker of light in the otherwise dark quarters, she used a penlight from her pocket and gazed at a small photograph taken from the side pocket of her backpack. Mateo was only thirteen when the photo was snapped—the only photograph she had left of him. His big, dark eyes beamed happiness. His wide, bright smile consumed his narrow cheeks and contrasted with his shaggy, black hair. The photo was taken the very day Havana sent Ñico to the beach.

She hadn't seen him for more than a few fleeting moments since. When she did, she was always under Ñico's vulturous eyes. Always under his rule. His control.

Tears flooded her face. She prayed he was well cared for—that somewhere in the despair around him he'd found some happiness. That he would know she was coming for him. That he would know how much she loved him and how hard she'd fought on the beach to protect him.

Afterward—after waking in the sand—she'd swore an oath to her keepers that she would complete her mission and be his mother again.

That had been a year—more than three hundred, sixty-five sleepless nights.

"Can I do this? Can I, Reynaldo?"

Only silence answered her.

Silence?

The stillness grabbed her heart and squeezed.

It was frightening. Telling. All night she'd been comforted by the night sounds of the dusty Cartago neighborhood. She had slept in short episodes for the past few hours, just a few minutes at a time. In the intervals, she laid awake listening for telltale signs of danger—footsteps on the stairwell, the rattle of the beer bottle she'd positioned as an alarm, even the idle of a nearby car engine too long in one place.

But silence?

This busy enclave was not unfamiliar to her. She'd used this safe house years ago during an operation. And while under normal circumstances, she'd never use a safe house twice, these were not normal circumstances. She prayed Havana would never think she'd violate that one rule. She had never known quiet to ever settle on this street—this building. On the first floor below her, an all-night bakery prepared the next day's sales. There had been the perpetual banging of pans, low murmurs passing the long hours in the hot kitchen, a radio playing soothing music for the bakers. Those sounds had been comforting and familiar.

Those sounds were now silent.

Reynaldo boomed in her head—*There is danger, Cat. You must go.*

"Stay with me, Reynaldo." She swiped away tears. "I am so alone. I fear so much."

For a long moment—a dangerous, vulnerable time—she couldn't move. She tried and failed to slide from her bedroll to gather herself. Instead, she waited, hoping the inevitable was a whimsy of her imagination.

Cat, you have to move—Reynaldo warned—*Now. Go.*

She jammed Mateo's photo away in her backpack and snapped up to her feet. She grasped the crucifix, said a prayer, and added—*Thank you, Reynaldo. I love you.*

A faint jiggle of the apartment doorknob met her ears. A pause. Another jiggle.

She moved with practiced speed and stealth—grabbed her backpack, pulled out her silenced Makarov, and vanished into the crawlspace above the bedroom closet. As the hidden hatch settled back into place behind her, she heard what she had feared all night—the clink and rattle of the beer bottle rolling across the marble floor that she'd positioned against the apartment door. If the door opened, it would unsettle the bottle's delicate balance and send it rolling away—a trick she'd seen in an old American spy movie.

It worked.

She scurried along a narrow plank positioned across the attic rafters to another concealed trapdoor leading to the roof. A few moments later, she had scurried two buildings over and dropped into an alley.

Sweat rained down her face. Her legs felt weak and rubbery as they carried her into the darkness. Now, she had miles to go before she could stop and rest—all on foot.

She had been mistaken. She'd believed two months in hiding was enough to make her trail cold. She was wrong.

The hunters had found her.

9

June 4, Late Afternoon–Tegucigalpa, Honduras

On a hill overlooking a seedy old district outside Tegucigalpa, Cat located the makeshift church where a line of worshippers threaded from the street through its front door. The church was in an old market and served migrants transiting Tegucigalpa northward among the never-ending herds of migrants trying for the US border. Its pastor provided clean water, a paltry meal, and spiritual comfort for the long journey ahead.

Cat needed more than spiritual comfort. She needed el doctor's next message—another clue on the treasure hunt to steer her safely on to another safe house. A place to rest, find solace and recharge her strength. Safety for a few hours just to close her eyes and rest.

Inside, numerous, old wooden folding chairs were arranged in rows. Ahead of those was a stack of packing crates three high and covered by a dirty, white linen cloth to act as an altar. People filled the rows of seats. The priest had not yet appeared; an elderly woman, worn from years in the hot dirty climate, sat in a chair beside a door leading to a back room.

Beyond her was their confessional.

Cat waited in the line of worshippers seeking confession. When it was her turn, she hefted her backpack higher on her shoulder, and walked casually through the doorway.

Inside, one of Doctor Montilla's contacts, a priest like so many of his others, held her next instructions. Those instructions would contain a route, safe stopping places—allies of el doctor—and her next haven. With each one, she drew one step closer to completing her mission. Each step made her stronger. More confident. Each step was one farther from her past and one closer to her target.

Washington was still far away.

Once inside the back room, she calmed. Believers lined the rows of chairs. None seemed a threat. They were there for what she sought: salvation. Theirs came from their God. Hers came from el doctor.

A sheet suspended over a rope partitioned the room into two sides. On this side, a tall, ladder-back chair awaited her. On the sheet, the silhouette of the priest who sat patiently on the other side waiting for her could be seen.

She sat, and whispered in Spanish, "He was an old man who fished alone in a skiff in the Gulf Stream and he had gone eighty-four days now without taking a fish." The opening line from *The Old Man and the Sea.*

The silhouette stood, moved away deeper into the room, and returned with something in his hand. He signed the cross on its tattered cover, bent, and carefully slid it beneath the sheet's bottom edge to her.

"*Vaya con Dios, mi niña.*" Go with God, child.

She picked up the small, dog-eared bible the priest had given her. "Gracias, Padre."

Behind her, two men rushed past the line of worshippers and into the confessional room. Both held pistols. One of them ran forward and yanked down the sheet that concealed the priest.

"You will die for helping this one, Priest." The gunman struck him but didn't unseat him. "But not before you tell us everything."

The priest jumped up, but the gunman pistol-whipped him violently across the face, knocking him to the floor.

"No." Cat moved to help him up. "Leave him alone. He has done nothing."

"Ah, but you, señorita. You are the one."

They had found her.

Her heart sank. Tears filled her eyes.

El doctor's entire network was in danger—life-threatening danger—and it was her fault. Somehow, they had followed her. She had been so careful. So meticulous. And now, they had the priest. They had her. They would find el doctor's message in her bible. Soon, they would torture everything out of the priest—names, addresses, code phrases and more. In the end, her mission would cost many lives and she would still have failed.

What have I done? I cannot do this. Why did I ever assume…?

Think, Cat—Reynaldo's voice whispered through her despair— *It does not have to be. There is time.*

"Reynaldo, can I do this?" she whispered. "Can I save them all?"

One of the gunmen spun around, searching for someone else in the room. "Who is it you speak to, *puta*? Where are they?"

"Por favor, I have money." She slid her backpack from her shoulder and reached into the side pocket. "Perhaps you might consider another way, no?"

"Give me the money, *puta*," one of the men ordered. "Or we take it from your corpse."

The gunman standing near the priest lunged for her.

She stepped back and fired her Makarov from inside the canvas pocket. Before the man hit the floor, she turned toward the second Dirección de Inteligencia, G2 operative, and shot him point blank in the chest. He faltered but didn't go down. She fired twice more.

It was done.

Her heart sank and she couldn't breathe. She was frozen— numb—staring at the men she had just killed.

Screams erupted outside the room.

She struggled for calm, finally achieving a long, deep gasp of air. She stood looking compassionately at the two men on the floor.

"Forgive me, Father, for I have sinned."

"No child." The priest embraced her. "You saved many."

Before she could reply, she pulled away and ran to the side window, leaned out, and vomited.

10

June 12, Morning–The Roman Catholic Diocese of Nuevo Laredo, Mexico

Gunfire in Nuevo Laredo was not unusual. Neither was the dissonance of mortal combat—the constant struggle between Federales, gangs, and the cartels. There was rarely any resolution, just the push and pull of factions trying hopelessly for domination.

At the end of each day, there were only bodies. Only sorrow.

Cat was not unaccustomed to such violence—a consequence of being a Cuban Dirección de Inteligencia operative—though her years absent from the field may have dulled her senses. She feared that. Some of her missions had been simple and smooth, utilizing surveillance that required no more than stealth, timing, and luck. On one mission, luck was absent, and it had taken Reynaldo's life and turned his best friend, Ñico, into a cold-blooded thug.

Her life had never been the same afterward.

The door to her small, barren room opened and a tall, thin priest rushed in.

"*Catalina, date prisa. Ellos están aquí. ¡Debes irte del santuario.*"— *Catalina, hurry. They are here. You must leave the sanctuary.* Father Martínez's face was anxious and worried. He was out of breath from running the hallways and stairs into the basement where the Diocese's residential rooms were. "Hurry."

Cat finished tying her long, dark hair in a ponytail down her back. She stood and deftly dressed in old jeans, a dark tank top, and running shoes. She stuffed her things into her backpack—suddenly tired of the chase, wishing it were over. Knowing it would never be.

But her mission was ahead. Behind her, Mateo's life was balanced against her success. She had to go on.

Time to be strong again, Cat—Reynaldo whispered—*Show no fear. No hesitation. No panic.*

"What about the others?" she asked. "Are they in danger?"

"*No habia tiempo.*"—*There was no time.* Father Martínez continued in Spanish. "They are safe. They are in the secret vault. Go, while you can. I will take care of everything. When it is safe, I will ring the bells three times. Return only then."

She slung her backpack onto a shoulder, placed a hand on her crucifix, and said a quick prayer. "Si, Padre. Be careful. I pray your kindness will not bring you harm."

Father Martínez reached out and touched the crucifix in her hand. "In my youth, I was once like these men—a guerrilla fighter in Honduras. Then, I found Jesus. Stay close to Him; He will be your guide."

"Padre, el doctor? He told me to meet him here...?"

"Si, si, he has arrived." Father Martínez glanced toward the doorway. "He is in the secret basement room with the others. For now, you must leave. The only access is across the courtyard. You cannot reach him without crossing the men who have come. For now, child, go."

So close to the doctor. How could she just leave?

As she turned, Father Martínez took her hand and pressed a folded piece of paper into it. "You have money?"

"Si, enough."

"Here are instructions I had for el doctor and you. Take them. If all goes well, you can both use them. If not..."

If not? Her stomach churned. The thousands of miles she'd already traveled might now all come down to three bell chimes. "I understand. Gracias, Padre. Tell el doctor I am coming back."

"I will." He gestured to the paper in her hand. "Beware, those coyotes are dangerous men. Where I send you is a dangerous place. Be careful. Very careful."

She kissed his cheek, slipped from the room, and jogged down the hall.

Voices reached her from the hallway stairs. First, fearful shouts. Gunshots followed. Then, silence.

The doctor was within reach—just a few hundred yards away—but he might as well be nowhere. She could never traverse the compound to the secret vault's entrance while gunmen searched the Diocese. To do so might place all those inside in grave danger. She would have to run, hide, and return when these men were gone. El doctor's last and final message had brought her here. Their next step was into the United States. Her mission was there.

So close.

More shouting. Panicked cries. A sporadic barrage of gunfire. *May God rest their souls.*

She deeply regretted the danger she'd brought to Father Martínez and those under his protection. For the first half of her journey, she walked in fear—uncertain if her once-omnipotent skills were still hers to wield. Years ago, losing Reynaldo vacated her tenacity. Despair consumed her. Her skills had languished and been hidden away—hidden so deep she thought she would never find them again. Tegucigalpa had forced her to summon those skills and step out of fear's grip. A trade: violence for survival. Since then, she walked a little easier. Slept a little sounder. Slowly discovering the operative she once was.

She was becoming the old Catalina Reyes, with steel and fearlessness.

It had been so long coming.

Now, after finally reaching Doctor Montilla, the hounds were close again.

She gripped the cross around her neck again and prayed el doctor and she would soon reunite. Then, she ascended the stairs to the main Diocese hallways. At the ground floor, she wound around the main hall that encompassed the inner courtyard. There, louder voices—angry, and raging—drew her to them. She knelt beside a hall window where she might see and go unnoticed.

Out in the middle of the compound, three armed men herded church staff together. One man strode behind them, ordering them about. The sight of him sent fear slithering through her. He was forty, dark-skinned, taut, and wiry. He was dressed in black jeans and boots, a black military field jacket, and a dark polo shirt. His face was shadowed with a day's stubble—always for appearance more than indifference—and his eyes were dark as coal and soulless. He held a small-framed, Russian Makarov semiautomatic pistol as he commanded his two ever-present, loyal minions—Ché and Mendo.

Ñico? Here? How was this possible?

She leaned close to the window and listened.

Father Martínez ran into the courtyard toward the men. Ché intercepted him and knocked him to his knees in front of the staff that was already corralled.

Ñico took something from his jacket pocket and held it up to Martínez's face. "I am looking for this woman. She has things that belong to me. Important things."

Father Martínez shrugged. "I am sorry. I do not know such a woman. Perhaps another church…?"

"No." Ñico pushed the photo closer to him. "She is here."

There was a muffled debate that Cat couldn't hear. As she peered through the window, Ché delivered a jackhammer punch into Father Martínez's solar plexus and drove the wind from him. A second punch crumpled him onto the stone courtyard as Mendo, the baby-faced gunman, grabbed two others nearby—another priest and a janitor—and propelled them forward.

Ñico lifted his pistol and shot the janitor in one knee, sending him down. He turned the pistol toward the janitor. "Father?"

"Stop. I beg you." Father Martínez stood, trying to shield the janitor. "The one you seek is not here."

Ñico's calm voice was difficult to hear as he shoved Father Martínez aside and raised his pistol to the janitor's head.

Father Martínez signed the cross and begged once more.

Ñico ended the old janitor's life.

Father Martínez cried out, "This is a house of God. Have you no shame?"

Ñico struck the priest's cheek viciously with his pistol. "What is shame, Father?"

11

June 12, Late Afternoon–Nuevo Laredo, Mexico

The Diocese bells never rang. Cat had waited in the secret tunnel for hours, just a block from the compound. Father Martínez had warned her, and she had obeyed.

She had moved quickly through Nuevo Laredo's streets, weaving and backtracking, lessening the possibility that anyone could trace and intercept her. With each pivot northward, she moved closer to the border. Focusing on her mission. Closer to her target.

She had spent the past fifteen years trying hard to move beyond Caracas and losing Reynaldo. Only Mateo had kept her from self-destruction. Each day of those years had brought her closer to this point—closer to her last, undeniable mission. She was so close to the border now. Once across, she had only to blend into the flow of immigrants fanning out across the US and make her way north. What waited for her there would decide her fate forever.

It would decide Mateo's, too.

The plan had been for Doctor Montilla to guide her across the border and northward. But that was not to be. Father Martínez had foreseen this possibility. He'd given her information on a coyote who would arrange her passage alone. All it would take was courage and money.

She had the money. Did she have the courage?

She located the seedy cantina, *Padrillo*—The Grand Stallion. She knew such places and dreaded what she must do. The men within Padrillo would claim the same vigor and machismo as a good horse. They made their living on other's dreams for America. They were cruel, duplicitous men. Dangerous men, but necessary.

The gruff man standing in the cantina doorway sent a chill through her as she walked up the street toward the building.

You can do this, Cat—Reynaldo said—*I'm with you.*

Inside, the cantina was everything she'd feared. A dozen Latinos sat at tables and perched on barstools. They were grungy and poorly dressed. A few played pool in a back room visible through an archway. The men at the bar turned in unison to gawk when she entered. Behind the bar an older woman leaned against a rickety rack of cheap Mexican liquor, smoking a hand-rolled cigarette and drinking a can of beer.

The air was heavy with tobacco, sweat, and despair.

With Cat's appearance, the men leered. One of them grabbed for her arm, but she pulled it away and continued to the corner of the bar where none of the men sat. Her breath quickened and sweat pooled on her forehead. She slipped her hands in her jeans pockets to hide their tremors.

"Por favor," she said to the poorly aging, haggard barmaid. "Por favor?"

The barmaid ambled to her, listened to Cat's request, and shook her head. In throaty Spanish, gruff from too many cigarettes and booze, she croaked, "You better leave, girl, before bad things happen. Go on."

"They are here." Cat handed her a twenty-dollar US bill. "I am in a hurry."

The barmaid shrugged, nodded toward the back room, and returned to her cerveza and cigarette.

Cat took a deep breath. She had to project strength. Anything less would leave her dead on the floor. She turned, hefted her backpack tighter on her shoulder, and walked across the bar to the archway. The men inside playing pool were cleaner, better-dressed versions of the gruff, older crowd behind her. All of them had handguns prominently displayed in their waistbands.

One Latino stood out. He was clean-shaven and wore a new cowboy hat and snakeskin boots. A bottle of Gentlemen Jack Daniels bourbon sat with him at a round table in the corner, and he sipped a glassful. He locked eyes on her, let them stray down her body and slowly back up, taking long, telling pauses at her groin and bosom.

This was the man she'd come to see. The dealmaker who American television called, El Jefe.

"I come to make a deal." She moved closer and handed him the handwritten note. "Father Martínez sends his regards."

"Father Martínez is trying to save the world," El Jefe said. "You, I don't know."

"This is who I am." She tossed a roll of US dollars on the table before him. "Do you like me now?"

"Si, very much." He unfolded Father Martínez's note and read it carefully. Then, he sized Cat up again. "How soon?"

"Tonight."

"Of course. But speed costs extra." He withdrew a pen and a small business card from his pocket. He scribbled on the card and slid it across the table. "This address is for my fastest men. They will take you across tonight."

"Bueno." She picked up his card and backed away. "I have put extra in your fee. I wish no one to know I was here."

El Jefe's face darkened. "There are others searching for you? ¿Policía? Federales?"

"Who is not important. There is one-thousand American dollars extra to forget I was here."

El Jefe considered the roll of bills in front of him, then looked back at her. "Perhaps I can triple that from those who wish to find you. No?"

"Do not change our arrangement."

"Or what?" He waved to the two men playing pool and waited as they dropped their cues and ambled over. "Do with her as you will, but keep her alive. There is money to be made."

They were on her. One grabbed her arms and pulled her backward to the pool table. The other stripped her backpack from her shoulders and dropped it next to her as they pushed her atop the table. One grabbed her shirt, popped buttons, and tore the fabric. The other grappled with her jeans, trying to pull them down for the assault.

She struggled to free herself.

The first punched her hard in the mouth, splitting her lip and steeling her resistance. He grabbed one leg and jerked it sideways, splitting her legs until she cried out.

Terror began to overtake her—it swelled inside and seized her—paralyzing her reason and ability to remain calm and ready. As they pushed and shoved one another for the right of first, she felt Reynaldo nearby and she smiled.

Cat, think…survive. They will not expect your skills. Wait for the right moment.

"Si, my husband."

As the two men struggled with their flies, the right moment arrived.

***

Ten minutes later, Cat reached the corner adjacent to Padrillo as the smoke started to rise through the cantina's roof. Flames escaped the windows and doors. The old, decrepit structure was a mass of flames. In moments, there was no evidence that she had ever been inside. No trail for anyone to follow. No one alive to betray her passing.

She glanced again at the address El Jefe had given her, tucked it into her jeans, and headed down the street.

12

June 12, Late Afternoon–Central Park, Manhattan, New York

The best defense…

Ana knew the idiom as well as anyone. She believed it to her bones. But here, now, was it true? Could she simply stalk Colonel Vergara and eliminate the threat he posed to Sarah and her? Could she dismiss the consequences? The laws? After all, this was Manhattan, not the jungle. Here, she was merely a college graduate, not a militant guerrilla.

At least, that's what she hoped.

Over the past days, she had wandered Central Park looking for Vergara. The closest man resembling him was a large, frumpy man feeding ducks and sipping a bottle of liquor without care who saw him. After covering some five miles of walking paths, she checked her watch and decided to return to the subway for the ride back to Queens.

Lobo would be waiting for his afternoon walk. Sarah would be ready for more homeschool studies.

At a small refreshment kiosk, she purchased an iced coffee and sat on a bench near an overpass. Beneath the overpass, a band of musicians played jazz and entertained a small crowd. The music was lively, and she listened as they broke into a string of forties tunes.

She was lost in the music in no time.

In college, she'd come to love forties music. Part of it was the history—she devoured all things from the era. Part of it was the purity of the instrumentals and vocals—the smooth, enticing tunes by Glenn Miller and the Dorsey's, and the clean, vibrant voices of Peggy Lee, Billie Holiday, and Helen Forrest. Poppi had introduced her to the music during the few months a year she'd spent with her. Ana's love of swing and big bands followed her back to Colombia where she wore out cassettes and thousands of batteries in her players.

Now, sitting on the bench sipping her iced coffee, she pined for her simple, carefree college days. For those short four years, she'd escaped the stress of her more illicit past and walked Manhattan as a normal young lady.

Since then, regrets and misadventures had haunted her.

Might those hauntings have caused her to imagine Vergara? Was it the nightmares and terrible memories that conjured Vergara into the park? An illusion of anguish and repentance?

Perhaps Yiayia Poppi had been right. Perhaps she hadn't seen Vergara at all. Perhaps it was someone else, someone void of violence and bloodstains—her bloodstains. Perhaps her fears simply manifested his presence to taunt her.

Perhaps.

On another bench across from her, a young couple cuddled as they listened to the music. They giggled, oblivious to those around them, as passion got the better of them. The girl, perhaps nineteen, had fiery red hair and an irresistible smile.

Ana caught herself staring. Familiarity nagged and squeezed her heart. Then, a face flashed before her and tears suddenly rained down.

***

Fifteen Years Earlier–December 12, Early Evening–

Jardin, Antioquia Department, Colombia–Fifty miles south of Medellin

Ana watched from across the street as the tourists sat sipping beers and cocktails on the veranda of the El Dorado restaurant. The dozen or more people laughed and mingled in groups, happy to be off the bus after the long, winding mountain trek from Medellin. Their excitement made them oblivious to the two men watching them intently from a corner table.

Ana saw them. She had been watching all along.

The men had arrived shortly before the tourists' scheduled bus—late by only two hours. But given the bus's history, they were fortunate the delay was not longer. Spotters along the bus route made the men's arrival at the restaurant anything but a coincidence. As they drank beer and nibbled at a basket of fresh bread, they kept a close watch on the tourist group, ready to move as soon as any strayed from the El Dorado to venture the dusty streets of historic Antioquia.

Before the men arrived, Ana had been waiting across the plaza at a small café where her line of sight allowed her an unobstructed view of the restaurant's veranda. She had witnessed the men taking their seats earlier and knew they required her complete attention.

These were dangerous men. Men on the hunt.

Early evening in Jardin meant music and laughter. It meant cooler temperatures, good food, and cold beer. There would be few vehicles or townspeople on the streets. Locals would be home or frequenting their own, local cafés where the food was savory and traditional, but the prices affordable. The expensive cantinas and restaurants were left for the tourists where barkeeps and pretty, smiling waitresses preyed on their American dollars and Euros.

Evening also meant the arrival of men such as those she watched now.

In Jardin, like the nearby jungles, evening was for the hunt.

A young couple, Europeans or Americans, climbed from a cab in front of the El Dorado and stood looking up onto the veranda at the other tourists. Then, they turned away and strolled into the main plaza, clutching each other as they kissed passionately and laughed. He was tall and thin with wavy, blond hair and a babyface complexion. She was much shorter, with fiery red hair and a smile that blossomed infectiously at his every word or touch. Too many cocktails elsewhere had enhanced their libidos and diminished their reason. They were out for an evening walk and perhaps some forbidden public romance where no tourist—or wise villager—would venture at that hour.

Ana sat quietly, observing them meandering around the quaint, picturesque square. Jardin's whitewashed restaurants, shops, and homes were framed in brightly colored doors and balconies—reds, greens, yellows, and blues that gave the pueblo a festive, friendly aura. It was early by local standards. Jardin's nightlife was already bustling.

Soon, the Federales and local uniformed policía would begin their sporadic patrols looking for drug runners and bandits targeting the tourists. They would also be on guard for others far more dangerous than mere bandits: FARC guerrillas. While Colombian policemen were often on FARC payrolls, Jardin's police had a reputation for integrity and grit. Tourist dollars were too valuable, and they took great pride in ensuring the turistas returned and their money flowed.

As Ana watched the young couple wander toward the end of the square, the two men on the El Dorado veranda stood. One dropped some pesos on their table, took a quick survey of a gathering of ladies near the bar, and then followed his companion slowly onto the square. As the second man stepped down on the street, his windbreaker fluttered and revealed a heavy pistol clipped to his belt.

Ana moved.

She edged along El Liberatado Plaza, getting ahead of the young couple when they stopped by the fountain to toss in coins and wishes for their blissful forever. Keeping to the shadows, she made it down Carrera 3 ahead of them.

She arrived just in time.

The couple stopped along the street for a long embrace. As passion blinded them, the two men appeared ahead of them and waited, watching. One of the men kept a hand inside his jacket; the other now slung a leather shoulder bag on his side, his hand resting just inside its flap.

"Por favor, debes venir conmigo ahora," Ana called, running to the couple. "Por favor."

The couple was startled. The man snapped up a hand to stop Ana. "What do you want? I don't understand. Speak slower."

"You speak English?"

He nodded and eyed her cautiously, pulling the woman tightly against him.

"I am Ana. We must hurry."

"Why?"

"Those men come." Ana threw a thumb over her shoulder toward the men lingering nearby. "They will take you. You must come with me. Now."

The young woman gripped her companion's arm. "Ted? What's going on?"

"I don't know, Cindy." Ted glanced back at the men. "Who are they?"

"FARC." Ana had a taste of fright in her voice. "Guerrillas. You must come with me and get off the street. There is no time."

The mention of FARC turned the couple pale. Ted glanced from the men to Cindy, and back to Ana. "Where?"

"With me." Ana grabbed his arm and pulled, leading them down a side street where her small, battered Nissan waited. They made it as the men came into view again. One pulled a pistol from beneath his jacket and the other a submachine gun from his shoulder bag. They looked around and began racing toward them.

"Get in," she ordered. "I'll take you away. Hurry."

"Wait, shouldn't we just go to the bar?" Ted looked at the

rusted, bald-tired sedan. "It'll be safe there, right?"

"No." Ana pushed him toward the passenger door. "Those men were there earlier. There could be others."

"How can we trust you?" Ted turned to his Cindy. "What do you think, babe?"

"It's her or them." Cindy released his arm and climbed into the car, pulling him in with her. "Please, take us to our hotel—the Hacienda Balandu. It's across town."

"I know it." Ana climbed in, started the Nissan, and sped from the curb and away from the two men just in time. "Stay down. Lay on the seat. Don't lift your heads."

Ted was atop Cindy in the back. She was frantic, almost crying as he whispered soothing somethings trying to calm her.

Ana made a violent left, sped another two blocks, and wrenched the sedan right into an alley. There, she continued one more block before slamming on the brakes.

"Oh, no. No. No."

Ted sat up. "What's the matter?"

"Trouble." Ana stared out the front window. "Be calm. I will try to help."

Ahead, bathed in the Nissan's one working headlight, four armed, balaclava-masked guerrillas waited. They aimed rifles and pistols at the car and waved for Ana to cut the engine.

"Oh, my God, Ted," Cindy cried. "What's happening?"

Ana spun in the seat. "Do you have money? Maybe I can pay them."

"Yes…at the, the, the hotel." Ted's voice was frantic and dry. "But…."

"Do not tell them yet. Let me see if I can—"

Ana's door flew open and strong arms pulled her from the car into the darkness.

***

Present Day–Central Park

Memories of Cindy and Ted were vivid and painful, as if she'd seen them only yesterday instead of many years past. They were casualties of Ana's life in Colombia following her parents on their dangerous misadventures. Those adventures seemed so foreign and obscure now. She'd been Ana Montilla then; her mother's daughter. Someone who had grown far beyond her youth and had done things others her age could not comprehend. Things no one so young—perhaps no one of any age—should bear.

But it was her past and it was as attached to her as a second shadow, one that didn't disappear with the sun. It was always a part of her. The shadow that was Ana Karras.

As much as she had tried to rid herself, it was Ana Montilla, not Ana Karras, who could do what was necessary to protect her family—to protect Sarah and Poppi. For that one reason, she could not allow her shadow to disappear just yet. As ugly as it made her feel, she needed her.

Bright, green eyes and an infectious smile flashed across her thoughts.

"My sweet, Sarah. My koúkla." She closed her eyes and let the music soothe her. "Forgive me, Yiayia Poppi. I must do this."

She finished her iced coffee, tossed a few dollars into the trio's open instrument cases, and listened to the last few notes of a tune. When she headed toward the nearest subway stop, the air rushed from her lungs as the nearby faces and surroundings blurred.

A dozen yards farther along a walking path, headed deeper into the park, were the three men.

Colonel Vergara.

13

June 12, Late Evening–Central Park West, Manhattan,
New York

Vergara would never see her coming.

Ana sat on a park bench near the 85th Street entrance. She wore black jeans, a dark button-down blouse that fit loosely to conceal her femininity, and black running shoes. She held her backpack tightly between her legs and her cell phone to one ear, pretending to have a conversation like the millions of other New Yorkers roaming Manhattan's busy streets.

Tonight was the night. It was time. Strike where no one expected her. Strike fast. Strike first. That was how Ana Montilla would defeat her enemy and save her family. Save herself.

She had reconnoitered the brownstone since spotting Vergara in the park again and following him home. She'd returned to Queens only long enough to gather changes for her appearance—a different coat, shoes, glasses, and hat. All of which were stowed in her backpack among her other mission essentials she'd returned with to Central Park. She considered the approaches to the brownstone from Central Park West, 85th Street and 84th, determining her moves and fixing her plan. Now, all she needed was time and luck.

A lot of luck.

Research on her cell phone told her enough to plan with. The brownstone, built in the late 1800s, proffered a Queen Anne exterior, a Guggenheim stairway leading up to its twelve-thousand square foot, single-family residence with a recent purchase price of more than twenty-eight million dollars. Over the years, the building had been home to a railway tycoon, numerous Wall Street pirates, and foreign elite and royalty. Now it was home to a Latino who spoke to no one, rarely ventured outside but for an occasional walk through the park, and who received no visitors and no mail.

A hermit in a new shell.

Ana knew only a few details of the building and the surrounding area that she'd been able to glean from the internet on her phone while sitting in the park observing the brownstone. She'd studied the street; the brownstone's physical layout. There was a bit of information from several past magazine and newspaper articles of architectural interests and stories of the rich and famous. All included an ample supply of photographs of the brownstone's interior that gave her an insider's view for her mission. Google Earth provided more excellent surveillance planning information. All this from a park bench two hundred yards from Vergara's front door.

It wasn't a perfect plan, but it was the best she could devise in a short time.

Surprise and stealth. Vergara would never expect her to bring the fight to him.

The brownstone had two closed-circuit television cameras mounted surreptitiously on its entrance. She stayed clear of those and knew that if there were two, there would be others. There might also be alarms and other defenses. Caution was paramount. One poor move and she could end up in jail—or dead.

Those two outcomes were not necessarily mutually exclusive.

She moved north along Central Park West and crossed to go east on West 86th Street. There, she crossed back south again and approached the brownstone along West 85th, a residential block of more historic luxurious buildings. A dozen yards from the rear of the brownstone, she stopped beside an unoccupied Mercedes parked with its emergency flashers on in front of a townhome.

Casually using the side window to check her reflection, she slipped a black baseball cap on and tucked her hair underneath it. Her appearance once again transformed. As she did, the reflection grabbed her heart and *squeezed.*

Ana Montilla gazed sadly back at her. The dark clothing and ball cap—stalking clothes. A backpack with rope, tools, gloves, and a silenced pistol—battle gear. She was again Ana Montilla, guerrilla fighter and…assassin?

The first time she'd seen death she'd only been ten. She'd been the decoy for a FARC kidnapping outside Bogota—a lost little girl seeking help at a well-guarded estate. A guard had taken pity on her and opened the estate's gates to take her in for water and shelter while he phoned the policía. A few seconds later, the kind young man lay dead inside his gate shack as Mamá and her team infiltrated the home and carried out their mission. Mamá celebrated her contribution—even bragged about her manipulation of the guard. On their return to the camp, fighters celebrated her initiation to their cause. Secretly, she'd wept as she would do many times again.

What am I doing?

For a moment she fought back eyefuls of regret. During the days she'd searched for Vergara, she'd convinced herself that she had to strike first and ensure Sarah, Poppi, and she were safe. Self-defense by offense. Now, her reflection in the Mercedes window knotted her stomach and filled her with shame and nausea.

She had planned a clandestine infiltration of Vergara's lair. She'd planned every move. Every possibility. Every outcome. She prepared an offense she convinced herself was premeditated self-defense.

Ana Karras was mortified by Ana Montilla's scheme.

"Dammit, Ana. What are you doing? You made a promise to Yiayia Poppi—to yourself. You don't have to do this. It's not too late."

She was wrong. It was too late.

As she scowled at her reflection, two men flanked her. Both were heavy-set, dark Latinos in business suits. They moved with surprising speed and deftness, grabbed her elbows and arms, and forced her into the seam between them.

A pistol prodded her side.

"Buenos noches, Ana Montilla," Tomãs taunted. "I see you have come as you promised."

14

*June 13, Very Early Morning–Central Park West,
Manhattan, New York*

An average-built man with sharp, striking features stood on the sidewalk across Central Park West from the brownstone. He'd been watching the cluster of New York Police Department cruisers for several minutes, deciding on his next moves. Several uniformed officers milled about near their cars while another stood on the stoop entrance to the multi-million-dollar luxury home controlling entry. At that hour, he wasn't sure who the police expected to control entry from, though, he was about to make their list.

The man had dark hair, unkempt and straggly, with a scruffy beard traversing a square jaw. He wore jeans and hiking boots, a tight-fitting black T-shirt, and a dark, military-style field jacket. As he approached the group of New York's finest, one of them held up a hand and waved him off.

"Keep moving," the officer said, stepping toward him. "Unless you live here."

"Special Agent Trane. Homeland." Trane flashed a leather credential case from his jacket pocket and continued up the stairs to the officer at the door. There, the officer at the brownstone's door glanced down at the first policeman, received a nod of approval, and stepped aside.

"What's this got to do with you?" the officer at the door asked.

"More than it does you."

Inside, Trane crossed the foyer and stood watching the rest of NYPD's response team working the room. No one had noticed his arrival. No one seemed interested in anything but the body on the floor in the middle of the room.

A dark-complexioned detective, with curly black hair and clean shaven, stood above the body lying on his back. Trane guessed the detective was of mixed descent, Latino—possibly Puerto Rican—and western European. The detective wore a dark suit with a black polo shirt, and he carried a notebook as he jotted notes.

Trane said nothing and listened to the conversation in the room. The detective—called Brennan by one of the crime scene techs kneeling beside the body—seemed to be in charge.

"Looks like a fireplug. Tough guy, right?" Brennan asked. "He's shorter than me but built. I'm five-ten and one-eighty. He's maybe five-five and over two hundred."

"Kinda weird," one of the techs said.

"Weird like he's wearing superhero underwear?" Brennan quipped. "Or space alien weird?"

The tech grinned. "Ah, then not weird by your standards. Dead from gunshot, probably a twenty-two from the entry wound. Right through the chest and probably clipped his heart. Two upstairs dead of gunshots, twenty-two caliber as well."

"What's the weird part?"

"Three big, armed Latino security guys, right?"

"Yeah?"

"This guy here," the tech gestured to the body, "got the only shot off. One. The shooter took all three out clean and snappy. Three big bruisers and they got whacked good."

"That's not really weird." Brennan shrugged. "Lucky, maybe. Shooter surprised them?"

"Maybe," the tech said. "Whoever killed them, surprised them I think, and got all three clean. I haven't found any brass or other trace of the shooter, either. Shooter's a ghost."

"Pro hit?" Brennan considered the dead man on the floor. "Maybe two shooters?"

"Maybe," the second tech said. "This guy got the crap kicked out of him, too."

"Tough guy like this?" Brennan cocked his head. "Looks like a fighter? A hard one to push around. I'm thinking two guys."

"That's your thing, Brennan," the first tech said. "We do the trace. You do the chase."

"That's so clever, man. Really." Brennan jotted notes. "Can I use that?"

"Excuse me, gentlemen," Trane said, stepping casually into the room. "I'll take over from here."

The room snapped silent.

"Who the hell are you?" Brennan looked up straight at Trane. "Who let you in?"

"I need you to round up your men and move them out, Detective." Trane waved around the room. "The faster the better."

Brennan stared him, unblinking. "Excuse me? The faster the better? Yeah, the faster you get out of here the better. You haven't told me who you are yet."

"Trane."

Brennan grinned. "Like a choo choo?"

"Very clever, Detective. I've never heard that one before." Trane held up his credentials again and kept them eye-level with the detective. "Special Agent Trane, Homeland Security."

"What's DHS got to do with my crime scene?"

"This is a diplomatic situation," Trane said. "National security."

"If it's diplomatic," Brennan said, "where's the State Department?"

Trane pocketed his credentials. "Have your men pull out and secure the outer perimeter until the rest of my team arrive. They'll be here shortly."

"Oh, they will?" Brennan's voice dripped with sarcasm. "This is a NYPD homicide scene, Trane. We're not going anywhere."

Trane held up a hand. "Hold that thought."

Another plain clothed detective, an Asian-American with slim, pale features and shaggy, black hair, came down the open spiral staircase from the second floor.

"What's going on, Brennan?" the detective asked. "I can hear you bitching upstairs."

Brennan jutted a finger at Trane. "Some suit from Homeland, or so he says, thinks he's kicking us out."

"It's for you, Detective Brennan," Trane said. "You'll want to take it."

Brennan's cell phone rang and he glanced at the screen. "One-P-P. Ah, shit. Sit on him, Chan." He wandered from the front room down a hallway toward the rear of the brownstone. He was gone only a few moments. When he returned, his face was red and tight and his eyes dissected Trane with rising contempt.

"Well, you got some juice," Brennan grunted. "I'll give you that."

Trane said nothing.

"You wanna fill us in on why DHS is stealing our scene?" Chan asked.

"Not really." Trane waved his hand around the room. "But if it makes you feel better, one of you can walk me through what you have so far. Everyone else needs to move outside the perimeter."

Brennan stood shaking his head. "You gotta be kidding me. You want me to give you the nickel tour before you boot us?"

Trane nodded. "If there's a problem, I can get One-P-P back to you."

"No, no problem, Secret Agent Choo Choo," Brennan sneered. "Hey, how'd you hear about our scene?"

"It's Trane, Detective, and it doesn't matter how I heard. I'm here and you're leaving."

Brennan's face reddened. "You know, Trane, I know a lot of the Feds around town. Do you know Agent—"

"No." Trane wandered the room, examining everything he saw. "I'm from DC. I don't care who you know. You have your orders. Move your men out."

"My orders?" Brennan nearly spit. "I don't take orders from you."

"Perhaps not, but you do from One-P-P. And they said out."

Chan shook his head. "This is bull and you know it."

"I don't have time for all this, Detectives." Trane thumbed toward the foyer. "No notes or memories or stories leave here. Got it? Everything they have stays here. Everything. This crime scene is classified."

"Classified?" Brennan snapped. "What about the vics? Are they classified, too? Transport's almost here to get them to the morgue."

"My people will handle the morgue."

Brennan aimed a gun-finger at Trane. "Something tells me your name isn't Trane and you're not DHS."

"Come on, Brennan," Chan said. "For once can't you keep your mouth shut?"

Brennan eyed Trane. "I ain't worried about this guy complaining about my smart Irish mouth."

"I thought you were Puerto Rican," Chan said.

"Only half—the sweet, lovable half on my mother's side. The Irish half gets me in trouble. Like now."

Trane held up a hand. "Detectives, don't make me call One-P-P again."

"Okay, okay," Brennan grunted and gave orders to the other officers to vacate the scene. When they had left, he took a deep breath and brushed back his curly hair. "We'll start with this guy. As you can see, he's dead."

The body in the center of the room was a Latino who was short and stout and dressed in a dark business suit. He had powerful arms that his sleeves strained against. He lay on his back with a single gunshot in his chest—a decisive center mass shot. His outstretched hand lay above the shoulder with his fingers a foot from the stainless steel nine-millimeter semiautomatic pistol lying nearby.

"I'm all ears, Detective." Trane folded his arms. "I'm hanging on your every word."

"Good for you." Brennan glared contempt but opened his notebook. "We got a call from the neighbors just after midnight. Old gal said she heard gunshots and saw someone running from the back of this place. We were here pretty fast."

"Of course you were," Trane said dryly. "I bet all the Central Part West millionaires get fast service."

"Screw you, Trane. One-P-P says I gotta turn this over to you. They said nothing of taking your shit."

"Touché, Detective." Trane grinned and mocked a salute. "Go

on."

Brennan checked his notes. "Three bodies. This high-priced suit down here and two upstairs in the master bedroom's sitting room. All Latino. The two upstairs were killed up-close and personal, too. Neat. Clean."

"Names?" Trane asked. "Anything?"

"Nothing. No IDs. No mail. Nothing in here yet that we found to identify them. Just lots of money dripping from the walls."

Trane nodded. "Okay. What else?"

"I bet all you Feds have digs like this, right Trane?" Brennan asked.

"Of course, and a Maserati, too." Trane gestured to the spiral staircase. "Show me the upstairs."

Brennan led him up the spiral staircase to the second floor and into the sitting room right off the landing.

The room was filled with lavish furnishings. Across from the entrance was a King George writing desk and chairs. A large, plush couch sat in the center of the room and faced a big-screen television mounted above a white marble fireplace and mantel. The walls were decorated with a variety of scenic Manhattan skyline paintings that reminded him of television shows of Hollywood elites. The walls were a rich, golden wallpaper with contrasting mahogany crown molding, and expensive Italian floor tile accented with deep-pile Turkish rugs. The room was lit with tasteful lighting that bathed the room in a soft glow that seemed surreal compared to the body on the floor.

Brennan pointed his pen at the body. "Corpse two."

The Latino body lay facing the center of the room, away from the large, heavy double-door that Brennan indicated led to the master bedroom and the third victim. While Trane had trouble estimating the age of Latinos and Asians, he guessed this one was in his mid-to-late thirties. He was an average-sized man, muscular but not overly powerful with tight, short hair. The body was facedown and sprawled out as though it had simply fallen forward onto the colorful Turkish carpet that was now matted in blood. There were no obvious signs of a struggle—just the bullet entry in the back of his head.

Brennan gestured to the body. "We were about to bag the hands up to the armpits to protect for residue and trace. But based on what I'm seeing, I'm thinking the shooter was a few feet away and popped him clean and neat from behind. Probably a twenty-two again. Just like downstairs."

"Got any actual evidence?" Trane turned in a circle, looking the room over. "Casings? Anything left behind?"

"A little."

Trane faced him and locked onto his eyes. "You'll leave it all downstairs before you go."

"Whatever."

Next, Brennan led him to the double doors and gestured to the doorframe where the wood was splintered and the door hasp had given way. "Forced entry here. Somebody kicked it in. Maybe there's a match down the road. Your guys should check for shoe prints on the door."

"I'm sure they will."

Inside the bedroom, another Latino body lay front and center among the lavish furnishings and artwork. He lay on his back just inside the doorway, sprawled backward. He was a pudgy, short man dressed in dark slacks and a pullover golf shirt. He looked like he'd just stood in the doorway when he was shot in the forehead with a small caliber round. A neat bullet hole was near perfect center in his forehead. The room was untouched—no open drawers on the dressers, no clothes or personal items strewn about. No indication of any altercation or misadventure anywhere.

Just the dead body.

"Corpse number three." Brennan moved carefully inside the room. "Bullet's still inside his skull. Looks like a twenty-two again. Small, quiet, and easily silenced."

"Anything else?" Trane asked after scanning the room. "Any leads?"

Brennan hesitated, then led him back out of the bedroom to the sitting room. There, he pointed to the wall beside the large, arched doorway and at a round, plastic device slightly out of arm's reach above the floor.

"At first appearance, we thought it was a smoke detector or

something." Brennan moved closer. "But it's a hidden surveillance camera. The house is loaded with them. Every damn room except inside the master bedroom."

Trane's body tensed. "Interior surveillance? Where does it lead?"

"There's a computer room in the rear of the house on the first floor." Brennan waved around the room again. "The whole house is bugged. The stiffs are all well-dressed and packing serious firepower. Something big is living here."

Trane nodded but said nothing. He wasn't falling for any bait to give an opinion or comment on what he'd seen.

"Let's go back downstairs." Brennan led Trane back down the spiral staircase to the front room where the first body lay. When they stepped off the landing, he turned around and faced Trane. "Want to know what I think?"

"Sure, why not, Detective," Trane said, stopping beside the body. "Impress me."

"Three guys packing at oh-dark-thirty in the morning. I'm thinking they're bodyguards for someone. Do you know for who?"

Trane shook his head. "No. I'm just getting here, remember?"

"If you don't know who lives here, then how'd you know to be here? And why is DHS stealing my case?"

Trane ignored him. "Anything else? You haven't impressed me yet."

"Look, this place is in filthy-rich central, right?" Brennan said matter-of-factly. "Maybe twenty, thirty-mill on the market. Yet these three corpses are wearing cheap threads—oh, nothing I can afford mind you—but cheap compared to this house. A guy who can afford this place isn't buying off the rack. The master bedroom closet has some expensive duds in it—several grand a piece. They're fifty-fours at least; Savile Row threads. None of the stiffs are fitting in those suits, either. Whoever owns them isn't one of our vics. He's missing."

Trane thought about that for a long time. "Okay, I'm officially impressed. Any ideas?"

"Nope. You took my scene, remember?" Brennan shrugged. "Look, this place is wired everywhere—cameras, listening devices, the works. Who watches their own house inside? Somebody's got bodyguards and inside surveillance. The house is owned by a corporation. No IDs or any personal stuff anywhere. This doesn't smell like Wall Street money to me, Trane. It smells like drug money."

"Okay," Trane said, "I'll pass it on to my team."

"And another thing—"

"Is all your evidence and notes here?"

"Everything should be right there." Brennan gestured to a decorative table near the foyer entrance. Then, he lifted up his notebook. "Except my notebook. Which I'm keeping to file my report with my lieutenant."

"No, you're not. No reports." Trane stepped forward and snatched the notebook from Brennan's hand. "One-P-P was pretty clear, weren't they? It's all mine."

Brennan cursed. "Jesus you're a jerk."

"I've been told that." Trane threw a thumb over his shoulder toward the front windows. "It's time for you to say good night, Detective."

15

June 13, Very Early Morning–Central Park West, Manhattan, New York

Trane waited until Brennan left and followed him to the front door, locking it behind him. Then, after watching through the window as the group of uniformed officers and detectives gathered on the street and commiserated over his arrival, he made a short call to a colleague a block south along the park. It took only a moment to pass on instructions.

He began a slow, deliberate search of the brownstone. He started with the ground floor and worked his way up, taking note of each room, closet, alcove, and access point—windows and doors. He had to move fast now. He had no idea how much time he might have before the wrong people returned—wrong being those who actually owned this brownstone. He found nearly fifteen other clandestine cameras and twice as many secreted microphones throughout the residence. If he didn't know better—and truth be told, he didn't— this could have been a CIA safe house. But the address, cost, and dead occupants made that possibility unlikely.

Not impossible. Just unlikely.

He knew much more about the brownstone than the NYPD

would ever learn. First, it was owned by a daisy-chain of shell companies and cutout ownership. All those led back to the Cuban government. Its current resident, or perhaps temporary guest, was one Raul Anibal Vacarro. Who that was, well…that was a mystery since that name didn't appear in any intelligence files anywhere.

Trane had received this current assignment nearly two weeks prior from his nemesis and boss, Alex McLaren. That assignment surrounded one Señor Raul Anibal Vacarro. Afterwards, Trane and his team had waited for a particular cell phone number—provided by McLaren in a cryptic operations order—to activate and signal its location. It had been silent since Trane received his first instructions. A few hours ago, that cell phone woke up and made a single call to the Cuban Consulate. That one signal pinpointed the user's location—Señor Raul Anibal Vacarro's location—and brought Trane through the Lincoln Tunnel to this luxury brownstone on Central Park West.

Just three hours ago, he'd moved on the target. Had he known the NYPD would be on his heels, he might have handled things differently. Their involvement had unexpectedly changed his play considerably.

Brennan's revelation of the brownstone's interior surveillance system was of serious concern. He hadn't expected that, though perhaps he should have. Now it was too late. Every movement in the house must have been recorded. If the surveillance feeds were transmitted to the Cuban Consulate, that meant they had the information, too. Of course, G2 wouldn't complain that someone killed their covert operatives who were living illegally on Central Park West. No, they'd handle this another way. A more direct and violent way.

The more immediate threat was the video and other recordings.

Trane located the computer room in the rear of the house and sat at the desk. He manipulated the keyboard to place ten camera feeds on the large screen in front of him. As he played the video captures made during the time the NYPD had been investigating the crime scene, he tensed when he saw Detective Chan sitting right where he was now, manipulating the surveillance system without concern that he was also being recorded into its memory. The last thing Chan did before leaving the room was locate a high-density USB backup drive from a desk drawer, insert its cable into the computer, tap a few keys, and wait several minutes before leaving with the drive.

"Dammit." Trane almost punched the monitor. "They've got it."

The NYPD had copied the events recorded at the brownstone. But, for how long back in recorded time? An hour? A day? Soon enough there could be other copies. Copies being distributed among detectives and the brass. Perhaps even outside the department to others in the community—the Manhattan intelligence community.

That was not good.

He continued watching the surveillance footage starting early evening and fast forwarding through the routine movements of the security men in and out of rooms. Then, later in the evening, he slowed the playback to normal speed when two bodyguards pushed a slender, darkly clad figure into the brownstone through the rear patio door. First, they stripped the figure of a backpack. Then, without much prodding, they negotiated the figure through the house, up the stairs, and into the second floor sitting room.

There, it all began to make sense.

The figure stood in front of the man of the house—the man Trane came for—Señor Raul Anibal Vacarro. Except Señor Raul Anibal Vacarro was actually Colonel Luis Vergara, Chief of American Operations for Cuba's Dirección de Inteligencia.

"You bastard, McLaren. You knew all along Vacarro was actually Vergara. What are you up to?"

More important to him than the games McLaren was playing, was why Vergara was there at all. Trane had last seen him in Cabrera, Colombia. A chance encounter that derailed Trane's mission to locate the elusive Hemingway.

Now, he was in Manhattan?

Vergara's presence was startling—especially under the cover name Raul Vacarro. He normally controlled Cuban Intelligence's operations from the safety of Havana. Occasionally, he made visits to El Salvador, Caracas, or larger Cuban outposts in South and Central America. As far as Trane knew, Vergara had never been inside the US. Such a trip was precarious; traveling into your enemy's country was asking for trouble. And here he was. At Central Park West. A revenge tour? Finishing Cabrera business? Something else?

Trane continued watching the camera footage as Vergara and his bodyguard stood and witnessed the mysterious figure being stripped of a disguise and transformed into a beautiful, exotic woman.

"Ana Karras. What the hell are you doing?"

Now things made sense. Ana Karras and Colonel Luis Vergara— both in Manhattan—both at the brownstone. There could be only one reason.

Hemingway.

Vergara groped Ana for a few moments before things changed dramatically and Ana Karras unleashed a maelstrom of violence on him and his bodyguard. In seconds, she had lured Vergara closer and the guard to become complacent. Then in a flash, she was the hunter, not the prey.

Ana Karras surprised even him. First by her tenacity. But perhaps more importantly, her skills. After all, *she* had found Vergara before Trane had. *She* had come to the brownstone. He had been too late. *She* had been right on time.

And now there were three dead Cuban operatives raising the NYPD and G2's blood pressure.

"Damn, lady, you should have left well enough alone."

Trane tugged his cell out and made a call to a nonexistent cell number. Nonexistent in that it appeared in no cell directories, no communication company listings, nothing. If one were to call the number accidentally and was not on the "approved caller" list, the sweet, mechanical voice gave the customary: "The number you have dialed is not valid." Then, in milliseconds, a reverse attack took place on the caller's phone and all associated computer records, devouring every possible bit of identifying information. Should the owner of the nonexistent number not be familiar or pleased with your identity, bad things—very bad things—might come next.

The call went through; Trane was a frequent "approved caller." Then, after a series of electronic ticks and tacks, a deep male voice answered. "We're clean now, Trane. Encryption and anti-intercept are on."

"Jesus, I hope so." In a few short, intense moments, Trane explained his situation. "No room for error, Rodin. Got it?"

"Child's play. Give me a few hours."

"Sooner is better. My ass is in a jam."

"Of course it is. But don't worry. I'll clean out every thread. It won't exist by breakfast. Best I can do."

Trane tapped off the call. As he watched the cameras playing the footage from the empty sitting room, he dialed another number and waited for the curt, grumbling voice on the other end to answer.

"You have something, Trane?"

"I found Raul Anibal Vacarro."

A pause. Then, "Something tells me there's a problem."

Yes, there is. "McLaren, Vaccaro is actually Colonel Luis Vergara."

McLaren nearly came through the phone. "What? How'd he get in the country without us knowing?"

Maybe he didn't know about Vergara. "I'm more concerned with why you sent me after him in the first place."

"Later. Do you have him?"

Trane waited a long minute to get McLaren sweating. "No. Three G2 operatives are dead. Someone else beat me here by minutes." Trane went on to explain his interaction with the police as he watched for the second time Ana Karras's confrontation with Vergara and his men. "I've—"

"Are we exposed?"

"It's possible."

Silence. Then, "Dammit, Trane. I sent you on a simple task."

"Simple? Nothing about this was simple—or clear." Trane cursed. "Someone got here first and stirred a hornet's nest. I have it under control now."

"But you don't have Vergara?"

"No."

"Find him." A pause, then, "Who stirred the pot?"

Trane hesitated. "Karras."

"Her? Sweet Jesus. This is the second time you let her screw things up. What are you gonna do about it?"

"I'll deal with it—her. And the cops."

A long, painful silence.

Finally, McLaren cursed loudly before asking, "Damages?"

"Not to me." Trane forced a laugh.

"Any links to us?"

"The Cubans had surveillance inside the house." Trane hated the words as they came out of his mouth. "I'm handling that, too."

"Interior surveillance? They're paranoid bastards, aren't they? And NYPD has that?"

"It's under control."

"It better be." McLaren was silent again. Then, "Clean that mess up. Don't leave anything behind that will connect us."

"Really? Why didn't I think of that?"

"Considering your performance, I'd watch my tone."

Trane said nothing.

"Is that all?"

"Isn't it enough?"

When the phone call ended, Trane considered the hidden cameras and other security devices around the brownstone. Someone had gone to a lot of trouble for internal security. What if there was more than simple electronic surveillance and digital contraptions?

He fast-forwarded the recording a few moments and saw what he knew was the answer. He pulled his silenced pistol from behind his back and climbed the circular stairs to the second floor.

16

"You're starting a war," Poppi said. "One that you can't win."

Ana watched her from her position leaning on the kitchen sink, standing post during the fight.

Sarah sat across from Poppi with a devilish grin, eyeing the stack of Bicycle playing cards between them. On her stack was the seven of clubs. On Poppi's was the seven of diamonds.

"Yes, I will, Yiayia Poppi." Sarah lay down three cards face up, ending with the six of hearts. Her face fell. "Oh, no. It's not a big card."

Poppi laid down two cards and readied for her third. She peeked at it—the nine of diamonds. She feigned a look behind Sarah, and when the child turned to see what was there, Poppi quickly found a lesser card—the two of spades—and laid it down on the pile.

"Oh, dear, I lost." Poppi put on a pout. "You got me."

Sarah spun around and looked at the cards. "I win. I win. I told you I'd win. You owe me another cookie, Yiayia Poppi."

"I give, Sarah." Poppi went to the cookie jar on the nearby island counter. "I cannot be beaten again. There aren't enough cookies."

"Sure there are." Sarah giggled and picked out a large oatmeal-raisin cookie. "Just one more game, Yiayia Poppi? Please?"

Poppi glanced at Ana. "Why don't you play, Ana?"

"Not yet," she said, glancing out the window. The dark van still sat across the street, three houses down. It had been there for two hours and it didn't belong in the neighborhood. Was Vergara watching them? "Maybe later."

"Are they still there?"

"Yes. They've driven around the block several times. But they always return. They're not very good if they're trying to hide."

"Maybe they aren't trying. Are they here because of last night?"

"What happened last night, Aunty Ana?" Sarah moved a kitchen chair and climbed up to look out the window beside her. "You got home late. Where were you?"

"I was visiting a friend, Sarah." Ana and Poppi exchanged uneasy glances. "I wasn't so late."

"I woke up and you were still gone, Aunty Ana. It was late."

"No matter." Ana scooped her from the chair and pulled her close, kissed her forehead, and gently sat her back on the floor. "Go get your new coloring books and we'll do some pictures."

"Or play a game?"

"Yes, a game. Hurry."

When Sarah ran up the staircase to her bedroom, Poppi confronted Ana.

"Tell me about last night."

That was something she wasn't prepared to do. "It's better I don't."

"I forbade you from going there and still you went. I forbade you from going to Colombia again and still you went. You're going to bring trouble to us, Ana. And for what? For parents who—"

"Stop." Ana held up her hands. "Please, don't start about Mamá and Pappa. They are my family, too—not just you. I want to find them and bring them safely home."

"Do you think confronting Vergara would do that?"

"I had hoped. But no."

"Of course not. And what of that large duffel bag you hid? More secrets you keep from me. No. If you live in my house, you live by my rules. Tell me."

"No." Ana folded her arms and turned to look out the window

again. "What you do not know cannot hurt you or Sarah."

"That bad?"

Ana stared out the window.

Poppi went to her and took hold of both her shoulders, looking deep into her eyes. "How am I to protect you and Sarah if I don't know what is happening? Should I call William?"

"No." Ana tried to look away but couldn't. Poppi had an unusual power over her—more so than her mother or father ever had. There was a bond between them. A bond so strong that it transcended blood and love and entered into something strange—a clairvoyance. Ana knew, as did Poppi, that once those eyes connected with hers, her secrets might be revealed. "I don't need protecting from anyone anymore."

"Ah, yes. Your mother and father again." Poppi closed her eyes. "You think what they taught you in the jungles makes you invincible. Is that it?"

Ana took Poppi's hands warmly. "Some of what I learned does make me stronger. Some of it—"

"Makes you dangerous. It makes you bad."

Yes, dangerous and bad. That was true. But sometimes, dangerous and bad were necessary. Last night, Ana Karras had every intention of confronting Vergara, and if necessary, ending his pursuit. Her promise—her conscience—got in her way. Until Tomãs captured her. Ana Montilla escaped. Without her, she would be dead.

Poppi's eyes filled with regret. "I am sorry, Ana dear. I should not have said that. I know you returned to me to leave that life behind. I only wish your mother had come home years ago, too. Now, she is lost."

"No. I don't believe that."

"She is."

Ana softened her voice. "Please try to understand. I went to see Vergara to stop him from hurting you and Sarah." She pulled back her shirt collar and showed her scars. "I wanted to find out what he knows of Mamá and Pappa. And yes, I used what I learned in the jungle. What I learned at college would not help with a man like him. Would it?"

"No, I do not suppose it would." Poppi went to the pantry across the room, opened the accordion doors, and looked for nothing inside. "So easily you become that person again. That's what nearly killed you in Cabrera—attacking one of Vergara's men."

What did she say? "How do you know I fought Vergara's men in Cabrera?"

"You told me when you first returned."

"No, I didn't tell you. Until just the other day, I didn't recall anything about Vergara and his men." Ana took Poppi's shoulder and forced her to face her. "William? You had William investigate after I said no."

"It doesn't matter, does it?"

"I can't believe you did that, Yiayia." Ana was furious. "What else have you done?"

"Nothing."

"Yiayia?"

Poppi changed the subject "Tell me, last night, did Vergara know anything about your parents?"

A memory flashed and made her pause.

"Ana? What is it?"

"I don't know." She closed her eyes and tried to will the memories from Cabrera. "Yes...as I told you, Vergara wasn't looking just for Pappa. It was also about finding someone else. Hemingway. Yes, that's it."

"You said that before." Poppi came closer and took her shoulder. "Do you remember something about Hemingway?"

What was it? Think Ana, think. Wait. "No, something else. After Tomãs attacked me, Vergara was upset; he said Havana would be angry with him."

"Really?" Poppi's eyes went wide. "How is that possible, Ana? I don't understand."

"Neither do I." She closed her eyes again trying to find those memories.

"Ana?"

"Wait." Vergara's words came to her—*I knew of this pretty one. I had my orders...*

"What, child?"

She turned and looked straight into Poppi's eyes. "I don't know how. I don't know why. But Vergara knew about Pappa. He knew about me, too. He wanted Pappa."

"Him again." Poppi's face burned red and her voice was tight and angry. "Your father went to Cuba several times with Irena. Perhaps he worked with Vergara. Your Pappa is behind this. He betrayed you and my Irena. That must be it."

Ana started to object but stopped, thinking. She had no other explanation for the events in Cabrera or how Vergara knew so much. But Pappa? She could not imagine her father betraying her. Not intentionally. Not accidentally. She simply could not believe it.

"Ana, what did Vergara tell you?"

The question shook her from her thoughts. "I never got a chance to ask him."

"Perhaps that is best."

Ana looked out the window again. The van down the street started up and began moving toward the house.

"They're coming." She spun around to Poppi. "Get Sarah. Keep her upstairs in my room. There's a gun behind my headboard."

"A gun? In your bedroom?"

"Yes. Now go. Quickly. They're coming."

Sarah ran down the stairs to them. "Aunty Ana, there's men outside." She collided with Poppi, who hefted her into her arms. "They're coming to our house."

"Ana, we should go out the back," Poppi said. "We should just go."

The front doorbell rang twice.

"No. They've been watching the house all morning." Ana moved swiftly and pulled her pistol from behind the living room bookcase and draped a kitchen towel over it to conceal it. "I won't run and hide anymore."

Two loud raps on the door.

"Upstairs, Yiayia. Please." She went to the front door and kept her pistol in hand, concealed beneath the towel as though drying her hands. After a calming pause, she opened the door. "Yes? What do you want?"

Two men faced her; behind them, a dark gray four-door sedan

102

sat in her driveway. The man to her left raised a hand. He held a badge.

"I'm Detective Brennan, Miss Karras." Brennan slowly moved his coat back and placed his hand on his holstered sidearm, gesturing with his other hand toward the towel in her hand. "How about you put that pistol down?"

"Of course." Ana backed up and placed the pistol, still beneath the hand towel, on the table beside the door. "I have a right to the gun. I didn't know the men watching our home were policemen. You scared us."

"Someone is watching your house?" Brennan glanced toward the street. "We just got here, Miss Karras. We haven't been watching you."

"The men in the van were not yours?"

"A van? No." Brennan threw a chin at one of the uniformed policemen beside him and gestured toward the street. As the officer went to investigate, Brennan said, "Did you get a license plate?"

Ana shook her head. *Stupid, Ana. Stupid.*

"We'll talk about that later." Brennan pointed at her. "For now, you have to come with us back to Manhattan, Miss Karras. We have some questions."

17

June 13, Late Morning–Midtown Manhattan, 20th Precinct, NYPD New York

"Lucius is your first name?" Ana sat across the gray steel interrogation table from Detective Brennan. "How unusual."

"I go by Luke." Brennan sipped his coffee. "Like from…."

"*Star Wars*?"

"Yeah, *Star Wars*. Just like him."

"You're named after a Wookiee?"

"Funny, lady. Real funny." Brennan jutted a finger at her. "You're in serious trouble, Ana. Maybe cut the jokes and cooperate. Things might go better."

"I'll cooperate." Ana smiled again; each time she did, his eyes lightened and his demeanor softened. It would be easy to forget he was a policeman had he not been interrogating her. She liked Luke from *Star Wars*. There was something kind and friendly about him. "But you haven't told me what this is about, Luke."

"It's Detective. Let's start with the gun you had at your house."

"My grandmother's gun?" She blossomed her best sheepish smile. Men always like that. "It's legal to have one in your own home. Is it not?"

"Well, sure, if it's properly—"

"You were watching my house and scared my grandmother and me. We must think of my niece. I had the gun out when you came to the door. How was I to know you were the police and not home invaders?"

"Do I look like a home invader?"

"Yes." Ana grinned and knew she had him hooked. "Well, maybe just a little."

Once, in Medellin when she was barely fifteen, she'd been picked up by a young policeman for questioning when she'd been seen with a known member of FARC. She'd been there delivering a message from her camp. The young policeman—Emiliano—was too thin and young for his uniform to fit properly. He tried hard to be tough and savvy, but all he did was make her giggle when he tried to bully her. Her smile and pretty eyes melted his façade and soon they were on a first-name basis. After just a couple hours, he allowed her to leave. She did, however, have to promise to have dinner with Emil soon.

"It wasn't us watching your house, Ana." Brennan watched her intently across the table. "We just arrived when we came to your door."

Then it was Vergara's men watching her.

Brennan leaned forward. "What have you done for someone to be surveilling you?"

"Nothing." She rested back on the chair and wrapped her long, black hair over her shoulder and around her neck. She wanted to flirt with Brennan, but not too noticeably. If he knew she was doing it, it would backfire. If he didn't, she'd lure him in like she had young Emil. "Really, Luke."

"It's Detective." Brennan opened a file—all interrogators know when to do that—and made a play of examining its contents. "When's the last time you were at Central Park?"

Uh, oh, he knew something. "Just the other day. Why?"

"What were you doing there?"

"I took my niece to play in the park." She slowly ran her fingers down her neck, adjusting her hair—drawing his eyes where her finger led. "She loves the park. Don't you?"

"Sure, yeah." He dropped his eyes quickly back to the folder. "Why not take her to one of the parks in Queens? There're dozens."

"Is there a law that says I can't go to Central Park?"

"No, but it's a long way to go for a park."

"And shopping."

"Shopping?"

She folded her arms closed. "Are you going to tell me I have to shop in Queens?"

Brennan's face reddened a little. "Only shopping and the park?"

Ana waited a moment and casually looked Brennan over. He was a handsome man and had Latino blood in him for sure—she could use that. But there was something else, too. His manner was smooth and confident, even pleasant and engaging. He smiled when she did. He took a joke about her *Star Wars* reference and seemed genuinely kind, even for a policeman. But still, he *was* a policeman.

"Actually, I was there last night. It was early evening. Is there—"

"Why were you there?"

Now for a lie. "I was looking for our little dog, Lobo. He escaped Sarah's leash earlier and we couldn't find him. I returned last evening looking for him. Yiayia Poppi and Sarah would be devastated if we lost him."

"Yiayia…your grandmother, right?"

"Yes." She smiled a disarming smile that had his eyes locked on her lips. "You speak Greek?"

"No." He shook his head. "But you can't live in this town without learning a little of a lot of things. Is that why you use the name Karras and not Montilla—your Yiayia?"

When Brennan said "Montilla" she tensed. How much more did he know about her?

"Ana?"

She pushed her concern away. "Yes, it is. My parents are missionaries in South America. I favor Mamá, so I took her last name. It's very common with Greeks."

"No, it's not. Come on, Ana. What are you into?"

She said nothing.

"Searching for your dog? Ever visit that nice brownstone on the corner of Central Park West and—"

"Oh, no." She dropped her eyes to the table, feigning embarrassment. "Is that what this is about? Did they see me?"

"See you do what, *exactly*, Ana?"

She looked sheepish and fidgeted with her hair as she stole glances between him and the table. "Um, I peeked in their windows. It's such a beautiful place, you know? I see it all the time. It was getting dark, so I snuck over and peeked in their foyer windows trying to see inside. No one was home. Or I didn't think there was...."

"Bull, lady." Brennan's voice got curt. "You didn't peek in any windows. You can cut the girlish-charm offensive, too. I'm immune."

"No man is that immune."

He sat back stone-faced.

Well, maybe he was. "I don't understand, Detective. I..."

"Do you know what the Lower Manhattan Security Initiative is?"

"No. Should I?"

"Yeah, you should." He leaned back and folded his arms. "The Lower Manhattan Security Initiative is very high tech. Virtually every street and store are covered by CCTV cameras and all types of sensors. You can't move in this town without us being able to see and find you—facial recognition software, too."

She had been foolish and hadn't considered that. "For people who look in windows?"

"No. For terrorists. You were casing the place."

"I'm no terrorist, Lucius." She slid back in her chair and folded her arms. "How could you say that?"

"It's Luke, and I didn't say you were."

"Then why am I here, Luke?"

"It's Detective."

"You just said 'Luke'?" She grinned and he grinned back. "Sorry, Detective. Tell me, what have I done?"

He studied her for a long time. "I traced you from that brownstone—the one you *weren't* peeping in through the windows at—all the way back to Queens. With facial recognition, we found you in the park several times. You, Sarah, and your grandmother. You know what?"

"What, Detective?"

"You're lying. Your grandma bought ice cream two weeks ago—on a credit card. That, Ana Montilla, aka Ana Karras, is how I found you."

She'd been careless. Something as simple as an ice cream receipt trapped her.

"Very clever, Detective Lucius Brennan, aka Luke Brennan, aka Chewbacca." She waited for a sign she still had him. She found nothing. "Why did you go to all that trouble to find me? And how did you get my picture to trace?"

His arms snapped folded again. "From the CCTV video cameras *inside* the brownstone."

She tensed. *Vergara had CCTV inside the brownstone?*

"I bet you didn't know the cameras were there. Did you?"

18

"I'll start with all the missing money," Brennan said, turning his notebook computer around so Ana could see the monitor with him. "Then we'll get to the really good part."

"The really good part, Detective?" The thought of what might be on surveillance video of the brownstone suddenly terrified her. "Surely you are being very dramatic."

The video was grainy and without sound. Brennan began playing it at the brownstone's sitting room with a view of a large duffel bag sitting atop a table off to the side of the camera view near the windows. Beside it were stacks of cash. A lot of cash.

"Lots of money there, eh, Ms. Karras?" Brennan asked, stopping the recording. "Know anything about that?"

She tensed. "No, I don't. What are you showing me?"

"I made a greatest hits recording." He tapped a few keyboard strokes and sat back, watching her. "Just watch."

The recording started again and sent shivers through her.

Two Latino security men burst into the sitting room. Between them, they dragged a smaller figure. The figure was dressed in dark clothes, wore a dark ball cap, and carried a backpack. The figure struggled, but the two men were unfazed. Once inside the room, they stripped off the figure's backpack and shoved him down onto the expensive Persian rug, driving a couple kicks into his torso. From the backpack, the Latinos withdrew a thick coil of rope, leather gloves, a lock pick kit that one of the security men quickly pocketed, a folding survival knife, and the crown jewel of the treasure—a silenced pistol and four magazines. The contents were tossed on the table beside the stacks of cash.

"Damn, someone did some planning," Brennan quipped, tapping the table beside Ana. "Maybe someone was going after all that money stacked up?"

"I wouldn't know." Though, she did. "Where is this leading, Detective?"

"Humor me."

On video, the Latinos taunted the intruder on the ground—a couple kicks and punches—until the bedroom door on the right of the screen opened and a third Latino—a large, powerful bull of a man—entered the sitting room. He was clad in dark blue silk pajamas and grinning ear-to-ear as one Latino yanked the intruder to his feet and quickly removed his black ball cap.

Flowing dark hair fell out.

Brennan faked a gasp. "Holy shit, do you see that, Ms. Karras?"

She shrugged. "So? A woman."

"It's you."

"It is not me." Ana fought the urge to expound on the denial—to reinforce it with an alibi or other lies. But to do that would make her appear afraid and guilty. "But I can see a resemblance, of course."

"No, Miss Karras. It's you."

Pajama Man exchanged words with his security men and sent one of them out of the sitting room, leaving the other holding a gun on the woman in the video. For a short time, Pajama Man carried on a tête-à-tête with her. Then, he stepped in close and began crudely groping her as his security man ogled and laughed. Then, the woman and Pajama Man exchanged more angry words—unknown to Brennan—in an animated confrontation.

It didn't last long.

Pajama Man slapped her hard across the face, viciously knocking her backward. Then he grabbed her arm, struck her again, and tried to pull her to her feet. The woman looked up and one of the cameras caught a full facial frame of her.

It was undeniably her.

"Still denying it?" Brennan asked, grinning. "These are bad men, Miss Karras. I know that."

"I can explain," she said, realizing she had no way out but a partial confession. "But it's not what you think."

"Okay, you can explain it all later." Brennan pointed at the notebook screen. "After the best part that's coming up."

The video started where it had left off, with Ana being pulled toward the bedroom doors. She leapt forward and kicked Pajama Man in the groin. As he faltered, she wheeled around to the security man behind her and snapped another kick to his outer knee, sending him rocking sideways, off balance. Her movements were almost a blur. She spun, lowered herself on bent legs, and swept the Latino's legs from beneath him. As he fell, she twisted, rolled sideways and up, and drove a bone-shattering heel into his solar plexus. The security man's arms flapped outward and he went limp.

As she finished the man, Pajama Man got to his feet and retreated into his bedroom, slamming the door behind.

Ana scooped up the fallen security man's weapon and she headed for the bedroom, kicking at the door several times to break it open. When it surrendered, she disappeared inside.

She was gone only a moment and reappeared in the sitting room. There, she checked the downed Latino before moving to the table near the window. She reloaded her backpack with all its contents, then stuffed it and the stacks of cash all into the large duffel bag. Finally, she retrieved her silenced pistol, tucked it into her waistband, and left the room.

"So tell me, Ana, who's Pajama Man? Is he dead? Where'd you put him? I didn't find him at the scene."

He restarted the video and watched Ana disappear from the second floor sitting room carrying the duffel full of cash. She appeared next on the first-floor camera coming down the stairs to the front room. In the center of the room stood the other security man who had helped drag her into the bedroom earlier. The man turned as Ana stopped at the bottom of the stairs. He faced her and reached for his pistol tucked beneath his suit jacket.

"Uh, oh," Brennan said with mock surprise. "What's happening?"

In one smooth, lightning-fast movement, Ana dropped the duffel and launched herself at the Latino. She caught him with a violent sidekick at the apogee of her attack. The kick crushed into his solar plexus and sent him reeling backward. She landed deftly on both feet in a hand-to-hand combat stance.

The Latino hit hard but rolled sideways and got back to one knee, tugging his weapon out.

He fired one shot.

He missed because she was still moving—spinning in a violent arc toward him. She twisted and deftly kicked the gun from his hand, landed, twisted again, and lashed a vicious heel-kick to his face. The Latino's head snapped back, and he hit the floor sideways. The gun dropped from his grip.

Ana moved quickly for the gun, but the man rolled up and caught her with a right cross as she bent to retrieve it. It surprised her and sent her backward against the stair railing. He snapped out two more punches at her. Neither landed as she deftly danced away, bobbing and weaving like a skilled fighter. She evaded the assault, spun back around, and connected a heel beside his left knee. As he faltered, her left fist lashed out and caught his jaw. A right knife hand slashed at his windpipe but collided with his cheek instead. Her movements were quick, controlled, and violent. Only luck had kept the man's throat from being crushed.

As the Latino tried to regain his balance and continue the fight, Ana delivered a crushing front kick to his midsection and doubled him over. He tried to recover but couldn't. She lunged forward, drove two more lightning punches into his face, and dropped him where he stood.

She sprang back, grabbed the duffel, and ran out of camera view.

Brennan paused the recording. "See what I mean? This stuff is great. Where'd you learn all those moves, Ana? Are you some kind of assassin? A ninja thief? Damn, you're really a bad ass, aren't you?"

"No." Her mind spun, groping for a strategy. "They grabbed me from the street. I was trying to escape."

"Escape? With a few hundred thousand in cash?" Brennan tapped a key on the notebook. "What about your accomplice?"

Two minutes on the recording clock ticked by before the Latino began to stir on the floor. It took him another thirty seconds to stand. When he did, he grabbed his pistol from the floor and started for the stairs. Something caught his attention off camera to his right down the first-floor hall. He turned away from the stairs and backpedaled as he lifted his pistol to fire.

At that moment, the video began to scramble and went black.

"No, no, not now." Brennan fumbled with the keyboard to control the image. By the time he regained a picture barely able to view, the Latino was dead on the floor with a gunshot in his chest, blood already pooling.

The video scrambled again and the program abruptly closed.

Brennan went to the interrogation room door and called out: "Chan, the video's going bonkers. Can you hook me up? Hurry."

"Hold on." A few seconds later, Chan entered the interrogation room, grabbed the keyboard, and went to work. It took him a minute or two, but he finally brought the video software back on and restarted the image. By that time, the video clock was already five minutes later. "There's something going on with the servers, Bren. I gotta check it out."

"Good. Miss Karras and I were really enjoying the show." He turned to her. "Weren't we?"

"No, I was not." Just then, relief began settling in. "I was being held against my will. They grabbed me off the street. I told you that."

"Sure, sure. Hold on. I got something else to show you." Brennan's fingers flew over the keyboard. "What the hell? Everything's gone."

Ana leaned forward. "Gone, Detective? I don't understand."

Brennan's face blanched. "Neither do I."

A few moments later, Chan appeared in the interrogation room doorway. His face was ashen, and he held a cell phone to his ear. "Something's up, Bren. The entire video management system is going crazy on the network."

"Find that video, quick. Ms. Karras and I—"

"There's no video, Bren," Chan said. "That's what I'm trying to tell you. The entire folder and all the backups were wiped. It's all gone."

"Define 'gone.'"

"Gone-gone. Like it was never there. Somebody just deleted the backup drive, the folders I set up on the net, and those backups. Gone. Poof. We've been hacked."

"Poof? Hacked?" Brennan slammed his hand onto the keyboard, sending his second cup of coffee splashing across the table. "Somebody hacked the entire NYPD?"

"I guess. Hell, I don't know."

Ana stood. "So, it seems you think I am the person in the video stealing money and fighting those men."

"You are, Ana." Brennan leaned back in his chair still staring at the black computer screen. "We both know that."

She relaxed a little. "You said you traced me using your facial recognition software? Obviously, that information was wrong."

"It's not wrong, Miss Karras." Brennan leaned back and locked his eyes on her. "I saw you in that house. We both watched the video of you being manhandled in that sitting room. We both watched the video of you inside the house with the dead Cubans."

"Dead? Vergara is dead?" She couldn't stop herself. She'd fallen into his trap, but it was too late. "He was alive when I left. Truly. All of them were. I swear."

"So, you admit you were there?" Brennan pushed the computer out of the way and leaned forward on the table to face her. "Who is Vergara?"

"You don't know?"

"If I did, I wouldn't be asking you." He softened his tone. "You're surprised they're dead."

You have no idea.

"What about Trane?"

"Who?"

"Trane." Brennan nodded. "You know, smooth talker, kind of frumpy dresser. Claims to work for Homeland Security."

"I don't know any Trane." Her expression matched her confusion. "Those men grabbed me from the street. You saw me fight them off and leave. I killed no one."

114

"No, but Trane did. He killed those three Cubans at the brownstone. It's all on the video. He took them out like they were nothing."

"Three?" She thought a moment. "This Trane man killed three men at the brownstone? It was on this video?"

"Yes, it was." Brennan nodded. "And imagine this, their bodies never showed up in the morgue this morning. Your pal, Trane, said his guys from Homeland Security were taking care of that. I guess they really did, huh?"

Ana sat back in her seat. *What was going on?* "They're missing, too? The bodies?"

"Yep, just like our video evidence. That makes you our only evidence." Brennan tapped the table. "You're a material witness—or a conspirator. I can't decide which one."

"You lost the bodies? And the video you claim shows me in the house just disappeared. Is that what you're saying?" She looked at him as a thin smile breached her lips. Calm settled over her. It was going to be all right. "I don't know the law well, Luke, but I'd say you have nothing to hold me on."

"You're unbelievable, lady. You know that?" Brennan stared at her before contemplating the file on the table again. "I'm holding you as a material witness. Get comfy."

"I wish to go. Now."

"What about all the money? What did you do with that, Ana?"

She looked straight at him, silent.

"There must have been a few hundred grand in that duffel." He narrowed his eyes on her. "Where'd it come from? Drugs?"

She held his eyes and smiled. "What money?"

"My guys will be searching your house within the hour. We're getting a warrant right now."

She lifted her chin. "I hope they're not trying to get a warrant without evidence, Detective. You just admitted you don't have any left."

Brennan started to speak but stopped.

"May I go now?"

"Who's Vergara?"

"Vergara who?" She watched his face twist. "I'm sorry, Detective.

But you have no bodies, no evidence, and no video. I wish to leave."

"Here's the thing, lady." Brennan steepled his hands. "You're not going anywhere until I get these videos back."

"You can't hold me…"

"Watch me."

19

June 13, Midday–The Caverns, An Undisclosed CIA Compound, Bayonne, New Jersey

"Explain to me why you sent me after Vacarro and I ended up in Colonel Vergara's living room?" Trane sat across McLaren's desk staring bullets at him. "That's not an easy mistake."

"I don't explain to you, Trane." McLaren glared back at him. "You do what I tell you."

"Explain it anyway."

"I can't." McLaren slammed his palm on the desk. "My source gave me a name and the assignment. Someone from the Venezuelan embassy vouched for Vacarro and said he had important intel. He turned it over to me."

"Who turned it over to you?" Trane smelled bullshit. Of course, he smelled bullshit whenever McLaren was around. "Who exactly? And don't give me that 'Capitol Hill' bull again."

"You do what I say and that's all you need." McLaren changed the subject. "How long until the locals figure this out? Or have they already?"

Trane wasn't sure and said as much.

They sat in one of the modestly furnished executive offices

they'd assumed weeks ago when they first arrived in New York. The complex was a self-contained command center—albeit a secret one—with workspace, equipment and communications, and living quarters. Located in New Jersey just a short drive from Manhattan, it was buried in the bowels of an indistinct building resembling a construction company. But unlike the other nondescript compounds in the Bayonne industrial area, this one was named the "Caverns" for its five subterranean levels. Unlike its neighbors, the Caverns was protected by the latest technology, surveillance systems, and armed CIA operatives.

"NYPD isn't known for subtlety." Trane sipped a cup of coffee. "Three corpses vanishing from their beat will piss them off. They are already hostile about me taking their crime scene. Will DHS cover us?"

"Our liaison is on it. It shouldn't be a problem."

McLaren, one of the CIA's Deputy Directors of Operations, had been Trane's boss for ten years. Together, and with a small team of other field covert operatives, they manned a new, special operations unit for domestic terrorism. The unit was rather special, too, since it was by all legal interpretations, *illegal*. By law—the National Security Act of 1947—the CIA cannot operate on US soil. They're an "over there" outfit. Except, since 9/11, the rules had become mere guidelines and were often ignored. That's why Trane was recruited into this unique unit. Since Iraq, Afghanistan, and Syria, he had a reputation for ignoring rules but getting results. McLaren, aside from rule-breaking himself, was good at other things, most notably hobnobbing with the powerful elite, and according to Trane, staying out of the fray of fieldwork.

Trane unwrapped a roast beef sandwich and watched the pickle fall from the wrapping onto his lap. He cursed, wiped the vinegar off his jeans, and stuffed it into his mouth. "I've already taken care of the video the NYPD grabbed—and their other files. I've also flagged everything I can think of to alert me if they get too creative."

"Knowing and stopping are two different things."

"Brennan has no corpses. No video. Nothing."

"Are you sure about all that?"

"I'm sure. My guy took care of the NYPD computers."

McLaren frowned. "I'm worried about Brennan."

"You want me to kill him?"

McLaren stopped chewing.

"It's a joke." Trane eyed him. "But you haven't said no."

"No."

"You will as soon as this is over, though, right?"

"Ask me then." McLaren returned to his lunch. "And not with anyone around."

"I will." Trane opened a bottle of spring water, took a long mouthful, and replaced the cap. He didn't like McLaren. Truth be told, he hated him. McLaren was a spoiled rich kid trying to prove himself in all the wrong ways. First, he used colleagues as rungs on his ladder to advancement—Trane had the heel marks on his back to prove it. Second, he didn't care who ended up as collateral damage—who might get injured or killed. Third, and most importantly, his overseas exploits had caught others' attention. That wasn't good. There could be casualties.

Trane could well be one of those casualties.

There was one thing about McLaren that Trane appreciated: his friends. More appropriately, his allies. Those who could look after him when things went wrong. By extension, that also meant looking after Trane—unless he was slated to be a casualty. After all, McLaren was no saint. In fact, if there was a sliding scale and 'saint' was on one end, McLaren was on the other.

Still, ever since Syria, they had been a team—master and servant. Albeit a reluctant one. Trane doing the doing. McLaren taking the credit. Yin and Yang.

"I'll deal with Brennan if necessary." Trane took a bite of his sandwich and tossed it back into the wrapper when mayonnaise erupted from the bread like a tsunami. "It's Vergara that'll cause problems."

"How so?"

"Havana won't be amused. He's in charge of Cuba's Americas operations. They won't appreciate his disappearance. He's a big fish these days. He came from South American Operations years ago and got promoted to colonel almost overnight. They'll also be wondering where all their money went."

"He was living in a thirty-million-dollar pad on Central Park West. I don't think a little bag of money matters."

"Little bag? It's at least a half-million."

McLaren leaned forward and locked eyes with him. "You didn't lift that out of that brownstone yourself, did you?"

Trane ignored him.

"You know, to even things with me?"

"No." Trane bristled. "If you'd bother to watch the video, you'd know what happened to it."

McLaren grunted something unintelligible. "Montilla's kid took it?"

"Yes. And I don't blame her after what they did to her."

"I don't give a crap what they did." McLaren dropped the tail of his pickle into this sandwich wrapper. "She screwed us for the second time."

"Look—"

"No, you look. You should've let Karras die in Cabrera." McLaren split the air with his finger. "You had one assignment—find Dr. Manuel Montilla. Instead, you found his daughter. You opened us to scrutiny we don't need. What are you going to do about it?"

"I'm working it." Trane cursed. "She was apparently looking for her father, too. I was on her tail all the way to Cabrera. How was I supposed to know Vergara would show up?"

"It's your job to know."

"Really? My *job* is to find Hemingway. My *job* is to break that bastard from the brownstone. My *job* isn't to be second-guessed by you or anyone else. If you can do it better, take your rich, lazy ass out of the office and into the field to get dirty."

Ten weeks ago, NSA intercepts and a deeply placed asset inside Havana reported a Cuban G2 operative infiltrating South America and heading north. Cuban Intelligence went immediately into high gear and their communications chatter was off the charts. The operative's mission, whatever it was, was being unleashed ferociously.

That operative—Hemingway—had gone deep.

McLaren, seeing an opportunity for another promotion, seized the assignment to capture Hemingway. In turn, he sent Trane and a team to accomplish just that. Their first encounter with anything potentially related had been in Cabrera, where a normally secretive G2 intelligence officer was suddenly away from his desk and getting his hands dirty.

The only reason was Hemingway.

"Your job is whatever I say it is." McLaren's teeth clenched so tight the muscles in his jaw began to pulsate. "How the hell did Ana Karras or Ana Montilla or whatever her name is find Vergara in Manhattan? If that's what happened?"

"My guy ran facial recognition across the city. He traced her off and on for a couple days. Vergara and Karras literally ran into each other in Central Park two weeks ago."

"Bull."

"It's true."

McLaren scowled, muttered something to himself, and set his hands on the desk in front of him. "I can't believe any of this."

"Yeah, but maybe you can." Trane held McLaren's gaze. "You said some Capitol Hill big shot sent us to find Raul Anibal Vacarro—who turned out to be Vergara. Who is it?"

"I've been over that. It's confidential and you don't need to know."

"Look, the Havana asset says Doctor Montilla has connections to Hemingway. That's why I went to Cabrera. Sources said he was there. Ana was there, too. Vergara arrived and tried to kill her. Something's odd about that. If your guy knows something else—?"

"He doesn't."

"Bullshit."

McLaren's face tightened. "If Vergara was meeting Dr. Montilla in Cabrera, why would he try to kill Montilla's daughter?"

"I don't know. We're missing something." Trane had asked himself those very questions since that day in Cabrera. He hadn't any more answers now than he had then. "Maybe she was in the way. Maybe she learned something she shouldn't have."

"Or more likely, she's part of it." McLaren stared at the desktop. "Why else would she, Vergara, and Doctor Montilla all be in Cabrera together?"

"But Montilla wasn't there. And if Karras is involved with

Vergara, why kill her?"

"I don't know."

Trane eyed him. "How exactly did your Washington contact get in the middle of this? It's no coincidence that he sent us after Vergara—whether he knew it was Vergara or not."

"I don't know."

"We need to know." Trane gulped a mouthful of spring water. "Ana nearly bled out by the time I found her and the kid that day. My medic got to her just in time. Once I got her back home, she stayed with grandma. I snuck her into the country, so there's no way Vergara should have known she was alive and back home. Then, a few days ago, you got a mysterious assignment and, presto-change-o, its actually Vergara who later runs in to Karras at the park."

"I don't like it."

Trane snapped forward. "No kidding. One of those intersections is your secret DC big shot. Now tell me who it is. How can I sort this out with half the intel I need?"

"Just find Hemingway, Trane. Your best lead is in the cells."

"No, our best lead is Ana Karras."

McLaren grunted. "Have we ever used a missionary before?"

"Missionary?" Trane laughed. "Karras is no missionary. She was a FARC guerrilla trained by mommy and daddy."

McLaren considered that. "Who's handling your intel?"

"Rodin."

"Rodin? More silly hacker-nickname crap. What's his real name?"

Trane grinned. "Frank Augusta. But he likes Auguste Rodin instead. He thinks his hacking skills make him like *The Thinker*. You know—"

"I know who Rodin was."

"Liar." Trane loved pissing him off. "Anyway, I've got him looking for Dr. Montilla and Hemingway. So far, no trail of them anywhere."

"Not many computers in the jungle." McLaren thought for a moment and changed the topic. "Our man downstairs?"

"He's playing 'possum."

McLaren turned to his computer, tapped a few keys on its keyboard, and brought up an image of a security cell five floors below. In the cell was a large, robust man gone mostly bald but for well-groomed gray hair on the sides and back of his head. He would have been distinguished looking, except for his rumpled suit pants and white dress shirt now unbuttoned and untucked from his pants. Even after four hours of harsh interrogation, he seemed strong and ready, lying face up on an old metal army cot.

Colonel Luis Vergara had been their guest since Trane had found him hiding in a second-floor safe room at the brownstone in the early hours that day. The safe room—a secured, hidden room protected with ballistic steel and advanced security systems for the residents to hide in during a home invasion or other emergency at their home—was concealed behind the large walk-in closet off the brownstone's second-floor master bedroom suite.

"How'd you find him, Trane? You said he was gone when you got to the brownstone."

"I thought he was. It's a big, swanky place. Sophisticated security setup. I figured there was a safe room somewhere. On the video he went into the bedroom and never came out. So it had to be in there."

"I bet he was surprised to see you when he popped out." McLaren allowed a laugh.

"I think he expected to find a security team from the Cuban consulate there to rescue him."

"What do you have from him so far?"

"Nothing. I dropped those names on him and showed him the video. He never blinked. Nothing."

"Get something. Time is short." McLaren cocked his head. "Any more intercepts on Operation Perro or Hemingway?"

"No. I've expanded the search into historical data going back years. It'll take time."

McLaren watched Vergara on the computer monitor. "It's nearly three months since we began receiving those intercepts on Hemingway and Operation Perro. Then they mentioned Doctor Montilla. You blew that lead in Colombia."

"I saved his daughter. She's the best link to him."

"Maybe." McLaren grunted. "Get Vergara to talk. Whatever it

takes."

Trane knew that "whatever it takes" meant McLaren didn't want to know or be involved in "whatever it took" to extract information.

"If he doesn't talk, I'll shift over to Ana Karras." Trane didn't like telling McLaren his strategy, but after Cabrera, it was already out in the open. "My working theory is Ana leads us to Daddy, then Daddy leads us to Hemingway."

"Can you convince her to help find dear, old dad?"

"I don't know. It'll mean her going back south." He thought a moment. "We might have to make a deal—a big one."

"And when this is over," McLaren said in a quiet but stern voice, "you'll have to clean this up."

"Define 'this'?"

"Karras has to go."

"All of them? The kid? I suppose you want me to kill the three-legged dog, too."

McLaren waved dismissively. "You'll do what's necessary to contain this."

"You're a real bastard, McLaren."

There was a knock on the office door and a young, pretty intelligence analyst walked in.

"Sorry, sir." She strode to McLaren's desk and handed him a thin, manila file. "You need to see this right away."

"What, for Christ's sake?"

She cleared her throat. "We have more NSA intercepts concerning Hemingway. They're deeply disturbing."

"Disturbing how?" Trane asked.

The analyst addressed McLaren. "First, we found older comms at NSA on Operation Perro and two additional items—Herrera and Espino—in the same comms. They're from fifteen years ago."

"Chase all that to its source," Trane said. "What else?"

The analyst gestured to the file in McLaren's hand. "The Cubans have moved another G2 team into Central America. Satellite imagery suggests that Cuban Special Forces are being readied in Havana, too."

"Damn." Trane eyed McLaren. "Whatever Hemingway's mission is, it's big. We have to find him."

"If the Cubans start sending troops in strength into Latin America, we'll have to respond." McLaren glanced up from the file. "This is gonna get ugly fast if someone makes a mistake. Whatever we're going to do, we better do it fast and quiet. I don't want to be responsible for a damn war."

Trane's cell phone vibrated and he took it out. After reading a text message, he frowned. "I gotta go, McLaren. You deal with the war. I'm headed to Manhattan to fight one of its battles."

20

June 13, Early Afternoon–Midtown Manhattan, NYPD 20th Precinct

When the interrogation room door opened and a man with sharp, hard features walked in, a memory floated into Ana's thoughts—a blurry vision, like a dream nearly lost after waking. Why, she didn't know, but a wave of ease embraced her and she found herself staring at the man contently. She suddenly felt…safe.

"Hello, Detective," the man said casually as the color drained from Brennan's face. "I see you've found my missing material witness."

"Oh, hell no. Not you." Brennan jumped to his feet. "Agent Choo Choo?"

"Choo Choo?" Ana looked from Trane to Brennan and back. "Who is this, Luke?"

"Special Agent Trane, Homeland Security." Brennan stabbed a finger at Trane. "Or so he claims. He's probably CIA. Doesn't matter. He's under arrest for triple murder."

A CIA man? Could it be him? A face sifted through a haze of memories and formed before her. His face; Trane's face. He was leaning over her, speaking softly and gathering her up from the desert floor in Cabrera.

"Murder?" Trane forced a laugh. "I don't think so, Detective."

That voice…

"I told you to drop this," Trane said. "One-P-P told you that, too. Ana Karras and I are leaving."

"No, you're not." Brennan called out through the open interrogation room door for backup. "You're under arrest. I saw the brownstone's video. I saw all of it. You killed those three—"

"There's no video," Trane said coolly. "We both know that."

"You killed three people." Brennan stabbed the air with his finger as two uniformed officers waited just outside the door. "Then you hacked NYPD computers and stole three bodies to cover it up, Choo Choo."

"I did all that?" Trane laughed. "Before or after I was in your Chief of Detective's office at One-P-P?"

Brennan's face fell. "Ah, bullshit."

"We're outta here." Trane gestured for Ana to stand. "This time, Brennan, I want all your files, recordings, and every damn note you took on this case. *Everything.* Do I make myself clear?"

"Take him, boys." Brennan waved to the uniforms. "He's my murder suspect."

"Based on what?" Trane asked coolly. "A video you weren't supposed to have? You have no bodies; I just heard you tell Ana that."

Ana couldn't take her eyes off Trane. "Luke thinks I killed some Cuban men on Central Park West."

"Oh, he does? No worries, Ana." Trane faced Brennan. "Your Chief of D's went batshit crazy when I told him what you were up to. You might reconsider your career choices."

The two uniformed officers exchanged glances as they entered the room and took Trane's arms in hand. One said, "Bren, you sure about this? This guy's a Fed."

Before Brennan could answer, a uniformed police lieutenant appeared in the hall and pushed past the two policemen. "What the hell is this, Bren? I just got my ass handed to me by One-P-P. Get your ass in my office now."

"Hold on, Lieutenant Devitta," Brennan said. "I saw a video of this guy gunning down those Latinos at the brownstone's crime scene."

"Show me the video," Devitta ordered. "Now."

"I can't." Brennan's face twisted. "This guy hacked the system and killed all my evidence. Ask Chan."

"I already asked Chan," Devitta said. "He told me what the hell you're up to. Just about the same time my phone rang and One-P-P summoned me."

"Lieutenant, listen—"

"No, you listen. Cut these two loose. Then get your almost-suspended ass into my office. You're coming to One-P-P with me."

The uniformed officers released Trane and backed out of the interrogation room.

Devitta turned and strode away, muttering expletives.

"You bastard." Brennan turned back to Trane. "I don't know what you're up to, but I'll find out."

"No, you won't." Trane grinned. "Take some advice, drop it now while you still have a pension."

Brennan and Trane stood nose to nose. Brennan's face was red and raging; Trane's was passive and taunting.

Ana only saw Trane. *It was him.* "In Cabrera, you saved me."

"Yes, I did." Trane turned and looked straight into her eyes. "Do you remember?"

"Wait, Cabrera?" Brennan looked from Trane to her. "What the hell are you talking about?"

She ignored him. "I remember. You found me. You knew my name? How was that possible?"

"Whoa now." Brennan held up a hand. "Someone want to clue me in? Please? He saved you? Saved you from what?"

"Don't worry about it." Trane calmly went to the door. "Let's get you out of here, Ana."

21

June 13, Late Afternoon–The Caverns, Bayonne, New Jersey

"So, you're Ana Karras." McLaren stood across the dimly lit room with a scowl on his face. "You've caused a lot of trouble for such a pretty lady."

"Only ugly women cause trouble?" Ana said with an edge in her voice.

Trane laughed. "What he means—"

"I know what he means." She stood from behind the interview table. "He's a sexist asshole who cannot believe dainty, lil' ol me could be a problem for him." She spun on Trane. "You rescued me from Cabrera two months ago and the police this morning. Now, you hold me here? Do you want a real problem?"

"At least we agree you're a problem," McLaren snorted. "That's progress."

"Where am I?" she demanded. "CIA?"

"Great guess." Trane's voice was easy, calm. "Relax. We won't hurt you. We need your help."

"My help?"

The walls were cold, gray concrete and devoid of anything

personal. There were no pictures or paintings. No certificates or commendations. Nothing.

"We call it the "Caverns,"" McLaren said.

"How clever."

McLaren scoffed. "You could be at Rikers."

Trane hadn't tried to conceal their location from her. There hadn't been any dark hood or blindfold. He'd simply driven her across lower Manhattan, through the Holland Tunnel, and into Bayonne. Once in New Jersey, she hadn't recognized much, and when he suddenly wheeled the Suburban off a side street into a small, high-fenced compound, she knew she was in trouble.

The facility's fence was fifteen feet high and topped with concertina wire—not uncommon for the lower port area where crime was rampant. The building was over seventy-five hundred feet square with no windows and only a single doorway in the center of the front wall. The added motion sensors, CCTV cameras, and armed, black-clothed security men made it far less hospitable than the many cargo facilities and junk lots nearby.

This was exactly what she had envisioned of a CIA field office. Her mother had often lamented she'd end up in one if she didn't learn their lessons carefully.

Mamá had been right.

Trane slid his chair around the table nearly beside her. "I saw the brownstone's video, Ana. You've got serious skills."

Icicles stabbed her. They had seen the same video Brennan had. How could she have been so careless? While she'd meticulously reconnoitered the outside and considered every camera and alarm possibility, she'd never considered surveillance inside. Stupid.

"Ana?" McLaren prodded. "Why did you go after Colonel Vergara? You're lucky to be alive."

"Am I?"

"Don't worry. This isn't about him," Trane said. "Frankly, we don't care about him—well, not much."

"Then, what?" she asked. "Tell me or let me go."

McLaren cursed. "You don't make demands here, lady."

Trane snapped a glance at him that sizzled the air between them. Then, he turned back to her. "The brownstone was wired with cameras. I saw everything. Even things Brennan hasn't seen and won't ever. He didn't have all the recordings. We do."

"Then you know I didn't kill Vergara."

"Too bad. He needs killing." McLaren forced a laugh. "Although the Cubans might be a little upset with you."

She didn't react.

Trane said, "If we work something out, you can keep the money. It's, what…half a million? That'll go a long way raising Sarah."

The money. The cash that Vergara's men had been packaging at the brownstone. At first, they'd thought she was there to steal it, but learned quickly they were wrong. The inside CCTV surveillance must have recorded her every move. A wave of fear flowed over her. In Colombia, she rarely worried about electronic surveillance. Well, except for the banks and government offices she'd raided. Never in the jungles. That type of security was rare in the estates and hotels, too. Some, but few. In Manhattan, she should have considered it.

That mistake might be her end.

"You're pretty gutsy going after Cuban Intelligence," Trane said casually, watching her for a response. "Real gutsy."

Cuban Intelligence? She believed him Cuban military and that was bad enough. But Cuban Intelligence? What had Pappa done that would bring such a man as Vergara after him?

"You didn't know, did you?" McLaren asked. "Then why did you and G2 duke it out at the brownstone?"

She gave them nothing. Not a word. Not a frown. Nothing.

Trane leaned closer with a sympathetic face. "Are you working with your father and Vergara? Is that why you were in Cabrera?"

"What? Working with Vergara? For what? No. I was searching for my pappa. My parents went missing in Colombia. I was trying to find them. Vergara was there to find Pappa, too."

Trane looked over at McLaren but said to Ana, "Vergara is hunting your father?"

"Yes." How much did they know? How much should she tell them? She wasn't sure how much she truly knew, but for sure, she knew she was in trouble. Trane had saved her and Sarah in Cabrera. Would he use Sarah against her, now? Would the CIA take her little girl? If they tried…

"Your father's in Latin America," Trane said. "I was searching for him, too. That's why I was in Cabrera. It's a good thing, too. I saved your life."

Silence—her best defense...for now.

"We know all about you, too, Ana," McLaren said coolly. "We know all about your parents. We know you're FARC."

Her chin snapped up and she faced McLaren. "You know nothing."

"Nothing?" McLaren took out his cell phone and found the data file he'd sent himself earlier. "Ana Montilla, born September 1, 1990, in Bogota, Colombia, to Dr. Manuel Montilla and Irena Karras. Montilla is a Cuban national sent to Colombia by the Cuban government to work with FARC. Irena is a Greek American born in Queens to Penelope and Theo Karras. You grew up in Colombia and spent summers with Penelope Karras—Yiayia Poppi—in Queens. But you always returned to Colombia. You travel under the name Ana Penelope Karras, using your Greek passport. You were educated at New York University, majored in political science with a three-nine-three GPA. Not bad for a jungle-schooled kid. How am I doing?"

Cold, steely fingers crept up her spine. Her chest tightened and made her ache. Thoughts swirled and collided. *What to do? What to say?*

McLaren continued, "You participated in at least eight kidnappings against the Colombian government. Five of those involved other foreign nationals: two French, two British, and one American group. You aided the assassination of two Colombian military officers. Granted, they were brutal bastards, so we won't hold that against you. You also carried out or assisted in at least four major bank robberies, raids on government facilities for weapons and munitions, and other sundry supplies. My, my, you're a hellion, aren't you?"

They knew everything.

Her face dropped and her eyes filled with a mixture of fear and regret. She had tried to escape it all—believing if she left it behind and didn't return, it would somehow disappear with time. It had not. To hear it all now—recited aloud like the charges of a condemned prisoner—were daggers plunged into her heart.

Thank God that Yiayia Poppi and Sarah were not here to hear it all. Poppi knew some of her past, but she had been kept from the details. And Sarah…what if Sarah learned that Aunty was once a guerrilla, a terrorist? Would she lose the love of the child who had saved her life as much as Trane had?

Tears glistened on her cheeks.

"Ana?" Trane said in a soft voice. "That's in the past. That's why you returned to New York. Your father—"

"Pappa did nothing. Mamá made me a soldier." As she spoke the betrayal, her heart broke. "I will say no more."

For a long time, no one spoke. Then McLaren stood and hovered over her.

"On your recent trip to Colombia," McLaren said, reading from the cell phone file again, "you used a different name to keep yourself out of Colombian prison. Too bad it didn't keep you from almost dying."

Trane picked up the thread. "You say you went to find your father. We need to find him, too." He reached out and touched her hand. "We can work together and help each other. It's very important."

"Is that why you saved me in Cabrera?" She welled with anger now and spun around to face him. "So you could use me? You're no better than Vergara."

"I saved you because you needed saving." He squeezed her hand gently. "I saved Sarah—and Lobo, too. I saved you all because I could."

Because he could? His words shook her like she hadn't expected. For a moment, she was back in the hot, steamy square in Cabrera. Trane's face hovered above her as she lay bleeding, slipping in and out of consciousness. He was smiling; a desperate attempt to calm her. His voice was foggy and faint, but he spoke kind, encouraging words. As she had looked around, Sarah sat beside him, clutching his side with his arm around her. She had felt…safe.

Could she be safe with this man? Even after Vergara?

"I have no reason to help you." She folded her arms. "There is nothing you can say—"

"Ted and Cindy Cooper." McLaren watched her melt before them.

***

2005–Fifteen Years Earlier, Morning, FARC Encampment, Antioquia Department, Colombia

Sitting inside the steamy canvas tent, Ana was flanked by Ted and Cindy—Massachusetts tourists she'd found at the El Dorado restaurant in Jardin. She'd learned their names and home in their nervous chatter following their abduction. They'd been driven miles into the mountains and delivered to a FARC camp that was tucked away in a small jungle valley. They'd been blindfolded, bound, and laid face-down in the rear of a pickup truck for hours. Sometime before dawn, they were dragged through brush and tangle and tied to three rickety wood chairs. For two hours, no one dared speak, but as the morning sun raised the temperature and turned the tent to a humid sauna, Ana found her voice.

"Ted, Cindy, are you all right?"

Cindy finally released her tears. "I…I…I think so."

"What's happening?" Ted's voice was raspy from the lack of water. "Are they going to kill us?"

"Not if we can bargain our way out." Ana remained calm. "You said you have money. How much?"

Cindy blurted, "Two thousand dollars. It's in the hotel safe."

Ana said nothing.

"Ana? What?" Ted tried to turn on his chair but cut his wrists on the bindings. "What's the matter?"

"That's not enough." Ana lowered her voice, "Do you have more? Somewhere else? Somewhere you can get it?"

"No. Not really," Ted said. "Not easily."

"I do." Cindy choked on tears. "I have savings back home. Almost fifty thousand dollars in a college fund."

Ana nodded. "Yes. I can work with that. You will have to transfer it. Can you do that?"

Cindy sniffled a yes.

"All right. Let me try." Ana shifted in her chair. "Do you speak Spanish? Either of you?"

Ted sighed. "Very little—enough to be polite. I can't understand any of them here."

"We relied on our tour guide," Cindy said. "Won't the police come looking for us?"

"The policía are often FARC," Ana spoke in a whisper. "And those who are not won't venture into the countryside without the military. We're on our own."

"Dear God," Cindy cried. "Please, Ana, can you help us?"

"I will try."

They could hear movement outside and then voices entered the tent. A moment later, Ana's blindfold was slipped off. She faced two men dressed in ragtag jungle camouflage military uniforms and dark green berets with Che Guevara's emblem on the molded crown.

"Hablas demasiado."—You must be silent. The guerrillas kicked Ted's chair and made him flinch. The man continued in Spanish. "Especially you, chica. You have a big mouth."

Ana ignored him, and in English said, "They have money. They can pay for their release. Let me speak with your commander."

The guards exchanged glances. The first said in broken English, "Tell me. If good, I will report this for you."

"No. I will speak only to the commander. And bring us water. We will be ill if we do not get water."

Ted coughed. "Please. We won't give you trouble."

The second guard backhanded Ted viciously across the mouth, knocking him from his chair. "¡Cállate!"

Cindy cried more tears and began shaking.

"It will be all right, Cindy," Ana said calmly. "Trust me. You will not be killed."

Cindy sniffed back the tears. "What about…?"

"Shh," Ana said. "I will speak with the commander."

The first guard bent and untied Ana from her chair. "You are lucky, chica. My commander is a kinder man than me."

Thirty minutes later, Ana returned to the tent. She brought water and a loaf of bread. She untied both Ted and Cindy, gave them the water first, and placed the bread on a nearby folding table in the rear of the large tent.

"Listen to me very carefully." She guided them to the table. "We are many miles in the mountains. There is nowhere for you to go. Drink. Eat. Stay in this tent and be silent. I have arranged for the commander to allow Cindy to go with him to Medellin and arrange for your money to be transferred here. It will take time—a day or more—but he gives his word she will be safe."

"No," Ted nearly yelled, then caught his tone and lowered his voice. "She's not going with anyone alone. We go together."

Ana shook her head. "They will not allow that. They want guarantees she will not cheat them. You are the guarantee."

"What about you?" Cindy said between gulps of water. "What will happen to you?"

"I will be released eventually." She looked to the ground and thought about that. "My father is a doctor. He travels through this area. They know him. He often treats the camp's children in exchange for free passage from the guerrillas in Colombia."

Ted ripped off a chunk of bread. "Is that why you tried to warn us? You knew these men?"

Ana nodded. "I was too late."

"They trust you?"

"No. They do not. But they have a deal with my father. Once I told them who I was, they know they must not harm me." Ana's voice was a whisper, "Do as I say. If you don't, you could get us all killed—and my father. Understand?"

Cindy and Ted exchanged glances. Their sweat-streaked faces were pale and tired, cheeks raw from the dirty, ragged blindfolds, and their nerves frayed and unsettled.

Ted closed his eyes. "Yes, of course. What do you want us to do?"

"Don't fight them. Don't try to escape. Go with them and transfer your money. It is the only way you might leave this place."

Cindy clutched Ted's hands in hers. *"No. I won't leave you alone. I don't want to go with them alone, either."*

"What if you went for us, Ana?" Ted asked. *"If we gave you the information, you could go and Cindy would stay with me. I'd know she was safe. Would they allow that?"*

Ana looked from Cindy to Ted. *Their fear had consumed them, and they were clutching to the hope that they might still survive together. Both knew the risks of separation—once the money was transferred into the FARC coffers, there was no reason for them to live. Ana knew that, too. She had to find a way to save them.*

"Perhaps. Give me your information." They did from memory. *"It might take longer, but I will try. If the commander allows me to leave with his men, I'll be back in no longer than two days. Remember what I said. Don't fight them. You can't win. Do as they say. Try to stay calm. My father will be at this camp in a few days. We'll all get home."*

Cindy jumped up and hugged Ana tightly. *"Thank you. Thank you."*

"How can we repay you, Ana?"

"Just do as I say." Ana stood and walked to the tent entrance. *"All is not lost. If you don't do anything stupid. If you don't trust me, you will kill us all."*

***

Present Day, The Caverns, Bayonne, New Jersey

Tears betrayed Ana again, not for the first time, but at the most serious time. She stared at nothing on the metal table, trying to regain control. She couldn't. There were things she had learned in the Colombian jungle—things she had done for a cause she thought had been hers. The truth was, despite the many dangerous and evil things she'd done for that cause—FARC's cause—it had never truly been hers. In a desperate attempt to gain Mamá's favor, she had embraced it. Her young, naive mind wanted desperately to believe in it—for her mamá, if for nothing else. Something so important it would rebuild the bridge between mother and daughter. In theory, perhaps it was meaningful and justified back then. But in practice, the violence and evil were a different story.

The cause had been a virtue; a theme of propaganda, goals, and dreams. How those would be achieved had been only words for the longest time. In time, came training. Her unit had taught her military tactics, weapons and combat. There had been tradecraft to spy on government officials and gain their trust with whatever wiles required. Often, those wiles helped steal money and information. A kidnapping here or there for extorting resources from Bogota and throughout the region. For a few short years, it had been an adventure born of ideals and lofty goals. Defeat the oppressors. Install the heroes. Save the people. Bask in her mother's love.

Until Ted and Cindy Cooper.

Ted and Cindy were the day she realized those adventures were no longer hers. Ted and Cindy had died simply because they were Americans. Because their money had run out. That, and they had seen too much. Heard too much. Knew too much.

She had murdered them—not with planned malice—but she had killed them all the same.

When she looked up from the table, she had no idea how long she had sat in silence. McLaren stood across the room staring at her. Trane sat beside her with hands folded on the table, his eyes on hers. Quiet. Patient. Perhaps knowing even before she did, what she was about to say.

"What must I do?"

22

June 13, Late Afternoon–The Caverns, Bayonne, New Jersey

"You tracked your father to Cabrera?" McLaren slid a fresh cup of tea across the table to Ana. "What was he doing there?"

She shrugged. "I'm not sure. Maybe meeting my mother. Pappa left the FARC camp last year. My mamá left later to find him. I followed their trail north but lost it at Cabrera. I have no idea why they left the camps."

Trane asked, "How did you know they had left at all?"

Ana glanced from him to McLaren and back, taking time to think. "I received a letter from Pappa saying he had to leave. He didn't want me to return there—ever. I spoke with him several times a year by phone, but this was different. He begged me never to return no matter what."

"What about your mother?" McLaren asked. "Did you hear from her, too?"

"No. Despite his letter, I returned to look for Pappa. I knew something was wrong. By the time I reached the camps, Mamá was also gone too. No word. Nothing."

"I'm sorry, Ana. Truly." Trane sipped his coffee. "Vergara was at Cabrera. Do you know why?"

"Yes." She looked between the two. "To find my father and others."

"Others?" McLaren didn't shift his eyes off her. They were like a viper's eyes, focused and deadly. "What others?"

She sat watching him, thinking, trying to find a way out of this. She found nothing. What the CIA men wanted might well lead to her betraying her parents. Such a betrayal could get them killed. It could get her killed, too.

McLaren snapped forward. "Look, you have Sarah—"

"No, McLaren." Trane flashed up a hand. "Leave the kid out of this."

"Then all she has to do is help."

Sarah. There it was. Betray Mamá and Pappa or lose Sarah.

"I've answered all your questions." Ana sat back defiantly. "There's nothing more I can do."

"You can help us." McLaren tapped the table with his fingers. "So far, you haven't told us anything we don't know."

Twinges of pain sliced up and down her scars like she was being cut all over again. "Vergara was in Cabrera looking for Pappa and someone that looked like me."

"Looked like you?" Trane asked, narrowing his eyes on her. "I don't understand."

"Neither do I." She explained about Tomás's photograph and Vergara's concern for finding the woman. "That is all I know of her."

Trane exchanged glances with McLaren, who said, "Did your father and Vergara know each other?"

"I don't know." Ana shrugged. "Mamá and Pappa went to Cuba several times."

"We know that, too," McLaren said dryly. "But you never went."

"No. They went whenever I was here with Yiayia Poppi. Pappa's family was in Cuba. What they did in Colombia has nothing to do with America."

McLaren cursed. "Of course it did. Your mother is an American citizen. But for now, we won't worry about that."

"Ana, think carefully," Trane said in a matter-of-fact tone. "Do you know someone named Hemingway?"

"No." Hemingway—it took them long enough to get there. "Vergara was looking for him and said my father knew him. That's who they really want. I guess the woman they were searching for knows Hemingway as well."

Trane shot a glance at McLaren. "Wait, you said that before, that Vergara was searching for your father and others. By others, you mean Vergara was searching for Hemingway, too? They weren't there to meet him?"

She shook her head. "No. I'm sure they were looking for him. That's why they wanted my father, too. They think he can lead them to this Hemingway."

"That doesn't make sense," McLaren snapped. "Hemingway's their operative and they were looking for him? Are you sure?"

Ana's chin raised and her eyes bore into McLaren. "Stop asking me that. I am sure or I would say so."

"Okay, okay." McLaren changed direction. "Did your parents ever speak about Hemingway? Ever?"

"I first heard that name—other than the author, of course—from Vergara in Cabrera."

Trane asked, "What else do you recall from Cabrera, Ana? Anything might be helpful."

She thought a long time, unsure if it was important. Unable to decide, she told them anyway. "In Cabrera, Vergara knew I'd be there. He was concerned that his people in Havana would be upset by my injuries after his men beat me."

Trane held up a hand. "How did he know you were there at all?"

"I don't know. He said something about expecting me. Someone told him I was searching for Pappa and betrayed me…"

McLaren stopped her. "Someone betrayed you?"

"I'd used my parent's old contacts in Bogota to track Pappa's movements throughout Colombia. That's how I learned he might be in Cabrera. One of those contacts must have betrayed me to Vergara. There's no other way."

McLaren and Trane had a subliminal conversation with their eyes.

She broke their silence. "Who exactly is Hemingway? What is this about?"

"We don't know," McLaren said. "We hoped you did."

"I don't."

"All we know is that Hemingway is a Cuban operative. Colonel Vergara is involved but we're not sure what's going on. You think he's searching for your father and Hemingway both. That's confusing since Hemingway is their man."

"That's why we need your help." Trane touched her arm, and oddly, she didn't withdraw. "We have to find Hemingway and figure out what's going on."

"I've told you all I know. I can't help you. And I've done nothing wrong for you to hold me."

"Oh, really?" McLaren forced a laugh. "Don't forget, we know everything about your family. Help us and you'll skip death row."

"Death row?" Ana tensed. "We've done nothing against the US. Pappa is a doctor—a Cuban doctor. I was a child—"

"Daddy's a FARC doctor aiding guerrillas. Your mother's FARC—like you." McLaren's voice was taut. His eyes bore into hers with the intensity of a laser. "I didn't say we'd execute you. But the Colombian government sure will. A terrorist is a terrorist. Maybe they're Cuban spies, too."

"No." Ana jumped up. "It wasn't like that."

"It wasn't like that with Ted and Cindy?"

She spun on her heels and faced the wall. Tears exploded from her eyes and she fought for control. He was right. He was right about all of it. Mamá and Pappa were not just aiding the cause with medicine and care. They had helped—planned and executed—many operations. They had joined the guerrillas and done terrible things in the name of revolution. The truth—the cold, tear-streaming truth—was so had she. Willingly.

"There's nothing I can do." She backed away from the table. "I don't know where Pappa or Mamá are. I can't help you. Can't you leave me alone?"

"No, we can't." McLaren slammed both hands on the table and startled her. "Sarah won't like a Colombian orphanage, lady. So, start thinking."

Trane glared at him. Then, he reached over and touched Ana's arm again, but this time, she pulled away.

"Don't touch me."

"Ana, I won't let anyone harm Sarah or you." Trane's voice was soft, almost fatherly. "We'll help you find your parents. Together, help us find Hemingway. After, we'll get them back here—home. What do you think?"

The offer stunned her and she dropped onto the chair, looking between the two men again. Her eyes flowed with emotion and she had to look away. "What happens to us when they get here? Immunity? A new life?"

"For you, maybe." McLaren shook his head. "For mommy and daddy, jail up here is better than a firing squad down there. You know what the Colombians do to FARC guerrillas, Ana. Take the deal."

Life in prison or death? That had been the very choice Mamá warned her about a hundred times. Now, she faced that choice for real. At least for them. Maybe for herself, too.

"And me? If I do this for you—find Pappa and help find Hemingway—what happens to me?"

"A new life," Trane said. "New name. New life for you, Sarah, Yiayia Poppi, even Lobo. I'll even get him a new name."

Nerves made her smile.

McLaren started to object, but Trane shot him a cold, chilling look.

After thinking for a moment, McLaren said, "All right, we can do that. But we have to move fast. We find your folks. They help us find Hemingway. Mom and Dad do some time but skip a firing squad. You get a new life."

She didn't need to think. "Where do I start?"

***

Ana walked into the gray-walled cell three stories beneath the administrative offices where Trane and McLaren watched her on camera. She stopped inside the doorway and readied herself.

Colonel Vergara sat upright and stared at her. "You? You are one of them? The little chica?"

No reaction. She looked at the big, powerful man, now

downtrodden and ragged. Whatever Trane and McLaren had done to him had chilled some of his bravado. Still, he hadn't talked to them—not one piece of information they so desperately needed.

He would talk for her, though, to Ana Montilla. He had to. Sarah was in jeopardy. Mamá and Pappa were in jeopardy. Yiayia Poppi, too. Trane and McLaren offered the chance of a normal life—something she had craved since leaving Colombia. All she had to do was break him. She had broken strong men before—often by her wiles, sometimes by her wits. When those failed, Ana Montilla broke them with ruthlessness.

"Chica? First you come for me at the brownstone. Now here? Can you not resist me?"

She watched him, considering her play.

"Little chica?" He grinned an evil grin. "You going to use your waterboarding? You going to beat me? Go ahead. I know these things. Why not screw me instead? Maybe I talk then, no?"

Nothing. Silence was unnerving. Waiting for the unknown was often more terrifying than the known.

"You wish to know about your mamá and pappa?" He laughed raucously. "I tell you that much. We have your mamá, Ana Montilla. What is her life worth to you? Hmmm?"

Sharp claws etched at her scars and ended in a fire in her stomach.

"*Puta*, I will tell you nothing more." He threw his head back and laughed. "Long before they are done with me here, your mamá will be dead. We will have el doctor next. Then, he will be dead." He laughed again and ran his finger across his throat.

Ana Montilla will change your mind.

"Colonel Vergara," she said in a calm, steady voice, just louder than a whisper. "Tell me of my mamá and pappa. Tell me while you still live."

Vergara was taken aback; for a moment he just stared, open-mouthed, considering her cool, calm delivery of the threat. After a long moment, his eyes widened and he laughed raucously, shaking his head.

"Where do you keep Mamá?"

Vergara sat, staring. "I tell you nothing, you FARC bitch."

"Yes. I was a FARC bitch. That was a long time ago." She stayed at the doorway, leaning casually against the wall. Her eyes were locked on him, unblinking. "But don't worry, I haven't forgotten my training. Tell me of my parents."

Nothing.

"Tell me."

Vergara folded his arms defiantly. "Your parents can go to hell and wait for you there. When this is all over, I will be free. We will hunt you and your family like rabid dogs. And that brat you have, the little bitch from the village, she'll die the slowest."

Ana rapped her left palm on the cell door. "No. That will not be."

The door opened and three guards entered. They descended on Vergara, grabbed his arms, and violently crushed him backwards onto his cot. Two pinned him down on his back holding his arms and legs while the other grasped his head and held it firm.

"Now, Colonel," Ana said softly, slipping a small glass vial from her pocket and holding it up. "Tell me, before I must use this. Mamá? Pappa?"

The more Vergara struggled, the tighter the two guards held him down. His eyes froze on the vial. "What is this now? A trick? I tell you nothing."

"Then I pity you." She removed the vial's top and moved to the cot. "Do you know what thallium is, Colonel?"

"Thallium?" Vergara's face tightened noticeably. "It is a poison of choice by, shall we say, foreign friends of my Cuba. Are you suggesting…?"

"It was provided by my new friends upstairs." Ana allowed a sly, cold grin. "It has no taste or smell. It causes vomiting and diarrhea—painfully so. In a special form it will destroy the heart and liver quite quickly, too, I am told. It is a terrible poison. Let us see."

"You lie."

Ana held up the vial. "Nearly impossible to detect during an autopsy. Not that there will be one."

Vergara's eyes widened. "You lie. No one here would allow you—"

"Wrong." Ana nodded to the guard holding Vergara's head. When the guard gripped Vergara's jaw and pried it open, she leaned down and poured the vial's contents into his mouth. "In the end, you will tell me."

The guard clamped Vergara's mouth tightly closed and pinched his nose, forcing Vergara to swallow as he tried to resist.

Vergara instantly began to writhe. His body arched and twisted. His eyes were darting about. As the guards released him and stepped back, he sat up grasping at his throat.

"It burns," he yelled. "You bitch, what have you done?"

"Forgive the taste. It does not dissolve well in water. But rest assured, it is a simpler alternative to the beating and pain I could cause you. Though it is more permanent." Ana returned to her place at the door as the guards filed out. She removed another vial from her pocket. This one filled with a bluish liquid. "And this, Colonel, is Prussian blue. It is an antidote that works *most* of the time. Assuming, of course, you have it within an hour."

"I don't believe you. Get the hell out of here. I will tell you nothing."

"As you wish."

Ana slipped the vial back into her pocket and joined the guards in the hall, locking the door behind her.

Twenty minutes later, even through the steel door and echoing down the concrete walls, Ana could hear Vergara vomiting violently in his cell. A few seconds later, he pounded on the door and called out for her.

She entered alone and stood beside the cell door, leaning on the wall as she had earlier.

"You wish to speak with me, Colonel?" She stared impassively at him as he crouched over the small toilet in the far corner of the room. "Something about Mamá and Pappa?"

Tears streamed from his eyes as he turned on his knees to look at her. He whispered something that she had to move closer to hear and she leaned in, taking his hand in hers. When she was sure of what he said, she whispered back to him and lessened the pressure she'd placed on his hand.

"Good." She pulled several handfuls of toilet paper from the roll and tossed it to him. "Now, tell me of Mamá and Pappa. Tell me of Hemingway."

Vergara lifted his head and looked up at the camera. It took him several moments to complete each sentence as he stopped to vomit every few words. His eyes became bloodshot and his face sweaty and pale.

"Hemingway is dangerous…our best assassin…Havana is not in control."

She held his eyes. "What do you mean, you are not in control?"

"We did not sanction Hemingway's mission." He choked back sobs and wiped the tears and bile from his cheeks. "Hemingway can destroy the White House—perhaps start a war. Your father is an old contact of Hemingway's. I wished your father to help us stop this madness."

Through the speaker in the CCTV camera, McLaren asked, "What is Operation Perro? Who are Herrera and Espino?"

"I do not know those names. I only know Hemingway is very dangerous. Our countries could be at war if Hemingway succeeds." Vergara rolled sideways and looked up at the ceiling, trying to regain his composure. "The antidote. Get me the antidote now, or you'll never learn of Hemingway's mission."

23

June 13, Late Afternoon—The Caverns, Bayonne, New Jersey

Trane stood in the cell doorway holding a carafe of water. He set it on the small table and contemplated Ana across the room.

"He knows where my mamá is." She nudged Vergara's arm as he lay on his back on the cot. The vomiting and sweating had subsided, at least momentarily. "He wants to negotiate."

"Negotiate?" Trane asked. "What's he offering besides the whereabouts of your mother?"

"My assistance." Vergara wet his puffy lips and clutched his stomach, sore from the ordeal. "I offer her mamá. She will no doubt lead to el doctor. El doctor will lead to Hemingway."

Ana stood over him. "That has not worked so well for you."

"Not yet. But you are her daughter." Vergara contemplated the toilet. Then, slowly, he lay back down. "Perhaps she will confide in you what our techniques could not persuade her to confide in us."

"You tortured her?" Ana walked to the toilet with Vergara's eyes tracking her. She withdrew the vial of blue-liquid antidote and hovered it above the seat, getting ready to empty it into the bowl. "Where is she? Tell me."

Vergara reached out his hand. "A deal first."

"I want facts, Vergara," Trane snapped. "I'm not interested in negotiating. It's your choice. Die barfing your brains out or start talking. Soon, you'll start losing your vision. Then the headaches will be unbearable. You won't be able to stand the cramps and nausea. You'll be crumpled in a ball with vomit all over yourself."

"Promise me the cure!" Vergara rolled to a sitting position, staring at the vial in Ana's grasp. "I have what you wish to know."

"Your life for Hemingway," Trane offered. "Those are my terms. Ana made her deal with us. Now you must."

Vergara turned and glared hate at Trane. "We both know Hemingway is far too important to chance. Hear my terms."

"Ana," Trane said, "do as you please. I don't think we'll get anything from him."

"No, wait." Vergara's eyes fell to the floor. "Por favor, surely you can bargain a little?"

"I am not the one dying, Colonel." She let a few drops of the blue liquid escape from the vial and spill into the toilet. "Everything. Quickly."

"If I die, you will regret it." He spat bile onto the floor. "My people will slice your mother and father to pieces and feed them to the pigs. Then, they will come for the child you stole from Cabrera. They'll take their time with her...." The cramps seized him and he rolled to the floor clutching his stomach. "Por favor...por favor..."

She capped the vial and left it on the sink rim. "You have but moments left, Colonel. What will it be?"

He clutched his belly, crying. "Once a terrorista, always a terrorista, eh, Ana Montilla?"

Deep down, she feared that was true. "Perhaps."

Vergara crawled on his knees to the toilet, bent over it, and projected what little was left in his stomach. As he rolled back, he tried to snatch the vial from the sink, but Ana reached it first and snatched it away.

"My mother. My father. Hemingway." Ana dangled the antidote in front of him, swinging it back and forth to taunt him. "They will save your life."

Trane leaned on the wall beside the door. "I'd start talking,

Colonel. She's nicer than me."

"You are animals. Both of you." He sat back against the cell wall watching her. His eyes were glassy and red, tearing from the pain and mounting discomfort. "I know about you, Ana Montilla. You kill easily."

The words cut, but she'd gone too far to retreat now. She opened the vial again and let a few more drops spill to the cell floor.

"Enough, no, por favor…I will tell. I will." Vergara looked at the door, his eyes pleading with it as though expecting salvation to enter any moment. When it didn't, he dropped his head and cried.

He began slowly, still coughing. "Nearly three months ago, Hemingway disappeared from Cuba without a trace. We sent teams hunting throughout South and Central America. That is how I came to be at Cabrera."

"What's Hemingway's mission?" Trane eyed him.

"The antidote first."

Trane pressed him. "What other Cuban contacts or routes will Hemingway use?"

"None." Vergara shook his head. "Hemingway is not using our resources at all—avoiding them at all costs. To use them would mean we could stop this madness. Instead, Hemingway is using the routes that other South Americans use to travel to America as illegals."

"Blend in. Just another illegal among tens of thousands streaming north and into the US," Trane said. "A needle in a haystack. Jesus, an assassin off their leash."

"Yes. A dangerous needle." Vergara nodded again and nearly retched on the floor before getting control of himself. "Havana is worried Hemingway will start a war. It was not my government who sent Hemingway, it was those who do not want Havana to make peace with Washington. If peace comes, they lose their power. Hemingway is a provocateur to ensure there is no peace."

Ana's thoughts sifted and sorted everything she knew about Cuba and America—everything she'd learned from her parents as they jungle-schooled her, and then later at NYU. The viewpoints were not all that different.

The Cuba story was complicated. It started in the late 1800s when the US got Cuba—and other islands—from Spain after the Spanish-American War. About three generations ago, Fulgencio Batista and Fidel Castro were fighting for control of the island nation just ninety-something miles off the Florida coast. The problem was, the US initially backed Batista—a dictator. Later, Castro, a communist guerrilla, overthrew him. Castro didn't take well to US involvement and things devolved into turmoil. There were seizures of private lands. The military raided homes and businesses. Even mass executions took place. In retaliation to the US sponsoring Batista, Castro turned to the Soviets. There were embargos, threats, and irreconcilable differences. The truth was that Castro and Batista were both bad for Cuba. The US simply chose badly.

The rest was modern history. The disaster at the Bay of Pigs. The Cuban Missile Crisis. Tens of thousands of criminals and the insane reaching Florida on flotilla. Wet-foot, dry-foot…Fidel's death. His brother, Raul…on and on and on.

Over the past few years, a tiny hope sprang up that relations between Washington and Havana might warm. Most of it was a whisper campaign between then-President Obama and Raul Castro. A few olive branches waved in the air and hope sprang eternal—for a short time. Just when America thought things might actually normalize, Russia's Vladimir Putin increased trade with Havana and sent a realtor looking for nice digs for new Russian military bases. An administration-plus later, the US decided that any good relationship with Havana was counterproductive; President Cohen froze all pending engagements. The old ménage à trois among Havana, Moscow, and Washington reignited.

Trane moved closer to Vergara. "Why are you in Manhattan, Colonel? Did you come to grab Ana to use her to find her father?"

"I came for several reasons." Vergara shrugged. "If you wish to know them, I want the antidote and a deal. A good deal, too. But I want the antidote now."

Trane turned and opened the cell door. "I'll see what I can do, Colonel. I'll leave you to talk with Ana some more." With that, Trane left the cell.

"What of my mother, Colonel?" Ana dangled the vial in front of him again. "Have you tortured her and that is how you found me?"

"That is my secret." He coughed and wiped spittle from his mouth with the back of his hand. "I have many secrets. Like how I found you in Cabrera before, no? I knew you were there—somewhere. I was told many things. Many things to hunt down your pappa—and you. My secrets now. I will use them later, perhaps. After the antidote and my deal."

"Who? Who told you about me?"

"Yes, that is the question for you, no?" He waved a hand in the air. "Your mamá and pappa once worked with Hemingway. Did you know that?"

She didn't know but refused to react.

"Your pappa and Hemingway were friends. How do you Americans say it? An asset? Si, Doctor Montilla was Hemingway's asset. Si. One Havana could not trust. Hemingway has gone to your pappa for help on this mission. If they are successful—if your pappa helps Hemingway—we might not stop them in time. That is on you, Ana Montilla."

"You're lying. Pappa was no spy."

"No, no. He was a puta." Vergara coughed several times, raised himself to the sink, and took a few handfuls of water from the tap to drink. "Your mamá, she was different, no? Too bad for her. In time, she will tell us everything we ask."

"Where is she?" She shoved him from the sink and held up the vial—a few more drops escaped onto the floor. "Soon, there won't be enough of this to save you, Colonel. Talk fast."

He sucked in air and leaned back on the cell wall again, tears running down his cheeks. "Your mamá...she is in Mexico—Monterrey. My people have her."

"She is alive?"

"For now. For my life, I will tell you where to find her. I will make the arrangements for you—*only* you—to retrieve her. For my life and a new life for me here, I will help you find Hemingway. I will need her cooperation. But together, we can do it."

"What's Hemingway's target?"

"That is the question." For a long, chilling time, Vergara stared at her. "A good question, too."

"Tell me."

A bout of cramps seized him and he thrust out his hand for the vial. "I do not know who. I do not know the target, but it is very high up—very high. When Dirección de Inteligencia learned Hemingway was coming here, they tried to stop it. *Comprende?* They don't want war. That's why I spoke with your vice president's office. The Venezuelans helped me and—"

"Stop," McLaren called through the CCTV speaker. "I'll be right there."

The audible "click" preceded the CCTV camera turning off and the speakers and microphones going mute.

Ana glanced at the CCTV camera and held up her hands in a "what now" gesture.

Vergara leaned forward, wiggling his fingers for the antidote. "You wish to find your parents, Ana Montilla? Help me here and I will help you. Surely, this offer is worth my life to you."

"Tell me."

He glanced at the cell door. "For my life? You will give me the antidote?"

She nodded.

He motioned her closer.

Taking a chance, she leaned in and he whispered in her ear. When he was done and she leaned back, her face was steel.

"If I find this is a trap, Colonel, these men can do nothing to keep you from me."

"I believe you. Your mother's life for mine. Your father and Hemingway for asylum—a well-funded asylum."

The cell door opened and McLaren walked in with two armed agents.

"Ana, I've got it from here."

"But—"

"Out."

Vergara struck the air with his palm. "The antidote, Ana Montilla. You promised me."

She tossed him the vial.

He caught it, twisted the cap off and downed the remainder of the liquid in one gulp. His face instantly twisted. "Water? This is no antidote. I am to die?"

"Die? No, Colonel." She turned and left the cell, calling back to him as the door shut, "I gave you only Ipecac and some minor additives—something to induce violent vomiting and cramps. Ipecac is given to children and dogs when they eat bad things. It'll pass soon. You will live, Colonel. At least, for now."

***

Twenty minutes later McLaren burst through his office door where Trane and Ana waited.

Trane sat at the desk. Ana stood behind him. Both watched the computer monitor as Vergara sat staring at the CCTV camera.

"Well, that went well," Trane said to McLaren. "We need to…"

McLaren wasn't listening. He was already on the desk phone. "Get the jet ready for DC. Now."

24

June 13, Late Afternoon—The Desert, Southwest of Nuevo Laredo, Mexico

"Why are we headed so far into the desert?" Cat asked the gunman riding in the rear of the old school bus. She looked out the bus window at the sunbaked desert floor. "America is north. We go southwest deeper into the Nuevo Leon desert. We are many miles from the border now. Many miles farther southwest."

Cat had met the coyotes in Nuevo Laredo the day before. After paying four thousand American dollars—cash she had taken from El Jefe's body at Padrillo just before she burnt it to the ground—and after finding the coyotes, she'd waited almost a day to depart in the ancient school bus. Among the rough and dangerous men handling the busload of immigrants was *El Malvado*—'The Mean One.' His disposition thus far had proven the name appropriate.

"Do not worry yourself," El Malvado grumbled. "You will get to America."

Cat could not allow these men to take advantage of her. Not now. She was too close to America. Too close to the next phase of her mission. After all she'd endured, she would not be defeated now. She couldn't be. She was ready to fulfill her mission, save Mateo, and find a better life. Well, that was part of her mission. The other part—the dangerous and provocative part—was making them all pay.

Did she truly have what it takes? After the cantina Padrillo, she'd wretched for twenty minutes before her legs would carry her away. Fear had nearly crippled her. Nearly ended her life. Nearly ended her mission.

She could not afford the crutch of remorse any longer.

"Por favor," Cat said. "Why southwest?"

El Malvado stared back at her, trying to make her break her gaze. "I don't need your trouble, girl."

"I wish no trouble."

He moved toward her.

"Please, I want to know what we do." She glanced at the young girl, Lucía, sleeping on the seat beside her. "That is all. I wish no trouble."

El Malvado growled something and moved closer still. When he did, fear began ebbing inside again. But this time, she fought back. First, she reached inside her backpack pocket and gripped her pistol. The feel of the grip and the cold steel swelled confidence in her.

"Wait," a man at the front of the bus, a young Honduran, called out. "We all wish to know. Tell us why we go this way."

El Malvado glanced back at the two younger men, perhaps in their early twenties, who stood together facing him.

"Señor," Cat said, "we wish only information."

He shrugged. "The border at Nuevo Laredo is watched closely by the Americans for miles in both directions. They have spies inside Mexico to watch us, too. If we were to drive right to the river, they would be waiting for us. We are smarter. We drive southwest like we take you to day work away from the city. Then we will head north and cross farther north. No one will suspect we do this."

Cat watched him closely, looking for a lie that she did not find. It made sense. The farther from town, the less attention the Americans might pay. Before she killed him, El Jefe assured her that these coyotes were safe and competent. She prayed that was not a lie.

Every day delayed reaching her target meant more money. Hers was running low. For years she had syphoned cash away from her Cuban benefactors and her husband, hoping for a chance to escape with Mateo. After they'd taken him away last year, she used the money to prepare for this mission. Now, that money was nearly gone and she hadn't even entered America. The doctor's circuitous route from safe house to safe house also cost more than she had planned. There had been other paths—official G2 paths—that she might have used. But Havana was watching them, waiting for her to appear. Ñico was, too. In Cartago, she had made that mistake and used an old safe house that had not been used in a decade. She gambled that Havana had forgotten it. She was wrong. It was there that Ñico had caught her scent. Then, his spies found her again in Tegucigalpa. He was closing in. Her path northward would be far more precarious. The closer to the border she got, the more obstacles—the more danger—would be in her way. She only needed to make it across. Once in America, she would be just one more brown face among millions of brown faces as she approached her target.

"Thank you." She sat in her seat and glanced out the window. "I only wished to know."

El Malvado threw his head back and laughed, spewing spittle and rancid breath into her face. "Sit and shut your mouth or you can walk. You have paid your money and we will get you across the border. But anymore mouth and I will put you out on the road."

She glanced at the others on the bus. One by one they turned away and found things out the windows to keep their attention. Conversation stopped and the only sound was the crackle of the tires over gravel and earth.

One of the passengers sitting behind her, an older, frail woman, leaned forward and whispered, "You should be cautious, señorita. These men should be feared."

"I am not afraid," Cat replied. "Not anymore. It is they who should fear me."

25

June 13, Early Evening–The Desert, Southwest of Nuevo Laredo, Mexico

The bus was veiled in uncertainty and silence. Cat watched 'The Mean One' seated in the front of the bus. Her backpack was between her knees, one hand resting on the pocket where her pistol waited, the other placed on the seat ahead of her.

It had been some time since she'd seen any signs, houses, or even distant town lights. The bus just continued southwest. Finally, it slowed and pulled off the desert road, coasting to a stop several hundred yards after the turn.

The frail woman behind her leaned forward again—worry paling her face. "Why are we stopping in the middle of the desert?"

"Don't be afraid." Cat peered out the window. "Perhaps we stopped for the driver to rest."

El Malvado stood and opened the bus's folding door. He spoke with the driver, who climbed from the seat and disappeared outside. El Malvado followed him.

They were not stopping to rest.

Cat lifted her backpack onto her lap and whispered to the frail woman, "Do as they say. It will be all right."

"I am afraid," the woman said.

So was Cat.

What was happening lit the bus from both sides. It turned night into day.

The two dozen passengers jumped from their slumber when the bus's interior was abruptly illuminated from the headlights of several vehicles. The lights cast the interior with an eerie kaleidoscope of colors and movement.

Panic began to bubble into the aisles.

Two men, both armed with assault rifles and dressed in tan police uniforms, climbed aboard the bus. One strode down the aisle to the seat in front of Cat. He swiveled his rifle back and forth and ordered the passengers to stay still and quiet.

Everyone complied.

Cat closed her eyes for a second, gathered her thoughts, and searched for a plan.

Another man walked onto the bus and stopped at the front. He prodded the air with his hand. He was tall and thin, with an unshaven face and a large, bulky nose that didn't fit with the rest of his features. "Hola, mis amigos. Welcome. You will take your things and get off the bus. Everyone on this side," he gestured to the left side of the bus, "will line up outside, facing the bus." He repeated his command for those on the right side of the bus—Cat's side—ordering them to form a second line, facing away from the bus.

"Do this fast and quiet," the man commanded. "Do this now."

One of the younger men, the thin, short Honduran who had spoken up earlier, stood. "Por favor, what is happening?"

The man at the door walked down the aisle to the Honduran. He drew his sidearm and mashed it into the Honduran's face, breaking his nose in a gush of blood and crumpling him onto the floor.

"I am Capitán Alfonso Cortez of La Policía Federal. You are my guests."

26

June 13, Early Evening–The Desert, Southwest of Nuevo Laredo, Mexico

Captain Cortez paraded up and down the rows of immigrants as though he were reviewing military recruits. His men had herded them into lines and had forced them to stand there, vulnerable, imagining their worst fears were coming true. He wanted them to feel his power. Occasionally, he stopped and studied one of them—always a young girl. He moved slowly and silently; one hand poised on his belt holster as the other examined the captives' pockets. When he came to one of the women, his hand became an instrument to probe and molest, eagerly fondling a breast here, a groin there. Always lingering as he held their eyes and flaunted his power—daring resistance.

Cortez stopped in front of Lucía. "How old are you, chica?"

Lucía didn't look up. She didn't answer.

"How old?" He grabbed her chin and forced it upward. "I ask a question, chica. You answer."

Lucía managed, "Sixteen."

"Sixteen?" Cortez licked his lips. "I like sixteen."

Cat moved closer and slid an arm around Lucía. Her courage

was back but she didn't know why—perhaps it was Lucía. "Por favor, Capitán. She is afraid. Leave her."

"Shut up." Cortez ogled Lucía with penetrating, vile eyefuls of her body. "Sixteen is good. Still a child. Ready to be a woman."

He turned and caught Cat's eyes boring through him. He moved to her as his eyes and fingers mapped every inch of her body—a clumsy, guttural assault—while he continued grinning sadistically.

"What is your name?" he demanded. "Where are you from?"

For a moment, Cat couldn't recall the name she'd given the coyotes. Couldn't recall her cover story. When she turned and looked at Lucía beside her, her mind settled. "Maria. I come from Honduras."

Capitán Cortez continued eying her, studying her, dissecting her. Then something crept across his face that Cat didn't like. He said, "Honduras, eh? Si, perhaps you will make it to America. Perhaps not." He waved in the air, and one of his men trotted over and stood behind her. "Keep this one close."

Cat closed her eyes seeking calm. She did not resist. She knew better.

Fear was Cortez's best weapon. That weapon was powerful.

Cat knew the game. She understood it. Cortez was inspecting his bounty and deciding each's fate. In time, soon, he would come for her again. When he did, she would wait for an opening. Then, she would act.

When planning her mission, she had considered this danger—had prepared for it and decided just how far she was willing to go. Often, compliance meant survival. She'd learned that many years ago. To fight might mean death. Compliance offered at least a chance. Now, she faced that decision again. To fail when she'd come so many miles and faced so much danger was not an option. She would fight to the end if necessary. Cortez, with all his bravado and terror, was nothing she hadn't faced before…and survived.

There would be more Cortez's along her path. She would defeat them, too.

Be strong, Catalina. Strength is your second-best weapon. Intelligence is your first…outthink them.

"Capitán." She tensed as he grasped the crucifix around her

neck. "For safe passage, I would do anything you wished. Willingly."

Cortez's mouth opened, sending a foul smell of beer and bad breath over her. "I take what I wish. But it is good you understand your place."

"Do as you wish with me. Leave this young one—" she gestured to Lucía. "She is young—afraid."

"Yes, young." Cortez's eyes lingered too long on the young girl's bosom before he refocused on Cat. "We will see how good you will be."

"Gracias. You will not be disappointed."

Cortez laughed and strode away. He spoke to one of his men, who scurried away around the bus to one of the trucks waiting there. Its engine started and the truck pulled ahead of the bus.

"All the men go into that truck," Cortez ordered. "Pronto." The other truck behind the group started its engine. "The women and children in that one."

The men moved lethargically until one of Cortez's men swung his rifle and crashed its butt into the back of a young man. As he crumpled to the ground, two other men took his arms and lifted him, moving faster toward the pickup. The women needed no such prodding and were already climbing aboard the second pickup.

When Cat fell in line with the women, someone grabbed her by the arm and pulled her back, shoving her onto the ground.

The man growled, "No, not you. Capitán Cortez has plans for you."

"Now?" Cat got back on her feet and brushed herself off. "With all these others watching?"

Cortez turned to her. "You smell of the desert. I prefer my women to be fresh. Tomorrow will be soon enough. There is time. After all, each of you must work off your passage across the border. A month, perhaps. Maybe more if we do not get more volunteers by then."

"What?" It was what Cat feared. "We have already paid the coyotes so much money."

"What coyotes?" Cortez looked lazily around. "I have not seen such men tonight. Have you?" He pointed to one of his men.

"No, Capitán," the guard said, causing a ripple of comments

through the other guards. "I think we find these illegals alone. They have no coyotes."

"Put this one in my vehicle." Cortez pointed at Cat. "Oso will be very pleased by her. She will deliver a nice price."

One of the men grabbed Cat's arm. She tensed but allowed him to drag her to Cortez's Humvee. As she climbed in, the man tossed her backpack into a pile with other luggage. Luckily, they had not yet searched it. If they had, she might already be dead.

Her mission was in jeopardy, as was her life. She knew that the moment Cortez had stepped onto the bus. There were more men here than in Tegucigalpa. Better armed. Organized. Their captain watching and in control. She could not fight all of them and win. She'd need a plan. A strategy. A miracle.

"Reynaldo, be close to me," she whispered as the man closed the Humvee's rear gate. "I need you."

I am here, Cat. Be strong. I will tell you when it is time to fight.

27

June 13, Evening–The Eisenhower Executive Office Building, Washington, DC

"The chief of staff will see you now, sir." The young male executive assistant led McLaren inside the large, modern office. "I'll bring in coffee."

When the assistant left and shut the doors behind him, Danny Bianco jumped to his feet.

"What in the hell are you doing here, McLaren? And at his hour?"

"My job." McLaren dropped onto the chair facing the vice president's chief of staff. "Colonel Luis Vergara."

"Who?" Bianco was a barrel-chested man in his late sixties with penetrating, gray eyes and a square face and jaw. Currently, that jaw was clenched tight and his eyes were shooting bullets at McLaren. "Who the hell is that?"

"Your Cuban pal." McLaren folded his hands on his lap. "The one you sent me to find and interview, remember? Except you told me he was Señor Raul Anibal Vacarro."

"What's Vacarro got to do with this Vergara guy?"

"They're one and the same, Danny. Vacarro *is* Colonel Luis

Vergara from Cuban Intelligence."

"Cuban Intelligence?" Danny's face flushed. "I didn't know. What's this about?"

"You tell me. He called you." McLaren looked around the office and set his sights on an oversized globe in the corner of the room. He rose and went to it, opened the top and found what he was looking for—a well-stocked bar of the finest liquors. He selected a bottle of bourbon and poured two fingers each into two crystal glasses. Then, leaving the globe open, he returned to his chair and set one of the glasses before Danny.

"You'll need this."

McLaren sat, lifted his glass in a mock toast, and took a long, protracted mouthful. After savoring it in order to drag the moment on, he leaned back in his chair and watched Danny above his glass.

"We found Vergara in a thirty-million-dollar brownstone on Central Park West. Three of his men are dead and a half-million in cash was taken from him."

"Sounds like something you would do." Danny glared at him. "You have him?"

"Yes. Why is G2 reaching out to you—directly?"

"I have no idea. Well, not really."

"Not really?"

"I'm trying to recall what my staffer told me."

"Your staffer? Didn't you speak with him yourself?"

"Not the first couple times."

"Couple times?" McLaren took a long pull of his drink. "From the beginning, Danny. You said someone at the Venezuelan government asked you to contact Vacarro."

"Well, not exactly." Danny scooped up the drink McLaren had made, downed it, and went to the globe for a refill. "We got calls from the guy claiming to be Vacarro. The first two went to a staffer. Vacarro asked for me and dropped a name from the Venezuelan embassy. Someone I've known personally for years. His bona fides, I guess."

"And?"

Danny slugged back more bourbon, refilled his glass, and returned to his desk. "I contacted the Venezuelan and he confirmed that he knew the caller, declined to identify him, and told me to hear him out. Vacarro called the next day and I took it. He refused to speak on the phone other than to say he had rock-solid intelligence for the boss that we absolutely had to have. He said it was about the boss's initiative on Havana. He demanded I meet him in Manhattan."

McLaren cursed. "That's why you sent me there to—"

"Vet him." Danny's eyes hardened. "He's Cuban Intelligence?"

McLaren nodded.

"Then I expect you to deal with this, McLaren. Personally."

McLaren forced a laugh. "You know, Danny, your foot on my throat won't last forever. Be careful you don't overextend yourself."

McLaren met Danny Bianco in Kabul five years prior. McLaren had been running covert operations for the Agency. Danny had been in Kabul to discuss Afghan corruption and the continued threats against our presence. Someone in the Afghan government had a beef with McLaren and put a spotlight on him with Danny. Fifty million dollars was sent to buy a ceasefire with Afghan warlords and cooperation from corrupt Afghan officials during the US drawdown. Twenty-five million of it went missing, or rather, couldn't be accounted for. One particular Afghan official apparently didn't get the cut he felt he deserved and pointed a finger McLaren's way—privately, of course, so as not to ruin any chance of future stipends. Danny, always the political animal seeking advantage, saw an opportunity to corral one of the CIA's up-and-coming stars. One thing led to another and Danny got the upper hand. Whether Danny had any proof wasn't the issue—he kept their little secret and used it as a leash around McLaren's neck.

"What aren't you telling me?"

"Watch your insinuations." Danny slammed his palm on the desk. "I don't have the patience."

Danny leaned back and contemplated the ceiling. He was a powerful man in Washington. He'd made his bones in DC at twenty-five as a hard-working, tight-lipped, street fighter who grasped the political rule book with one hand and shredded it with the other. Still, Danny was well respected and courted by both sides of the political aisle. At one point in his career—a very important one—he had been appointed as the liaison between a powerful up-and-coming senator, Martin Cannon, and the US intelligence community. It was there that Bianco became an instrumental friend to Langley headquarters and the spearhead of Martin Cannon's political career—right up through Cannon's office down the hall as Vice President of the United States.

McLaren asked, "What do you know about Hemingway?"

"The author?"

"The Cuban assassin."

"Assassin? This just keeps getting better and better. What about him?"

"He's headed here."

"What?" Danny's eyes flashed wide. "Vergara told you that?"

"Yes."

"Sweet Jesus. Was he trying to warn us? Make a deal? What?"

"Oh, I think a deal is part of it. But there's something else, too." McLaren eyed him, getting ready to set the hook. "What's that something, Danny?"

"Screw you, McLaren. You work for me, not the other way around."

"I work for—"

"After Afghanistan, you work for who I say you work for." Danny surveyed his glass. "A few missing millions gets me that. Don't you think?"

McLaren stared impassively at him. "Hemingway?"

Under normal circumstances, Danny should have reported Vergara's phone calls to the intelligence liaison officer and on to CIA's top people, and to the Secret Service. But since Danny had found it necessary to seek McLaren's counsel in secret, there was something else that Bianco knew. Something that was making his ass twitch in the seat.

"I don't know anything about any Hemingway." Danny looked squarely at him. "What else has Vergara given you—all of it."

"Not much. He's still negotiating. But there's something big coming, I can feel it."

Danny's face tightened. "We need to keep it close hold, at least until I hear it first. Are you clear on this?"

"What's wrong, Danny? Do you know something I don't?"

"No. But I don't want the boss's plans screwed up by a leak somewhere. Got that?"

"I don't leak, but fine." McLaren leaned forward. "We need to get this to the Secret Service and the FBI. Domestically, they handle this sort of thing."

"Absolutely not. No way." Danny rose and walked across the room to the globe bar. He refilled his glass and returned to the desk with the bottle, stopping along his path to refill McLaren's drink. "Okay, Alex, this is all off the record. Got that?"

When Danny called him Alex, McLaren knew things were going to get interesting.

"I want—*need*—you and your people to handle this discreetly. We're coming into an election year. The FBI and Secret Service leak like sieves. It'll be in the *Post* and *Times* by morning if we screw up. Can you image the headlines? G2 calling the boss's office? My God, they'll label us Cuban spies and we'll be off again with the Russian collusion playbook."

"There's an assassin headed here to start a war, Danny. Screw politics."

"Listen to me." Danny's tone softened and he seemed almost imploring. "The boss has been a big advocate for maintaining Cuban isolation until Raul Castro improves his human rights. He supports the president's position on normalized relations only after concessions. The president thinks it's achievable. We're not so sure. Either way, this raises big questions."

McLaren sat listening, considering, analyzing. So far, his bullshit meter was pegged.

Danny continued, "If G2 is coming here to stir up trouble, it might have something to do with the boss's recent maneuvering. He's been using his old contacts for unofficial dialogue with Havana at the president's request. There are indications that Castro might be willing to capitulate a little—release a couple dissidents, return some family properties, and maybe even clean up their act overall. Castro may even request a formal state visit within the year to discuss terms to reopen Cuba to full US diplomatic relations and trade status. Having said that, it doesn't make sense that the Cubans would sabotage their own peace initiative."

"The hardliners don't want to lose power, Danny. Either way, that's why we need to bring the Agency into this officially—to get those answers."

"No. We're keeping this close hold." Danny waved his hand. "The president wants to make sure my boss takes the Oval Office next term. Part of that is to make this Cuban peace deal totally our success—making him President Martin Cannon down the road."

"You're lying, Danny. You know, the old Washington Deception Dance."

"You're lecturing me on deception?"

"Ever hear the names Herrera or Espino?"

Danny thought a moment and shook his head.

"Operation Perro?"

"Vergara gave you all this?"

"No. We started getting NSA intercepts on Hemingway nearly three months ago. That's how we knew to start looking for him. At first, we thought it was a Cuban operation gearing up. Now, from Vergara, we know the Cuban's aren't behind it. Not the government, at least." McLaren went on to explain the little that Vergara had told them in the cell earlier.

Danny frowned. "And you believe him? This isn't some kind of provocation?"

"I don't believe anything until I can prove it," McLaren snorted. "But the Cubans have sent G2 teams into South and Central America. They've got their special forces gearing up for something. It has to be to find Hemingway."

"Sweet Jesus. What a mess."

McLaren agreed. "Then there's the others. Just recently, the names Herrera and Espino were connected, too. We started hunting down the information on them and someone named Doctor Manuel Montilla. Apparently Montilla's an old pal of Hemingway from Cuban Intelligence. We know Vergara was in Colombia and Central America hunting Montilla and Hemingway. His mission in Manhattan is still unclear and he wants to bargain before he tells us."

Danny's face flashed a touch of panic before he smoothed it over with more bourbon. "The Cubans know the boss is working hard to broker a peace accord with Havana. Maybe this was a back-channel attempt to influence him."

"Influence him how?"

Danny steepled his hands. "We have considerable experience in Latin America that began during the Bush-43 years. My boss sent me on a lot of trips down south. Most of them are paying dividends now. But listen, that's all classified—*very* classified."

"Perhaps Vergara and Operation Perro are related." McLaren didn't care for coincidences, and those facing him were huge ones. "Unless you already know the answer to that."

"I told you no." Danny pointed a finger at him. "You better get to the bottom of this fast, McLaren. There's a lot at stake."

"There are bigger considerations, Danny. Huge ones—war-starting ones." He explained about the recent NSA intelligence regarding Cuban operations moving around the border. "Someone gets twitchy and we're in a shooting match."

"Then handle it." Danny gestured toward the office windows overlooking Washington. "I'll alert everyone myself—the Service, Bureau, and Langley—as soon as we know more details. But I do that; not you."

"I don't like any of this, Danny." McLaren looked down at the desk. "When this is over, my slate is clean. Got that?"

"Of course." Danny stood. "We're done."

The office door opened and two dark-suited men entered. One remained by the door and the other approached them at the table. "Mr. Bianco, the vice president is here."

28

June 13, Evening–The Eisenhower Executive Office Building, Washington, DC

"The vice president?" McLaren said, aiming a gun-finger at him. "I'll be going."

"Relax, the boss will want to meet you."

McLaren turned as a suave, sandy-haired man in his late forties entered and walked directly to Danny. Vice President Martin Cannon resembled a young Robert Redford. He clutched Danny's hand and turned to McLaren.

"Alex McLaren." Cannon gave him a broad, Hollywood smile. "I'm glad to finally meet you. Danny has spoken of you often. Why is it we have never met before?"

"Our circles are quite different, Mr. Vice President." Powerful men didn't intimidate McLaren. Yet, while he despised most of them, he aspired to become one. "I was just leaving. It's a pleasure to meet you."

"No, stay." Cannon extended a hand, warmly shook his, and gestured for him to return to his seat. He turned to Danny and pointed to the bottle of bourbon on his desk. "I'll have what you're having, Danny. But larger. The Good Lord doesn't mind a drink now and then."

Danny retrieved a glass from the bar.

"What brings you here, Mr. McLaren?" Cannon asked. "You have the new domestic response team, correct? Very hush-hush."

Danny answered him. "That's right. We were just discussing your initiatives with Cuba and Latin America, boss."

"Oh?" Cannon squinted at him. "I thought we were keeping that in a close hold, Danny."

"We are, boss, but something's come up. I think it would be better if you leave it to me, though."

"I see." Cannon turned to McLaren. "Do you agree with that?"

He shrugged. "It's your show."

"I think it best for now, sir." Danny sighed.

"Well, dear Lord, what do we have going on?" Cannon said. "Does it have to do with those odd phone calls you were receiving, Danny?"

"It does."

Cannon considered that and glanced at McLaren. "You're on top of this?"

"I'm trying."

"Good. Then Danny's right, I'll stay clear of it." Cannon smiled. "He told me you were a good asset for us. Don't disappoint us, McLaren."

"No, sir."

"Well, you'll advise me when it's appropriate, I'm sure." Vice President Cannon took a long pull on his drink and walked to the office windows to gaze out. "McLaren, I'm sure Danny has explained that I'm leading an effort to crack the ice around Havana. God willing, we can improve human rights and gain other concessions. I believe we're within reach of a huge diplomatic coup."

McLaren watched him. "I'll leave politics to you, sir."

"Of course. But if the Cuban government screws this up, I'll build a wall around them so high it'll block out the sun."

McLaren glanced at Danny, who smiled and nodded.

"My pleasure to meet you, Mr. Vice President." McLaren stood and turned to Danny. "Let me get back to Manhattan."

"Right."

"Alex?" The vice president walked to him. "Do you need anything from us?"

Alex again. "Time."

"Only God can grant that, I'm afraid." Cannon smiled thinly. "However, if you require anything else, my office will deliver. Keep Danny in the loop. I know, I know, you people all have your rules and protocols. However, Danny tells me you're known for decisiveness and action. You're the man to make problems go away."

McLaren shot a cynical glance at Danny. "He has no idea, sir."

"Good."

As McLaren reached the door, Cannon turned him around. "Alex, could this little matter you're working on be dangerous to us here?"

"It already is, Mr. Vice President."

29

June 13, Evening–Queens, New York

Ana burst through the rear door and ran into the living room where she found Poppi sitting on the couch. Sarah was curled up on her lap, fast asleep, with Lobo at her feet.

"Ana, what is it?" Poppi whispered. "Where have you been? I've been worried sick since you called earlier."

After Trane secured her in his New Jersey haven, the first thing he'd done was return her cell phone. She'd called Poppi to reassure her that she was safe and out of police custody. Despite Trane's insistence she did *not* explain she was going into CIA custody, Ana gave her brief details that she was helping someone else from the government. She didn't elaborate and promised to return home as soon as possible.

That was hours ago.

"I'm sorry, Yiayia, but we have to hurry." Ana flew around the room gathering items from drawers and retrieving a large rolling suitcase from the hall closet. "You must leave. Tonight. You must take Sarah somewhere out of the city for a few days—maybe longer."

Lobo was on his feet now, watching Ana's flurry through the house, pivoting and cocking his head with each foray she took into a different room.

"Away? What is it?" Poppi slid Sarah from her lap and stood. "What is going on? Have they discovered you?"

Yes, they have. "There's no time. The man who got me from the police—Trane—will be back. He expects me to help him find Mamá and Pappa and Hemingway. It could be dangerous for you and Sarah until I return. You must go."

"Dangerous? Who is Trane?" Poppi's face twisted with confusion. "And what have you learned about this Hemingway? What is it, Ana?"

"Trane is CIA."

"The CIA?" The words burst from Poppi's mouth like she'd taken a mouthful of ghost peppers. "What do they want? Is this about Vergara?"

"They have him. I've seen him." Ana ran up the stairs to the second floor. After several minutes, she returned with a heavy suitcase stuffed with Sarah's clothes and a few toys. "I'll explain everything later. Please, pack enough for a week or two."

"No."

"Yiayia, please. There's no time…"

"No, child. Not until you tell me everything."

"I can't. You must go. It's dangerous to stay here."

Poppi stared at her with a strange intensity on her face. "Ana, I must know what you're doing. Please. If there is danger, then…."

"Aunty Ana?" Sarah stirred on the couch and lifted her head, smiling widely at Ana across the room. "You're home. I missed you."

"I missed you, too, Sarah." She went to her, kissed her several times on the cheek, and hugged her close. "You're going on a little trip. It's a surprise. So, go back to sleep."

"A trip? Really?" Sarah rubbed her eyes and yawned. "Is it a secret trip like the last one where you found me?"

"Yes, but much better. You, Lobo, and even Yiayia Poppi are going together."

"I like trips…" Sarah closed her eyes, fought valiantly to open them, but drifted toward sleep again. "I like being a family with you. Lobo does, too. Can I…" She was asleep.

Ana turned to Poppi. "You have to get Sarah somewhere safe until I can figure out what to do."

"We'll go to Williams." Poppi still didn't budge. "But call me when you are on your way. You must tell me everything or I will fear the worst. Please, child. Don't make me wait in silence. I could not bear it."

"Yiayia, they know." That thought made her shudder. "They know who I am; the things I've done. They know everything."

"Oh, Ana, that's in the past. Perhaps…"

"No. It's not far enough in the past." She looked into Poppi's eyes as hers rained. "They want me to do it again. For them. If I do as they want, they'll save Mamá and Pappa. I have to go to Monterrey, Mexico. I have to help them find Hemingway. I have to be Ana Montilla again."

***

2005, Evening, The Jungle, Antioquia Department, Colombia

"You can do this, Ana." Irena Montilla stood behind her between two guerrilla fighters from the camp. She shifted a pistol at the rear of her waistband. "You must. I know it's difficult, but the commanders will not trust us again if you don't."

"I don't know, Mamá. The commander believes I failed—that I'm not ready." Fear gripped her. Not fear of the jungle or the guerrilla fighters sent to ensure the mission was completed, but fear of what she must now do. "Perhaps I'm not ready."

"You're not weak, as he said. No. But he blames me for the failures. He's a hard man, Ana, but a good leader. Our fighters are blessed to have him. He will not be defeated, and he will protect his camp no matter what. We must do our part. All of us—Pappa, me, even you."

"But Mamá, they did as we asked. They gave us their money and promised to be silent. Cindy and Ted—"

Irena raised a hand. "Ted and Cindy? I have warned you, Ana. You should not learn their names."

Ana's heart fell but she nodded. Yes, she had allowed herself to become too close to them.

For hours, she'd followed Mamá and the FARC guerrillas into the jungle—climbing hillsides, struggling along nearly impassable trails—deep enough that no one would find them. Along the journey, Mamá had been silent, watching her. The guerrillas led the way, pushing Cindy and Ted ahead of them, tied hand-to-hand with a rope tether as a leash held by a guerrilla fighter called Jaime. After a nearly three hour walk from their basecamp, Jaime stopped and waved at Irena.

This was the end.

"Ana," Irena said, taking her shoulders and whispering so the fighters would not hear, "Jaime is here to watch you. If you can't do this, he will. But then, he'll report to the commanders that you failed—that I couldn't make you. We'll both answer for that."

Ana lowered her head and tried to fight back the tears— the coldness invading her. She felt so out of control. So alone. So evil. It was like she was elsewhere, the shell of her body marching through the jungle, readying to do the unthinkable.

Can you, Ana?

She looked at Cindy and Ted, trying desperately to steady herself. Then, she looked at Jaime and the other guerrilla fighter as they untied their leash and allowed their captives to sip water from a canteen.

Cindy and Ted had steeled themselves to the fate they knew was coming. During the jungle hike, they'd spoken little except an occasional word of solidarity between them. A prayer. An 'I love you' shared repeatedly when the group stopped for a break, fearful that each pause was their final step. Never did they resist or try to run. Never did they beg or pledge a promise that everyone knew they could not deliver.

They were strong, these two. Brave. Doomed.

"No, Mamá. I can't. Let me go back into town and see if I can get more money somehow." She wiped the tears from her cheek. "Maybe—"

"No, Ana. It is too late for that." Irena slowly shook her

head. "If you do not do this, then none of us will ever go home again."

Ana lifted her eyes to her mother's. Hers were as cold and empty as some of the fighters she'd come to know. Once, when she was younger, she marveled at how full of life and kindness her mother had been. Now, there was nothing left.

"It's not too late, Mamá. We can all go together; Yiayia Poppi will help get us home."

"Stop it, Ana." Irena pulled the pistol from her waistband and forced it into Ana's hand. "If you don't, then it's too late."

"Mamá…"

"Pare," the second guerrilla cried out. He was loosening Cindy and Ted's bindings—perhaps to allow them to relieve themselves in a last act of decency—when Cindy threw herself onto him and bit deeply into his neck. Blood flowed over them both.

Ted lunged at him, twisted his rifle away and smashed the butt of it down on the man's neck.

The guerrilla dropped to the jungle floor.

"¡Pare. Stop!" Jaime swung his rifle off his shoulder. "No. No."

Ted spun around and shot him squarely in the chest. Then he turned and took aim at Ana and Irena.

"Please," Irena said, trying a calm voice to still Ted. "Do not hurt my Ana. We are only following orders and did not want to do this."

Cindy's arms flailed and her cries were guttural and savage—the rage of terror unleashed by hope. She tugged Jaime's Beretta pistol from his belt and turned on Irena. "Bastards. You took us. You stole our money. Now you want forgiveness for trying to kill us?"

"We trusted you, Ana." Ted's face was pale and blank; his voice was coarse and unsteady. "We thought you were helping us. We thought you were a captive like us. You were one of these animals all this time."

"Put the gun down," Irena said calmly. "You need us to escape the jungle. You'll never make it out alive without us."

Ted closed his eyes and fired.

The bullet struck Irena and toppled her sideways onto the ground.

"Mamá?" Ana dropped to her knees beside Irena and grabbed her head. "Mamá, no."

Cindy screamed, "Ted, let's go. Let's go."

Ted's face blanched. His eyes were vacant. He didn't move.

"Ana, I am all right." Blood oozed from Irena's shoulder, but she managed to get onto her elbow. "Kill them."

"Mamá, please…"

She shoved her away. "Do it. Fight."

"Ted, let's go," Cindy cried again. "Let them be. Let's go."

Irena lay back, staring at Ana.

You will not run, Ana Montilla.

Ana watched it happening. Cindy tugged on Ted's arm. His eyes were dead and his movements slow and robotic—his hands lifted his rifle.

Now, Ana. Now.

In one swift motion, she lifted Irena's pistol and fired wildly, diving away and rolling into the bush.

Ted fired three shots, chasing her across the jungle foliage as she rolled into the darkness. Then, he turned back and steadied his aim on Irena.

No.

Ana's next shot struck Ted in the stomach. Another in his chest. Her final shot hit Cindy a split second before she focused her pistol on Ana's head from five feet away. Cindy's shot whistled past her innocently into the jungle behind. Ana's shot did not; it hit its mark just above Cindy's chest, burying itself into the small of her throat.

As Cindy lay dying beside Ted, Ana eased from the bush and walked calmly toward them.

"Fools. I would have let you go. Now look what you have done."

***

Present Day–Early Evening, Queens, New York

"Then we have to go." Poppi headed for the stairs. "I'll get my things. William will protect us. I'll call him from the car."

"Good. I'll join you later."

"Ana, come with us now. You don't have to help the CIA. There are other ways—"

"No. I have to make sure you and Sarah are safe." She glanced out the front window. "Then, I must help Trane. Just a day or two in Mexico. If all goes well, I will return with Mamá and Pappa."

"What? No. It is far too dangerous. You should not trust this Trane person or any of the others. You cannot go, Ana."

"I know what I'm doing." Ana shooed her up the stairs. "Go pack. Take your car from the garage. Trane's men are out front, watching. I'll distract them so you can go."

Poppi was up the stairs and back in moments while Ana finished packing Sarah's things. Sarah would be heartbroken when she woke up and didn't find Ana with them, but Poppi would explain. She'd join them soon enough. A day. Maybe two. Nothing more.

She'd made a promise to always keep her safe. *Always.*

Ana carried Sarah to the rear door and handed her to Poppi as she piled three bags there.

"Protect her, Yiayia. I'm trusting you." Ana kissed Sarah's head and allowed her fingers to glide down her auburn hair. "She is like my own."

"I must tell you something." Poppi's voice was strained. "Something important. It's about your mother and father."

"No. Not again. Not now." Ana kissed Sarah's cheek long and lovingly again. "I can't bear it. Go while it is still safe. I'll do what is necessary."

"Please, Ana, listen—"

"No. Get Sarah to safety."

"You are as stubborn as my Irena. William will take care of us. We'll be safe. Then, he'll fix this."

"William cannot fix this." She hardened herself. "But I can."

She followed Poppi outside and into the rear garage carrying their bags. Then, she secured Sarah into her car seat, kissed Poppi's cheek, and stepped away.

Poppi backed the car out of the garage and was gone.

Ana watched the car disappear down the alley and looked for someone following them. There was no one. Collecting herself, she returned to the house and locked the rear door behind her. As she walked into the living room, she stopped.

Standing across the room, holding a silenced pistol, was a familiar face.

Tomãs.

30

June 14, Very Early Morning–Queens, New York

The kitchen door splintered at the same moment the rear door crashed in.

Trane and his men breached the house in a tactical swarm—speed, overwhelming numbers, and superior firepower. They blurred into the room with lethal focus. He was the first into the house—coming directly through the front door—as his team rhythmically cleared the house room by room, floor by floor.

Ana sat in the living room sipping her tea. She didn't react. Didn't flinch. She'd expected it. Anticipated it. She'd waited for it in her favorite overstuffed chair since she'd found Tomãs in her home last night.

"I'm here," Ana called out. "It's all right. I'm alone."

A laser sight swept from the side wall and tracked across the furniture to eventually rest on her chest.

Trane yelled, "I've got her."

"You're late," she snapped. "Where were you last night? I needed you."

"What happened?"

"I had a visitor."

***

Last evening, Tomãs had stood in her living room, barely ten feet away. He had a cold, dangerous grin on his face as he taunted her with his silenced pistol. "Buenos noches, Ana Montilla. Just because Colonel Vergara is gone doesn't mean I have forgotten you."

"How did you find me?"

"That is unimportant." He holstered his pistol beneath his leather jacket and slid a knife from his pocket—flipping open the six-inch blade. "We have to finish what we started in Cabrera, no? Before you die, you will tell me where your father is. That will make me a hero. Perhaps I will replace Colonel Vergara."

"You shouldn't have come here, Tomãs." She stood calmly, waiting for his attack. She knew he would taunt and bluster—a false belief that her demise was a foregone conclusion. "You can still stop this. You can leave."

He laughed and stepped closer—predictable.

Just before he lunged for her, she clapped her hands twice and plunged the room into total darkness.

Tomãs's knife sliced only air.

She wasn't in front of him any longer. When the lights flashed off, she spun away, rolled deftly over the overstuffed chair, and landed behind him. He slashed away at where she had been and that cost his life.

She drove a heel into the rear of his knee and dropped him backward. As his hands flailed to regain balance, she seized his knife-holding wrist, ratcheted it backward and up, and plunged the blade into his throat.

"¿Que?"

"Adiós." She twisted it deep until she felt the blade touch his spine.

It was over that quickly.

***

"Where is he?" Trane looked around. "The body, I mean."

"In my neighbor's garage."

"Your neighbor's garage?"

"Of course. You didn't expect me to put him in *my* garage, did you?" She moved to the coffee table and hefted a large, black backpack. "He's away on vacation."

"Well, thank God for that." Trane issued orders to one of his men, who jogged to the rear door and headed for the neighbor's garage. Trane turned back to her. "Are you all right?"

"Yes, of course." She pulled a cell phone from her back pocket and tossed it to him. "Tomãs had this. Perhaps it will explain how he found me so easily."

Trane caught the phone. "I'll have my people go through it. Never know what might be valuable on it. Where's Sarah and your grandmother?"

"I sent them away where they can be protected. You already broke our deal, Trane. You were supposed to protect them. You told me you'd have people watching the house."

"I did." His face paled. "My men are dead."

"Dead?"

"Someone killed them during the night."

A pang of guilt stabbed her. "I'm sorry."

"Where did you send Sarah and your grandmother?"

"Somewhere safe."

"Where?" Trane waved his men outside. "I'll have my men—"

"No." She glared at him. "If your men were any good, things might have turned out differently."

Trane said nothing.

"Let's go." Ana held up a gun finger. "Mamá's waiting."

31

June 14, Very Early Morning–Queens, New York

Outside, Trane's operatives were strategically posted throughout the neighborhood. They took tactical positions on both ends of the street, around the house, and near the sedan where Trane's two agents sat dead in the front seat. Tomãs had executed them without a struggle. He'd shown no mercy.

Ana had shown him the same courtesy.

She stopped on the front stoop and surveyed the area. "I'm sorry about your men."

"So am I." Trane looked down the street where his team was working the sedan with the two dead operatives inside. "I'm sorry, too, Ana, for you having to send your family away and for having to involve you in all this. But you're our best chance of stopping Hemingway."

If Trane's people weren't his best chance, could she truly handle what was coming? Vergara's Cuban operatives were pros—evidenced by Tomãs's lethal success against Trane's team in the sedan. Tomãs's weakness had been overestimating himself. If he hadn't been so overconfident, she might be dead. Yet, Trane felt she was his best chance. Was she?

"I'll do my best. But understand, I'm in this for our deal, nothing more. Remember that."

"Got it."

Ana knew that if she was going to survive this dangerous game with Trane, she'd have to dig deep and employ all her skills from her past. Everyone wanted Hemingway: the CIA, the Cubans, who knew who else might be in the game. The Cubans already showed they were willing to kill in order to win. Back in the Caverns, she'd learned the stakes. What she couldn't fathom was why and how her parents had become entwined with a Cuban assassin heading to America. Joining FARC was one thing. She'd understood, for the most part, how they could join a cause fighting a corrupt government oppressing its people. For too long, she'd believed she was a revolutionary too, fighting the good fight. Her disillusionment had come when she'd witnessed the defenders of justice become no better than their enemy.

Still, what they'd done had little direct impact on her home—on America. Hemingway was different. There was no misunderstanding what would happen if Hemingway succeeded in assassinating Washington leaders. There would be retaliation against Havana. It could escalate ferociously. There could be war, and not just with a small Caribbean island.

For her, however, the crisis was not communism vs. democracy. Not Havana vs. Washington. It was simpler than that. It was a little seven-year-old orphan. It was Mamá and Pappa. Yiayia Poppi. It was about a new life. A safe life. Family.

All that was impossible if Hemingway succeeded. If that meant traveling to Mexico and hunting Hemingway—even with the CIA—then that is what she was going to do. Her family for Hemingway.

It was no choice at all.

"Let's go, Ana. In my Suburban." Trane signaled his men they were ready. "I've got transport waiting."

"What about McLaren?"

"Yeah, him." He guided her toward a large black Suburban parked just outside the fence gate. "McLaren wants you at the Caverns until I have your mother. I'm to take my team to Monterrey and retrieve her. Then, and only then, you'll help gain her cooperation to find your father. In turn, you'll get him to cooperate to find Hemingway."

She stopped dead in her tracks. "Vergara said my mamá was being held in Monterrey. So, I'm going with you to Monterrey."

"No. McLaren doesn't want to chance you running off on your own."

Perhaps McLaren wasn't as stupid as she first thought. "It wastes time keeping me here. Mamá will not speak with you or your men. She might well fight back against you. You'll need me there when you find her."

"You're not a field agent, Ana." Trane held up a hand. "You're not trained for what we have to do. Hemingway is too important."

"Mamá and Pappa are important, too. Do you think she'll talk to you after resisting Vergara's methods? And, Trane, I was instructed by those who have beaten you for decades. Tomás killed your men." She gestured toward the sedan down the street. "And I killed him."

Trane stood watching her. He started to speak twice but stopped and continued thinking. He didn't take his eyes off her; his stare was penetrating.

"If Mamá and Hemingway are so important," she said, "then I must go to Mexico, too. Or, we have no deal."

"Listen, Ana, it's not that simple."

A series of *whoop-whoops* erupted down the street. Two marked police cruisers sped around the corner and screeched to a stop outside the house. They blocked his Suburban against the curb as four officers jumped out and took up tactical positions over the hoods of their cars, pistols drawn. Behind them, an unmarked sedan rolled in with flashing lights in its grill and window visors.

Trane grunted, "Now what the hell is this?"

Detective Brennan stepped out of the sedan, took a slow, panoramic scan of the area, and waved at the uniformed officers. "Hold here, guys. I know this character. Keep your eyes on his cronies."

"Trane?" Ana whispered as his hand locked around her upper arm. "What's going on?"

"Relax, I got this."

"Secret Agent Choo Choo." Brennan ambled over. "Why am I not surprised?"

"Detective?" Trane gestured for his men to lower their weapons.

"You need to withdraw. We've been through this before."

"Sure, sure, I remember. Except as always, I got a homicide scene and you're in the middle of it. And look, Ms. Karras is involved again, too. She's either in custody again or being kidnapped."

"It's neither, Luke." Ana tried to smile but failed. "I'm helping Mr. Trane."

"'Mr.' Trane?" Brennan's face scrunched up. "Help with what? Obstructing justice? Stealing bodies from crime scenes? Overthrowing a government, maybe?"

"It's classified." Trane's words were ice. "Move out."

"Sorry, Choo Choo, this is Queens. There's no diplomatic anything. We got a call about bodies in a car. I see them right over there." He jutted a finger at the sedan down the street. "Dead bodies draw you like flies, Trane."

Trane fumed. "I don't have time for this. I'll have your job."

"Good. It's long hours and lousy pay." Brennan stepped closer. "Let Ms. Karras go and you and your circus clowns can leave."

Ana held up a hand. "I'm all right. Really, Luke."

"It's detective." Brennan flashed a grin like that was their new secret passphrase. "What's happening, Ana? I can help you."

"No, I don't think you can." She caught herself feeling a familiarity with him that startled her. What was it about him? A smiling, handsome memory made her smile and tune out Trane's debate with him. Brennan's easy smile and quirky personality reminded her of Tommy Robert Sawyer.

The autumn when she turned seventeen, Tommy, the nineteen-year-old son of a visiting British missionary, arrived in a small remote village where her camp received supplies. He'd come to Colombia with his widowed father to set up a reading program in the village. Ana's mamá had sent her to infiltrate Tommy's group and gather information on his father—concerned he might be a spy or threat to the camps. Each week, she ventured to the village as instructed but soon found it more pleasure than assignment. Having someone new to talk to—someone not connected to the camps—was exhilarating. Tommy was bright, cheerful, and worldly. By the end of that first month, they were in love.

Since Tommy, Ana had never loved again.

"Ana?"

"Right, it's detective. Sorry." She pushed the memory away. "Please don't interfere."

Trane relaxed his grip on her arm. "See, Detective? She's fine. I'm fine. Everything's fine."

"Those two stiffs in the car aren't fine," Brennan said. "Let her go and you and me will have a little parlay."

"No." Trane left no room for negotiation. "Last I checked, Queens wasn't Midtown Manhattan. You're a little out of your patrol area, aren't you?"

Brennan grinned. "I got special dispensation. When the call came in on this address—*poof*—they called me. And what do we find? You, her, and more bodies. Shocking, isn't it?"

"It's still classified." Trane took out his cell phone and hit a speed dial number. "McLaren, I need some juice. I'm with Karras and Brennan just showed. Yeah, I warned him already…I'll be waiting."

Brennan stepped forward again, but two of Trane's operatives grabbed him, spun him around, and shoved him onto the hood of the Suburban.

"Take your hands off me, dudes." Brennan tried to push off the vehicle, but he was pinned. "You're assaulting a cop. Let me up."

Neither man budged.

Trane waved them off. "Let him go."

"Yeah, let me go." As the operatives released him, Brennan shoved both away and turned back to Ana. "Where you going with this guy? Remember, you're a material witness in my case. I need your help."

She said nothing.

"I want to see your grandmother and niece. Right now, Ana. Get them out here."

"Detective—Luke." Her voice was soft and pleading. "You can't help. I think you truly want to, but you can't. Let us go. It's for the best."

Brennan's eyes probed as his lips parted but he said nothing. Then, his cell phone rang in his pocket. He took the phone out, glanced at the screen, and shook his head in disgust. "Son of a bitch. Not again."

"Again," Trane snickered. "One-P-P."

Brennan said to Ana, "If you're not in custody, come with me. I know you like me better."

She smiled, though she tried not to. Perhaps in another place… another time.

"Come on, Ana," Brennan said, lifting the cell to his ear. "What's he got that I don't?"

"Her." Trane pulled her to the Suburban, waited while she climbed in, and a second later, drove away.

32

June 14, Early Morning–The Bear's Den, Sixty Miles Southwest of Nuevo Laredo, Nuevo Leon, Mexico

Cat woke abruptly and sat up. She hadn't slept well on the dirty, thin mattress she'd been assigned the night before. A couple missing hours intermingled with trepidation had been her night. Each noise tormented her.

Last night, Captain Cortez's caravan of trucks delivered the busload of immigrants to a compound hidden among the low hills set deep in the Nuevo Leon desert. As they dismounted the trucks, harassed and prodded by many guards, she paid careful attention to her surroundings, looking for weaknesses in security and avenues of escape.

There were fifteen or twenty buildings—some little more than shacks or overhangs—and numerous SUVs and pickup trucks. The few buildings that were lighted last night revealed a large desert compound split in the middle by a long, dirt road. On one side of the road were the shacks and shanties—one of which the guards were tossing the immigrant's belongings into from the bus. On the other side were cabins, garages, and work structures in good repair. Slave-labor to one side; paid cartel to the other. To the right of the entrance sat a two-story hacienda that was well groomed and looked like a diamond among the rough. It was a grand, adobe structure with a flat roof and a large front veranda. There were at least two armed sentries patrolling the front nearby and Cat knew that meant more in the rear. At the far end of the dirt road was a large, wood, two-story barn that was both illuminated and well-guarded.

There were at least a dozen armed sentries in view and perhaps that many more elsewhere out of her line of sight.

This was a cartel stronghold. Which one didn't matter. There were many in Mexico and they all had commonalities—drugs, the sex trade, extortion, corruption, and terror.

Cat had taken it all in when they arrived. The immigrants had been herded down the gravel road where they were separated into small groups and assigned sleeping quarters in the dilapidated shacks and lean-tos. She hadn't resisted—she needed rest and time to think—and was one of the first to find a corner in one of the shanties. She dropped onto the ancient, grungy mattress and went instantly to sleep.

After just a couple of hours, she became restless, and sleep evaded her.

Her first thoughts after waking were her failures. She'd successfully exfiltrated Cuba and fought her way across South America and north to Mexico. She'd evaded the devil in Cartago. Killed others in Tegucigalpa. Escaped still more in Nuevo Laredo. Some of them were Havana's operatives; others were simply evil men seeking a bounty. She'd survived all that only to fall victim to a coyote's deceit. Now, she sat on a lice infested mattress facing an uncertain future inside this cartel compound. She was surrounded by too many guns and too much desert. Too much security. Too few options.

How was she to complete her mission now? Was it over? Just miles from the American border and unable to reach it?

No, Cat—Reynaldo's voice was soothing—*you have made it this far. Months now. Don't stop. Mateo needs you to succeed.*

She closed her eyes and willed her nerves to calm.

The room smelled of sweat and filth; human waste and defeat. The air was stagnant but for the occasional hot breeze blowing through the unsealed board walls. There was so much to be afraid of here. So little hope to calm the fear. So much uncertainty.

"No, Reynaldo. I will go on. I must."

She moved to the plank door. Locked. She peered through a small window. The sun wasn't on the horizon yet and the darkness was only broken by the compound's sporadic lights. A guard sat, head down, asleep, just outside. Behind her, across the room, a faint light spilled through a window five feet above the floor facing out of the compound.

At the window, she jumped and grabbed the sill, easily pulling herself up to look out. Holding herself with one hand, she checked the window—closed and stuck tight. She struck the frame with her palm several times and dropped down to her feet to rest and check that the dozen others in the room were still fast asleep. Satisfied she was unobserved, she confronted the window again. After repeating her assault several times, the window surrendered and opened. After another brief rest, she pulled herself through the window and dropped outside, as agile as an acrobat.

She stayed close to the shack wall and moved to the corner, carefully surveying all around her, listening for voices or footsteps, watching the corners of her vision for telltale movement. Each step unnerved her. Each sound seized her. Each moment made her wonder if it was her last.

There were two sentries at the compound entrance. They leaned against the fence, talking. No lights were on in the shacks or guard quarters. Even the hacienda was dark but for two outside lanterns on the front corners. A guard leaned wearily beside its front door, dozing. At the barn at the end of the compound, a wisp of movement caught her eye; the stir of dust revealed two sentries as they moved around its entrance.

She crept to the lean-to where the guards had stored the belongings stolen from the other captives; her backpack among them. Inside, she was devastated. The dirt floor was littered with clothes and personal items, all savaged by the guards as they rutted about for anything of value. Her backpack was shredded in the corner of the room, its entire contents missing.

"*Oh Dios mío, no*," she whispered. "All gone."

Disheartened, she slid back into the pre-dawn darkness and moved from shanty to shack, deeper into the compound, looking for anything that might aid her escape. She hugged the shack walls, staying secreted in their shadows. She advanced carefully—lean-to after lean-to. She peered in high windows, through wall cracks, and beneath hastily hung blankets and canvas used as partitions.

"You can do this, Catalina," she whispered to herself. "You can. You must."

At the end of the line of shacks, there was a hundred feet of open ground to reach the barn. She reasoned any supplies usable in her escape might be inside: weapons, transport, equipment. Luckily, the two sentries at its entrance seemed more concerned with chatting than concentrating on their duties. They were smoking and leaning against a pile of boxes, looking away from her.

Cautious of her footing—knowing that the crunch of gravel or a dislodged rock might betray her—she picked her way to the barn's corner and crushed into the darkness. She continued around to the rear, stopping to check for other sentries. Finding none, she stopped to catch her breath.

There were two windows nearby. They were located three feet above the ground and four feet square. At the far corner, she could barely make out a large set of doors—perhaps a loading dock. Keeping to the shadows, she reached the closest window and peeked in. A wall of boxes a few feet inside the window blocked her view. They were stacked high, nearly to the roof, and lined up as far as she could see along the rear wall.

She was about to try the window when a Hummer rolled out of the desert in the distance. It traversed the far side of the barn, made a U-turn, and headed toward her. Its lights bounced along the ground coming closer and closer.

A perimeter patrol.

Quickly, before the lights caught her, she lifted the window, slid up over the sill and dropped inside. She quickly slid the window back into place and waited.

The patrol passed without notice.

She crouched behind pallets of boxes, unable to see anything but the narrow channel behind them running along the barn's rear wall.

A dull, rhythmic metal scrape whispered above her: ventilation fans.

She searched around and found a loose foot-long piece of pallet wood and broke it off. Then, she shortened it enough to hide it inside her waistband. The piece was broken to a point and sturdy enough for combat; a useful dagger. Years ago, her training had taught her survival skills. Among them was how to find weapons where none existed. A rock. A stick. Even a piece of broken pallet. Anything to increase your chance of survival.

It would have to do.

Working as quietly as she could, she used the dagger to cut into one of the cardboard boxes and peel a panel away. Inside were containers of ether. She moved along the rows of pallets and repeated the foray—one pallet after another. By the time she'd checked eight pallets, she found a hefty supply of hydrochloric acid, alcohol, and other chemicals. Another pallet was stacked high with burlap bags labeled *granos de café*—coffee beans. But when she ripped open a bag, quart-size plastic bags filled with rolls of brown gum fell out.

Opium. Raw, opium resin.

There was enough raw opium to make several fortunes in the heroin trade.

She and the other illegals had been taken for labor, drug mule-distribution, and human trafficking. Young boys and men for the barn work; women and girls for the streets. The compound was the center of a major Mexican industry—drugs, slavery, and prostitution.

She wiggled out between the pallets enough to see deeper into the barn. Near the center, beneath a large exhaust fan and low-hanging lights, were tables and cabinets stacked with plastic and glass bottles, chemicals, and rows of packaging materials. On the opposite side was a framed office with glass windows overseeing the work area. On the barn's far end near the loading dock were hundreds of shrink-wrapped bundles stacked and ready for shipment.

The barn was a heroin processing laboratory.

A plan was suddenly born. A plan that would keep her captors occupied and allow her to escape. It wasn't an easy plan. It was her only plan. She'd create a diversion and escape the compound while the guards were responding—as simple as an old American movie. All she needed was transportation and better weapons to defend herself.

Engine noise told her that the patrol was making another pass outside. If she were to escape, she had to draw the patrols in from the desert surrounding the compound. She had to get clear of the barn and find a vehicle to escape with, evade the guards, and run.

It would be light soon. She had to hurry.

She returned to the window she'd entered through. There, she stopped, listened, and dared to peek over the sill.

The Hummer was already heading out into the desert again.

She slipped over the sill and dropped onto the desert floor outside.

As she hit the ground and turned, her plan evaporated.

A short, stubby man stood at the corner of the barn, grinning. He aimed an M16 rifle at her. Another sentry joined him.

"You dumb bitch," the first spat. "You trouble. Oso no like no trouble whores."

33

Cat stood in the middle of the hacienda's great room feeling much like a Colosseum prisoner awaiting the lions. The room was two stories tall with a second-floor balcony overlooking it on three sides. The room was decorated with Incan artifacts, fine Mexican furniture, and tasteful paintings of local landscapes and village scenes. While the cartel kingpin might be a vile, dangerous man, he had good taste.

She'd been there for nearly an hour. Uncertainty and fear welled inside. She struggled with her waning courage that threatened to emit tears, but she fought them back. Weakness might destroy her. She could not allow that. Not now. Not any longer.

You can do this—Reynaldo whispered.

She lifted her chin feeling the solace of his presence. *Yes, I can do this.*

The man sitting on the couch sipped coffee and had appeared indifferent when the guards had dragged her before him. He'd barely taken notice of her over the past hour. He was a large man with powerful limbs and a robust, broad torso. Even sitting, he was foreboding. He wore tan slacks and a green cotton shirt. His hair was neatly trimmed. His face clean-shaven. While he sipped coffee, he flipped through screens on a tablet and occasionally frowned or smiled.

Finally, he looked up as though he'd just noticed her. "Who is this, Felipe?"

"Oso, we catch her in the barn," the guard, Felipe, said. "What shall we do?"

"Do?" Oso—the Bear—flipped through more screens before placing the tablet beside him. "Do for what?"

"She was in the barn and saw our processing."

Oso laughed. "You think what she saw is worse than what she has already experienced? Do you think if she had not seen our business that she would somehow forgive us for taking her?"

Felipe looked blankly at him.

"Leave her and go."

Felipe disappeared through the large double-doors and closed them behind him.

Cat stood rigid, watching Oso, waiting for his transition from indifferent to demon. It would come. It always did with men like him. She felt the danger. It settled about the room like a veil. Oso was a powerful drug lord. She hadn't known his name before now. It wasn't necessary. Such men were all the same, just with different names and placed in different settings. They shared the same methods. The same evils. The same moralities.

He studied her. "What is your name, chica?"

She said nothing.

"Come now, do not be rude. What is your name?"

Nothing.

"You are beautiful, *la chica sin nombre*." *The girl with no name.* "Why were you prowling around?"

She didn't hold back. "Trying to escape."

"Ah, you can speak, la chica sin nombre." He laughed heartedly. "Your name?"

"Does it matter?" Confronting him felt good. It invigorated her. It returned some strength and confidence. "I wish to go."

Oso set his coffee on a glass-top table beside the couch. He stood, straightened his shirt, and ran beefy fingers through his hair. He walked to her and leaned in close to smell her hair. He recoiled and grunted. Then, he meandered around her, ogling as so many had in the past weeks. Twice, he slithered his hands over her, probing and fondling. Finally, he stopped in front of her, facing her.

"You are lovely, la chica sin nombre. But you need a bath." He struck her violently across the face with his open palm and sent her sprawling to the tile floor. "And you need manners. This is the Bear's Den. I am the Bear. You will respect me. Your name?"

Cat's face stung. She gulped for air as her vision faded in and out—partially from the brutal strike, partially from panic. She ran her hand across her mouth and returned a smear of blood on her fingers. The warm, sticky ooze cleared her mind. It angered her. It focused her and pushed back the terror.

She stood and faced him again—oddly, a little stronger.

"You wish harsher persuasion, la chica sin nombre?"

"My name is unimportant." She raised her chin. "Your drugs and businesses are unimportant. I simply wish to leave and cross the border."

"I think no," Oso said flatly. "You will make me much money."

"I have business in America. If you help me across, you will be paid."

"Oh? This is so, la chica sin nombre? You must be very important, no? How much?"

"One-hundred thousand...*American*."

"Dollars?" His eyebrows lifted. "Not an insignificant reward, la chica sin nombre. But if I help you across the border, you will simply disappear and leave me unpaid."

"No." Cat casually put her hands into her waistband. "You can trust me. The danger, of course, is if you do not help. There are others who will come for me. They will do you harm. All that you have built here—all of it—might be destroyed."

"Destroyed? I see." Oso reached out and grabbed her by the throat. "You talk very tough for una niña sin nombre"—a girl with no name.

She struggled for balance, choking out, "Por favor...you'll regret—"

"No." He tightened his grip until she paled. "You are worth much to me. But your mouth may get you killed first."

Haze began replacing her thoughts. Her eyes fluttered. With her last strength, she pulled the wooden dagger from inside her waistband and plunged it into Oso's arm. When he screamed and released her, she fell to her knees, recoiled, and stabbed him again. The dagger sliced into his pants, heading for his scrotum.

Oso fell back onto the couch and grabbed his groin, screamed obscenities and bellowed for his guards.

"Pig." She scrambled to her feet and ran for the door.

It flew open.

She froze.

Felipe stood in her path. He held young Lucía by the arm with one hand, a pistol to her head with the other.

Oso screamed, "Look what you have done to me, la chica sin nombre. Look."

She stared at Lucía, her heart breaking as the girl's eyes pleaded with her for protection, salvation. A bruise was growing on her cheek.

Cat turned to Oso. "Let this young one go."

Oso stood holding his crotch and cursing. "You will pay for this, la chica sin nombre. You protected this chica from Captain Cortez, no? So now, you choose."

"Choose?"

"Si, choose." Oso limped forward and struck her across the face again, but this time, she didn't fall. "Will it be this little chica for me? Or will it be you?"

34

June 14, Morning–Linden Municipal Airport, Linden, New Jersey

Trane wheeled his SUV into the entrance of the small municipal airport just thirty minutes south of the Caverns. "My pilot will have the plane ready shortly."

"You have your own airplane?" Ana reviewed the rows of steel administrative buildings and hangars. It was all eerily familiar. "I think I've been here before, Trane. Haven't I? After Cabrera."

"Yes, you were," he said. "This is where we flew into from Colombia. My pilot can get us in and out of the country without a fuss. McLaren has a dedicated aircraft for our team, but I don't want to use it."

"Why?"

"I don't trust him." He was matter of fact. "My pilot is an old friend of mine. I keep him in business and in good bourbon. He's ready without notice, too. That helps. He does pretty good for a cowboy."

"A cowboy?"

"His name's Dallas."

She wondered aloud, "Should I remember him?"

"Maybe."

As Trane parked near the last bay at the end of a row of hangars, the hangar door slid open. A tall, lean man dressed in jeans and a dark cotton shirt appeared from the rear of a sleek Beechcraft jet sitting inside.

"That's Dallas," Trane said. "He's a good man. Trust him."

"Trust him?" Ana hesitated and glanced at Trane. "I am not sure I trust you."

"You can."

"How do I know?"

He turned to face her and a thin, friendly smile took over his face. His eyes found hers, and he gazed at her intently. "I saved you in Cabrera. I didn't have to. If I wanted to harm you, I could have. I could have left you to the NYPD, too. If I wanted to double-cross you, you'd be in Guantanamo in hours—no sweat. Trust goes both ways, Ana."

Yes, trust went both ways.

She slid out of the Suburban and contemplated the aircraft—a sleek, late model Beechcraft Premier jet. She'd flown a lot over the years, even as a child, in every conceivable aircraft. That included FARC's own twin-engine Cessna that barely made it off the ground most flights. She'd been aboard that airplane when it made its last landing—a crash into a mountainside. The pilot, Pedro Ruiz, had a heart attack en route to a mountain runway and she had been forced to make an emergency landing at the controls. Pedro's limited guidance and her sheer will saved them. She'd been lucky, limping away with a split lip and a wrenched knee.

Trane's Beechcraft was significantly better than FARC's Cessna. Dallas, on the other hand, was a younger, Texas version of Pedro Ruiz—scruffy, lanky, and underwhelming. How he came to pilot such an expensive jet was a mystery. But given Trane's line of work, that mystery was probably a long, twisted tale.

Trane's cell rang as he handed her the backpack from the rear of the vehicle. "I need to take this call. Check your things with Dallas."

As he walked away with the phone to his ear, she opened the bag and surveyed its contents.

A go-bag is the quintessential companion for those with an

eye toward survival in any situation—as it is for survivalists and preppers and all kind of doomsdayers. It's an emergency kit of whatever you think you'd need if you had to bug out fast. Hers contained cash, credit cards, a passport in a new fake name, energy bars, bottles of water, a compact Kimber .45-caliber semiautomatic pistol, extra ammo, and other personal and sundry items.

She slipped the backpack over her shoulder and walked to the front of the hangar, leaving Trane behind to his phone call. Each step was harder to take; laborious, as though she was exhausted from some long journey. Nerves were settling in. Things were moving fast. Almost too fast. Yesterday, she'd been arrested by the NYPD and then saved by the CIA. Then, the CIA manipulated her into confronting a Cuban Intelligence thug, and later was forced to kill one of his best operatives. Today, she was on her way to Mexico to rescue her parents and find an international assassin.

Even in the chaos that had once been her life in the FARC camps, it had never been this tumultuous. It's a good thing it was all moving fast or she might change her mind.

At the hangar entrance, she glanced back at Trane, wondering about him. Strangely, he kept her at ease, and she had been quick to trust him. Why? Had it been his kindness and compassion in Cabrera? The ease at which he stepped in and protected her from the police and McLaren? Truth was, she didn't know if those actions were his true character or manipulation tactics. Was he just using her to find Hemingway? Trane was a professional operative. An expert at manipulation. Was this all part of his play?

She didn't know anything about him and even less about McLaren. She was about to embark on a mission to hunt a dangerous Cuban assassin. And after? When they got Hemingway, would they honor their promise and give her family a new life? A safe life? Or would they spend their lives in a cell? Should she really trust *any* of this?

No. She could not. But she had been trained in manipulation, too. She would play by their rules. She would simply treat the situation as Ana Montilla would—use Trane as he was using her—a means to an end. Only that. No more. He had the resources to find Mamá and Pappa and bring them home. She had the ability to gain her parent's assistance to find Hemingway. She would use Trane's plan her way. If he betrayed her, she'd be ready.

After all, she knew something Trane didn't. Something very, very important.

"Miss Karras?" Dallas walked up. "Good to see you doing so well."

Ana studied his face, his frame, even replayed his words in her head searching for proof of familiarity. "You're Dallas."

"Yes, ma'am." He winked. "But Dallas ain't my real name, sorta."

"Karras isn't my real name, either—sorta." She took his extended hand. "Thank you for what you did for me before, Dallas. Call me Ana."

He nodded and grinned widely. "No worries, Miss Ana. I was just doing my job."

"Trane said we'll be ready to go shortly. He's on the phone. What can I do to help?"

"Nothing, Miss Ana. Just have a seat." He glanced back at Trane who was becoming animated on his call. "It doesn't look like a good conversation. Better get ready to go. It'll take us around six hours to get there, counting at least one stop for gas. Just give me a few to finish my pre-flight and then we'll roll her out."

"Okay, I guess."

As Dallas returned to the Beechcraft, Trane tapped off his call and walked to her. His face was strained, his eyes narrow and distant. Something was wrong.

"What is it?" she asked.

"A delay." His voice was chilly. "I have to go back to the Caverns. Something's up and McLaren wants us both back. Pronto."

The thought of being in that place again unsettled her. "I'm not going back there. I—"

"No, you're not. You're staying with Dallas. I should be back in a couple hours. Hang tight until then. There's food at the terminal where you can buy us coffee and sandwiches for the trip. Dallas has some petty cash."

"All right. But we can't delay too long. There's no telling what Vergara is doing with my mamá."

"I know."

Trane walked briskly away and spoke with Dallas. Their conversation was longer and more intense than hers, and that worried her more. A few moments later, Trane left the hangar, got into his SUV, and drove off. As he left, Dallas kept glancing at her like he expected her to run at any moment.

At that moment, she wondered if she should.

35

June 14, Morning–Linden Municipal Airport, Linden, New Jersey

Forty-five minutes after Trane left the airport, Ana was bored watching Dallas work on his airplane. She walked to the small terminal café and returned with a large bag of sandwiches and two quart-sized containers of coffee. She set the items down on the workbench and settled onto a steel folding chair to look around.

She felt suddenly, and completely, alone. It was a feeling reminiscent of the jungle camps.

In the camps, there were other women and girls, but true friends were rare. Trust was a dangerous and fleeting commodity in FARC. There, her parents wanted her focused on her duties and education. And there was the training. It had been long and hard, and it seemed a never-ending challenge. A constant test. In the little time she'd had to herself, making friends was difficult and ill-fated. Those that she'd made—anyone she'd actually confided in—left the camps for other FARC units. Later, she learned several had been killed or captured by the Colombian army. What became of them was heart-wrenching. She learned early on that friendships were a curse. After losing a handful of friends, the barriers she built to protect herself from their loss had never been torn down.

After returning to Queens, she'd never allowed herself to get close to anyone other than Poppi. Now, looking back, she was glad.

Sitting on the chair watching Dallas work made her feel as she had in the camps when preparing for a mission. Nervous. Anxious. Alone. She knew she must not trust Trane, but for the next few days, he might be all she had. She wished for a true ally—a partner, a confidant. Being Ana Montilla in the Colombian jungles was difficult, but at least there, on a mission—friends or not—she always had her comrades. She always had her parents.

Here, she had no one. She was alone. Strangely, that felt all right.

A vehicle passed the open door and pulled up along the side of the hangar. A moment later, Detective Lucius "Luke" Brennan strolled in with his jacket over his shoulder, whistling like he was out for a Sunday stroll.

Oh, no. How did he find me?

"Well, well, if it isn't Ana Karras. AKA Ana Montilla. AKA Agent Choo Choo's new partner." He walked up to her wearing a big, easy smile. "Where's your buddy, Ana?"

Her thoughts swirled trying to reason her next moves. The Beechcraft was ready for the long flight to Mexico. As soon as Trane returned, they had to leave. The clock was ticking and every second they were delayed put her mother and father in greater jeopardy. Every hour lessened the possibility they might find Hemingway. Now, Luke Brennan was intervening again which could further disrupt their plans.

Maybe not.

"Hey there, mister." Dallas climbed out of the Beechcraft with an M4 assault rifle leveled at him. "Just stop right there. Who are you?"

"Whoa, now." Brennan's eyes locked onto the rifle as he raised his hands. "Easy. I'm a cop. Well, I was a cop. I mean, I'm still a cop, but I'm not here as a cop."

"Huh?" Dallas walked over beside Ana. "This here's kinda Fed property and you're outta here."

"Kind of 'Fed property'?" Brennan said. "Is that a real thing?"

Dallas nodded. "Kinda like you're a cop but not a cop. Doesn't matter. You're not on the team, so you're leaving."

"You got a team now?" Brennan eyed Ana. "I just need to talk to you. Give me five minutes."

"Why are you here, Detective?" Ana asked. "Trane made it clear this morning to stay away from us."

"It's complicated." Brennan flashed a grin. "Let's just say I got suspended. Or maybe I was fired. Either way, Trane's boss called the chief, the chief called my captain, and…well, you get it."

"How did you find me?"

"Ah, that's part of why I got fired." He lowered his hands a little. "I planted a tracking device on Trane's Suburban when his boys were roughing me up at your place this morning. Anyway, my boss wasn't happy about getting chewed out by the brass. Some other stuff, too, but that isn't important. I'm—"

"Miss Ana?" Dallas prodded his rifle toward him. "What do you want me to do with him? Trane…"

"It's okay, Dallas," she said. "Detective Brennan is, well…he's okay. I'll speak with him."

"See, Dallas," Brennan said, "I'm okay."

Dallas nodded hesitantly and walked over to the Beechcraft where he stopped and watched Brennan and her from a distance.

"Ana, you gotta listen," Brennan said. "You're a material witness in a murder, and Trane's the murderer. So, unless you know something I don't, you need to come with me."

Yes, I do know something you don't. "If Trane killed those men at the brownstone, they deserved it. They were Cuban operatives here to kill me."

"Cuban spooks? Why are they after you?"

She said nothing.

"Did you join the CIA or what?" His face twisted and his eyes probed her, confused. "But hey, if it's like you say, I'm good with that."

"You should go, Detective. You can't stay here."

Dallas' cell phone rang and drew Ana's eyes away for a second. He took the call for several moments before waving her over to him. "Miss Ana, it's Trane. You better talk to him."

She walked to Dallas and took the phone. "Trane? Where are you? Brennan—"

"Listen to me, Ana. Carefully." His voice was hushed and tense. "I briefed Dallas already. Get on that plane and go. I won't make it back there today. I'll meet up with you in Monterrey later."

What? No. "What's going on? What happened?"

"I can't go into it. Just get going." Silence; then, "My people will meet you in Monterrey. Do as they say. They'll locate your mother and get her safe. Then, you take it from there. Hopefully, I'll be down with you by tomorrow. Either way, stick with the plan. Find your mom and dad and get them to help. Find Hemingway. Dallas will get everyone back here when the time comes."

"That sounds like you're not coming. Aren't you—"

"I can buy you forty-eight hours. After that, well, I'm not sure what happens. I've told Dallas to give you whatever you need. He's a good man. Trust him."

"What about your men in Monterrey?"

"They'll be there. Go now. And Ana…I'm trusting you. You have to trust me. Don't screw me."

The call ended abruptly.

She stared at the phone, half-expecting him to call back. Her heart pounded and her scars tingled, forcing her to rub them. A strange darkness fell over her.

What was happening? What could be so wrong that Trane wasn't returning? On one hand, it made her plan easier. She had a secret that she hadn't planned on sharing with him until they got airborne—a precaution in case Trane's people were not trustworthy. She didn't have to worry about that now. She only had to deal with Dallas. On the other hand, she would have to go up against Vergara's men in Mexico alone.

"Hey, Ana, you okay?" Brennan called, breaking the panic welling inside her. "What's wrong?"

She returned to him. "Leave, Luke. Now."

"No, I'm staying until I know what's going on." He leaned forward and held her eyes. "So, start talking, lady."

Dallas threw a thumb toward the airplane. "We have to go now, Miss Ana. Trane said vamoose immediately."

"Okay. Give me a moment."

Dallas turned, went to the Beechcraft, and disappeared up the stairs.

Brennan walked to the table and grabbed her backpack, opened the main compartment and looked inside, lifting out her .45-caliber pistol. "Whoa, now. What's all this?"

"You're not a policeman any longer, are you? So forget it."

"Nope. I'm just Joe Citizen." Brennan gazed at her with an intensity that pulled her in. "Ana, you're in trouble. Your grandmother and Sarah are gone from your house. Now, you're packing for a fight and jumping on a private jet headed for who knows where. You got me fired for doing my job. So I'm sticking with you until I knew why all of this is happening."

"This is my trouble. Not yours." She felt the heat in her cheeks. "I have to leave. It's important, Detective. Please."

"We're ready, Miss Ana," Dallas called from the bottom of the Beechcraft stairs. "Now or never."

Brennan stepped closer and touched her arm. "You don't know these people, Ana. You cannot possibly trust them."

"No, and I don't know or trust you, either." Strangely, she felt terrible saying that. "I have to help Trane. It's very important."

"Okay, but I'm like a puppy dog that won't let go of this bone." He grinned. "You might as well let me come along and help. You'll love me, I promise."

"No." She stood looking at him, feeling more alone than she ever had, wondering why she didn't just climb aboard the Beechcraft and leave. "I can't, Luke. I want to. But I just can't."

"Your pilot's right; it's now or never. If you get on that plane alone, whatever danger lies ahead you'll face alone." He squeezed her arm reassuringly. "Let me help you. We'll figure out what's next together. I promise. You can trust me."

Ana lowered her eyes. *What would Ana Montilla do?*

"Ana?"

Fine. "All right, Luke. But you won't like it."

"Try me."

Here goes. "Cuban Intelligence is holding my mamá hostage in Mexico. I have to rescue her. Then, I have to find my father and hunt down someone named Hemingway. If I don't…."

"Hemingway? Mexico?" Brennan's face twisted. "Cuban

Intelligence?"

"Yes."

"Really? That's the best you got?"

"Oh no, there's more." She backed toward the Beechcraft. "Hemingway is a Cuban assassin coming to America to start a war. I'm helping Trane stop him. Something has gone wrong and now Trane isn't coming; not today, anyway. But my mamá is still in trouble and I'm going to rescue her—*alone*."

"You're stopping a war all alone? This was all Trane's plan, right?" Brennan's eyes narrowed on hers. "This sounds like total bullshit."

Yes, I suppose it does. "The man from the brownstone—Colonel Vergara—came to New York to force me to help him find my parents and Hemingway. Those dead men at the house were Cuban operatives. They nearly killed me in Colombia two months ago."

"Right, when Trane saved you in Cabrera?"

She nodded.

"I mean, you're a bad ass ninja girl, but come on, why would the CIA, or the Cubans, need you? Seems like they have plenty of their own bad ass assassins. Or am I wrong?"

"Yes, they do." *Was he ready for this?* "But you see, Luke, I was raised in the Colombian jungles and trained as a FARC operative. I'm a guerrilla fighter; I was once one of their best. My father and mother were FARC, too. Somehow, they are involved with Hemingway. They're our only hope of finding and stopping him in time."

His eyes went big and his eyebrows nearly shot off his head. "Are you shitting me?"

"No." She extended a hand for her backpack that he still held tightly in his grip. "Now, kill me or leave. Choose."

"Choose?"

She nodded.

For a long moment, Brennan looked between her and the Beechcraft as Dallas revved the engine and checked his flaps and tail rudder.

"You're a FARC guerrilla? From Queens?"

She nodded again.

"Just great." He hefted her backpack over his shoulder. "You might have to hold my hand. I hate flying."

36

June 14, Morning–The Caverns, Bayonne, New Jersey

"I don't understand this." Trane stared at the computer monitor on McLaren's office desk. "How could this possibly happen?"

The image on the screen was a familiar one—Vergara's cell, five floors below in the holding level. This time, however, instead of the Cuban intelligence chief brooding atop his cot, he lay face down on his cell floor. A medical tech was prepping the body for removal under the watchful eye of an armed operative.

"He's dead, Trane," McLaren said with an edge in his voice. "You tell me what the hell happened. Someone stuck a needle of something into his damn neck and executed him."

"I went to Queens as we planned." He returned McLaren's stare in a contest McLaren wasn't up for. "What are you suggesting?"

"I'm not suggesting anything. I'm saying it's odd that you disappeared right about the same time our star detainee got hit."

Trane wasn't going to let McLaren lay this at his feet. Vergara was in a cell, under guard, and still someone got to him. Since that should have been impossible, they had a very serious problem at the Caverns.

"Or, McLaren, you could say, 'Isn't it good for me that I wasn't here when someone killed him.'"

213

"I tried to track your vehicle. It's off our GPS system. Why?"

Trane frowned. "I pulled the plug on your tracker three months ago, McLaren. I don't like being spied on."

"You're in the spy business."

"I'm in the spying business. Not the 'being spied on' business. There's a difference."

McLaren's face tightened. "That's the stupidest thing I've ever heard."

"Not as stupid as you accusing me of killing Vergara. Especially since you were going to order me to do it sooner or later, anyway." He casually watched McLaren as though they were discussing the weather and not a major breach of their security. "Where were you when all this happened?"

"Asleep in my quarters."

"What about the CCTV cameras and the security team on level five?"

McLaren fidgeted a little. "The camera system went off-line at oh-four-thirty."

"Convenient."

"Isn't it?" McLaren's face reddened. "Level five has one agent at those hours. Shit, all the cells are locked down. He checked Vergara hourly. Last at zero four hundred hours. He found him dead at zero five hundred."

Trane thought about that. "Where was the agent during that hour?"

"He was supposed to be there." McLaren frowned. "When the CCTV system went down, he went to check the system. He was gone less than fifteen minutes."

Fifteen minutes. Ample time to give Vergara his flu shot. "We have a problem inside our team."

"No shit." McLaren tapped the desk. "Can you prove where you were during those hours?"

"Can you?"

McLaren jumped up. "You watch your ass, Trane. I'm in charge here. I want answers."

Trane slowly stood and leaned over the desk, nearly nose-to-nose with him. "And you watch *your* ass, McLaren. You wouldn't want to start answering questions about twenty-five million bucks, would you?"

"Blackmail implies guilt."

Trane laughed. "And bullshit stands on its own."

"Screw you." McLaren slouched back into his chair. "This is a shitshow. Nobody leaves this compound until I know what happened to Vergara. Jesus, DC's gonna eat me alive."

"You mean the vice president is gonna eat you alive."

"What's that mean?"

"It means, for somebody who's all about spying on me and demanding to know what I had for breakfast every day, you sure tried to keep his holding your leash secret."

McLaren's face twisted. "It's his Chief of Staff—Danny Bianco. Not the Veep."

"Potayto, potahto."

"It's need to know."

"Vergara knew but I didn't?" Trane laughed. "The next time you send me off to kidnap someone like Vergara, I want to know who's pulling your strings."

"And if I don't tell you?"

"Then get dirty on your own." Trane sat back down. "Why don't you write me up for insubordination? Of course, I'll have to defend myself and explain to Langley that I'm insubordinate about you running a rogue operation without their approval."

McLaren's lips clamped. His eyes sent missiles at him as his fingers clasped together so tightly they turned white.

"I didn't kill Vergara, McLaren. Assuming you didn't—"

"I didn't."

Trane grinned. "Assuming you didn't, we've got a bigger problem."

"I know. Our best chance to grab Hemingway is dead, and someone here is working for the Cubans."

"That's half-right. Our best chance at stopping Hemingway is Ana Karras, and she just took off for Monterrey."

"What? I ordered you to bring her here. We'll never see her again now."

Trane shook his head. "No, she'll do fine. She'll be in Monterrey

215

in a few hours. I've got Robertson's team waiting on her there."

"Get her back here. Now."

"No. She's the only one who might get through to her parents and find Hemingway. The only one. She wants the deal we made. I think she'll stick to it."

McLaren sat back, staring at the ceiling, thinking. Then, he snorted like a bull about to charge. "You know, maybe this is better for both of us, Trane. Let her go on her own down there. Robertson is a good man—a damn good man. Let her find mommy and daddy and lead us to Hemingway. Then, Robertson will end this."

"Define 'end this.'" Trane folded his arms. "I hate word play. It smacks of deniability."

"He'll kill the bitch. He'll kill every damn one of them."

37

June 14, Afternoon–In-flight Over the Southern US

The Beechcraft was a sleek, fast jet that made the seventeen-hundred-mile trek to Mexico comfortable. With a planned stop in Louisiana for fuel, Dallas kept on track to complete the flight in about six hours.

It had taken quite a bit of persuasion to convince Dallas to allow Brennan on the flight. Ultimately, Ana convinced him that Trane insisted Dallas do as she asked, which included bringing Brennan to Mexico. Dallas had tried to reach Trane before takeoff, but when he couldn't, he relented, albeit reluctantly. She had no illusions that Dallas would not continue to try and ultimately reach Trane, but for the time being, they were airborne and headed southwest.

Early in the flight, Ana was surprised Dallas hadn't received orders to abort their mission and return Brennan to New Jersey, or dump him off at thirty-thousand feet. Whatever had happened at the Caverns obviously had Trane's full attention.

Ana and Brennan spent much of the trip in a back and forth. He demanded to know the details of how she became involved in a secret government mission; she gave him the high points only. She demanded to know everything about his investigation at the brownstone, why he'd tracked her to the hangar, and why, surprisingly, he'd volunteered to join her in Mexico.

"What do I have to lose?" Brennan stretched out on the luxury leather cabin chair. "You cost me my job already, Ana. If I stayed behind, Trane might put me in jail or worse. And it's the 'or worse' part that worries me."

"This is not some trick to arrest me or entrap me?"

He grinned. "I have no jurisdiction in Mexico."

"You had no jurisdiction at the airport, either."

"Touché."

She aimed a finger at him. "Then you do as I say."

"Yes, ma'am."

Ultimately, Brennan turned the conversation to less onerous topics—mostly about himself. As it turned out, Brennan was his own favorite topic to talk about. He was humorous and entertaining about his life's adventures in the NYPD and made the time go by quickly. The only time he seemed to stop talking was to refill his cup of coffee or open another package of in-flight snacks.

Mid-flight, Dallas allowed Brennan to sit in the co-pilot seat. Brennan chatted him up good-naturedly as he regaled him with more cop stories. It seemed to work, and Dallas allowed him a few minutes at the controls—under careful guidance. Brennan was a child in a toy store.

Ana, on the other hand, was concerned about Dallas and kept an eye on him. She considered that he was befriending Brennan for other reasons—nefarious ones. Brennan was a friendly, lovable sort of guy, but he was still a cop…or ex-cop. He was also not part of the equation Trane had set in motion. Trane and Dallas were long-time friends, and Trane relied on him heavily. That meant there was more to Dallas than his 'aw shucks' cowboy persona. He was probably a lethal, well-trained operative. What that might mean for the mission, should Trane change his mind, was unclear.

It was a long way to the ground from their cruising altitude.

After they'd refueled and settled back into the flight, Brennan poured more coffee for her and himself and returned to his seat across the aisle from her. "Okay, Ana. How about you give me the whole story. You know, the one with all the parts you left out the first go-round."

"You volunteered." She considered him over the porcelain coffee cup. "You know what I know."

"Well, not really. It's all that 'Mexico, mom and dad, Jules Verne—"

"Hemingway."

"Just seeing if you're listening." He winked. "It all sounds a little Alistair MacLean to me."

"All right, Detective…"

"Detective? Really?" He laughed. "You're taking me on a secret mission to Mexico to find your kidnapped mom and a Cuban assassin out to start World War Three. I think you can call me Luke."

"Well then, Luke, apparently you already understand everything." She took a long, drawn-out sip of coffee. "But I'll explain. I wouldn't want you to die in Mexico and not know why."

"Die?"

In the next thirty minutes, she told him everything, beginning with her past in the Colombian jungle. Life with Mamá and Pappa. Life as a FARC guerrilla. And later, life in Queens. During her vignette about Cabrera, that story was more difficult to tell. The fresh memories disturbed her and started her scars tingling, each time causing her to caress them into submission. Afterward, she stared out the aircraft window—refusing to look at him—and explained everything that had happened since then. Out of caution, she decided to "forget" the chapter where she killed Tomãs the evening before and left him in her neighbor's garage. After all, that *was* in his jurisdiction.

Luke, for his part, sat and listened intently. He traded his coffee for single-malt whiskey he'd found on his first foray for snacks. He was a good listener. Attentive. Sympathetic. Kind.

"So, you're Ana Montilla *and* Ana Karras? It's just a name thing, though. Right?"

She turned back from the window. "No, Luke. Ana Montilla is the other me—the dark, dangerous me. I loathe her. When I left Colombia and left my parents, I left her behind, too."

"Well, she was at the brownstone. I saw you do all your ninja stuff. It seems like she's handy to have around sometimes. Something tells me we'll need her in Mexico."

"Yes, we will. I only hope she does not stay once it's over."

"Well, that's up to you, isn't it?" Brennan looked understanding. "I mean, you can turn the switch on and off?"

"She has a mind of her own. It's complicated."

"Complicated? I think you make it complicated." He laughed. "We're headed into Mexico to carry out a secret CIA mission to un-kidnap your mom, find your dad, and hunt down an international assassin—all on Mexican soil. Now that's complicated."

She turned and gazed at him. She couldn't help but like him. She hated to admit it, but she'd been drawn to him since the first day in his office. He was a direct man, funny and pleasant even for a policeman. He put her instantly at ease—not unlike Trane—and she felt a comfort in confiding in him. Other than Yiayia Poppi, he was the only other person she'd willingly told of her tumultuous past.

Feeling that comfortable with him was dangerous and she knew it. To confide or care for anyone could be a disaster. She had cared deeply for Tommy Robert Sawyer—her first, and last love—to whom she'd lost more than focus.

...In Colombia, Ana had waited impatiently all year for Tommy's return to the village. When he did return, she made the trek each week as she had before. Except each week, it had not been for her mission, but for romance. To her mamá's ire, she often stayed the night before returning to the camps the next morning. Each time she'd conjured a new excuse for her absence, but she'd fooled no one. When Tommy was in Colombia, they corresponded through letters posted through the village school. It was a slow, painful love affair. But the mere thought of his return had her counting the days each year...

She'd only known Brennan for a few hours and already she wondered what that time was leading to. Across the cabin sat this policeman—ex-policeman—who just yesterday believed her to be a killer. Then, only a short time ago, he joined her on a dangerous mission with little understanding of what he'd gotten into other than her promise of danger. Why had he done that? Did he have an ulterior motive? Was there deception looming? Something else?

There were now two men she was forced to rely on: Trane and Detective Lucius Brennan. She shouldn't trust either man, yet, she had to.

"I need to trust you, Luke. I need to know you'll not turn on me. How can I?"

He leaned back in his cabin chair and set his eyes on her, unmoving for the longest time. His answer surprised her. "I really don't know, Ana Karras or Ana Montilla or whoever you are. All I know is this: I became a cop to help and protect people. Since I met you, I knew you needed both. I know you're a bad ass ninja jungle fighter, but you can't do this alone. The fact I'm sitting on this plane tells me you know that too."

She couldn't help but smile. "You're a kind man, Luke Brennan, AKA Luke the Wookiee from *Star Wars*. I hope you're telling me the truth."

"I am. I'd hate for you to have to kill me." When she didn't respond, he added, "Oh, come on, you wouldn't kill me. Right?"

Some questions are better left unanswered.

***

"It's another forty-five minutes to Monterrey, Miss Ana," Dallas said, as she came into the cockpit and sat in the co-pilot seat with another coffee. "We're starting our descent. Trane's people have a hangar for us. Everything's arranged."

"Put us down in Nuevo Laredo, Dallas," she said, matter-of-factly. "And no communications with your people in Monterrey or Trane until later."

"Huh?" Dallas eyed her quizzically. "Miss Ana, my orders—"

"Just changed."

"You can't do that."

Ana slid her Kimber .45 from behind her back, setting it onto her knee. "Yes, I can."

"Unless you can fly this jet, Miss Ana, that would be a bad idea."

"I can."

"Really?" His face crumpled a little. "You're rated for a jet?"

"I can fly a Cessna twin-prop. I'm sure I can get us down. With or without you."

"Without me?" Dallas's grin turned upside down. "Trane ain't gonna like this."

She changed tactics. "Dallas, Trane trusts you. He told you to give me whatever help I asked for."

He nodded.

"Back at the Caverns, you know what happened?"

"Yes, ma'am. Some Cuban big shot was murdered. McLaren thinks Trane did it."

"Do you?"

"No, ma'am." He shook his head vehemently. "Not Trane. Oh, he can get the job done, sure. But he's no traitor."

"Then someone on his team is." She was counting on Dallas seeing her logic. "I don't trust anyone. Those men in Monterrey could be okay, or they might not. Land in Nuevo Laredo. Brennan and I will drive to Monterrey. We'll call you when we need you, and we'll hold up until you can get there."

Dallas stared straight ahead, unblinking. "You think whoever killed that Vergara fella might have his compadres waiting at the terminal in Monterrey?"

"Yes, I do. Have you heard from Trane since we took off?"

He shook his head.

"Then he's in trouble. This mission is too important. You have to trust me. For all we know, if we land in Monterrey, the Cuban's might be waiting for us instead."

Dallas sat thinking for a long moment before he flipped a switch on his communications panel, called Nuevo Laredo air traffic control, and went through a series of communications with them.

"Miss Ana?" He gestured at her gun. "You don't need that. All you had to do was explain things. I'm not interested in dying in Mexico."

"Me either, Dallas. Will we have trouble with customs or the Federales when we get down?"

"No, ma'am. I gotta guy." Ease washed across his face. "He'll take good care of us. I'll have a car waitin' for you, too."

"Good." She tapped her knee with the Kimber. "I think we understand each other. But if you get silly and think you should call Trane or anyone else about our flight change, just know I can fly back home just fine by myself."

Dallas never took his eyes off his instruments.

38

*June 14, Afternoon–Quetzalcóatl International Airport–
Nuevo Laredo, Mexico*

"Understand, Dallas?" Ana put her go-bag on the front seat of the airport rental. "You can't warn Trane's men in Monterrey. If there's a traitor on his team—"

"I know. I know." Dallas flashed up a hand. "If there's a traitor working with the Cubans, you could be walking into a trap. I got it."

"Give the man a kewpie doll." Brennan slid into the rental's driver's seat. "Just stay close to your cell phone. Be ready to get us fast, Dallas. Okay?"

Dallas nodded. "I did you right so far. Didn't I?"

When the Beechcraft had taxied into the general aviation apron to meet Mexican Customs and Immigration, the usual uniformed Mexican Federales didn't greet them. Instead, a man in an expensive linen suit strolled up to the plane and waited for Dallas to cut the engines and climb out onto the tarmac. They embraced warmly and shook hands, laughing and cajoling one another. As the man leaned in to speak in a confidential manner, Dallas slid a manila envelope from his pocket into the other's suit coat. They chatted momentarily, embraced, and the suited man walked off. Fifteen minutes later, a rental car appeared, full of gas, with no paperwork required.

"Yes, so far." Ana smiled. "Thank you."

Dallas walked around the rental car and leaned in to her open passenger window. "There's a canvas bag in the back seat with some necessities inside."

"Necessities?" Brennan asked from the driver's seat.

Dallas winked. "Yup. A couple handguns, two MP-5's, ammo… those sorts of necessities."

"Good to know. Thanks."

Dallas took something from his pocket and handed it to Ana. It was a thin, metal neck chain. On the end dangled a Saint Christopher medal a quarter inch thick.

Dallas said, "Trane said to give this to you. Only as a last resort, Miss Ana."

"Last resort?" She examined the medal and popped it open, revealing two aspirin-sized pills inside. "What are these?"

"Suicide pills. *Cuban* suicide pills." He let the idea sink in. "If, you know, you can't bring Hemingway to us, make sure Hemingway's mission can't succeed. You get it? These are a quick and painless heart attack; untraceable. Since they're Cuban, too, if anybody gets suspicious, they'll take the blame."

She stared at the pills. She'd taken life before and for less reasons than stopping an assassin. But these pills changed her mission considerably. Finding and capturing Hemingway was difficult enough—even with Trane. She hadn't considered what her options were if returning Hemingway to the States was impossible. Trane had already contemplated that solution.

"Do I have a choice?" she asked.

Dallas shook his head. "Not really. If you run or double-cross us, well…you got family in the States. Think about that."

There it was: the threat.

Dallas eyed her. "I'm not saying it'll come to that, Miss Ana. Just don't go off the reservation. You get that? Find Hemingway and either deliver him or end him. If you end him, bring proof. That's the only way to get your deal."

Ana looked down at the two little pills as Dallas spelled it out. Of course it was a kill or capture mission. There was no way

Hemingway could be allowed to go free and enter the country unchecked. There were many possibilities how it might end, and a heart attack was better than the alternatives. Clasping the chain around her neck, she rolled up the car window.

"Do you trust him?" Brennan glanced in the rearview mirror as they drove off.

"No."

"Me neither. Do you think he'll call Trane?"

"Yes."

"Then we're screwed. Aren't we?"

"No, not yet."

Brennan rolled off the tarmac apron, waved at Dallas's linen-suited man waiting at the security gate to let them out, and sped onto the main road to Nuevo Laredo. Once out of the airport, he rechecked his rearview again and noticeably relaxed.

"Ana, it's almost three hours to Monterrey by car—a hot, long three hours. Do you know where we're going?"

She turned in the seat to face him. "We're not going to Monterrey."

"Huh? You told me that Vergara's men had your mom in Monterrey."

"That's what Vergara told McLaren." She dug into her go-bag and withdrew a plastic case, opened it, and lifted out a cell phone. "Before I left Vergara at the Caverns, he told me more that Trane and McLaren didn't hear."

"What?"

"His people do have my mother, but not in Monterrey. She's here, in Nuevo Laredo." She fiddled with a map program on her cell phone. "He told me the location."

Brennan looked nervous. "Do you trust him?"

"I don't trust anyone. Especially the CIA."

"Then what are we doing?"

She thought a long time. "We need to look the place over first. Then, we'll make a plan and rescue her."

"Alone?" A nervous grin cracked his face. "I'm not sure what scares me more: That you're lying to the people giving us backup in Monterrey, or that you still haven't said you won't kill me."

Both possibilities scared her.

A half-block ahead, two large, dark SUVs pulled out of side streets and stopped diagonally across their path, blocking their route. Four armed men jumped out.

"Luke, get us out of here." Ana tugged her pistol from her go-bag. "Quickly."

As Brennan slowed to find an escape, another SUV appeared behind them and slammed into their rear bumper, jolting them forward. A man hung from the passenger window, aiming a submachine gun at them.

"Is this because I was speeding?" Brennan quipped nervously. "I was, wasn't I?"

39

When Ana's hood was removed, the stark infusion of light disoriented her. A musty heaviness hung like thick fog in the hot, humid air. As her vision settled, the room came into focus. It was large and windowless. The walls were dull gray; the concrete floor was dusty and barren. There were rows of fluorescent lights hanging overhead, two-stories above where the roof was lined with pipes and ductwork. A wide, metal roll-up door faced them across the room.

There was nothing around her but two empty metal chairs—one facing her, and one beside her. The room was dim and eerily lit with a morbid, stale odor in the air. The overhead lights were dull and cast the room like an ancient mausoleum.

She glanced around. Four gunmen—the same Latinos who had pulled her and Brennan from their rental car earlier—moved in from behind and surrounded her. They were all casually dressed in open-collared business attire like it was casual Friday: khakis, colored pullovers, and dress shoes. None of the men wore jackets, revealing semiautomatic pistols strapped to their belts.

She'd been tied to a metal chair by her arms. One gunman

moved closer and tested her bindings before he stepped away.

Brennan was dragged into the room grappling with two other gunmen. He'd gotten his hood off and one arm free to fight. A third Latino joined the struggle and sent two powerful punches into Brennan's face to still him. Then, they slammed him into the metal chair beside her and tied his arms tightly.

"Ana?" Brennan grunted. "You okay?"

One of the gunmen backhanded him in the face and split his lip in two places. "Shut up."

"Stop, Luke," she said. "Don't antagonize them."

"Good plan. You okay?"

"Yes, for now."

The man who'd tied Ana to the chair stood across the barren room near the roll-up door. He spoke in a heavy, Cuban accent: "We wait a long time for you, Ana. Cooperate and maybe you live to tell stories of your stay with us, no?"

She lifted her chin. "You've been waiting for us?"

"Si, but you will know soon." The man laughed. "Be still. We will return with a very big surprise."

"Great," Brennan said dryly. "More surprises."

The man nearest him punched him in the side of his head and knocked him to the floor with the chair still attached at his arms. "Do not talk."

Brennan grunted as two men righted him. "Okay, okay. I'll behave."

The gunmen spoke quietly among themselves as they left through the roll-up door. A moment later, they returned, dragging another hooded figure between them. They repeated their process— tied the figure into the empty chair facing them and yanked away the hood.

Ana's eyes flashed wide. "Mamá?"

Irena Montilla's head bobbed against her chest as she slumped against her bindings. Her ragged, cotton shirt was torn partially away. Her shorts were soiled and ripped open in the front. Her once flowing, black hair was cut short above her shoulders—tangled and unkempt. Her eyes were vacant and staring at nothing on the floor in front of her. Swelling disfigured her left eye and jaw. A trickle of blood ran from her lips, down her chin, and onto her exposed bosom and tanned, dirty flesh.

"Ana? This is your mom?" Brennan watched the two men. "Hey, get her some help. A doctor. Some water."

One of the men—a dark Latino with big, bulging arms and a muscled chest—laughed. "Shut up, American. You're next."

The two men exchanged whispers. One made a gun-finger at Brennan and they left through the roll-up door again, closing it afterward.

"Mamá, are you all right?" Ana strained against her bindings. "Can you talk?"

Irena rolled her head twice and lifted it, looked around the room, and found Ana.

"Ana...my daughter? Oh, no. They found you, too?"

"Yes, Mamá. It's me. Are you all right?"

Irena licked her lips. "They hurt me, Ana. But I am still here."

"How long have you been here?" Brennan asked.

Irena glanced around, blinked several times and winced, trying to free her arms. She looked at him. "Who are you?"

"He's a friend." Ana tried to remain calm but the anger churned inside. These men would pay for this—somehow. "How did they capture you, Mamá? Have they found Pappa?"

"I don't think so." Irena looked to the floor and wept. "What has your pappa done, Ana? What they did to me...I don't know what to tell them. I haven't seen Pappa since he left the camps last year. I don't know what's going on."

"I've been looking for you both." She scooted the chair toward her several feet before resting. "Where have you been? No one had seen you in the camps. I looked everywhere."

Irena slowly shook her head. "Pappa left Colombia very quickly. I don't know where he went. He didn't tell me. I searched Colombia for many months. Then, I worked my way here. I heard he was in Monterrey. I went there three months ago. I didn't find him. A month later, these men found me."

"You've been captive for two months?" Brennan asked. "At least you're still alive."

"For now." Irena's face saddened as tears rolled down her cheeks.

"They're using me as bait. They've offered much money for Pappa. They've spread the word that they have me and will trade for him."

Ana scooted the chair a little closer across the concrete floor. "Can you hold out a little longer?"

"I don't know." Irena lifted her eyes to Ana. "How did they find you?"

"It's a long story, ma'am," Brennan said. "We came to rescue you."

"Rescue me?" Irena squinted at him. "There are others? Federales?"

"No, Mamá. We were sent here by someone else."

"Who?"

Ana glanced at Brennan who shrugged. She lowered her voice. "The CIA. A man who saved me in Cabrera sent me to find you. But now, it's just us."

"I don't understand. The CIA? There's no one coming to help?"

"No. I'm sorry." Ana watched the pain in her mother's face deepen. "They may have betrayed us, too."

"I'd like to get my hands on Dallas," Brennan said. "That bastard. I bet Trane is behind this, too."

Ana shook her head. "I just can't believe that. Not yet."

"Dallas? Trane?" Irena asked. "Who are those men? Why were you in Cabrera, Ana? How are you involved with the CIA?"

Ana gave her a brief summary of her past few months—her search for Irena and her father, her near death and her rescue in Cabrera. Then, she skipped the details concerning Colonel Vergara, and picked up again with her deal with Trane.

"The CIA wants someone named Hemingway, Mamá. Not you or Pappa. They said he was going to start a war between the US and Cuba. If we help them stop this, they will give us all a new life—all of us. You and Pappa can safely come home."

"A new life? Home?" Irena's eyes dropped to the floor again as she sobbed. "Even with everything we've…we've done?"

"Yes, Mamá. Hemingway is that important. We can go home when this is over. All of us."

Brennan said, "We have to get you out of here first. Then we'll find your husband."

"Yes, we must find Pappa." Irena looked toward the roll-up door.

"I don't know where he is. Do you?"

"No. I lost his trail before Cabrera. I have no idea where to look. But between us, maybe we can find him."

Irena shook her head. "We'll never get free of these men. Only if we tell them about your pappa. Everything. I never knew anyone named Hemingway. Did you?"

"No," Ana said. "What are we going to do?"

"Stall for time until I figure something out." Brennan looked around but his face showed the grim reality of hopelessness. "There's gotta be a way, right?"

Irena thought a moment. "Is there anyone in Mexico who your father knew well? An old contact? You know what I mean, Ana. Anyone he would go to? Anything might save us."

Ana thought hard. In the years she had worked with FARC, she didn't recall ever discussing contacts in Mexico. She'd joined the Colombian guerrillas on missions, but she was never privy to their intelligence methods. The truth was, neither of her parents ever discussed those matters with her. It was one of the important rules in the camps: compartmentalization so if one of the members was captured, they could not harm many others. Even among family.

"No, Mamá. Never. I thought Pappa was just the camp doctor. I thought it was only you and me who did...."

"Nonsense, Ana," Irena blurted. "Manuel was as much FARC as we were. Well, maybe not you. You were a disappointment to me. But now, Ana, now you can make up for that. Tell me about your pappa's contacts."

The harshness in her mother's voice startled her. The last time they'd been face-to-face had ended in a bitter argument. Ana was returning to Queens for college. Mamá refused her permission to leave. She insisted Ana stay and continue her guerrilla training. Pappa had intervened. In the end, Mamá banished her—wished her away to never return. When she did return after college, she'd hoped to mend their relationship and convince them both to return to the US. But Irena had refused to even speak with her. Ana had left, alone. That had been years ago and those wounds were still deep and raw.

Irena broke the awkward silence. "Ana, I'm sorry. Arguing over the past helps no one. How can we find your pappa or Hemingway?"

Ana sat, thinking. "I know nothing that will help."

Brennan said, "Ma'am, did you see any way out of here?"

Irena shook her head. "You're sure there is no rescue coming?"

Ana said, defeated, "We're on our own."

"Think, Ana. There must be something to tell these men," Irena pleaded. "They'll kill me. Kill you. The only reason I'm alive is they were waiting for you—hoping you'd know how to find your father and—"

"What?" Brennan's eyes snapped to Irena. "They were waiting for her?"

"No, no, I meant waiting for a way to find her father. Maybe they thought—"

"You said they were waiting for her." Brennan looked to Ana. "Something's all wrong about this."

Yes, there was something wrong, and Ana realized it too late.

First, the roll-up door opened and one of the gunmen returned and removed her mother's bindings. Then, they whispered between themselves as they watched her and Brennan.

Another gunman joined them. "They have found her."

"Reyes?" Irena spun toward him. "Are you sure?"

"Si. They found her. She is held not far from here. Ñico has gone to get her."

Ana finally understood everything when her mother said, "That is good, Mendo. These two know nothing of Hemingway. They don't even know where my traitorous husband is. They're worthless to us."

Her mother, the victim, was not one.

40

June 14, Afternoon–Somewhere in Southwest Nuevo Laredo, Mexico

Ana sat stunned, demoralized…defeated. Her scars burned; hot fingers of emotion trailed her flesh and stabbed her as she quivered with disbelief.

Irena Karras Montilla had betrayed Pappa. She betrayed her country. She betrayed *her*.

Irena led the gunmen from the room and left her and Brennan behind. For what? Beatings and interrogations? To die? How much more pain could she endure than the realization that her mother was a traitor—that her own mother had just left her to die? This was not the camps—an idealistic, misguided adventure battling a corrupt government and stealing to feed and educate villagers. This was her and Pappa and Mamá.

This was betraying family. Betraying her.

"Ana?" Brennan's voice was soft and concerned. "I'm so sorry. Really. But we have to focus on getting out of here. You gotta let all this go and—"

"I have it." Ana Montilla twisted in her chair. "Can you get over to me? Side-to-side; facing me?"

"I guess. Meet me halfway."

As quietly as they could, they scooted their chairs together so they were side-by-side, facing opposite directions. They positioned themselves with their hands alongside the rope knots that bound each other to their chairs.

"Rock your chair and fall against me," Ana said. "The knot will be nearly in my fingers."

It took Brennan three tries before he tipped the chair enough to balance it against Ana's without falling onto the floor.

"They took my knife when they searched us," he said. "It's always in my pocket."

"I doubt I could reach your pockets, anyway."

He grinned. "Maybe not. But trying would be fun."

She shot him an evil eye. "Really? Now?"

"What? No jokes? A time like this and I can't joke?"

It took her ten minutes. Her fingers were raw and sore, but she loosened his binding enough for him to slip his arm free. In another minute, he was free and untying her. Finally, after what seemed like hours, she rubbed her arms from the chaffing and ache.

"You're pretty good in a tight spot, Ana. Which one of you came up with that idea? Miss Montilla or Miss Karras?"

She allowed a thin smile. "It was a team effort."

"Does the team know how to get through this roll-up door without getting shot?"

No, they didn't. "We have to get them to open the door. The control is on the outside."

Brennan lifted a finger. "Get back into your chair and play dead."

"What?"

"Just do it."

She did, and as she draped the binders around one arm to appear she was still bound, Brennan took one of the empty chairs and stood alongside the roll-up door, out of sight.

"Okay, Ana, scream."

She did like she'd never screamed in her life, praying Brennan would not get them killed.

The roll-up motor clicked on and the door began to rise.

When it was eighteen inches off the floor, Brennan lifted the metal chair. As the door reached about two feet off the floor, he knelt and found his target—a gunman standing just outside the door near the controls on the wall. A few more inches and he swung the chair with all his might, smashing it into the man's legs.

The gunman cried out and crumpled sideways on the concrete floor.

Brennan dove half-beneath the door, grasped the man's legs as he clutched them in pain, and dragged him inside. Once there, he pummeled him with four brutal punches to the face. The man's head rolled to the side and he slumped back, unconscious. Brennan grabbed his nine-millimeter pistol, checked the chamber, and pivoted out the door to search for other gunmen.

There were none.

"Not bad, Luke." Ana searched the fallen man. All she found were two more high-capacity magazines for the man's Glock. "Is it clear?"

Brennan scanned a long, wide corridor outside the roll-up door.

Their room was at a junction of three hallways. The hallways to the left and right were pitch dark and uninviting. The corridor straight ahead had overhead lighting and several doors on each side, disappearing far ahead at another junction.

"I think so," he said. "Straight ahead seems our best bet. Maybe find our gear and a way out."

"Or more guards."

"Yeah, there's that."

She tossed him the spare magazines. "Are you ready?"

"Follow me." He set off down the hall.

The first two doors were locked and no sounds emanated from within. The third opened to an empty office. The fourth surprised them.

The door was ajar. Ana pressed herself against the wall, listened, and peeked through the opening. Inside, a man sat with his back to the door and an AK-74 assault rifle resting on his lap. He was threatening someone out of her view.

"I would gut you like a fish if not for your pappa."

"He is not my pappa, Che." It was a young voice. "I am not afraid. I will not do as you say."

"You will or I'll beat you half to death."

Che suddenly stood, leaned the AK-74 against the nearby wall, and moved out of sight.

The young voice choked cries of pain and anguish as a brutal beating ensued.

No more.

Ana Montilla burst into the room, grabbed the assault rifle, and slammed its butt into the side of Che's face when he whirled to confront her. As he went down, she smashed him again behind the head.

"Dammit, Ana." Brennan moved in behind her. "Warn me next time. Okay?"

"There wasn't time." She faced a young teenager cowering against the far wall. He was slight and handsome, perhaps thirteen or fourteen years old, with black, shimmering hair. His face was ashen and tear-stained—red and puffy from the beating Che had just delivered.

She lowered the assault rifle and motioned for Brennan to shut the door. Then, she turned back to the boy and smiled an easy, friendly smile. "I'm Ana. This is Luke, like in *Star Wars*. Are you all right?"

The teenager watched her carefully but didn't speak.

"Please," she said, reaching out to touch the boy's face with a mother's attention. "You're hurt. Let us help you. We're leaving. We'll take you wherever you wish. What's your name?"

The boy pulled away from her touch.

"Che and other men kidnapped us off the street," she said. "We're escaping. We'll keep you safe."

The boy watched Brennan guarding the door. Then, he looked back at Ana. "I came here to find my mamá. Che and Mendo are holding me until my stepfather returns with her. I am afraid they will kill her. Can you help us?"

"I don't know, kid," Brennan said. "But we'll do what we can."

"I am not a kid." The boy lifted his chin proudly. "I am Mateo Reyes."

***

As Brennan opened the door to check the hall, he whispered to Ana over his shoulder, "What are we going to do with him?"

"I don't know." Ana held the assault rifle with one hand, and held Mateo's hand with the other, pulling him safely behind her. "We can't bring him to the police. For all we know, they're working with these guys. They're not to be trusted."

"Nice town, Nuevo Laredo." Brennan motioned for Ana and Mateo to follow him down the hall. "What then?"

As they neared the intersection at the far end of the hall, two large metal doors up ahead banged open. Two gunmen burst through, assault rifles at the ready.

"Go back." Brennan spun around, looking to retreat.

Behind them, two more gunmen appeared.

Nowhere to go.

41

June 14, Afternoon–Somewhere in Southwest Nuevo Laredo, Mexico

"Any ideas, Luke?" Ana pulled Mateo close as the gunmen closed in from both ends of the hallway. "Now would be a good time for a plan."

"I know." Brennan looked from the men behind to the men in front. "But I got nothing."

"Put your weapons down," one of the gunmen ordered. "Mateo, come to us. Come here, boy."

Mateo clung to Ana. "Don't let them take me, please."

"It'll be all right, Mateo," she said, shielding him behind her. "You'll stay with us. I'll protect you."

"I'm afraid," he whispered.

"Me, too, kid." Brennan moved around so Mateo was sandwiched between him and Ana. "We'll figure this out. You'll see."

Yes, it would be all right.

The two gunmen in front of them dropped to the floor, one after the other, as loud, mechanical "coughs" rattled from somewhere behind them.

Brennan grabbed Mateo's shoulders and pushed him to the

ground, kneeling over him with his Glock pistol ready.

As the two gunmen behind them spun to engage their target, both of their heads snapped back—one after the other—and they fell to the ground, dead.

Ana lifted her AK-74 and swung it left to right searching for the shooter.

"Easy now, Miss Ana," a familiar voice called. "I'm coming out. Don't shoot me, okay?"

At the far end of the corridor, at the junction of the three hallways, Dallas appeared around the corner near the roll-up door. One hand was chest high in surrender. The other held an M4 assault rifle with a long, tubular suppressor affixed to the end.

"Ya'll okay, Miss Ana?" he asked. "Took a chance firing around you like that. Sorry, didn't want to whistle or anything to get you out of the way. But I'm a pretty good shot most days."

"Yes, you are, Dallas." Brennan helped Mateo to his feet. "Not bad at all."

"How did you find us?" Ana moved from gunman to gunman, checking them. Each had a bullet hole in their foreheads. Neat. Clean. Instant. "We thought maybe—"

"That I set these bandits on you?" He walked up the hall to them, checking the open office where they'd found Mateo. "I reckoned you did. My man at customs saw somebody follow you from the airport. He warned me and here I am."

"But how'd you find us?" she repeated.

Dallas grinned. "Ah, well, I slipped a tracker into your go-bag, Miss Ana. Don't get all upset and all. It saved your lives." He gestured to Mateo. "Who's the boy?"

"I'm not a boy," Mateo said. "I am fourteen. I am Mateo."

Dallas nodded. "Well now, I didn't know. You're right, amigo. You're a young man."

"You handled yourself real well, Mateo." Brennan patted Mateo's shoulder. "Your mom will be proud of you."

Mateo tried to smile but it was lost in the paleness spreading over his face as he looked down at the four dead men. "I've not seen men killed before."

"It's ugly." Ana put her arm around him and hugged him tightly.

"There was no choice, Mateo. But I'm sorry you had to see this."

Dallas picked up the gunmen's weapons and spare magazincs, distributing them to Ana and Brennan. "We need to move. I counted seven foot soldiers and one el jefe when I got here. El jefe and one of his boys left a bit ago—that's how I found my way in. These four and the one you got in the office account for all of them. But there could be others I didn't see."

"We'll follow you," Ana said. "But first we have to find our things."

"I got plenty of everything you'll need on my airplane, Miss Ana." Dallas gestured to Mateo. "What's his story? You got a plan?"

"No."

"Mateo," Brennan asked, "you said you're looking for your mother and that your stepfather is here somewhere?"

"Yes." Mateo looked to the ground. "My real pappa is gone. I have never met him. My mamá is here, somewhere. My step-pappa and these men were holding me until they found her."

"Mateo?" Ana stopped and faced him. "Where are you from?"

"Cuba. My stepfather, Ñico, brought me along to find my mamá."

Brennan and Ana exchanged looks. "Ana, are you thinking…?"

"I am." She turned to Dallas. "Mateo will go with you to the aircraft. He'll be safer with you until this is over."

"Sure, okay. Something else I should tell you." Dallas gestured down the hall. "There were two SUVs sitting out back. I was worried they might move you before I could stop them, so I plopped a GPS tracker on each one. El jefe and one of his men already left in one of the vehicles."

"You're tracking his stepfather?" Brennan asked. "He's headed to find—"

"My mamá," Mateo said. "Ñico is a bad man. I hate him."

Dallas nodded. "GPS should make it easy to find them now."

"I take back everything I thought about you, Dallas," Brennan said. "You're all right. Even for a horseless cowboy."

Dallas grinned and gave him a mock salute.

"Mateo, you go with Dallas. Brennan and I will join you later." Ana gave him a reassuring hug. "You'll be safe with him."

Mateo smiled. "You will help find my mamá?"

"Yes, Mateo, we certainly will."

42

June 14, Afternoon–The Eisenhower Executive Office Building, Washington, DC

"This better be good." McLaren sat staring impatiently at Danny across the office meeting table. "I've got pressing matters elsewhere."

"I don't care what you've got elsewhere," Danny snapped. "I beckon. You come. Besides, that's why you have a private jet at taxpayer expense."

McLaren's teeth ground.

Danny stood and walked to a coffee server across the room. He picked up two cups, a carafe of coffee, and returned, filling his own and pushing the empty cup and carafe across the table to McLaren.

"How bad will this Vergara mess get, McLaren?"

"You mean because he's a Cuban Intelligence officer with your phone number in his pocket?" McLaren shrugged. "Or because he's dead?"

"Dead? How?"

McLaren sat stoically. Silence was a powerful intelligence technique. Silence could mean truth or deception. It could bring on confessions. It could raise alarms. It could quell an adversary by sheer inference of superiority. Now, it simply allowed him time to think.

Danny rapped the table with his knuckles. "How?"

"We were working on him and he died." McLaren didn't give him the facts. Those would just complicate matters. "He was a link to Hemingway."

"Hemingway, the Cuban assassin?" Danny dropped his face into his hands. "Sweet Jesus. How in the hell did you screw this up so bad?"

"Excuse me?" That irritated McLaren to no end and the fire in his voice didn't conceal it. "If you'd been square with me from the beginning, we wouldn't be in this mess. What aren't you telling me now?"

"McLaren, I told you all I know…well, except one thing." Danny tapped the table in front of him. "It has to stay between us. No playing games with this. Got it?"

"What is it, already?"

Danny steepled his hands. "I told you about the calls we got from Vergara a little over two weeks ago. The first two went to an intern for handling. Vergara—remember, I didn't know who it was at the time—tried to get through to me but this intern blew him off. All the caller said was 'we must discuss Hemingway.' Afterward, I took the next call. He demanded to meet me. I decided to send you."

McLaren watched him. Danny was as nervous as the proverbial cat in a rocking chair factory. "Yeah, and?"

"The intern's name was Sean Finley."

"Was?"

"He didn't show for work this morning. I sent someone by his place. Clothes cleaned out. Bags gone. No one has seen him." Danny slid a piece of paper across to him. "Here's his address. I have someone there in case he returns."

McLaren took the paper, glanced at it, and set it on the table. "We have to find Finley. He might know more than he told you. If he does, or if someone is pulling his strings, that's more trouble."

"For you. Not me. Remember, I have your strings firmly in my hand, McLaren."

McLaren gritted his teeth again. "Just be careful no one wraps them around your neck and strangles you with them."

The two sat in silence. The air between them was cold and tense as McLaren stood and went to the office window. He took out his cell, made a call, and relayed Finley's information to a loyal operative at the Caverns.

He turned back around. "What else, Danny? You look like you're about to give birth."

"I know the targets. It's me and the boss."

"You and the vice president?"

Danny nodded.

"You think Hemingway is coming to kill you and the vice president? That would mean war, Danny. A big, fat, ugly gunfight. Why him?"

Danny looked away. "I've already told you that since becoming vice president, he's led the negotiations for the president—behind the scenes—with Havana. He's taken a very strong position on improved relations with the Cubans. No negotiation without dramatic improvements and benchmarks on human rights—release of political prisoners or restitution for land and assets seized in-country. Dramatic requirements, I tell you. No equivocation. No capitulation."

"Hurrah for him. That wouldn't necessitate his assassination, however. It must be the other thing."

"What other thing?"

"The thing that's going to piss me off. The thing you're still not telling me."

"Well, yeah. Okay." Danny leaned back. "As I've told you, I led a team that spent considerable time in Latin America for Bush-43. We were trying to broker deals with Venezuela involving oil and improved regional stability. It was a very difficult endeavor, to say the least. You recall how Chavez was."

"Yeah, insane and he hated us. Get to Hemingway and the part you're avoiding."

"It's complicated."

"Of course it is."

Danny sighed. "While we were in Caracas back in the day, the Cubans ran an operation against us. They ran hard, too. It got ugly."

"How ugly?"

"Very ugly. My security people handled it. They kept it out of the media and, well, out of our records, too."

McLaren watched him for the lie; Danny was twitching. "What the hell happened?"

Danny crossed the room to a small server beside the coffee and poured himself a tall bourbon, plopped in some ice and offered one to McLaren, but was already sitting back adjacent to him before he received a curt shake of his head.

Danny went on. "Havana sent a team of agents to compromise us. They tried to sabotage our mission."

"And?"

"Twice, a young agent—her name was Catalina Reyes—made moves on us. You know the type, what do you call it…a honey trap?"

"Did…?"

"Absolutely not. We knew what it was about. And believe it or not, I'm very ethical."

"Yeah, me too."

"Screw you." Danny took a mouthful of bourbon. "Both times we stopped Reyes's provocation and turned it on them."

"Why did you allow it to continue once you identified her as a threat?"

"We wanted to compromise *her*." Another mouthful of bourbon. "We needed someone to get us access behind the scenes of the meetings we were holding. She was perfect for it."

"Bad decision." McLaren shook his head. "You weren't trained for that, Danny. I doubt your security people were either."

"Hindsight. Anyway, one evening, we caught Reyes in one of our suites trying to plant surveillance devices. There was a confrontation."

McLaren's radar pinged wildly. "Ah, crap."

"One of the Cuban agents with Reyes was killed." Danny held his glass to his lips, watching McLaren over the top. "Purely self-defense."

"Killed? And none of this went to State or the CIA station in Caracas?"

"Hell, no. We never expected it to escalate to that level. Jesus, McLaren, things got out of hand fast. We didn't dare go to State or to you guys. We weren't even supposed to be doing what we were doing, remember?"

McLaren took hold of Danny's eyes. "Was Cannon involved?"

"No, thank God." Danny eased a bit. "I led the team in Caracas, and he handled the effort back here in DC. He was never there."

McLaren sat digesting it all. "Reckless, Danny—and illegal."

"Yeah, well, you have no room to talk about illegal." Danny's face reddened. "It was fifteen years ago, dammit. Look, we had Reyes dead to rights bugging our room. The next thing we knew, this other agent crashed in and there was a fight. Our security guys killed him."

"Unbelievable."

"His name was Reynaldo Reyes."

McLaren snapped forward in his seat. "Are you telling me…?"

"Catalina Reyes's husband. It was unfortunate."

"Unfortunate? Sweet Jesus." McLaren closed his eyes. Revenge was a powerful motivator. Catalina Reyes was highly motivated. Could she be Hemingway? "You have a knack for the obvious, Danny."

It was not uncommon for intelligence operations to employ husband and wife teams. They were plausible and more easily put into deep cover. Over the years, many of these teams had been discovered operating in the US. They were neither the cliché James Bond spies nor the lone wolf operatives of a John le Carré novel—and that was the point.

Danny said, "Our people had a few locals who were on our side at the time. They made it all go away. They made everything go away."

"Obviously, not all of it. You think Hemingway is connected to this?"

"I don't believe in coincidences."

"Why, after all these years, would they be gunning for you?" McLaren thought a moment. "How does the fact you were involved in Reyes' death make the vice president a target?"

"I think they're using this as an excuse to hurt him." Danny frowned. "They don't want the boss elected president. They think they'll do better with someone softer on human rights. They believe they can get at me and ruin him. Revenge for Catalina Reyes; political win for Havana. It's that simple."

"This is not simple, Danny. This makes Afghanistan look like sandbox bullying."

"Yeah, yeah." Danny took a long swallow of bourbon. "Things didn't work out exactly how we planned. Ultimately, Bush got some of what he wanted with Venezuela back then. So, in the end, it all worked out."

"Except for Reyes." McLaren stood. "So, Hemingway is an assassin coming to balance the books against you and, in turn, ruin the vice president. They pop you—maybe the vice president—and leak what happened in Caracas as justification. Next, someone says 'charge' and we're invading Cuba."

Danny shrugged. "Look, even the worst peaceniks around Washington won't sit still for the assassination of a US leader by a foreign government. Before the funeral, Havana will be a smoldering ash pit."

"And maybe us, too, depending on the Russians." McLaren's brow furrowed. "I assume the Secret Service is aware of this by now?"

"No. I already told you what I think of the service. Every move they make is scrutinized by the media, down to the color of their shoes. All we need is for any bit of this to go public and we could forget the Oval Office. The media would turn this into a nightmare. You handle it."

"Me, handle it? We need the FBI on Hemingway and protection on—"

"No. We've already discussed that." Danny came around the table closer to him. "Look, you have what you have to work with. I'll worry about protection and the rest."

"This is insane, Danny."

"We can do this." Danny opened his palms to him. "I want Hemingway brought in. I want the intel from this to beat the Cubans over the head with. I don't want some two-bit revenge play…"

"If Catalina Reyes is Hemingway, we're in trouble." McLaren lifted his chin. "She's an assassin on a revenge tour. And her sights are set on you."

43

June 14, Afternoon–The Bear's Den

Cat stood at the second-floor window watching the activity in the dusty compound below. She'd been in the bedroom for hours. She took the opportunity to shower and change clothes—an unexpected gift from Oso. Felipe had brought her a stack of clothes of varying sizes and styles to choose from. She'd selected a simple combination of clean jeans and a loose, button-down, cotton shirt. The variety of clothes made her wonder how many women had been forsaken by Oso in the recent past. In the short time she'd been in the compound, she'd only seen two Latina servants downstairs and several migrant women slaving for his drug business. What had been the fate of those who'd once owned these outfits?

She'd been locked away in the second-floor room for hours, waiting and wondering when Oso would appear and take his revenge for her failed escape attempt.

The thought of him touching her—forcing her—made her wish for a fast end. Perhaps she should find a way to end it quickly and alleviate his pleasure of killing her slowly. Anything would be better than what she knew him to be capable of.

No, Cat—Reynaldo whispered—*do not fear what you cannot control. You must survive. Think of me…of Mateo. Survive for us.*

Your mission is not lost.

"Yes, Reynaldo. I will try. Stay close."

The bedroom door swung open and Oso strode in wearing fresh khaki slacks and a polo shirt. He had shaved and showered. A gesture that sent shivers through her.

"Ah, la chica sin nombre," he said in a friendly, pleasant voice. "Hot water and clean clothes are wondrous, don't you think?"

She lifted her chin but said nothing, waiting on his assault.

"No?" Oso wandered to the side of the king-sized bed and sat, facing her. "Forgive me, you are no longer *la chica sin nombre*, are you?"

What?

"It seems you are worth much money to Cuba. Isn't that right, Catalina Reyes?"

44

June 14, Afternoon–The Bear's Den

"Come, Catalina," Oso said politely. "Downstairs. We will eat and talk."

She took a moment to summon her confidence. *Steady, Catalina, you can do this.*

"Fine. I will follow you."

Oso led her down the winding staircase to the foyer, through the great room, and out the French doors onto a rear veranda. There, the sun baked the tile beneath her feet and the arid smell of dust and wildflowers lingered in the air.

Posted on both sides of the veranda were two well-armed guards.

"Por favor, join us at the table," Oso said, gesturing toward a man already seated at a large, round marble table. "He has been waiting patiently to meet you."

"Who?" Even as she spoke the words, fear began stabbing her. "What is this?"

The man at the table stood, turned, and faced her. "Buenos días, Catalina. It has been too long. This mischief you have gotten yourself into, so bad, no?"

She went ridged in mid-step. Her fire and strength evaporated.

Her confidence withered and died. A sudden rush of tears filled her eyes as she stared into Ñico Guerro's dark, deadly eyes.

No, no, no.

"I see you are delighted to see me." Ñico walked around a heavy planter, grabbed her, and kissed both her cheeks. "We have much to discuss."

Oso threw his head back and roared, "Such a surprise. Wonderful. Come. Sit."

She stared blankly at the man who had been her husband for fourteen years. A husband that had been anything but. A man dedicated to self-preservation and vice, inflicting as much pain and despair on her as he could. Their marriage had been a match commanded by Havana's G2 spymasters to produce one thing and one thing only: a facade. A marriage to maintain the ruse of normalcy. But it was about strategy and deception. Subterfuge. Mostly, though, it was about control.

Ñico always controlled her. By fear. By violence. By intimidation. It never ended. After leaving Cuba, she had hoped life would be different after she had escaped him. Now, however, he had found her. Looking at him—grinning like a jackal preparing for the kill—she knew his torment would return, and after festering for all these months, she bet it would be ferocious.

She had hoped after the Diocese that he'd moved on and sought her elsewhere along the American border. Instead, he was standing in front of her.

Be strong, Cat—Reynaldo was close—*show no fear.*

"Pig." She pulled away from his grip on her shoulders and slapped him hard across the face. "How have you left Havana?"

Her resistance shocked him. His eyes went wide and surprised… confused. It had been years since she had the strength to defy his presence. He stood there, uncertainty saving her from brutal retaliation. Finally, he stepped back with a dull, bewildered look on his face.

"I came for you, Catalina." He recovered his swagger. "You will return what you have stolen from us and come with me home to Cuba."

"I will not."

"Oh?" Ñico's face washed with rage and he struck her across the face, knocking her down onto the stone floor. "You are hundreds of miles from our home. You are on a mission to destroy everything. I have you now and still you defy me?"

"Yes." She returned to her feet and faced him again. "You are here to kill me, Ñico. You would do that to our son?"

"Mateo is *your* bastard son. You are a whore; I am your master." He grabbed her arm, twisted it violently, and pulled her close. "You left Cuba without permission. Without *my* permission. For months our people have hunted you—to stop this foolish mission. You have done well, I see. But it is over. You will return with me."

"You will have to kill me. Then where will that leave you with Havana?"

Ñico grinned menacingly. "I have Mateo. Here, with me. In truth, that is all I need."

Mateo? "You cannot possibly—"

"He is here. Close by. You see, Catalina, just like before, you need me to survive. If it were not for your failures in Caracas so many years ago, none of this would have happened. Reynaldo would still be with you. You would be Havana's star still today. Instead, you have become a traitorous *puta* shunned by everyone."

"You bastard." Cat's eyes were raining a brew of hate and memories. For an instant, she was back in Caracas fifteen years before. "I was doing what was asked of me and it took my Reynaldo. It left Mateo fatherless. For that, Havana sentenced me to you."

Ñico pulled her nose-to-nose with him. "Without me, you would be on cold streets or dead. You will return what you took from us—everything. Do you understand? Everything."

"I would rather die."

"¿Si? Just say the word."

She trembled inside—a boil of fear and anger. "You betrayed us—Mateo and me. The things you did to us will haunt me forever. You brutalized Mateo. You are a jackal. A demon. You tormented your family for pleasure and power."

"You were never my family, Catalina. You were Havana's property under my care. That is all."

Not able to hold his gaze, she and looked away. She had to think of Mateo. She had to find the strength to fight back and survive. Somewhere, nearby, a young boy waited…scared and confused.

Time. Patience. Escape.

"What did you think?" Ñico released her, walked casually back to the table, and sat facing Oso again. "Did you think Havana would let you live a normal life? Do you think you can simply steal the power we have?"

"Where is my son?" she asked, following him tableside. "Let me see that he is all right. Please, let us go. I beg you. For Mateo."

Ñico lifted his lemonade and toasted her. "I think not. You will both return with me."

Wait. How was he here with Mateo? Havana would never allow him…. The realization struck her. "You took him without their permission. You brought him to lure me back. But Havana did not know, did they?"

Ñico's face tightened. "They will forgive me upon my triumphant return. They will praise me for my initiative and strength."

"They will kill you."

Oso flashed a hand up. "Enough."

"It is not enough," Ñico growled.

"Let us be very clear, Ñico Guerro," Oso said coldly. "This señorita will not be leaving unless I say so. And she is right. Your people in Havana are not pleased with you."

"What?" Ñico slapped the table between them. "How do you know anything about this?"

Oso grinned. "Where is the boy? You will bring him to me."

"No, I will not. He is mine to do with as I wish." Ñico stood again, grabbed Cat by an arm, and shoved her into the chair alongside him. "He is not your concern."

Cat pulled from Ñico's grasp but stayed seated. "What is it you want, Oso? What deal is there to be had for me?"

"Ah, now we have some fun, no?" Oso looked from Cat to Ñico and back. "You offer me one-hundred thousand American dollars, no?"

She nodded.

"Really?" Ñico snorted. "I have already offered you two-hundred fifty thousand. I…"

"Hmm." Oso poured another glass of lemonade and slid it across the table to Cat. "Havana has offered me one million. You did not know I was in communication with them, did you, Ñico? I was already aware of Señora Reyes's treachery before you arrived. Havana's hunt for her was well known in my country. And for some time, too. They have spread much money around to find her. And yet, it was I who did."

Cat snapped forward. "If you return my son and me to Cuba, we are as good as dead. Get me across the border and there will be much more money. This I promise."

Oso considered that. Then, he turned to Ñico. "Is this true? They will be executed?"

"The boy will be fine. Her, I cannot guess."

"Then, it is true." Oso looked at Cat. "What have you done so treasonous, girl?"

Before she could answer, Ñico shoved her out of her chair onto the ground. "She is a traitor. She was once one of our best operatives—trained as an assassin and very skilled. I know; I helped train her myself. If she does not return to Cuba with me, America and Cuba could be at war soon. That will be on you, Oso."

"War?" Oso's eyes widened. "Truly, señora? A pretty, young thing like you wishes to start a war with the Americans?"

Cat climbed to her knees, struggling against the panic welling inside. "He lies."

"Yet my country hunts her, Oso." Ñico raised a hand but didn't strike her. "She calls *me* a liar?"

"Enough. I don't care about any of this." Oso shrugged indifferently. "It is only about how much."

"Let me contact Havana," Ñico said. "I will secure you more money."

"Havana will not speak with you." Oso locked on Ñico's eyes. "You came here of your own accord, operating...how did they say, *rogue*. They care not if you return, but I am to secure the boy and his mother for them."

"No. They will return with me."

Oso lifted his glass. "You displease them, Ñico. They are angry—very angry—that you took this boy, Mateo. They told me to do with you as I pleased. If you return, so be it. If you do not, well…it is of no consequence to them."

"They will understand," Ñico said. "I brought Mateo as bait to find her and return her and what she stole from us. The boy will stop her resistance."

"Yet, it was I who stopped her. Not you." Oso grinned. "The price is two million American dollars."

Ñico's face blanched. "Two million?"

"Cash. Each." Oso stood and headed for the French doors. "American dollars."

Ñico jumped up and tried to follow him but one of his guards stopped him. "Four million dollars? Are you insane? Havana—"

"Havana will pay," Oso said. "They know the consequences of refusing."

"Consequences?" Cat asked. "You would kill us; a mother and her son?"

Oso shrugged. "I have killed mothers and sons before, señora. Still, it will not come to that. If Havana won't pay my price, the Americans will."

"The Americans?" Ñico yelled. "Do you know what would happen if you made a deal with them?"

"That is not my concern." Oso waved a hand. "From them, I might get five or ten million dollars. I might also get, what is the funny term, a 'get out of jail free' card. No?"

"Oso, listen to me," Ñico pleaded. "Give me time…"

"It is done. I await Havana's decision."

45

June 14, Around Midnight–The Bear's Den

Hours later, Cat stood by her second-floor window watching the dark compound below. Somewhere, perhaps in the compound itself, Mateo waited. Oso had demanded Ñico retrieve him to the compound earlier. While Ñico had resisted, she doubted even he could defy Oso's pressure and demands for long. Since then, she'd kept her focus on one strategy: find Mateo, escape, and return to her mission. Finding Mateo might be the hardest part, but she was closer to him now than she'd been in a year. She'd brave whatever hell Oso and Ñico could bring to find him. She could never leave Mexico otherwise.

Without her son, there was no reason to go on. Her life—her mission—was all about Mateo.

Find Mateo. Complete her mission. Disappear. It seemed so simple.

Surveying the compound, only a few guards were on patrol that she could see. And while Mateo waited somewhere, there were others held captive here, too. Sleeping in the crumbling shanties and huts were dozens of others enslaved, praying simply for survival, let alone freedom. They waited for either an end to their slavery, or death to escape it.

The sights she had seen in the camp—the misery and hopelessness—reminded her of life in Havana without Mateo. Oso's slaves were without a future. Without hope. She had felt those pains and lived those endless days herself.

Could she escape and abandon those other souls?

She studied the compound below her—contemplating an escape. Oso's patrols came and went. Most of the time, the vehicles traveled to the barn and disappeared around back, only to reemerge later. Supplies in; product out. Other vehicles patrolled the perimeter of the compound. At least two were farther in the distance, just headlights and taillights against the black horizon, roaming the desert for distant threats.

Since nightfall, she kept the room dark, using only the outside ambient light to move about. The room's two windows were narrow and opened horizontally. One window overlooked the road running through the middle of the compound, and the other overlooked the side of the house facing the compound's entrance. Both views gave her a look at the patrols milling around.

Her training in Havana had been nearly twenty years ago. She'd been very young, barely a teenager, but she recalled it well. She'd learned street survival, escape and evasion, and clandestine urban warfare. But it was Reynaldo who had taught her the most. His dedication to her was both an act of love and survival. They'd be working together and, if she was not the best she could be, she could kill them both. One of his lessons was to learn to start your mission with nothing. No weapons. No supplies. No support. Steal what you require. Fight with what you find. Operate alone. In the months learning those lessons, she had excelled. Excelled so much that Havana eventually assigned her to Caracas and a very, very special mission—Operation Perro.

That was fifteen years ago. Now, tonight, it was time to test all her forgotten skills.

The bedroom door was locked, and she knew a guard waited just outside. The windows offered long drops to the hard desert ground. There were at least two guards posted at the front of the house and most likely others in the rear. She couldn't simply drop to the ground. The guards would find her in seconds.

The most impossible route was up. Up might afford her a chance to reconnoiter and find the best escape out of view of the patrols. Up was also the route no one would expect her to take.

She would go up.

The roof overhang was a foot above the top windowsill. That morning, moving through the compound, she recalled the roof was flat and she hadn't seen any guards atop it. Still, certainly there'd be one, perhaps two at night, watching for Federales raids or incursions by competing cartels. Waiting on the roof might be weapons and communications. Perhaps other needed supplies.

It was a start.

She examined the window, devised a plan, and went about the room to gather the few needed supplies. At the window, she worked carefully so not to catch the attention of any guards below. The window had two large sections—a lower and an upper half. She used medical tape and bandages from beneath the bathroom sink to cover as much of the glass as possible. Working quietly, she used the edge of a metal shower hanger and dug away the window putty and dried wood from around the glass. Once she'd loosened the panes, she secured bath towels with more tape over the glass panes. When she was certain the guards were not nearby, she pressured the glass panes until they cracked; the towels muted the high-pitched fragmentation to mere faint "crackles." The tape kept them from falling down to the ground. Once cracked in multiple places, she worked the shower hanger tool and removed the glass entirely.

She repeated the process on the top window.

When she was done, she used her shower tool to dig around the wood and dismantle the remaining glass framing so she could slip through unscathed.

Carefully, she slid the small dresser into position tight against the window. It was barely three feet from the top of the dresser to the top of the window, giving her a good anchor point to move through the window and reach the roof overhang.

Before she began her climb, she cracked parts of the windowpane into long, narrow shards—eight inches long, two inches wide, and tapered to a jagged point. Using the last of the medical tape, she wrapped the glass shards together halfway up at one end, leaving about six inches of exposed, jagged glass. At the other end, she wrapped the tape to form the grip of the glass dagger. Then, she slid it into the rear of her jeans, climbed onto the top of the dresser, and started up.

Part of her G2 training had been physical fitness. She had excelled. Over the years she continued to stay in shape even after her missions were only a memory. Part of it was to control her anxiety. Part of it was to hasten the healing from Ñico's barbaric treatment. A toned, fit body was more resilient to his abuse. Bruises faded. Bones mended.

She slithered out the window and reached for the roof overhang. Twice she nearly toppled out where a two-floor fall would surely break bones. On her third attempt, she found a handhold on the roof and secured a second handhold. She paused, listened for anyone sounding the alarm, and finally pulled herself up to breach the roofline. She peered over the edge like an alligator surfacing in the water.

She tensed.

One armed sentry.

The man sat on a box halfway across the roof with a ladder at his feet. His rifle leaned against the box. His chin was down on his chest, unmoving.

Sleeping?

Would one of Oso's men dare sleep on duty? Perhaps. No one could see him. No one could reach the roof without him dropping the ladder, and in the darkness, he was safe from observation below.

His dereliction was her only chance.

She swung her hips left to right and back—once, twice, three times—and swung her legs up to grab the roofline with one foot. Swiftly, she levered her body up and over the edge. Once there, she lowered herself prone and froze.

No movement from the sentry. No calls for alarm.

She watched and waited for him to rise to his feet, turn, and kill her.

Nothing.

She remained unmoving, settling herself and preparing for a fight. Her breath came faster, not from exertion, but unease. This was not Tegucigalpa. She had no silenced weapon. She would have to take the sentry by hand.

Was she ready? Did she still have the skills?

You must try, Cat. For Mateo—Reynaldo whispered.

She kept low and stepped toward the sentry.

He didn't move.

A second step.

Nothing.

Three, four, five steps…ten…

The sentry coughed and lifted his head. He reached for his rifle but only laid a hand atop the barrel—a comfort check. For a moment, he gazed out over the black desert in front of him, turned to his left and did the same. Before the last turn of his head, he yawned, coughed again, and rested his chin back on his chest.

Her limbs tingled. Her chest was ready to explode.

She slipped the glass dagger out and held steady.

The guard settled. A snore was released.

She lunged.

Two steps before she reached him, he jarred awake, twisted around, and caught her approaching.

She dove for him, plunging the glass dagger deep into his neck. Her right hand wrapped around his head and clamped his mouth tightly closed.

Darkness and the sentry jumping up caused her dagger to miss his carotid artery. Instead, it sliced into his shoulder, glanced off bone, and broke apart.

He attempted to call out, but her hand was clamped too tightly over his mouth. He whirled around with her latched tightly to his back. He was not a large man but lean and spry. He twisted side-to-side, trying to shake her free. His arms flailed, trying desperately to grab hold of anything to pull her free.

She clung to the remains of her dagger and wrapped her legs around him, locked her ankles at his waist, and fixed herself for the struggle. In his frenzied throes, his head snapped back and struck her face, stunning her momentarily and nearly weakening her control. She countered with a ferocious assault across his neck and face with the dagger shard, trying for his eyes, holding his mouth and stunting his breath.

Stabbing. Stabbing. Stabbing.

The sentry faltered. He dropped to one knee.

She rode him down and held firm.

He shuttered and stilled.

She relaxed her legs and dropped to the ground behind him. Then, she reached over his shoulder to deliver the *coup d'état* to his throat.

He suddenly twisted and grabbed her hand. He snapped forward, wrenching her over his shoulder, tossing her in front of him. As she hit the roof, he clambered for her, grabbed her throat, and plunged his fingers deep into her windpipe.

The counterassault stunned her. As his hands encircled her throat, she slashed upward with her dagger, stabbed over and over, and prayed for flesh. Prayed for survival. A warm spray of blood wetted her face and hands as she continued the onslaught; each flailing attack grew weaker and weaker as her brain screamed for oxygen and her eyes fluttered toward obscurity.

With her remaining strength, she stabbed upward and found nothing.

Her eyes flickered closed—fluttered open. Movement in the night somewhere beyond the perimeter strangely caught her attention. Her thoughts melted away.

The sentry's fingers tightened more than she could bear. He grunted once. Twice.

Her eyes fluttered open as her body tensed for its last throe.

I'm sorry, Reynaldo, I have failed you.

Nothing.

46

June 15, Very Early Morning–The Bear's Den

Cat awoke next to the rooftop sentry. His hands still clutched her throat, but their strength had passed with his life. He lay limp and unthreatening. She gasped and sat upright, yanked his dead fingers away, and rolled free. She lay still for a moment to regain her strength before she stood.

I knew you could do this, Cat—Reynaldo said—*you are strong again.*

The sentry lay on his side where he dropped. Both eyes were gouged and bloodied—only dark ooze remained from her assault with the glass dagger. His cheeks, ears, and throat were equally disfigured. While he found the strength to counterattack, blood loss and shock ultimately took him—perhaps seconds before he ended her life first.

Only conviction and will had saved her.

She searched the dead guard. She discarded a half-empty package of cigarettes and his billfold with a few pesos stuffed inside. What she found next was a treasure trove—a sturdy hunting knife and sheath which she slid onto her belt, a small pair of binoculars, and a miniature two-way radio with an earbud and a microphone. She slung the binoculars around her neck, pushed the radio earbud into her ear, and slid the radio into a pocket. Her most important find was the two full spare magazines for the rifle lying on the ground where it fell during their scuffle.

She rested a few more minutes as she listened intently to the radio but heard no chatter. One by one, she checked the other channels but found no radio traffic, either. While listening, she used the binoculars to scan the area for roads and any landmarks that might aid her escape.

She found none.

Staying low to keep her profile invisible, she moved along the roof from corner to corner, taking care to peer over and look for sentries below. There were four in the far distance along the perimeter, but none were nearby the hacienda now. Her sightline was dim and obscured most details, though she thought she saw two additional sentries on the far side of the compound sitting near the shanties where the other captives slept. All total, there were nearly a half-dozen visible. That meant there were many more invisible to her.

She focused the binoculars on the barn. There were no outside lights on, and the night offered only a big, imposing silhouette. After her incursion yesterday, the bulk of Oso's forces might likely be there protecting it. There was at least one vehicle patrol that she knew of, probably out in the darkness patrolling outside the perimeter. That was what she'd seen in the daylight. By now, in the early morning hours, Oso might have twice that many patrols.

The ladder used to access the roof lay nearby, and she considered it. It posed problems. First, she'd be vulnerable longer if she used it to descend to the ground. Second, if it were found propped to the roof without the rooftop sentry nearby, it might raise the alarm.

She would descend without it.

At the rear of the hacienda just above the veranda, she slithered sideways over the edge, dropping her right leg and arm down the wall. Using her left foot and one hand to grip the roof ledge, she stretched her body down the wall like a spider—clinging with her left side, stretching with her right. When she was fully extended, she swung her left leg down, righted herself, and dropped easily another two feet to the rear veranda roof. She adjusted her rifle over her back and almost, without stopping, gripped the veranda roof and swung down to the ground with a gymnast's finesse. There, she moved to the house wall and flattened her form among the night shadows for better concealment.

She stopped, daring not to move in case a sentry returned too quickly.

Safety.

Now, to find Mateo.

Peering through the French doors into the hacienda, she saw no one at first, then two armed men wandered in, did a cursory check of the room, and exited into the main hall.

Searching the hacienda was out for the time being. While Oso and Ñico might keep Mateo inside, there was no way to safely search for him there now. She would search the remainder of the compound first, and if she failed to find him, she would have to form a plan to search the house later.

Moving in short, smooth movements, she sneaked away from the hacienda and traversed the narrow opening to a single-story ranch house probably used by the guards. Twice she was forced to slip deeper into the shadows when she feared sentries nearby. Both times she was right, and they walked by within a half-dozen steps of her. Luckily, their focus was away from the compound, not within. Their senses—dulled by the late hour—missed her.

At each hideaway along her path to the barn, she listened for radio calls that might bring danger. There were none.

Except for those captured at the hacienda, the compound was asleep.

After twenty minutes working her way down the row of buildings, she neared the barn. At the corner of a small shed—the last structure before the barn—she stopped.

A shadow moved through the darkness straight at her.

She slipped the hunting knife from its scabbard; the rifle would be her last resort.

The shadow was nearly on her.

A coyote sniffed along the ground, foraging for food. It saw her, chattered surprise, and scampered off.

She grinned and took a long breath.

You are doing fine, Catalina.

She took care to move her eyes in freeze-frame snapshots, looking off-center from objects, as human vision created blind spots in the dark. Satisfied the sentries were elsewhere, she crossed to the barn's nearest corner and melted into the shadows.

She was about to traverse the length of the barn to the window she'd entered the day before when truck lights broke the horizon ahead. A few seconds later, they touched the far corner of the barn and inched toward her. The lights bumped and jiggled along the wall, closing the distance too rapidly for her to retreat.

She was caught.

47

June 15, Just Before Dawn–The Bear's Den

The patrol's lights bumped along the desert and headed directly at Cat.

Her chest tightened. She struggled to quell the raging adrenaline and ease the tension tightening her muscles. Without control she was vulnerable.

The Hummer's lights arced across the barn wall. In another few feet, they would be on her.

She crawled backward to the corner of the barn and wedged herself into the darkness against the wall. She'd have a split second to judge the light's path before being forced to run or fight. If the Hummer drove west to east, she was safe. If it turned and approached her corner of the barn, the lights would pass over her. The sentries would find her.

Ten more feet. The lights drifted away.

No. The Hummer turned. The patrol made a quick arc and swung back toward her corner of the barn. Its lights grew larger.

She quietly reached for the M16.

As the beams reached her, the vehicle stopped. The lights went dark. A door opened.

The sentries were talking inside. One laughed and said

something. The other grunted something. The door closed.

Footsteps.

She lay still, tucked against the barn wall on the desert floor, hoping for invisibility. Praying she had it.

The sentry stopped at the corner. He stood just feet way—perhaps mere inches. He sighed, shifting his weight from side-to-side.

She gripped her rifle, readying to roll sideways and snap into a prone shooting position—a combat exercise she'd rehearsed thousands of times. If necessary, she'd take the sentries one by one. First the man standing nearby; then the one inside the Hummer. From the moment she squeezed the first shot, she'd have seconds to disarm them, take the vehicle, and escape.

No, that wasn't an option. That would mean abandoning Mateo.

Her mission was in peril.

Failure.

Reynaldo whispered, *Cat, do this silently. As I taught you.*

She released the rifle and silently drew the hunting knife.

The sentry grunted and leaned back from the barn wall; his silhouette wavered like a bear posturing for a kill.

She braced herself, ready to spring. The knife in hand. Trying hard to steady her breathing…find her control.

A sprinkle of urine splashed off the barn wall just inches from her. The man groaned and continued relieving himself, wavering side-to-side, and each time he did, she caught a passing glimpse of him around the corner.

Gracias a Dios.

She waited for him to straighten and return to the Hummer.

When he climbed in, he did not shut the door. Instead, he lit a cigarette and blew smoke out of the open door.

Five minutes passed.

Ten.

Would they stay parked there for the remainder of their patrol?

Breathe, Catalina. Patience.

She considered crawling backward along the barn to the southern corner, but that was risky. The path would carry her into the view of the main compound and make her vulnerable from three sides. At any point, one of the sentries might discover her.

She waited.

Five more minutes passed before the Hummer's engine started. Then, the lights turned on as the patrol made a slow U-turn and headed out into the desert.

She waited a few more minutes; listening to the radio for activity, she heard none. Then, she crawled to the rear of the barn and stood. Satisfied the patrol was gone, she moved slowly along the wall to the window she'd accessed the day before.

Taking care not to slip or bump the sill—the slightest noise could bring trouble—she slid open the window and climbed inside behind the familiar wall of boxes. Once there, she crept to the end of the pallets where the laboratory lay. She used the sounds of the ventilation fans resonating to cover her movements to a point where she could view the lab.

As she cleared the last pallet, voices fluttered from the opposite end of the lab. The words were low and indistinguishable, partially obscured by the ventilation rattle. They were nervous and angry. When she dared peek around the corner pallet, she understood.

Several workers stood halfway to the end of the barn around the metal tables stacked with chemical containers, glass paraphernalia, and bags of heroin. They were poorly dressed and wore protective goggles and surgical masks. Two women without masks stood away from the group, and Cat recognized them from the coyote's bus. They had joined the busload of those trying to cross the border the same afternoon as she had. They had ridden together into the desert on the bus three seats in front of her.

They were now drug slaves.

A guard stood against the wall with his back to Cat, sipping a bottle of beer. He half-watched the workers and half-watched what had their attention. His rifle leaned against a stack of chemical containers and the pistol on his belt hung low on his hip like an old Western movie villain. The workers were staring into the small office only a few yards away.

The office windows faced the lab, and inside, a large, powerful man stood with his back to them. There was someone else inside, too.

Lucía—the scared teenager from the bus.

One of the workers choked back a cry when the big man reared back and struck her across the face, sending her plummeting backward. More cries when he lunged forward, grabbed her and tore her shirt, leaving her cowering and crying. When Lucía cried out, the man struck her again and pushed her down. As he did, he realized the workers were watching, went to the windows, and dropped the shades to cover his depravity.

Enough.

Cat strode from her hiding place beside the pallets, raising her rifle as she closed on the lab. She made it six steps when the nearby guard saw her and grabbed for his rifle.

A man from the group—dressed in dirty slacks and a bloodied dark shirt—lunged out and tackled him, ripped the rifle from him, spun it around, and smashed it into his midsection. As the guard faltered, the man bashed his face with the rifle, and followed him to the ground with a third strike into his windpipe.

The guard was done.

Cat continued to the office.

Inside, the big man was atop Lucía now—slapping her each time she wailed in terror—trying to control her arms to begin his assault. When the door opened behind him, he didn't stall but turned his head and barked over his shoulder.

"*Lárgate.*"—*Get out.*

Cat dropped her rifle onto a rickety desk, pulled the hunting knife from her belt, and descended on him.

It was over in seconds.

The man rolled from the teen, grasping his throat. Blood spewed between his fingers, and he fell onto his back, staring up at her. His lips parted but no sound took flight—just the gurgle of blood and surprise.

"Get up, Lucía." Strength was important now. "You are all right. He did not take you. You must be strong."

Lucía whimpered, but Cat grabbed her arm and tugged her to her feet. "You are alive. There is no time for grief."

She had saved her from the horror by mere seconds. She offered a quick, strong embrace to steady the teen before guiding her through the door and into the lab.

As soon as they emerged from the office, they stopped.

The workers all lay on the floor. A man dressed in tattered black clothes stood behind them, facing her. His hands were chained in front of him. His head was down—a mat of bloodied hair and filth covered his dark skin' his body was withered and hopeless.

Four gunmen stood behind him. Their guns were leveled at Cat. Their eyes were hard and fixed, revealing what was about to be her fate—all their fates.

She gripped Lucía's shoulder. "Turn away, Lucía. Close your eyes."

48

June 15, Just Before Dawn–The Bear's Den

The four gunmen spread out across the room. One moved beside the black-clothed man and waved another guard into the office behind Cat. "You cannot escape us."

"Kill her." The guard emerged from the office and grabbed Cat's hair, pulled her backward, and knocked her rifle to the floor. "She killed Antonio in the office."

"Antonio is dead?" The first guard turned, grabbed the black-clothed man by the hair and jerked his face upward. "You know what this means, Padre? Do you?"

Father Martínez's bruised and bloodied face looked sorrowfully at her.

"Father Martínez?" She tried to go to him, but the gunman behind her pulled her back against him. "Let him go. Let them all go. It is me you want."

"We already have you." The first guard spit on the floor. "We have all of you."

You must fight now, Cat—Reynaldo's voice was all around her—*strong and confident—It is time. Fight as I taught you to fight.*

Cat abruptly stepped backward and snapped her head back, crashing it into the guard's face behind her. Then, she spun around and grabbed his pistol, twisted it free, and shot him in the belly.

The first guard, surprised and unprepared, swung his rifle up awkwardly, but Father Martínez leaped onto his back and wrapped the chain binding his wrists around the man's throat. He thrust his knee into the guard's back and wrenched the chain violently backward, snapping his neck in a dull crack. He followed the man to the ground and tugged a pistol from his belt.

The other two guards were reacting, but far too slowly.

Cat shoved Lucía to the ground, scooped up her rifle off the floor, and shot a guard charging toward Father Martínez.

The last guard grabbed one of the young boys in the crowd of workers and dragged him to his feet as a shield. Then, he backed toward the barn door. As he did, Father Martínez raised his rifle, juggled it in his chained hands, and aimed. As the guard raised his weapon, Father Martínez shot him neatly in the head. He released the boy and fell dead.

Cat and Father Martínez turned in circles, searching for more targets. They found none.

It was over.

Cat gazed down at the dead man at her feet. For a second, she shook—from adrenalin, not fear—until she commanded her nerves to settle and regained control. She had not felt this level of adrenaline and intensity of battle for fifteen years. Her life as an up-and-coming Cuban operative seemed like another lifetime, another person. Her skills remained, but her heart had warmed by Mateo—a child that made her a mother and drove away the cold and emptiness. Now, some of that callousness had returned, just in time to save her life.

Lucía threw herself into Cat's arms. "They, they…"

"You are fine, young one. They didn't succeed with you." She brushed a lock of hair from Lucía's eyes. "You and the others must run from here."

"Yes, but what of you?"

"My business is not over." Cat waved to Father Martínez and gestured to the teen. "Father, please."

"Si, of course." He came to Lucía and clutched her to him, comforting her in whispers. He called for someone to give her a jacket and herded the others around him. He spoke rapidly but sternly, offering prayer and issuing orders at the same time. He was taking command. Forming his resistance. Mounting an attack.

Cat looked to the teen. "Lucía, you will go with these people when they escape. I will find you again, soon. I promise. Be brave and trust me."

"I'll be all right."

As Lucía rejoined the others, Cat gathered the dead gunmen's weapons and carried them to Father Martínez.

"Father, I believed you were dead. I thought Ñico...?"

"He killed Father Christopher and took many of my people. I demanded to be taken, too, to look after them. He saw more value in my imprisonment than my death."

"You must get the others to safety. I must find my son, Mateo. He may be here in the compound. Oso might have him as a hostage."

"If Oso has your son, he is not here, child. Perhaps the hacienda—but that is suicide."

Cat lifted her chin. "He is my son."

Father Martínez nodded and moved to the group of workers huddled together. There, the man dressed in dirty jeans and a bloodied pullover knelt to treat a worker suffering on the floor from a bad beating he'd received from one of the guards.

"Father, it is too late for this one," the man said. "Please."

"Of course, Doctor Montilla." Father Martínez knelt beside him and whispered his last rites. When he was through, he stood and guided the doctor to his feet. "Doctor, treat those in desperate need. Then, lead them away out back. I must stay for a short while and get everyone out. I will cover you as you escape."

"Montilla?" Cat stared at the doctor, unable to recognize him through the grime and filth covering him. "Doctor?"

The doctor turned and faced her. A smile cut through the camouflage of grit and dirt. "Catalina?"

"I have been looking for you."

"Catalina, you are safe, thank God. How did you find me here of all places?"

"Oso's men captured me and brought me here." She told him a short vignette of her recent travels. "I received your messages along my journey. You saved my life many times over."

"Thank God." Doctor Montilla repeated, embracing her tightly. "I feared you would be found and returned to Havana. I had to keep moving to ensure your safe houses were ready. I, too, am a wanted man. More so than I thought. Since your departure from Cuba, your people have been hunting me. I had to move quickly ahead of you or be taken. I am so sorry I was not there for you."

"Sorry? No. I would not have made it this far if not for your assistance. But there is no time. Ñico has brought Mateo here. I have to find him."

"The boy is here? In this place? Madre de Dios." Doctor Montilla's face went grim. "Catalina, Ñico Guerro cannot leave this place. He is an animal—a beast. Get Mateo and run, but Ñico cannot follow. Do you understand?"

She did.

She turned to Father Martínez who was blessing a wounded man. "Father, there is no time for religion. It's time to fight."

"Yes, it is." He waved his hand toward the workers. "It is time I stepped away from the cloth and defended those who cannot defend themselves. I pray God will forgive me."

"He surely will, Father." She kissed his cheek. "Get these people to your sanctuary. I will come for you. I will find a way."

"Do not worry about us, child. Go. Find your son and run."

"I'll find a way." She looked at Doctor Montilla again. "Stay with them, Doctor. Please."

"I will. Catalina, remember what I said." Doctor Montilla waved and returned to the wounded. "Ñico Guerro cannot leave this place."

49

June 15, Just Before Dawn–The Tsolias Café, Falls Church, Virginia

Trane sipped his coffee and contemplated the plate of eggs and sausage in front of him. For months, he'd ventured to this all-night eatery every week to establish himself as a regular. A casual, routine appearance would draw less attention than a change in habit should someone be surveilling him.

Even at home, caution and tradecraft were important.

Tsolias was one of his favorites in the DC Metro area. On the outside, it looked like a Jersey diner—a robust, highly-polished chrome exterior trimmed in neon lights and boasting the best food in town. Inside, the restaurant was layered with tall-backed booths sporting leather bench seats in the 1950s style. The long lunch counter was guarded by red vinyl swivel stools right out of a Norman Rockwell painting. In contrast to its 1950s Americana, its walls were covered in paintings and photographs from Athens—Greece, not New York—with a prominent photo of the famed traditional Tsolias soldier guarding the Greek Tomb of the Unknown Soldier. The picture depicted the soldier on his ceremonial march—one straight-leg extended forward, rifle shouldered, wearing his kilt-like tunic—referred to as the *chiton*—and red fez.

Trane had operated in Greece many times. He'd visited the Tsolias guards and often used the tourist crowds nearby as cover for a brief meeting or to pass information to another operative.

Such was the purpose of this visit.

In the time it took him to spread cream cheese on his bagel, a tall, wiry man wearing an ancient bomber jacket entered the eatery and slid across from him into the booth.

Trane held up a finger and waved for more coffee from the counter waitress reading a paperback thriller—*The Consultant*—and hoping for more tips than she had a right to receive. When she responded with a clean cup and a fresh pot of coffee, he waited for her to return to her grueling workload.

"This better be good, Rodin." He put his bagel down. "I had to drive all the way from the Caverns to get here."

"You'll thank me. I got five biggies for you." Rodin gulped his coffee, picked up half of Trane's bagel, and grinned at the enormous glob of cream cheese. "I haven't eaten."

"What do you have?"

Rodin chewed, gulped coffee, and pulled several folded papers from his breast pocket. "You're gonna love this, Trane."

"Eat, drink, or talk." Trane took the papers from him. "Not all at once."

"First, the vice president's intern, that Finley guy? A Chesapeake sheriff found a body in the bay a few hours ago. It's him, but they're keeping it under wraps. Thank me later."

"That's one."

Rodin held up two fingers. "Operation Perro is suddenly a very popular hit on the dark web."

Trane began reading the papers.

"Perro was a G2 operation in 2004-2005. Deep stuff, too. Nothing in our current files about it. I had to hack some old NSA intercepts from the Venezuelan mission."

"I expected that."

"G2 targeted several of our diplomats begging Chávez to stop rocking the boat down there and for oil deals. Back before he died, Chávez was messing with the Latin economy, and that was spilling over into ours. He was pretty formidable before Venezuela went totally in the shitter."

"Right. Great. I knew that, too."

Rodin fixed his eyes on Trane's plate as he pointed to something on the page in Trane's hand. "Hemingway's a big surprise."

Trane read the passages—twice. "Hemingway?"

"That's three." He sprinted through a few details on Hemingway, finally coming up for air with, "You going to eat that sausage?"

"Give me the highlights." Trane slid his breakfast plate across the table. "I'll read the details later."

"Thanks." Rodin jutted his fork toward the folded papers. "Two days ago, a dark web site popped with Perro again. Some super-secret message board the Cubans are using to communicate with their people. I was able to pull some threads from that."

Trane sat…waiting.

"Sorry, right." He wiped his mouth, chugged some coffee, and tapped the papers. "I snooped around some more—other places, like, um…Cuban intel signals computers; I backtracked the dark web posts to them."

"You better not have left a footprint."

"Me? No worries there."

"Good, get to Catalina Reyes."

"The Cubans are going batshit crazy trying to retrieve Hemingway. And some has-been operative, Ñico Guerro, is on your gal Reyes' trail, too. Funny thing is, Guerro is Reyes' second husband."

Trane nodded, thinking. "Okay, they're keeping it in the family."

"Not just them, but Montilla, too. Doctor Manuel Montilla and his wife, Irena, were primarily based in Colombia at the FARC camps. But they moved around Central and South America, too. Their favorite spot, outside Colombia, was Caracas. They liked Havana, too. That's number four."

"Did you confirm they're both G2 operatives?"

Rodin shrugged. "Working on it."

"Good work, Rodin." He waved for his check and pointed to Rodin's face. "Try a napkin. Maybe a sponge. How about number five?"

"Last couple pages." Rodin held up five fingers. "Those other names—Herrera and Espino—are Consuelo Herrera and Nina Espino. It's weird, brother. They don't fit the rest of this at all. I found the names in archive newspapers—Caracas newspapers."

Trane flipped to the last two pages of Rodin's package and scanned the report. Then he reread it, slowly. He pointed to a line in the report.

"Is this correct? Verified?" He tapped the passage several times. "You can prove this?"

Rodin nodded. "Of course. It's all there in the details, brother. I've got flight records, hotel receipts, cell phone bills…*everything*. All the evidence you need. *De facto*."

"Excellent." Trane leaned back. "I wish all my ops were this easy."

"Easy? This wasn't easy." Rodin tapped his forehead. "Oh, one more tidbit. A freebie, too."

Trane stared. "If I have to ask, I'll be pissed."

"Oh yeah, right." Rodin lowered his voice. "Early on, when we were hunting that Raul dude…."

"Raul Anibal Vacarro."

"That's him. I dug way, way deep into Operation Perro. His name popped in the fine print. Deep G2 intel stuff, too."

Trane's interest peaked. "Define 'popped'?"

"Vacarro was Colonel Luis Vergara's code name when he was just a pup G2 operator back in the day. But he only used it for Operation Perro. No trace of it anywhere else. It's in the file. There are details about who he was in touch with down there and everything else I found."

Trane let it sink in, and as it did, the entire affair became clear. What he saw now worried him to the bone. "Good stuff, Rodin. Real good. When this is over, I'll tip you."

"Not like McLaren tips, I hope." Rodin lowered his voice. "He'll have you 'tipping' everyone involved over this—you know, his wet work."

"We don't really use that term, Rodin. We just say 'kill.'"

"Okay, right. Kill. Is Karras, the cop, or anyone else on the 'kill' list yet?"

Trane looked away. "Be happy it isn't you making McLaren

nervous…yet."

"Yet?"

Trane just looked at him.

"I'll take 'yet.' Hey, I had to lay out some cash on this one; that'll be billed later. With interest. Lots of interest."

Trane cocked his head. "Do you have that other thing lined up yet?"

"You bet I do. Just say when."

"Good. Stand by on that."

Rodin slid the empty plate back across the table. "You promised to get the Feds off my ass, remember?"

"When I'm done with you." Trane pocketed the folded papers, dropped some cash on the table, and stood. "Not until."

"What am I supposed to do until then?"

"Stop hacking the Federal Reserve."

50

June 15, Very Early Morning–The Bear's Den

"Where do you think Hemingway will be?" Brennan slipped through the darkness behind Ana. "There must be a couple dozen buildings here. We can't search them all."

"We shouldn't have to." Ana found a dark recess behind a tall stack of firewood near the rear of a long, single-story building. She tapped on the screen of the cell phone Dallas gave her to replace the one taken by Irena's people. She concealed its glow inside her jacket. "Dallas's GPS tracking signal says the SUV is just on the other side of the hacienda."

Brennan crawled to the end of the woodpile and peered out, instantly backing away and patting the air for Ana to get lower.

"A guard," he whispered. "Coming our way."

"I'll take him. Cover me."

"You?" Brennan half-turned toward her but she'd already slipped by. "Wait...don't."

The guard—a tall, lanky Latino armed with an M16 rifle—lazily walked toward the woodpile on the opposite side. He had his rifle in one hand and a cigarette in the other. Like any sentry posted alone in the early morning hours, he seemed weary and disinterested in his duties. As he reached the woodpile, he leaned against it, rested his M16 on the ground beside him, and lit another cigarette from the stubby one in his mouth.

Ana Montilla stepped into the open and struck.

She moved with lightning speed and precision, whirling around the end of the woodpile and crashing the butt of her M4 rifle—another gift from Dallas—into the guard's jaw.

A dull crack broke the silence and he dropped to the ground, unconscious.

While Brennan dragged the guard behind the wood and concealed him beneath a heap of logs, Ana quickly broke his M16 down and tossed the charging handle and bolt carrier group out into the desert grass. Then, she searched him, found four thirty-round magazines of 5.56 ammunition, plus the one from his rifle, and slipped them into her jacket pockets.

She knew the American M4 carbine was the close quarter battle version of the original M16. Its receivers are identical, as are their magazines and ammunition. Dallas had only four magazines for Ana out of his stash on his Beechcraft; "emergency toys," he'd called them. With the extra ammunition from the guard, she had two-hundred seventy rounds of firepower. Given the security at the compound and the nature of Mexican cartels, she would need every round.

"I found a radio and headset." Brennan slipped the earpiece into his ear. "I'll keep track on it. Oh, and remind me to never get you mad at me."

Ana grinned. "Ana Karras likes you, Luke from *Star Wars*."

"How about Ana Montilla?"

She shrugged. "We'll see."

"We'll see?" Brennan followed a few feet behind her as she maneuvered through the dark toward the hacienda set a hundred feet away.

As they reached the corner of the house, movement behind spun them around.

Ana lifted her M4 before Brennan could react.

It didn't matter. It was too late.

Two gunmen stepped around the corner of the hacienda and leveled rifles down on them. A third man, dressed in a tan police uniform, stepped forward and motioned for his men to flank them.

Ana lowered her weapon and let it slide to the ground. Brennan followed suit.

The policeman was tall and lanky with dark, gruff features. The thing about him Ana noticed, even in the darkness, was that his nose was flat and too big for his face.

"I am Capitán Cortez of La Policía Federal." The policeman had a touch of mirth in his voice. "You are my guests. Ah, you must be señorita Ana Montilla and your, what do you American's call it—sidekick? Si, your sidekick, ex-policeman Brennan." He laughed at his own joke.

Brennan raised his hands. "Sidekick?"

From behind, someone cracked Brennan's head with the butt of a rifle and dropped him to the ground.

"Leave him alone," Ana snapped, kneeling beside him.

"Yes, leave the poor policeman alone," a voice said from behind Cortez. "They are outnumbered and outgunned. There is no need for violence now."

Irena Montilla appeared beside Cortez.

"Mamá?" Ana should have expected it. That fact sickened her. "First Cuban Intelligence and now a cartel?"

"Oh, no, Ana dear." Irena gestured for Cortez's men to help Brennan up. "I am here for the same thing you are: Catalina Reyes. She is called Hemingway. She is a guest of Oso, as am I."

51

June 15, Dawn–The Bear's Den

The guards had no sooner shoved Ana and Brennan into the hacienda's great room when a symphony of gunfire and explosives rocked the compound outside. The French door windows rattled and a desert skyline painting fell from the wall beside them.

"What is going on outside?" Captain Cortez shouted at his men. "Sergeant, go find out."

The sergeant, a short, plump, bald man, disappeared without a word.

After their capture, Ana and Brennan had been searched; their weapons, ammunition, and other equipment was now stacked up on an expensive mahogany card table near the French doors. Now, they stood in the hacienda's great room surrounded by Cortez and four gunmen.

Irena Montilla had disappeared deeper into the house when the first chorus of gunfire erupted outside.

Cortez faced Ana. "Now, what of you, señorita? I have heard so much about you. How is it you escaped so easily from town? We have not heard you were missing."

Brennan forced a laugh. "Your men weren't very good."

A guard beside him punched him hard in the stomach and

doubled him over. "*Silencio.*"

"Stop this," Ana pleaded. "It is me you want."

Irena reappeared in the foyer doorway, walking in beside a large bull of a man wearing a night robe that hung to his ankles.

"Captain Cortez, there is trouble in the compound," Irena said casually. "Perhaps you and your men can aid our host, Oso, in ending it. Leave two men behind with me."

Cortez waved dismissively. "I have already sent my sergeant."

Irena raised her eyebrows. "Captain?"

"Si, si, of course. I will go myself." With that, Cortez and two of his men left through the foyer.

The large man in the night robe walked to Ana and looked her up and down in a slow, deliberate assault. "I am Oso, the Bear. This is my den. You are the Americans I have heard so much about?"

"We are." Brennan pulled Ana close to him. "I'm—"

"I was not speaking to you, policeman." Oso stepped closer to Ana. "Your CIA friends are not coming from Monterrey. I have many Federales friends. Those in Monterrey have arrested your men there. So, as you can see, you are all alone."

The question of trusting Trane's team was now irrelevant.

Ana said, "What do you want of us? I came—"

"Be silent, Ana," Irena said coldly. "We don't want you. Now that we have Mateo and his mother, that is all Havana wishes. Soon, Oso will be paid, and I will return them home. You don't matter any longer."

Ana's eyes burned through her. Her mother and she had never had a mother-daughter bond. It had always been master and servant, teacher and pupil—commander and soldier. Despite Ana's constant attempts to earn her love, her only affection came from her pappa. Now, after having been captured and preyed on by her, that dull coolness between them turned to fire and anger in her gut. Perhaps even hate.

"So, Mamá, you are one of them?"

Irena shrugged. "Havana sent me to find your pappa. I was to make him bring me Catalina Reyes; he was aiding her. Did you know that? Afterward, I learned her husband stole their son, Mateo, from Havana and brought him here, hoping to lure Catalina out directly. I have them all now."

"You have Pappa?"

Oso lifted a hand. "Yes, we do, girl. But he is of no consequence any longer."

"The boy is of consequence," Irena said. "As is his mother. We have them both."

"Are you sure?" Brennan asked, regaining his wind from the beating. "If you're sure, then okay."

Oso eyed him for a long time. Then, he stepped forward and whispered something to one of the guards who ran from the room just as gunfire once again erupted out in the compound.

Ana said, "It seems, Mamá, the trouble in this place is getting worse. Perhaps the Federales—"

"The shooting? No." Oso laughed. "It is just a little skirmish. That is all. My men will squash it very soon. And the Federales are mine. If they came here for anything, it would be to kill those who struggle against me now."

"A struggle?" Brennan said. "Sounds like a revolution."

"No, Detective Brennan, it is not."

"You know my name?" Brennan's face flashed surprise. "All the way down here?"

Oso jutted a finger at him. "Yes, I do. But it was not from your reputation. It is from your previous misdeeds."

"My misdeeds?" Brennan shot a glance at Ana. "I think you mean her misdeeds. Right? She's the guerrilla fighter. Ask Captain Cortez; I'm just a sidekick."

Another punch to the stomach sent Brennan to his knees again.

Irena gazed indifferently at Brennan, turned, and confronted Ana again. "You are CIA now? That is a far cry from our FARC comrades."

Ana said nothing but wished she hadn't fallen for her mother's theatrical performance back at the warehouse. Now, she knew everything. Guilt stabbed her. Why hadn't she seen that coming? That ploy—a wolf in sheep's clothing—was a play she'd used on Ted and Cindy and dozens of others herself. She'd played on their fear, their hopes, even their love between one another. Mamá had played her the same way and defeated her the same way.

Deception was a tool of the cunning and a poison to its victims. Shame embraced her, and for a moment, she felt sick.

"Come now, Ana. Surely you cannot believe the Americans."

"We have a deal," she said. "I came for Pappa and you, Mamá. I came to bring you home."

"Home? Ah, yes, your deal." Irena laughed sarcastically. "The Americans offer you a deal to retrieve Catalina Reyes."

"The Americans? You're an American, Mamá. At least, you were."

"I gave up my branding many years ago, Ana. Of anyone, you should know this."

Ana dropped her eyes. "I had hope."

"Hope? Foolish girl. That was always your problem. Hope is for the weak. Strategy is for the strong. Power is for the winner."

"Mamá, please. Let Pappa and I return home. It is not too late. Trane said—"

"This man Trane?" Irena turned to Oso. "The CIA man who controls my former daughter. Shall I tell her?"

Oso shrugged. "Of course. She should know how badly she was played."

Irena took hold of Ana's chin and lifted it. "You know the Americans will kill you—kill us all—the moment they get what they want."

Ana pulled her chin free.

"If you had succeeded in capturing Reyes, we would all die, Ana. Don't you see it?"

"Hey, lady." Brennan got to his feet again and moved close to Ana. "Trane's a prick, sure. He'll kill me in a heartbeat. But he wouldn't hurt Ana. He has a thing for her. A big thing."

"A thing?" Ana looked sideways at Brennan before addressing Irena again. "Trane saved me in Cabrera, from *your* people who tried to kill me. Why would he save me then, just to kill me later?"

Irena laughed. "Because he needed you to complete his mission first. You're a simple girl, aren't you? You always let your heart get in the way of your mission. Always. Do you think the Americans would give you a medal? Money? Anything? You are FARC. A terrorist to them. A traitor. Of course, you are a traitor to us, too.

You are alone, Ana. Alone."

She said nothing. A crack—a thin, tiny sliver of doubt—crept into her and chilled her to the bone. Could she be right? Would Trane and McLaren betray her? Mamá was many things, but a fool was not one of them. Was she right?

"How does it feel to have no one, Ana? To be completely alone?" Irena slapped her hard across the face. "You come here working for the CIA. You make a deal for me and your father. All they will do is take what they want and kill us. You would bring us to them?"

Words stung her as much as her mother's assault. Could she be right? Had Trane sent her here with a promise that was a lie? Embrace her and her family only to lure them all to an execution?

The sliver of doubt swelled into a crevasse.

Mamá was right and that burned a path along her scars. Why had she trusted Trane? That he'd dangled the right temptation before her and waited for her to reach for it? Was she again learning one of Mamá's lessons that she'd forgotten so long ago?

Anger seared her cheeks. "If you are so sure of yourself, Mamá, let us go. We'll leave here together and return to the jungles."

"What?" Irena stepped back and contemplated her. "If only I could trust you, mi hija. Perhaps you and your father would live."

"Then just let Pappa come with me, Mamá. Please. It's of no consequence to you now. You have Hemingway. Let us go."

"No. Oso has your pappa well employed. Isn't it ironic how all of us have come together here? Perhaps it's fate or perhaps—"

"Oso, she is gone." The guard Oso had sent away earlier burst into the room. "Señora Reyes is not in her room."

"What? How could she escape?" Oso's face was on fire. "Get more men. Search everywhere."

Outside, the compound erupted with several more explosions and the sound of rampant gunfire.

"Bitch," Oso screamed at the ceiling. "This is you, Catalina Reyes. What have you done now?"

52

June 15, Dawn–The Bear's Den

A taut, wiry Cuban stormed into the room and went immediately to Irena, thrusting an angry finger toward Ana. "Is this her? Is this Ana Montilla?"

"Yes, Ñico. What's wrong now?" Irena asked. "Oso and I have a deal. It does not concern you."

Ñico pushed past Irena and grabbed Ana by her shirt, lifted her into the air, and slammed her backward onto the mahogany card table near the French doors. The weapons and magazines stacked there tumbled to the ground as he followed her down and pinned her to the table.

"Where is Mateo?" Ñico demanded. "Where?"

"Whoa, now." Brennan grabbed him by the arm, spun him around, and landed a powerful right hook into his face, downing him instantly. "Back off, jackass."

Two guards instantly responded, pulled Brennan away, and forced him face down onto the floor.

To Ñico, Oso said, "What is it you say? You have lost the boy, too?"

"Too?" Ñico was on his feet and delivered two sharp kicks into Brennan's side. Then he returned to Ana at the table and grasped her throat. "Where is Mateo? Tell me or I'll snap your neck like a twig."

Ana managed to pry his fingers loose, roll off the table, and backpedal away. "Nowhere you'll ever find him."

"Stop this." Oso grabbed Ñico's arm, yanked him away, and pushed him backward into the arms of one of his guards. When he turned on Ana, his face was red and angry, like a bull ready to charge. "Think carefully, Ana Montilla. Your mamá has disowned you. Your pappa is in my grasp. You are here, in my house, surrounded by *my* men. Think."

"Mateo is already in Laredo," Brennan blurted. "There's nothing you can do."

Yes, Laredo. Ana said, "That's right, Oso. Mateo Reyes was flown to Laredo a few hours ago. He's in CIA custody now. Whatever you wanted from him is theirs. Give us Catalina Reyes and let us go; for that, we will pay a large bounty."

"A bounty? You sell my wife and her son back to me?" Ñico pulled away from the guards and charged at her again, but Oso stepped in the way and knocked him back. "I will kill you slowly, Ana Montilla."

"No, you will not." Oso aimed a finger at Ñico. "If there is a bounty, it is mine, not yours, Ñico. Now shut up and mind your manners."

"What is your price?" Ana asked coolly. "I am authorized to negotiate."

Brennan stood, stunned. "Huh?"

Oso looked from Ñico to Ana. "Ten million dollars."

"Five," Ana said. "I am authorized to pay five million. No more."

"Ten." Oso sized her up. "You are a brave chica, Ana Montilla. What your mother has told me does you no justice. You bargain like a car salesman in my own house. I have men and guns and still you negotiate?"

Ana glanced at her mother. "My mamá doesn't know the real Ana Montilla, Oso. Neither does the CIA. I will contact them. I will tell them, hmm…I will say fifteen million."

"Ana, that's not negotiating," Brennan whispered to her. "You're going in the wrong direction."

"Trust me." She stepped away from him. "They will refuse; they will offer ten or perhaps even twelve. I will pay you three-quarters of that. You will give me the rest. Brennan, my father, Reyes and her boy, and I will take the extra money and disappear. No one—not Havana or the CIA—will ever find us."

Oso's eyes brightened as he threw his head back and laughed raucously. "Why, you *la puta*. You are a devious one, no? But I like how you play."

"Are you insane, Oso?" Ñico raged, jumping forward to face him nose-to-nose. "If you do this—if you do not return Catalina and Mateo to me to go to Havana—then Cuba will send more men and destroy you."

"Oh?" Oso jammed a deadly finger into his chest. "Then they better offer me more. No? Say, all fifteen million."

Ñico's face flushed. "You said four before? Four million American. Now you demand fifteen?"

Irena had been standing aside watching Ñico and Oso argue. Finally, she raised her voice. "Oso, I will contact Havana. I'm sure we will provide you a number that is good for everyone."

Oso considered that. "You have one hour, Irena. After that, I will take your daughter's proposal."

As Irena swiftly left the room, Oso looked at Ana. "Make yourself comfortable, Ana Montilla. We are all safe in my home. My men are quelling the disturbance outside and soon Catalina Reyes will be back in my grasp. In one hour, you will either be dead, or you will be rich."

Ñico grabbed Oso by the arm. "Listen to me, Oso. This is insanity to deal with the Americans."

As Oso lifted a hand to silence him, the world turned upside down.

53

June 15, Dawn–The Bear's Den

The world was indeed upside down. Of that, Ana was sure.

A pretty, Cuban Latina charged through the French doors firing an M16 rifle; the shots were barely over everyone's heads. Once inside, she aimed the rifle at Oso. "I will kill you if anyone moves."

"No," Ñico bellowed. "You will not, Catalina."

Catalina Reyes—Hemingway—had made her entrance. "Shut up, Ñico, I am through taking your orders."

Blood red anger spread across Ñico's face.

Ana turned slowly to Brennan and held a hand close to her body, patting the air. *Don't move. Let this play out.*

Brennan's face went blank with confusion as he nodded.

"Ah, pretty Catalina." Oso held his hands up at his chest. "Put the gun down. We are negotiating for your release. Surely that is better than to die by my guards."

One of Oso's men ran into the room with his rifle out, but Cat twisted, fired, and turned the gun back on Oso. The guard dropped where he stood, a blossom of red spreading across his chest.

"Send your men out, Oso," Cat ordered. "Do it now."

"Of course." Oso waved and the guards filed from the room. "It is done. Drop your weapon."

"I want Mateo," Catalina said in a calm, steady voice. "Bring me my son."

"Catalina?" Ana stepped forward with both hands raised chest high. "I am Ana Montilla. We have Mateo and he is safe."

"Montilla?" Confusion twisted Cat's face. "You have my Mateo? I don't understand."

"My father is—"

"Montilla? El doctor?" Cat asked in a cautious voice. "Doctor Manuel Montilla?"

Ana nodded. "I came to find him."

"He is here. I left him in the barn not long ago with Father Martínez. They fight their way out of this place and then will take all those imprisoned here and go."

"Let me go to my pappa, please."

"Us, Ana," Brennan said. "Let *us* go to him. And you come too, lady." He gestured to Cat. "We can all get the hell out of here together."

Ñico pushed Oso's guard away from him and walked up to Cat, stopping an arm's length away. "The CIA sent them. They came to kill you, Catalina. They have Mateo as bait…"

"As you did." Cat tried to put on a tough face but Ñico's eyes and nearness chipped away at her edges. She could feel his intensity—his power—and see the confidence in his eyes. She prodded the rifle toward him but he didn't retreat. "Get back with Oso."

Ana said, "Catalina, Mateo is safe. I'll explain everything later. Let's get out of here. Now, before this madness goes any farther."

"You will go nowhere, Catalina," Ñico sneered. "Do you hear me? Nowhere."

Oso raised a hand. "Por favor, Catalina, put the gun down. We can all sit and discuss this. My men will stop the fighting soon, and—"

"Your men are dying, Oso," Cat said calmly. "Father Martinez and the others are fighting back. The barn is destroyed. Your drugs are burning. You are through. Done."

"What?" Oso's face went wild and he lunged for Cat. "No!"

Ñico spun around, pulled a Makarov pistol from beneath his shirt, and shot Oso in the forehead. He walked to him and stepped over his body like he would a sleeping dog. Then, he turned back around and aimed the pistol at Cat, watching as her strength melted before him.

"No more negotiations," Ñico said to Cat. "Now, bitch. Put your rifle down. Do not, and I'll kill you."

"You should not have come for me, Ñico." Cat lowered the rifle ever so slightly. "Stay away from me. Stay back."

Ñico moved closer to her again. With his first step, her rifle lowered more. With each next step, Cat's face paled. As the monster of her life closed in on her, her courage and conviction waned—slowly failing her, leaving her submissive and vulnerable. By the time he reached her, her face was ash and her eyes could not hold his. When he was a short step away, she took a hesitant step back and looked to the marble floor for refuge. The monster that had controlled her was seizing her again.

"Catalina, you will come with me now. I will make Ana Montilla and the policeman give Mateo to us. Do not fight me. You will lose, as always. You will be punished for this."

"No…no, Ñico." Her voice was a whisper. "No more. I beg you… please, let us go."

"Your short freedom is over. You will return to me what you took from Havana. All of it." He reached out, grabbed her face in one hand and lifted the pistol toward her with the other. "If I fail to bring you and Mateo home, I am a dead man. I will see you dead first."

Cat pulled her head free and turned it as though listening to someone beside her. "Yes, Reynaldo, I understand."

"Que? Reynaldo?" Ñico followed her gaze to nothing, lowering his pistol to his side. "Have you gone mad, Catalina? Reynaldo is long dead."

Cat nodded to no one beside her, turned, and leaned closer into Ñico. She smiled. "You will never hurt Mateo or me again. Ever."

"What is this?" Ñico's eyes dropped to his belly as Cat's hunting knife ripped upward and twisted into his heart. "No…"

Two of Oso's guards rushed into the room, ready to fire.

Brennan dove for the weapons that littered the floor around the card table, slid one to Ana, and opened fire with another. His first shots struck one of the guards in the chest. His second volley missed altogether.

Ana's didn't. She hit the second guard with a three-round burst, dove sideways to avoid his return fire and landed on one knee, drilling him with two more shots into his torso.

A third guard rushed in and his rounds chattered across the marble floor heading for Brennan.

They never made it.

Twisting back, Ana adjusted her fire and easily ended the guard's life just before his shots would have reached Brennan. The guard dropped and his weapon slid across the floor.

"Jesus, that was close," Brennan called. "Thank you."

"Bastard," Cat screamed and let loose a burst of automatic fire that shredded Ñico at her feet. "You bastard. No more."

Ana and Brennan exchanged glances, slowly raised their hands, and prayed she was out of bullets.

54

June 15, Morning–The Bear's Den

"Do not move." Cat swiveled the rifle between Ana and Brennan, watching them with big, dull eyes. "I have many bullets."

Ana and Brennan lowered their weapons at the same time.

Ana said, "Catalina. We're friends. We rescued Mateo from Ñico's men and he's safe."

Upon hearing the name, Cat's eyes cleared. "Where is my son?"

"Close by," Ana said calmly. "Please, hear me out."

Outside, gunfire and explosives continued to rock the compound. The combat was centered deeper inside the area at Oso's barn. Outside the hacienda, vehicles drove down into the compound and voices shouted orders and acceptance. More of Oso's men were joining the fight.

"Easy now, I'm just checking outside." Brennan backed to the French doors and peered out. "We can't stay here long, Ana. Whatever we're going to do, we need to get it done fast."

"Tell me where Mateo is," Cat demanded. "Tell me and you can go."

Ana nodded. "He was in Nuevo Laredo. We rescued him from Ñico and my mamá…"

"Your mamá had my son?" Cat's face showed even more

confusion. "She helped Ñico?"

"Yes." Ana's eyes fell to the floor. "She was working with your people in Havana."

Cat nodded knowingly. "Yes, and your pappa has been such a good friend to me. He helped me escape Havana and led me here. He would have helped me across the border, too, but Oso caught him first. He is a good man, Ana Montilla."

"Yes, he is." Ana's eyes softened. "My mother is a traitor to him and my country. Even to you. But don't worry, Mateo is safe. I promise."

Cat studied her. "What about you? Will you betray your pappa for what the CIA has sent you to do?"

The question stunned Ana. It first surprised her with its simplicity and sent a tingle of hot stabs along her belly scars. Why hadn't she considered that question before? If her father was involved with Hemingway, would he truly help her start a war between Cuba and America? He was never a true believer in FARC's war. He was a doctor and a sympathizer. A tentative collaborator at best. It was always Mamá who had fallen deep under FARC's control and had a hot fire of anger constantly waging in the jungle. So, the question—would she now betray Pappa—was a good one.

What would her answer be?

"I don't understand any of this," Ana finally said in a soft, slow voice. "You're headed to America to start a war. Why?"

"I go to America for justice, Ana Montilla. Your pappa understood that. That is why he was helping me."

Ana's brow furrowed. "But—"

"Tell me where Mateo is."

"No. Not until you explain. We came to find my parents."

"And me."

"Yes. And you."

"You came to kill me." Cat took a step toward her and shot a cautionary glance at Brennan who instantly stepped back and raised his hands. "Now, you have my son."

"It isn't like that, Catalina," Ana said solemnly. "We were kidnapped at the airport and taken to a place outside Nuevo Laredo. My mamá was there, working with Ñico and his men. When we escaped, we found Mateo with someone named Che."

Cat's eye lit up. "One of Ñico's pets."

"Che's dead. We rescued Mateo before we knew who he was. I swear to you."

"Where is he?"

Brennan said, "We have an airplane nearby. It can get us across the border to safety, your boy is with our pilot."

Cat turned the rifle on him. Her face hardened as she studied him, perhaps contemplating his honesty. Perhaps contemplating the trajectory of the bullet to kill him.

"Easy now, lady." Brennan held up both hands, palms out. "We're friends. We saved your kid. That's gotta count for something."

"Friends? You are Americans," Cat said. "I have no friends in America."

Something vibrated behind them on the floor for several seconds. It stopped. Then, it vibrated again.

As Ana and Cat turned toward the sound, they spotted a cell phone laying on the marble floor beneath the card table—the phone Dallas had given Ana the evening before.

"That's my pilot." Ana gestured to the phone. "If we're getting out of here alive, I have to speak with him."

Cat backed up to the table and bent down; keeping her rifle aimed between Ana and Brennan, she retrieved the phone and looked at the screen.

"What is your pilot's name?"

"Dallas," Brennan said.

"I am putting you on speaker." Cat tapped on the call. "Who is this?"

Silence.

Ana called out, "Dallas, it's Ana. Where are you?"

"Miss Ana?" His voice was tentative. "You all right? Who's that with you?"

Ana glanced up at Cat with a question on her face. When Cat nodded, Ana said, "Catalina Reyes. Is Mateo safe?"

"Reyes? You got Hemingway with you?"

"It's complicated." Brennan stepped closer to the phone. "Dallas, put Mateo on the phone. Fast."

Silence followed, then, "Mamá? Is that you? Are you there?" It was Mateo—vibrant and excited. "Where are you, Mamá? Have Ana and Luke saved you, too?"

"Luke?" Cat's face softened and she glanced at Brennan, who nodded. "Mateo, are you all right? Are you safe?"

"Yes, Mamá. Hurry, please. Dallas and I are waiting for you."

Cat tapped the speaker off and walked backward across the room, keeping her rifle raised and ready. She spoke quietly with Mateo for several minutes. With each moment, her face lightened and her rifle lowered a little more. Finally, she returned to Ana and Brennan and handed the phone to her.

"You have two minutes to speak with your pilot. Then, we are leaving."

"Yes, of course. Thank you." Ana snatched the phone and put it to her ear. "Dallas, I—"

She didn't get a word in. Dallas delivered a quick, staccato message. As he spoke, her stomach knotted and her thoughts tumbled and fell. She knew now why Catalina Reyes was headed to Washington. She knew why she was willing to start a war. And as she hung up the phone, Ana wondered if she would do the same if it was her and not Catalina, standing across the room just then.

"Dallas is twenty minutes by vehicle across the desert," Ana said. "He's sent his GPS coordinates. We can find him easily."

Cat stepped close to her. "Mateo says you saved him. You have been kind to him. He does not believe you knew who he was before that."

"We didn't, Catalina."

"If we go with you, what happens to us in America?" Cat asked tentatively. "You may do with me what you must. But Mateo…."

"I know why you're headed to Washington," Ana blurted. "I understand. I know about Reynaldo and how he died."

"Oh, you do? You think you know so much?" Cat said. Then, she glanced at Brennan, who shrugged and looked back to Ana. "Tell me what you know."

Dallas had delivered a quick briefing on Catalina Reyes and her exploits in Caracas fifteen years prior. Dallas relayed the message Trane had sent for her, and while she knew it was not the entire truth, it was some of it. It had to be enough.

"You and Reynaldo were working against American diplomats in Caracas in 2005. Things got out of hand and Reynaldo was killed. You blame the diplomats for his death, and you are headed to Washington for revenge."

"Is that it?" Cat asked. "You know nothing more?"

"Well, lady, that's more than I knew," Brennan said. He turned to Ana. "What the hell, Ana? When were you going to share?"

"Dallas just told me. You know what I know, Luke."

"Then we go." Cat motioned for Brennan and Ana to take up their weapons. "But know this, Ana Montilla: I trusted el doctor; I do not necessarily trust you. You do not know all of what happened in Caracas. Your pappa does. Soon, you will, too."

Pappa. "Catalina, we have to find my father. I came for him. I need him to return with us."

"Just Pappa?" Irena Montilla stood in the doorway with two of Oso's gunmen behind her. She held a pistol up, aimed steadily at Cat. "What about me, Ana dear?"

55

June 15, Morning–The Bear's Den

Ana stared at Irena and didn't recognize the woman behind the raging eyes. She had lost her mother years ago to the jungle camps, even though she'd never lost hope that one day, Irena Montilla would lose her hate and find her maternal connection. Looking at her now—standing with her pistol in the company of two cartel gunmen—she knew that day was a fantasy.

"Ana, you would leave without saying goodbye?" Irena walked into the great room. "I know Pappa was your favorite, but he was weak. I am the stronger one. If you had only stayed"

"I would have turned out just as you have," Ana snapped. "I left to be with Yiayia Poppi. She educated me. She made me see what I left behind was evil. It was you who kept Pappa there—away from me. Still, I came here to save you."

Irena laughed. "Save me? From what? I do not need saving. I am a fighter. I am a revolutionary. Havana has treated me very well over the years. They scoffed at Pappa. They knew he was weak and could not do their bidding. It was I who they chose to lead our camp. Me, Ana. Me."

"Yiayia Poppi blames Pappa for everything." Ana's heart fell and she wondered if she would live to tell the truth to her yiayia. "She warned me about returning for you."

"Warned you? Really?" Irena grabbed Ana by the chin and pulled her in close. "You are such a stupid girl, Ana. You take after your father. You deserve each other."

"I'm proud to be Pappa's daughter."

Cat and Brennan looked on. Brennan was trying to understand the debate between Ana and Irena. Cat was trying to find an opening for escape.

Irena ended both debates. She waved to the two guards behind her. "Take my daughter and lock her up somewhere. I will take this one." She aimed her pistol at Cat. "She will come with me. I must retrieve the boy and arrange transport to Havana."

The two guards walked into the room, keeping their rifles up and ready.

"Where is Pappa?" Ana asked. "I wish to see him now."

"Gone. Dead. I don't know. I don't care." Irena's voice was cold and indifferent. "Forget him. You'll be staying here for quite a while. Oso may be dead, but I'm sure someone will be taking over. Perhaps that pig Cortez. He's somewhere killing workers who dared to defy Oso."

Catalina had said she'd seen Pappa in the barn. Was he now gone or dead? She prayed it was the former. Though, with all the gunfire and explosions, reason said it might be the latter. She was no longer on a mission to find her parents and capture Hemingway. She was on a mission to simply survive—survive against the hand of her own mother.

"You will allow them to kill me, Mamá?"

Irena shrugged. "You are not my daughter. You are your father's child. I renounced you when you left us the last time."

"Damn, lady," Brennan said, "that's hard core. Maybe there's a middle ground. How about—"

Irena turned and shot him from her hip. "You are not in my plan."

"Luke!" Ana ran past Irena and knelt down beside him. He'd dropped against a large, leather sofa; half on, half off. Blood oozed from his waist and she tore his shirt open to check the wound. After a moment, she said, "I have to stop the bleeding."

"Damn, it hurts," he blurted, holding the wound. Blood oozed between his fingers as Ana tore his shirt farther away. "How bad, Ana?"

"The bullet went all the way through. So, that's good."

Irena stared down at him. Then, she turned to her men. "Take her. Leave him."

One of the guards moved forward, aiming his rifle at Ana. The other shoved Cat toward the open great room doors leading to the foyer.

Cat swiftly dropped to the floor, spun in a ferocious arc, and kicked her guard's legs from beneath him. At the same time, she grabbed his rifle and yanked it away. As the guard hit the marble surface, she deftly rolled away and came up on one knee to a shooting position. As the other guard turned to fire, she snapped off a shot and hit him squarely in the chest. Still shooting, she hit her guard twice, pivoted, and let loose a burst at Irena.

Irena was already moving. She leapt over a large, elegant chair, hit the floor and rolled up, firing at Cat. Without stopping, she bolted toward the door and disappeared into the foyer.

"Luke?" Ana lay atop him. She'd thrown herself over him the moment Cat made her first move—anticipating the battle and fearing her mother would try to end his life in the crossfire. "Are you all right?"

"Yeah, I'm good," he grunted. "Hurts like hell though. Is it time to go? I'm done with Mexico."

"Do not leave without me," Cat ordered and raced after Irena.

A moment later, gunfire echoed in the house. Someone called out—just a loud cry distorted by gunfire. Two more shots.

Silence.

Ana continued tending to Brennan's wound. The bullet entered his side waistline above his belt and out his back. It bled heavily as she stuffed pieces of his torn shirt into the wound to cease the blood flow.

"It looks worse than it is, Luke." She jammed a padding of material against the entry wound. "I'll stop the bleeding and we'll get out of here."

He cried out as her fingers kneaded the fabric against the bullet hole. "Jesus, you're not stuffing peppers, Ana."

"Stay still. It's too close to your side to have hit anything important."

"It hit *me*. That's important."

"Shut up. Your jokes are not funny right now."

Cat ran back into the room, agitated. "Irena is gone. There's an SUV outside and the keys are in it. We should go."

"I need a few minutes on this. Then I must find my pappa."

Cat stabbed a thumb over her shoulder. "There is no time to find your pappa, Ana. To go down to the barn or into this fight would be our death. We must leave now."

Ana worked quickly on Brennan's wound. Her mind reeled at the thought of leaving her father behind. The barn was so far away. Brennan was badly wounded. Moments counted, and if she took too many to find her father, she might condemn them all to death...or worse.

"Let me finish up Brennan's wound first," she said. "I'll come back for pappa."

"Fix him on the way to your plane." Cat took Brennan's arm and lifted him up. "Irena will bring more men. We have to go *now*."

Guilt gripped Ana as she glanced toward the main hall and the sound of growing gunfire. To no one, she whispered, "I'm so sorry, Pappa. I'll be back. I will."

Cat prodded her. "Now, Ana. There is no more time."

"Yes, all right." Ana grabbed Brennan's other arm. As she did, the Saint Christopher medal slipped from beneath her shirt and dangled out. She reached to tuck it back in, but Cat grabbed it first. "It's—"

"I know what it is, Ana Montilla." The air between them sizzled. "I have seen them many times before."

56

June 15, Morning–Highway 1, North of The Bear's Den

"Where is your plane?" Cat asked from the SUV's front passenger seat. "I do not see an airstrip. I see a highway."

"Right now, it's all we have." Ana took out her cell phone and checked the map program. "We'll stop just up ahead. Dallas will be here shortly."

"He has not yet landed? He's not waiting on us?"

Ana pulled the SUV off the four-lane highway. On the left side of the highway was a train track that followed the road all the way to Nuevo Laredo farther north. She tapped on the cell phone and hit the speed dial number 2. "We're here."

Dallas's voice came back loud and clear. "Fifteen minutes. When I land, get in fast and we'll make a run for it. There's not much traffic, but there's a train coming a few miles back. It'll be dicey but I can do it."

"Good. We're ready."

Ana turned off the engine and leaned over to check Brennan in the back seat. "Are you all right, Luke?"

His eyes fluttered open. "I'll be okay. It was just a bullet, right?"

"It was."

Cat eyed the highway as a tractor trailer drove by. "Your plane is landing here? On the highway?"

"Yes. There's no safe place in the desert to land. He's afraid the engine will get clogged upon landing and we'll never get out."

"He is either a very brave man or a fool," Cat said.

Brennan tapped the seat. "I hope he's just good. I need a doctor."

"You will be fine," Cat said. "I have seen worse on ten-year-olds."

"That's harsh." Brennan tried to sit up but cried out and lay back down. "Have you ever been shot?"

"Yes. And worse."

"Worse?" Brennan asked. "What's worse than getting shot?"

"Many things, Luke Brennan," Cat replied. "Some you will never experience."

"Like?"

Her face paled and she lowered her head. "Let me tell you of my mission. Perhaps then you will understand."

Ten minutes later, Cat turned back around and stared at nothing out the front window.

"Dammit, Catalina," Brennan finally said, "I'm sorry. I'm really sorry."

Ana thought she understood Cat after hearing Trane's message. Since finding Sarah, she'd become a surrogate mother and felt that bond grow every day. Now, after hearing Cat's story, she felt a strange connection to her—mother to surrogate mother. And while she'd never been married or even been close to it, she could not imagine losing a husband under any conditions. The violence that took Reynaldo Reyes's life had been unmerciful. Now, hearing what Trane didn't know, churned inside her like a storm brewing.

"Catalina, I cannot imagine what this has been like for you," Ana whispered. "I thought I understood. I didn't."

"No, you didn't. No one could understand. Reynaldo was everything to me. They took him. They butchered him."

Ana started to speak but the tears flowing down Cat's face silenced her. What could she possibly say to ease her pain or show understanding?

"That night changed my life. If not for Mateo…well, if not for him, I would never have survived all these years alone."

Ana reached for her arm but Cat pulled away. The tears had

stopped; in their place were now cold, hard eyes. "What now, Ana Montilla? We escape Mexico in your plane. You take me to America. Then what? They kill me? They kill my Mateo?"

Ana had no answers. She simply wasn't sure what she was going to do.

"Or do you do it yourself?" Cat said, pointing at the Saint Christopher medal around Ana's neck. "You could kill a mother and her son?"

"I have a little girl who needs me too, Catalina." Ana looked away, searching the sky for Dallas as a means to shield herself from Cat's unyielding glare. "If I don't do what I promised, they'll take my little girl away. Havana will want revenge on me. I cannot hide from Cuban operatives and the CIA the rest of my life. My only chance is with the deal I made for a new life."

"And what of my life? What of Mateo's?"

"I don't know."

Cat's eyes held Ana's. "I will do anything for my Mateo—anything. I came on my mission to save him. Havana took him from me a year ago. It was Havana who forced me on this mission. So, see it for what it is; those who could threaten your family cannot be trusted. Do you really think that if you do what they demand they will live up to their promises?"

That was exactly what her mother had said. Was she the only one who hadn't understood that before?

"I know these men, Ana. You do, too…perhaps in your past life. You know I'm telling you the truth."

Ana could only nod as tears began to well in her eyes. Had she fallen for the biggest trap of all—false trust? Was that failure going to cost her Sarah? Yiayia Poppi? Everything?

Cat held onto her shoulder, connecting on some maternal wavelength that seemed to sear an understanding between them.

"A year ago, I began planning my mission," Cat said. "Part of it was to have your father help me through South America, into Mexico, and then into the United States. He had his own contacts, his own pathways. He helped me all along my route even though he was never with me. In doing so, he brought the wrath of Havana upon himself."

"Cat, my father is a good man. And you came so far alone."

"Yes, but my Reynaldo guided me." Cat's eyes welled up. "Now, I fear losing Mateo."

Ana gazed at her. Cat's loss and the fear of losing Sarah and Yiayia Poppi bonded them without another word. What words could describe the loss of your loved ones? Of a child?

"Hey, ladies? Hello?" Brennan said. "There's a big, pretty airplane landing up ahead. Maybe we should get out and be ready. You know, before I bleed to death?"

Ana climbed out and opened Brennan's door. Cat came around and the two of them eased him out of the back seat, while he groused constantly, and leaned him back against the SUV for balance.

Amidst blaring horns and shrieking tires, Dallas made a very low pass along the highway and sent cars and trucks skidding off the road into the desert, opening a long band of vacant tar. Then, he made a sharp turn and brought the Beechcraft down on the open road, taxiing through the dust to stop opposite their SUV. Before the plane stopped rolling, the side passenger door opened and the stairs slowly descended.

"Mamá! Mamá!" Mateo called from the top of the stairs. "Hurry, we must go."

Cat flew up the stairs and embraced Mateo, ravenously kissing his cheeks and head, all the while whispering to him.

Their reunion was short lived.

A shower of bullets rattled across the road and shredded the hood of the SUV behind Brennan. A second foray of rifle fire shattered the window and ripped apart the doors and tires.

"Go," Ana shouted, "go."

Cat leapt from the open aircraft door and darted across the road to her. She grabbed Brennan's arm and pulled it over her shoulders. "Come, Ana. We have no time."

Ana turned toward the gunfire as a dark Hummer smashed its way through the glut of vehicles and plowed toward them. It skidded to a stop just a few car lengths away where a large delivery truck had attempted to turn from the carnage but inadvertently stalled, blocking its path forward.

Irena Montilla jumped out from the Hummer, firing an AK74

rifle as she ran for position.

Drivers and passengers bailed from their vehicles and ran into the desert, searching for cover.

"Catalina, take Brennan and go." Ana crawled to their vehicle's rear passenger door and pulled one of the M4s and several magazines from the rear seat. "I'll cover you."

"No." Cat shifted Brennan's weight on her shoulders. "We must all go."

"We'll never get airborne with their gunfire. I'll cover you. Go. Save Mateo. Now. Go."

Cat hesitated, glanced up at Mateo still standing in the Beechcraft's door, and ran for the plane's stairs, dragging Brennan beside her; bullets followed her the entire way.

Ana jumped up, leaned over her SUV's shredded hood, and opened fire. Her bullets rattled across the stalled delivery truck's rear tandem wheels where Irena had taken cover. Each time Irena leaned out to shoot, Ana fired and forced her back again.

Two more of Irena's gunmen joined the melee and pinned Ana down.

She knelt behind the SUV, waved at Dallas to leave, and changed magazines in the rifle.

As Dallas sped down the highway, Ana popped up from beside the SUV and sprayed a long barrage at Irena and her men.

She gave Dallas the few seconds he needed to escape the assault.

Ana ducked down behind the SUV to reload. Her heart sank—weighing heavy with the thought of Sarah waiting for her in Queens. She might never see her again.

"I'm sorry, Sarah. I'm so sorry." She knelt, changed magazines, and popped up firing again as tears rained down her face. "I love you."

Far down the highway, Dallas lifted the Beechcraft and made a steep climb out of range.

Irena's men charged from cover trying to shoot the plane from the sky, but Ana popped up, sprayed half a magazine of bullets at them, and sent them diving back for cover.

The stalled delivery truck's explosion split the air with a deafening thunderclap. One of Ana's bullets had struck its cargo bed and ignited a maelstrom of anger. The rear of the truck cratered and fragmented across the highway. A fireball erupted. The blast wave knocked Ana backward from the SUV and onto the ground. Hitting hard on her back, she lost her wind as her head cracked against the roadway.

Ana tried to rise…but the darkness overtook her.

57

June 15, Afternoon–Cruising Altitude, Crossing The Rio Grande

Ana's eyes fluttered open. After a moment glancing around, they focused on Cat. "Catalina?"

"Lay still. You're in shock."

"What happened?" Ana's eyes struggled to focus. "Where…?"

"You are safe." Cat dabbed Ana's face with a wet compress. As unsure of Ana as she was, the truth was right beside her and she smiled at her son. "You saved my Mateo. You saved me, too."

Ana glanced around the Beechcraft's cabin. Her eyes still showed confusion.

"We went back for you," Cat said. "When we saw the explosion, I knew what had happened. Your pilot had to make three passes to find an opening to land along the railroad tracks. But he did it. He's a crazy man."

"I remember the explosion. I hit something on that truck."

"Yes, you saved us. You are your father's daughter. You risked your own life to save Mateo and me."

"And me," Brennan added from across the aisle. He was propped up on two pillows watching them. "Ana, Cat forced Dallas go back for you. You're both crazy Kung Fu ninja chicks."

Ana closed her eyes. "Mamá? Did you see...?"

"No," Cat said. "No one was shooting when we returned. The explosion stopped their attack. There were several bodies near the cars when Dallas landed. We couldn't get too close; he had to turn around on the highway and take back off quickly. When we did, no one tried to stop us."

"Oh." Ana's face fell and she spoke in a low, painful voice. "The explosion killed them all."

"Perhaps. But you saved us, Ana Montilla." Cat leaned forward and took Ana's hand. "I am so sorry. You sacrificed your own mamá for Mateo and me...and Brennan and your pilot. That is not the act of a FARC guerrilla. That is the act of a mother. No?"

Ana glanced at Brennan. "Are you all right?"

"Peachy. Dallas had some morphine in a combat med kit onboard. I'm good. Actually, I'm *real* good."

Ana lay back and rested.

Mateo moved to sit on the floor at Cat's feet and lay his head on her hip. He stayed there, staring at nothing.

"Mateo, are you all right?" Cat asked. "Did someone hurt you? Did—"

"No. I am fine. Dallas was good to me while we waited for you. He even let me sit in the co-pilot's seat." He never raised his eyes to her. "Is this over?"

"Is what over, mi hijo?" She stroked his hair. "We go to America now."

"What of my step-pappa; Ñico? Will he find us there?"

"No, mi hijo." Cat leaned in close and whispered, "Ñico Guerro will never hurt us again."

"Good." He refused to look at her. Instead, he gazed at Ana. She smiled; he smiled back. "Luke and Miss Ana rescued me from Che. They saved me."

"Yes, they did." Cat exchanged glances with Ana. "She saved us just now, too."

He shrugged.

"Mi hijo?" Cat asked. "What troubles you?"

Mateo looked away.

"Mi hijo?"

He faced her, his eyes red and tearing. "Why did you leave me in Cuba? Why didn't you come for me and save me, Mamá?"

The words struck her like a bullet to the chest. Everything around her seemed to quiet and wait for her response. She had none.

"Why did you let Ñico take me from you last year? I have missed you so." Mateo's eyes rained as the tension of their highway escape disappeared and old fears rose to the surface. "Ñico said you could not protect me. He said you were bad for Cuba. Bad for me."

"Mi hijo, you know the truth about what Ñico did to me—to you." She hugged him tight. "It was he who was bad for you. He and Cuba are bad for us both."

"Then why didn't you rescue me?" he demanded. "I have been so afraid. So alone."

Brennan's hand reached across the aisle and touched Mateo's shoulder. In a faint, almost singsong voice, he said, "Hey, pal. Easy on Mom. Sometimes moms and dads just can't do what you want. They really want to, but they can't. What's important is that you're with her now. She came for you."

"Mateo, he is right," Cat said. "Ñico would only let me see you those two times. He threatened that I would never see you again if I fought him. Instead, I took this mission. For you, Mateo. To save you."

"Mission, Mamá? You weren't running away?"

"No. I would never run away from you." Cat's eyes flooded as her mouth gaped, shocked at his belief. Her hands trembled as she touched his face. "I love you. I went on this mission to save you. To save us." She whispered to him. When she was done, she leaned back and took his face in both her hands. "It is the only way we can survive. I must do this. Do you understand?"

"I think so, Mamá." He watched her sob. "Is it safe for us to go on?"

Cat turned to study Ana. "I don't know."

This strong, dangerous woman sitting just an arm's length away was the key to her answer. She was so much like el doctor—strong but compassionate, steadfast and brazen. But was she trustworthy? Could she trust her not to simply turn them over to the Americans as soon as the airplane touched down? Would there be CIA and policemen waiting to whisk them away to some prison, or worse?

If all that were waiting for her, why had Ana Montilla risked her life to save them back on the highway? Surely, by doing so, she'd risked never seeing her own little girl again. Were they so different?

Cat said to Ana, "What is it to be Ana Montilla? Will you sacrifice a mother and her son? All for a deal that may very well be a lie?"

"Did I sacrifice you back in the desert?"

"No. But...."

Ana's face paled. "The truth is, Catalina, I don't know what to do."

Mateo moved across the aisle and hugged Ana. "Thank you for saving me. Thank you for saving my mamá."

"You're welcome, Mateo. You're a strong young man."

Mateo released her as his face showed strain and heartache. "Americans killed my pappa, Miss Ana. We go to America for justice. After what you and Señor Luke did for me and Mamá, can we trust you?"

"You can, Mateo," Brennan said in a hazy voice, dazed from the morphine.

"Then, you will help us get justice?" Mateo glanced between Brennan and Ana. "We cannot go back to Cuba. We must stay in America."

"I know," Ana said.

"Do you?" Cat pulled Mateo back to her side. "Will my mission mean prison or freedom? Perhaps death?"

"I cannot allow you to start a war."

Their eyes met and a chill settled between them.

Cat stood. "Come, Mateo, I will find some food for you."

"Dallas has some in the back," Mateo said, and he followed her to the storage compartments at the rear of the aircraft.

Once there, Cat whispered, "Listen carefully."

He glanced back at Ana and Brennan in the front of the plane.

She whispered close to his ear, "You must be ready, my son. Stay close to me always. My mission is the only chance we have. When it is right, we will escape. Be ready."

58

June 15, Afternoon–Cruising Altitude Over Kentucky

The flight went on uneventfully. Cat and Mateo continued their reunion, sitting in the rear of the aircraft alone. Forward, Ana recovered and monitored Brennan. His wound was stabilized, and he was now sleeping soundly.

At Big Sandy Regional Airport in Kentucky, they landed for fuel and food. In just over an hour, they were airborne again.

As they climbed to cruising altitude, Ana glanced back at Cat. Catalina Reyes was a G2 operative—an assassin. That fact was undisputed. She wanted justice; not just revenge, but justice. In the New Jersey countryside, at an estate set in the rolling hills, a little seven-year-old with bright green eyes and an irresistible smile waited for her, probably scared to death she wouldn't return and she would be alone again. Mateo had lived that fear for a year. She, herself, had wondered for years if she would ever have a family again with her mamá and pappa. Just a few hours ago, that question was answered—first by her mother's evil betrayal, then by a fireball that snuffed Irena Montilla out.

Sarah and Poppi were her only family now. Mateo and Cat were not, but they were a family. Could she find a way to fulfill her agreement with Trane and not destroy them at the same time? With all that had befallen them, was there a way to grant justice without igniting a war? If by simply trying, would that destroy any hope of her safety? Of Sarah and Yiayia Poppi's safety?

What am I to do, Ana Montilla? It is an impossible choice. One family for another.

Brennan woke and gripped her hand that was resting on his hip. "Hey there, Ana...whoever. Thanks for taking care of me. I've never been shot before. It sucks."

"You'll be fine, Luke." She squeezed his hand. "Just rest."

He gestured over his shoulder toward Cat and Mateo. "What are you gonna do?"

Yes, Ana Karras, what will you do?

If she could turn back time, what other option would she have given Ted and Cindy Cooper? How could she have carried out her mission back then and still let them live? She could have secreted them away and never allowed FARC to execute them. Had she, they would have lived; she would have been executed instead.

Life had come full circle.

She turned in her seat and looked back at Mateo and Cat playing cards. Then, she turned back to Brennan and squeezed his hand again.

"I have little choice, Luke. You must stay away when we get back. Promise me."

"Why? I already got shot. What's the worst that can happen now?"

The words brought back a memory—one that could still bring tears to her eyes, and did. Brennan didn't know it, but that was the last thing Tommy Robert Sawyer had written to her, nine years ago...

...Tommy's third mission trip to Colombia ended tragically. The bus that he and his father took from the airport to the village was ambushed by guerrillas just outside Bogota. They'd been dragged from the bus and executed along the roadside. The Federales were mobilized to hunt those responsible and Ana's FARC camp had to relocate miles away as a precaution. She was devastated. The missionaries had paid fees to the camp to be granted access to the school.

Strangely, no FARC unit took credit for the attack. Each of her letters were always ended with her customary plea for caution just before her closing heartstrings: Be careful, Tommy, this is a dangerous place. I love you—Ana. His last reply had simply been: You made me fall in love with you. What's the worst that can happen…?

Tommy's fate was never explained.

Now, Ana watched Luke reclining on the airplane's seat. He was acting tough, but she knew he was in terrible pain despite the morphine.

"Just stay out of this from now on, Luke. I hate to do what I am about to, but I have to protect Sarah and my grandmother."

"Look, I'm a cop—sorta." He smiled faintly. "Trane says Cat's going to DC to take out the vice president. She hasn't exactly denied it. It's terrible what happened to her and her family, but starting a war won't change that. If we let her go, it's treason. Getting shot's one thing, but I'm too young to hang."

She thought long and hard about that. "When we get to Linden, stay aboard the plane with Dallas. I'll deal with Trane."

"No, no, hold on," he said. "Just the other day I was saying, 'Lucius, you need more excitement in your life.' Then, *bam*, I met you and I got shot. I gotta see this through."

"No, Luke. I must do this alone."

He started to argue but she injected him with another dose of morphine and sent him back to sleep.

She brought Dallas some coffee, slipping into the co-pilot's seat. "We'll turn them over at your hangar, Dallas. Don't say anything to them in the back. I don't want them to know until it's over."

"Well, Miss Ana, Trane wasn't wrong about you," he said, nodding. "I know it's tough, with the boy and all, but you're doing the right thing."

"I pray so, Dallas. I do."

***

A little over an hour later, Dallas brought the Beechcraft in for a smooth landing on the general aviation strip at Linden. As soon as they were down, he taxied the Beechcraft off the runway to his private hangar and stopped in front, turned the plane, and faced back toward the apron.

Four large, black SUVs roared around the administrative building, down between the hangars, and screeched to a halt in front of Dallas's hangar. Black-clad commandos leapt out and formed a tactical line facing the Beechcraft.

Trane sprang from the lead vehicle, waved at Dallas in the cockpit, and walked slowly toward the Beechcraft.

Ana stood on the stairs watching his approach, then turned back to Brennan. "I'll have you to a hospital soon. Don't worry."

"Good, the morphine's wearing thin again." He gestured toward the cockpit. "Everything okay in there?"

"It is."

Cat and Mateo came forward and stood beside Brennan's seat. When Cat saw Trane's men approaching, her face was fiery.

"I trust you," she said to Ana.

"I know."

Ana climbed down the aircraft stairs and onto the tarmac, closing the stairs behind her. As soon as the hatch was locked, the Beechcraft taxied back onto the apron a hundred yards away; its engines powered up.

"What is this, Ana?" Trane called out. "What are you doing?"

Ana confronted him. "Do I have my deal?"

"Yes, of course. What's going on?"

She held up a hand. "My father is in Nuevo Laredo—somewhere. I want him brought here safely. My mother is dead. You promised me new lives, protection, and money. I can deliver Hemingway. Prove we have a deal."

"I gave you my word, Ana. What makes you think it's no good?"

"Who killed Colonel Vergara?"

Trane paled. "You think I…?"

"I don't trust anyone, Trane." Ana waved at the aircraft and a hand waved back from the window over the wings. "But now, I have no choice. You should know that everything that has happened to me has been recorded and saved."

"Really, Ana?" Trane said, smirking. "Did you see a good inflight movie or something? My word is solid. As soon as Reyes and the kid are in my custody, you've got your deal."

The Beechcraft's engines revved, but instead of turning toward the hangar, the side door opened, and the stairs lowered again. Cat stood behind Brennan in the open door. She held a pistol on him as he tripped down the stairs, fell to the tarmac, and rolled away from the plane.

"You betrayed me, Ana Montilla," Cat yelled, and she pulled the stairs up and secured the door.

As Ana and Trane watched, dumbfounded, the Beechcraft accelerated down the taxiway.

"What in the hell, Ana?" Trane sent his men after the Beechcraft. "Secure the aircraft."

Dallas never slowed; he hit the runway, and was airborne.

"Oh my God." Ana ran to Brennan. "Luke, are you all right?"

Trane caught up to her. "Ana, this was not our deal. What the hell is going on?"

"I don't know." She knelt and lifted Brennan's head onto her lap. "Luke, it's all right now. You'll be fine."

"What?" His voice was barely a murmur as Trane leaned over him. "Catalina went forward right after you got off, Ana. Next thing I know, I'm falling down the stairs. What happened?"

Trane growled, "What the hell am I supposed to tell McLaren? That the Cuban assassin you captured just flew away in her own airplane?"

"Secret Agent Choo Choo?" Brennan said. "Hey, I need a job. I got shot catching that Cuban assassin for you. So, don't be unappreciative."

Trane ignored him. "Was this your plan all along, Ana?"

"No," she said. "But it seems it was Hemingway's. We need to talk. I think I know her next move."

59

June 17, Early Morning–Number One Observatory Circle, US Naval Observatory, Official Temporary Residence of the Vice President of the United States, Washington, DC

McLaren waited in the sitting room looking out over the rear gardens still lit with decorative ground lighting. On the outskirts of the yard, a Secret Service agent stood post in the faint light, secluded near an arbor.

McLaren wondered about this morning's meeting and the impact of events from Caracas fifteen years ago. Had those events not happened, he wouldn't be standing in the sitting room. Had those events gone differently, perhaps Martin Cannon wouldn't be living in this house at all.

The sitting room door opened and the vice president strode in. "Don't you sleep, McLaren?"

"Not well, Mr. Vice President." He turned and contemplated the man who might be the next president. "Regrettably, sir, this could not wait."

"You look grim." He motioned for McLaren to sit at a small table as he did.

"Yes, sir." McLaren sat and gave the vice president a short

summary of what had transpired in the past few days, ending with: "We haven't located Reyes again."

"Dear God, McLaren. You were supposed to be better than this."

"Yes, sir."

"Pretty poor performance. Wouldn't you say, McLaren? Danny spoke so highly of you, too. How in God's name did you screw this up so badly?"

McLaren tensed. "You forbade me from involving my people or the FBI, sir. Otherwise…"

"Oh, that's how it is?" Cannon thrust an angry finger at him. "You're blaming *me* for your incompetence? Danny shared some pretty damning facts about you, McLaren. If this goes south, you'll be in a federal prison before it's over."

"I'm not blaming anyone, sir. Reyes simply outfoxed us. Otherwise, yes, it is my responsibility."

Cannon sat, watching him across the table. His face was blank. He was a good poker player, for sure. Just when McLaren thought he'd berate him again, he eased and smiled.

"Fine. Fine. I hope you can still handle this so you can be, well…a more integral part of my team. We'll have to sort out that mess from Afghanistan, of course. But that's easy enough. I have the contacts." Cannon put on a wider, faker smile. "Now, what's your plan?"

"We are exercising every option. We know Reyes wants revenge for her husband's death in Caracas. We believe she's headed here to kill Danny; perhaps, even you. And sir, Danny may be more deeply involved than you know."

Cannon's eyebrows rose. "Dear God, no. When he returned from Caracas, he briefed me on some of the details but he held most back. He didn't want me involved. You understand, for deniability. Now, it seems he has me deeply involved anyway. That is, if Reyes wants me dead too."

"That's what we believe, sir. For now, we must ensure Danny and you are secured. I can't locate him. Where is he?"

"Reyes is really a viable threat?"

"There's no doubt."

Cannon considered that. "A lone wolf operative is more

dangerous than any other. That's true, isn't it?"

McLaren nodded.

"Dear Lord, I can't believe this." Cannon folded his arms on his chest and leaned back. "I don't know all that Danny did down there, but I cannot imagine it's worth all this. Can you?"

"Revenge is like wine, sir. It matures with age."

60

June 17, Morning–The Army Navy Club, Arlington, Virginia

The Army Navy Club was established in 1927, in the scenic hills of Arlington, Virginia, five miles from Washington, DC. The Club is private, members-only, for civilian and military. Aside from hundreds of acres of golf courses and tennis courts—among other amenities—the Club has a historic, stone clubhouse that has had such members pass through as Admiral Chester W. Nimitz, General Omar Bradley, and Presidents Eisenhower, Johnson, Nixon and, most recently, Clinton.

Ana knew all this because while she waited in the employee lounge, she found a brochure on the desk that contained the Club's rich history. A note on the bulletin board beside the brochure read: *A knowledgeable employee is a proud employee.*

Perhaps after this morning the brochure would require revising.

She sat at the supervisor's desk and turned on the computer monitor. With the keyboard, she brought up the CCTV camera in the Williamsburg Room, a second-floor private dining room reserved for special occasions. The cameras were used by the staff supervisor to ensure the esteemed Club guests had immediate service and attention whenever they required—a dropped fork, an empty water glass—without the staff hovering nearby. Now, the system afforded Ana the ability to observe an older man with graying hair, whose square face was focused on a small notebook computer, at a back table littered with files and a coffee service.

She was about to adjust the camera when the large, double oak doors opened from the grand hallway. Five men entered. Four were earwig-wearing Secret Service men who quickly checked the room and Martin Cannon, Vice President of the United States.

Ana turned up the volume and watched.

"Sir, this is a bad idea," the lead Secret Service agent said to Cannon. "We haven't done a proper advance."

"Give it a rest, Mike," Cannon snapped. "You've said that Off-the-Records are less risky because nobody knows where I'm going. If nobody knows where I'm going, how can they possibly get me?"

"OTRs are less risky, sir. But we don't have to do an OTR. We can—"

"Enough, Mike." Cannon waved his Secret Service detail from the room. "Wait outside—everyone. I don't want anyone in the room. Just Danny and me. You got that?"

"No, sir, I—"

"Out, goddammit."

The Secret Service detail left and secured the room's double doors behind them.

Across the room, Danny Bianco stood beside the large, round table near the windows where he had been working. He finished manipulating his notebook computer and projected meeting slides onto a large screen hanging from the ceiling a few yards away.

"Martin? What are you doing here? The donors—"

"Screw the donors, Danny." Cannon strode to him and jammed a steel finger into his chest. "What have you got me into?"

Danny reeled back. "What are you talking about?"

"Your boy, McLaren, lost Reyes. He came to me early this morning. She's still loose and probably in town. You told me you had this under control. You told me McLaren was the right guy for this."

"He is. Trust me." Danny's voice was a little unsteady. "He'll take care of this, Martin. We're good."

"We?" Cannon slammed his palms on the table and nearly toppled a cup of coffee onto Danny's computer. "She's coming, Danny. Do you know what that means?"

At the side of the room, the service area's double doors opened and Club waitstaff rolled in carts adorned with dishes and carafes of coffee. A young, Latino wait staffer held up his hand for the other two to stop.

In thick, accented English, the wait staffer said, "Excuse me. Do you wish us to come later to prepare your tables?"

"Yes, for Christ's sake," Danny bellowed. "Get out."

"Of course. We will make sure no one disturbs you." The young Latino spun on his heels and directed his setup crew out of the room.

As the other two wait staffers maneuvered their carts back into the kitchen, a third walked to the front of the room and locked the entry doors from the inside. Then, the staffer returned to the kitchen entrance, shut the doors, and engaged the top and bottom locks with a key. Finally, the staffer turned around and faced Cannon and Bianco.

"Buenos días, mis amigos." Catalina Reyes, Dirección de Inteligencia operative, lifted her left hand; in it was a thin, cylindrical device that resembled a cigarette lighter. In her right hand, she held a gun. "The room is wired with explosives. Do not call out. If you do, you will die before they breach the doors."

Vice President Martin Cannon's mouth dropped. "Now, miss, I've got a dozen agents outside that door."

"Then they will all die too."

61

June 17, Morning–The Army Navy Club, Arlington, Virginia

"Don't do this, Reyes." Danny stepped away from the table. "Think about your kid."

"Mateo? How do you know of Mateo?"

Danny glanced sideways at Cannon. "Colonel Vergara told me about him."

"I see. Then you know Mateo is all I think about as I stand here."

Cannon asked, "What's she talking about? Who's Mateo?"

"Don't worry about it, boss. She's as good as dead already."

"It's you?" Cannon studied her. "You're Hemingway?"

"My name is Catalina." She crossed the room and stopped just feet from them. "I am here for justice. Justice for what was done to me. Justice for my Reynaldo." She tipped her hand with the device toward Danny. "Justice for Mateo."

"You'll die," Cannon said. "There's no need for that. I can arrange asylum. I can give you a new life."

"This is about my new life."

"What?" Cannon glanced at Bianco. "Do something before this gets out of hand."

***

Yes, let's not let this get out of hand, Ana Karras.

Ana silently disengaged the two serving entrance locks and slipped inside the Williamsburg Room. She relocked the doors behind her, turned, and leveled her .45 pistol at Cat.

"Don't move, Cat. Don't make me use this."

"You?" Cat turned ever-so-slightly toward her. "Ana Montilla?"

"I can't let you do this." She carefully moved around the room, getting into a better position near Bianco and Cannon, but all the time keeping the pistol trained on Cat. "Put the detonator down."

"Shoot her," Cannon ordered. "Now. Kill this lunatic."

"Hold on." Ana gestured to Cat's hand. "Her finger's on that detonator."

"Yes, it is." Cat lifted her left hand and wiggled her thumb above the device. "If you try anything, I will kill us all."

Ana eased closer to Danny. "McLaren sent me. Everybody be calm, okay?" *Yes, Ana. Be calm. Especially you.*

"Sweet Jesus," Danny said, "do something."

"Catalina, it's so sad." Cannon calmed. "This entire unfortunate—"

"Unfortunate what?" Cat pivoted toward Danny. "You bastard. You know what happened. What you did to them all. You did not have to kill my Reynaldo. He was everything to me."

"Hey, lady," Danny said to Ana, "if you're with McLaren, then you know what side you're on. I mean, you know how this has to end."

Do you know, Ana Karras? Ana Montilla knows.

"Of course." Ana waved her pistol at Cat. "Put the detonator and gun down. We'll listen, but you have to meet me halfway. I'll count to three; on four, I shoot."

"You will die." Cat tapped her thumb on the device. "All of us will die."

"All right, all right," Danny gasped. "What do you want?"

"Justice." Cat waved him and Cannon away from the table where Danny had been working. She sidestepped over to it and set her pistol down in front of her. Then, she pulled her crucifix off her neck, twisted the cross piece, and revealed a USB flash drive. She inserted it into Danny's notebook computer on the table. "Justice for my Reynaldo."

The flash drive launched a color video taken by a camera hidden somewhere in the corner of a plush hotel suite. The date-time stamp put the video in Caracas, Venezuela, fifteen years before. The playback lagged a moment before it projected full and large on the big screen hanging from the ceiling behind her.

The first video clip was fragmented and difficult to see. The camera angles were often blocked by a man in the hotel room. The second was better. The hidden cameras had been adjusted and captured cleaner recordings. When Ana saw them, she half-wished they hadn't. In each video, a hotel maid entered the suite and began her daily work. A security man followed her in. At a point early in the video, the security man grabbed the maid, struck her and wrestled her to the floor; he then held her for another man who entered from the second room of the suite. Through the entire video, the identities of the two men were obscured and unrecognizable. Still, what took place sickened her—their brutality and debauchery. At the end of each video, a newspaper clipping was displayed that pronounced the victims—Consuelo Herrera and Nina Espino—were found dead along a lonely ghetto street frequented by prostitutes and pimps.

"There's more." Cat tapped computer keys and changed the video on the big screen. The readout said it was in the hallway outside the same suite as before, at the same hotel in Caracas.

There was no audio, and Ana thanked God there wasn't.

Danny Bianco was easily identifiable in the hotel corridor. He dragged a young Catalina Reyes from a hotel room and threw her violently into the wall, kicking her as she lay on the corridor's carpet. His assault continued until she sprawled out, unmoving.

The elevator door opened and a wiry man with handsome features stepped out, witnessing the attack. He launched himself down the hall and tackled Danny. They struggled.

Two security men—they had earpieces and were clean-

cut, powerful men—joined the fracas from outside the camera's view and took control of the man. They held him as Danny gave animated commands. Then, Danny landed several punches into the man. A kick. More punches. Finally, the man succumbed and collapsed beside Cat.

They lay there as Danny gave more orders.

The two security men forced the wannabe hero to his feet. One shoved him toward the elevators, as the other dragged Cat by the arms. When the elevator doors opened, they rolled her inside; her body was half-in, half-out of the elevator, keeping the door from closing. The man was shoved inside but he turned and fought back. His surprise attack knocked down the security men. The man paused as Danny moved in, drew one of the security men's pistols from beneath his jacket, and took aim at the stranger.

The man stood his ground—toe-to-toe with Danny. Neither would retreat.

Finally, Danny lowered the pistol and waved for him to leave. The man bent and tried to slide Cat safely inside. Danny leaned down and helped him with her—lifting her legs and easing her inside.

As the elevator doors began to close, Danny lifted his pistol and fired three times into the car.

As she watched the video, loss rained down Cat's face. She picked up her pistol again and swiveled her outstretched hand with the device between Danny and Cannon. For a moment, her hands quivered as she relived those horrific moments over again.

Danny's face was blank and his eyes fixed on nothing. "What do you want, Reyes?"

"I told you. Justice."

"Danny, I thought you handled this years ago," Cannon said. Then, he faced Cat. "They sent you to destroy him—us? With this?"

"No one sent me. I escaped Havana. They want all of this for evidence to blackmail you."

"Blackmail? You're an assassin. A spy. You got—"

"Herrera and Espino were no spies. They were simple maids trying to make a living. Their only sins were youth and beauty.

Their only mistake was to be assigned that hotel suite."

"Bull." Danny spun on Ana with large, crazy eyes. "Shoot this bitch or get McLaren in here. Now."

"Pretty damning stuff, Danny Bianco," Ana said.

"No, no." Danny waved his hand dismissively. "It's all a Cuban provocation…"

Banging came on the dining room doors behind them.

"Mr. Vice President. Is everything all right?" The large, oak doors began to rattle as the Secret Service agents outside tried to force them open. "Mr. Vice President?"

"Tell them all is well, Cannon," Cat said. She moved closer to him and Danny. "Or I push the detonator."

"Tell them, Mr. Vice President," Ana urged. "Quickly, before she loses it."

Cannon hesitated, then yelled, "It's all right, Mike. It's fine."

"Come to the door, sir."

"Five more minutes."

"Sir, come to the door."

There was another brief rattle at the door…more voices. Then, silence.

"Danny?" Cannon stepped away from him, shaking his head in slow, disbelieving movements. "What is all this?"

"Shut up, Martin." Danny pivoted and grabbed Cat's gun. He twisted it away and stepped back, firing three rounds at her. "I told you that you were dead, bitch."

62

June 17, Morning–The Army Navy Club, Arlington, Virginia

Cat was not dead. She stood, holding the device in her hand, staring pure hatred at Danny.

Earlier, Ana had loaded Cat's pistol with blanks—at Trane's direction—just in case Cat or she changed their minds about *their* plan. This elaborate scheme had been all Ana's conception. An idea to give Catalina Reyes her justice and still met Trane's demands. Though, it had been under Trane's rules. A simple ounce of prevention.

"Drop the gun, Bianco." Ana aimed her pistol at Danny. "It's all blanks anyway. Mine, of course, are not."

"I…." Danny's face went from a deep, angry red to a stark white. "How did you…? Who…?" His eyes were big as saucers and his mouth fell open. He squeezed the trigger again. That exaggerated *thwack* reverberated but no bullet fired.

"Ana Montilla promised justice," Cat said to Cannon. "As did her people. I am here for that."

"It's all over." Ana looked at the ceiling where the surveillance cameras were hidden. "Trane?"

Behind them, the double doors opened and five heavily armed men entered, followed by Trane and McLaren. Of the troop, one was the vice president's Secret Service detail leader, Mike; two were FBI agents; and the last two were McLaren's operatives. The FBI was there to conduct business. McLaren's team was there for support. Trane was there to make sure everyone played nice together.

"Well done, Ms. Karras." McLaren stopped beside her. "When Trane briefed me on this operation, it was already in motion and scared me to death. He didn't give me much choice, but it worked. When this is over, we'll have to debrief you. Trane has given me the details of our arrangement. I will, of course, honor it."

"I will hold you to all of it," Ana said. "With what you have on the CCTV recordings this morning, and this, it ought to be enough."

"Not quite, but we're close." Trane threw a chin at two FBI men who proceeded to grab Danny and force him face down on a table to cuff him. "Nice to finally meet you, Danny. McLaren has told me so much about you."

"Screw you. Get these men off me."

Danny squirmed and tried to free himself from the agents. As he did, he turned sideways and found McLaren watching him. "Damn you, McLaren. This is all bull. It started with Colonel Vergara. He's a provocateur."

"No, Danny, he's not," Trane said. "He's a thug and a predator. Just like you."

Danny stopped fighting the agents. "No. No. This isn't right."

"Hold a minute, gentlemen." Cannon brushed past one of the agents to Danny. "I'll get our lawyers right on this. You've been loyal and hardworking for me. I'll get you all the help you need. You deserve that."

"Lawyers? Fuck your lawyers. This is all on you, Cannon. You're a—"

"I'll take care of you, Danny." Cannon's face was pale and tight. "I'll take care of all of this."

The FBI men walked Danny from the room.

McLaren turned to Cannon. "Thank you for cooperating, sir. We couldn't have done this without you."

"Damn terrible thing, Alex. I've known Danny most of my

professional life." Cannon wiped his brow and turned to Cat. "I'm sorry, miss. Truly. I will—"

"Miss?" Cat's face darkened. "You don't remember me, do you, Martin Cannon?"

"Remember you? No, of course not." Cannon looked confused. "I've never seen you before in my life."

63

June 17, Morning–The Army Navy Club, Arlington, Virginia

"Never?" Cat taunted. "Too many women? Too many tragedies?"

"What are you talking about?" Cannon's eyes darted between Cat and McLaren. "McLaren, get her the hell out of here. Now."

"Hold on," Trane said. "Show's not over."

Cat returned to the computer and its keys. Before she hit 'enter' to start a new video, she looked sadly at Cannon and spoke in a faraway voice. "That night, at the hotel—before Danny murdered my husband—I was in your room. Do you remember me now?"

"I don't know what you're playing at. I wasn't there." Cannon's face paled. "I never went on the Caracas missions."

"Yes, you did," Cat snapped. "I was there to check the cameras in your room—not install them. You thought you caught me in time. You believed I was just installing the surveillance devices. As you will see, our equipment was already working. Just as they were working many times before. They were, perhaps, not as clear during your previous visits to Caracas, but we have the autopsies of the others—Herrera and Espino. It is all here on these files in my crucifix USB drive."

A video sprang to life and returned them to the same plush Caracas hotel suite as before.

Cat's face blanched. "This is what happened in the room just before you had my Reynaldo murdered in the elevator and left me to die."

Cat faced the camera and adjusted something on the lens before moving systematically around the room, inspecting several other hiding places to utilize for eavesdropping devices—the lamp, the telephone, and a dresser mirror. She had finished manipulating something in the nightstand when the suite door opened and two men walked in: Danny Bianco and then-Senator Martin Cannon.

Danny charged across the room and grabbed her. "You, bitch. Bugging us? Stupid move."

"Oh, sweetheart. You just couldn't take no for an answer, could you?" Cannon had a drink in his hand and his speech slurred slightly. "What are we gonna do, Danny?"

"I don't know, boss. Any ideas?"

Cannon downed his drink and threw the glass against the wall, shattering it. "Give her to me."

"No, no. I will go." Cat struggled to get free. "This is a mistake. I will go."

"You're damn right it's a mistake." Cannon crossed the room and struck her in the face. Her body faltered. He struck her again. "Leave her, Danny."

"Okay, boss." Danny shoved her limp form onto the bed. "I'll be right outside."

Cannon was on her in seconds—tearing at her—throwing another punch. Another.

Her rape was brutal and unimaginable.

With tears streaming down her face, Cat pulled the USB drive from the computer and held it up with the other device in her hand. "It is all right here, Cannon. The hospital reports. Photographs. Video. Everything. You killed others, too—like Herrera, Espino— and more. It's all here."

Cannon stared blankly at the large screen. The video was paused with Cat lying unmoving on the bed.

"Moments later, Danny Bianco shot my Reynaldo in the elevator—all for trying to save me. I nearly died from what they did to me. If not for Doctor Montilla—" she smiled meekly at Ana. "I would have."

The remaining Secret Service, FBI, and CIA men stared at the big screen, some with mouths open in amazement, and others with angry, dismayed expressions. None of them moved to arrest Cat or Ana.

Cat slammed her palm on the table to regain Cannon's attention. "That is why Reynaldo was there that evening, because of what you had done so many times to the other women. We were there to spy, yes. As you do. As all countries do. Rape and murder…they are something else."

Cannon's voice was strained and unsteady. "No. That's not right. None of this is right."

"When I did not return to the bar as planned that evening, Reynaldo came to save me…from you. He found Danny beating me in the hallway just outside your room."

Cannon opened his mouth, but no words found voice.

"We have the evidence, Cannon," Trane said. "We have your flight records, hotel receipts, cell phone bills, and more. You were there. And every date corresponds to one of the Caracas murders. You're a regular Jack the Ripper."

"That's impossible." Cannon's face was exploding as his eyes darted wildly between Trane and Cat. "This is bullshit."

Trane shook his head. "The evidence was buried in miles of passwords and secret handshakes. But once it's in computers, it's there forever. That, and I gotta guy." Trane winked at Ana. "A guy who makes confetti out of cyber security. You're done, Cannon."

Ana put her arm around Cat's shoulders. "Justice, Cat. You have it now."

64

June 17, Morning–The Army Navy Club, Arlington, Virginia

Rape is an ugly word; perhaps the ugliest Webster ever recorded. Yet still, there's no other word that more adequately describes the horror it defines. To Cat, it should be answered with swift, definitive justice—a needle in the arm or a bullet in the brain. The latter was good by Ana Montilla, and it was justice—even to Ana Karras.

Catalina Reyes agreed.

The FBI men closed on Cannon, as Trane and McLaren looked on.

Trane said, "You won't be running for president. But you will be going to prison. Especially if Danny cooperates with us. I think he will. Don't you?"

"You fool. Who cares if it's true?" Cannon sliced the air with his hand toward McLaren as his voiced strained and his chest heaved. "Who cares what happened to this spy-bitch fifteen years ago? She was after us. She got what she asked for."

"Reynaldo?" Ana asked. "Consuelo Herrera? Nina Espino? The others?"

"Screw all of them," Cannon screamed. "They came at me."

"They were innocent. Reynaldo did not even have a weapon." Cat's voice cracked, and she paused to regain control. "You took him from me—killed him like an animal. You didn't need to do it. Even after what you did to me. You didn't need to kill him."

"No. No." Cannon rubbed his eyes and shifted his weight from side-to-side. His face twisted, and for a moment, he looked like he might collapse. "Vergara told Danny—"

"Vergara was a hustler," Trane said. "He knew you and Danny from Caracas. You should remember him. He bought drinks for you in the bar. Oh, wait, you knew him by his cover name back then: Raul Anibal Vacarro."

"Vacarro?" Cannon looked from Cat to Trane as something ignited his recollection. That memory started him trembling.

"Ah, you do remember him," Trane sneered. "Earlier this month, he arrived in Manhattan to get Ana. But he saw an opportunity to make a few bucks and called Danny. He wanted money to keep quiet about what you and Danny did in Caracas. Havana didn't know about his little side scheme. But Danny blew it. Instead of meeting him, he sent McLaren—who sent me. Isn't that right, McLaren?"

"Yes, correct." McLaren had been hovering off to the side and the question sent a milky white sweat over him. "But we didn't know about all this at the time."

"All lies," Cannon murmured. "Vergara said—"

"Vergara is dead," Ana said. "You should fear us more than him."

Cat moved close to Cannon, and as she did, the FBI men took hold of his arms. "Havana was going to blackmail you with all this information I have. But I took it and escaped."

"Screw you," Cannon snapped. "You're a Cuban spy. No one will believe you."

Cat recoiled and slapped him hard...once, twice, three times. Then she took the device in her hand and stuffed it into his pocket, but not before holding it up and flipping the plunger to ignite the cigarette lighter's flame. "You took everything from me."

"Easy now, Catalina." Trane gently took her hand and eased her back from Cannon. "It's over."

She spat at Cannon and stared hate.

"Do something, McLaren." Cannon looked at McLaren and the

339

FBI men standing around. "I'm the Vice President, goddammit. Do something."

"I spoke with President Cohen this morning, as I have each of these past couple of days," McLaren said. "He was, to say the least, disappointed. What you and Danny confessed on camera and audio recordings this morning will be all he needs. That's why Trane was allowed this unusual operation. He needed firsthand, undeniable proof. You've confessed."

Cannon started twitching—his eyes darted from person-to-person—his lips opened and closed. "It's not too late. I can…"

"Ah, yeah, it is," Trane said. "It's actually overdue."

McLaren turned to the FBI men. "You have President Cohen's orders. Execute them."

The biggest FBI man gripped Cannon's arms. "Sir, I don't want to use handcuffs."

"Hold on, guys." Trane turned and waved to someone in the hallway. A moment later, two of his tactical operatives walked in escorting Mateo Reyes.

"What's this?" Cannon scowled at the boy. "Who's he?"

"Martin, I am not Hemingway." Cat took hold of Mateo's shoulder. "This is Hemingway—your son."

65

June 17, Morning–The Army Navy Club, Arlington, Virginia

"Your son and I did not come to kill you, Martin Cannon," Cat said in a slow, deliberate tone. "I started for Washington to ask for your help to rescue him from Havana. They took him from me and were holding him to blackmail you later. I could not bear that and went on this mission to reach you. But as you see, that is no longer necessary. Now, we need protection. Havana will do anything to enslave him as their propaganda puppet. They will simply kill me on sight."

As the shock rippled through the room, Cannon's face contorted. His entire body quivered and he nearly lost his balance. The two FBI men stood beside him, as much controlling their prisoner as steadying him from collapse.

"I wish to speak privately to him," Ana said to Trane, gesturing toward Cannon. "May I?"

Trane and McLaren exchanged glances, then McLaren nodded to the FBI men beside Cannon and they backed away, out of earshot. "Make it quick."

"Thank you." Ana's fingers manipulated the Saint Christopher medal around her neck. "Mr. Vice President, a moment?"

Cannon glared at her.

"I have a message for you." She walked up to him, still holding her Saint Christopher medal in one hand. "A copy of those Caracas videos is already with the newspapers. Before you reach your lawyer, you'll be international news."

Cannon's trembling was now uncontrolled. "You wouldn't."

"I have." She leaned in and grabbed his hand, shaking it tightly in both of hers. "Are you really going to put your family through this? Danny Bianco is making a deal right now. Do you think he'll go to prison for life because of you?"

"Danny?" Cannon's eyes darted around. His breathing began to flounder. For a moment, he looked at the ceiling and his eyes rolled back. He mumbled incoherently. "Jesus, help me."

"Yes, pray." Ana leaned into him again, squeezed his hand, and whispered, "Regrettably, I'll never meet Jesus. But I will see you in Hell."

His face contorted and he tried to grab her, but the FBI men came close again, pulled him away and walked him from the room. He was still mumbling and gyrating, like he was having a nervous breakdown, as he disappeared from sight.

Moments later, Ana stood at the Williamsburg Room windows overlooking the Club's front entrance. Martin Cannon was lying on his back outside his limousine. Four FBI and Secret Service agents surrounded him. One agent talked furiously on a cell phone as two others tried in vain to resuscitate him. Seconds later, they stuffed him into the limousine and dashed away for the hospital.

"Dear God." McLaren was beside her watching. "What have you done, Karras?"

She tossed Trane the Saint Christopher medal.

He opened the compartment. The two suicide pills were gone. "Christ, Ana. Tell me you didn't...?"

"Ana Montilla wanted real justice." She refused to look at him but there was a hardness in her voice. "Today, she received it."

Trane's eyes closed and he sighed deeply. "Jesus, Ana, what have you done?

To Cat, Ana said, "You have justice, too, Catalina Reyes. For

Reynaldo. For Mateo. For you."

"I never told you how your pappa saved me." Cat's face lightened a little. "Your mother was in Caracas to meet Reynaldo, by chance. I was there to work Operation Perro. She and your pappa were nearby when this happened to me. Your pappa treated me at a hotel. He saved my life. What Cannon did to me.... There was nothing he could do for my Reynaldo."

Ana watched the memories fill Cat's eyes. She hugged her tightly, holding the embrace—sister to sister, mother to surrogate mother. Both fighting for a cause long ago thought lost. Both saved by the same man: Doctor Manuel Montilla.

"Cat, you did well. Everything will be better for you now. Trane will make sure."

Cat looked around the room, listening, hoping for Reynaldo to tell her what to do next. When he didn't, she realized she didn't need him any longer.

She whispered, "Goodbye, my love. Thank you."

66

June 19, Dawn–Roman Catholic Diocese of Nuevo Laredo, Nuevo Laredo, Tamaulipas, Mexico

When the Black Hawk dropped down inside the Diocese courtyard, Trane turned to Ana as the doors began to open. "Legally, we just invaded Mexico."

Ana shrugged. "It's nothing I haven't done before."

Trane's tactical team—eight of Trane's most trusted commandos—fanned out from the Black Hawk and took defensive positions around the aircraft. A moment later, the courtyard gates opened and a large tour bus pulled in, led by a black Suburban.

The Suburban stopped and waited.

Trane spoke into his microphone: "Execute."

Catalina Reyes jumped from the Black Hawk and led four of Trane's men into the building, leaving the other four securing the perimeter. She was gone twenty minutes—five minutes longer than Trane's op plan allowed. When she emerged, she led Father Martínez and nearly forty raggedy, terrified people—Latin American families of all nationalities—with their meager possessions to the tour bus where she directed them aboard. Beside her, holding her hand, was a young, pretty teenager.

"This is Lucía," Cat said to Trane and Ana. "She goes to a family somewhere in Oklahoma. Can we help her find them?"

"Of course we can, Lucía. Jump aboard," Ana said. "Everything is going to be all right now." For the first time in a long time, she was sure it wasn't a lie.

At first, Lucía's face was taut and fearful, but when Ana winked at her, it blossomed into a smile. "Gracias, señorita."

Ana turned toward Cat. "Did you see my father?"

"No. He has already gone. He disappeared right after they returned from Oso's. Father Martínez didn't know he had left. I'm sorry."

"I see." Ana looked away and wiped her eyes. "Thank you."

Trane glanced at the front courtyard entrance. "We've got company."

A large black Hummer screeched around the street corner into the courtyard and skidded to a stop behind the bus. Two tan uniformed men jumped out carrying rifles and headed for the line of immigrant families. They made it only two steps before Trane's tactical team swooped into a line between them and the families, blocking their approach.

A familiar face climbed out of the Hummer and strode past his men to Trane, Ana, and Cat.

"I am Capitán Cortez of La Policía Federal…." His face contorted when he recognized Cat and Ana. "You two? You are back? What is this?"

"Save it, Capitán," Trane said. "We're evacuating foreign refugees seeking asylum. Tell your men to stand down."

"I will not." Cortez snatched his pistol from his holster, seemingly oblivious to Trane's team standing just a few feet away. "I am—"

"Capitán, no." Father Martínez walked up to Cortez. "You have taken their lives. Broken their families. Killed husbands and enslaved wives and daughters. Today, what is left of my flock is saved from you by God and the Americans."

"Never," Cortez barked. "Nuevo Laredo is mine."

"Stop," another voice boomed from behind them. "I am taking command here." A well-dressed, older Latino, with immaculate silver hair, stepped from the Suburban that had arrived with the bus.

Behind him, two armed Mexican commandos wearing balaclavas followed. The well-dressed man walked up to Trane and the group.

Trane said, "This is General Felix Pérez Ortiz of the National Defense Ministry."

"What?" Cortez looked from Trane to General Ortiz. "I was not informed you were in the area. I—"

"Take him," the general ordered, then waited for his two Mexican commandos to whisk Cortez—protesting loudly all the way—into his SUV. "It is done."

"Thank you, General," Cat said. Then she turned to Father Martínez, who looked on in surprise. "Your biggest problem is solved, Father."

"Si, it appears so. Thank you."

Trane shook General Ortiz's hand. "Always a pleasure, Felix."

"Si, it is, my dear old friend." Ortiz grinned. "I shall now consider my debt to you paid. No?"

"In full, sir."

General Ortiz returned to his vehicle, and in a moment, drove out the gates.

The Black Hawk's rotors began to turn, as Trane walked to the bus where Father Martínez, and Cat waited. "You're staying, Father?"

"Yes." The priest smiled. "Who would provide sanctuary for so many after me? My best staff have been killed. I cannot leave. I must rebuild."

"My personal number." Trane handed him a business card with just a phone number scrawled on it, shook his hand, and walked to the waiting Black Hawk.

Cat followed him aboard the helicopter. She sat beside Ana and quietly took her hand. "Thank you for all you did. Now, I must build a new life. I will always be in your debt, Ana Montilla."

"Stay close to Trane until you're settled," Ana said, glancing at Trane in the co-pilot's seat. "He's a good man."

"Yes, I see that." Cat nodded. "So much tragedy. It is a shame about your vice president. I did not wish him harm. That was not my mission."

"No, I guess it wasn't. Still, it was a tragedy. An up-and-coming politician Cannon's age having a heart attack. Shocking."

67

June 26, Morning–William Tillson's Estate, Western New Jersey

Ana woke late as she had for the past few days. William's guest room—one of four—was large and comfortable and furnished with fine things. Things she would never be able to afford. As she slipped gently off the bed, she looked back amidst the covers and smiled. Sarah was still asleep on the other side of the bed, tied in knots within the bedsheet from hours of twisting and turning and all manner of childhood sleep wonderment. Ever since Ana joined her and Poppi after the vice president's death, Sarah had been glued to her. They ate together, slept in the same bed, and went on walks several times a day on William's lush, landscaped property. She was rarely more than six feet away.

Sarah was not having any more separations.

Ana showered and dressed before carefully untangling Sarah from the bed linens. Then, she tucked her back into bed and smoothed her covers. It was a difficult task, given Lobo was curled up beside her, half-wrapped in the same blankets as Sarah. Ultimately, Lobo woke and hopped off the bed to follow Ana down the winding staircase to the main floor.

There, they walked together onto the rear patio where Poppi and William were eating breakfast.

"Ana, good morning." William rose and kissed her cheek. "Bonnie, would you please get Ana some breakfast? Thank you."

"Yes, Mr. William." His housemaid brought her a porcelain cup and saucer, poured Ana coffee from the porcelain carafe on the table, and disappeared into the house.

"I've turned into a bum, Yiayia," Ana said, yawning. "You two are spoiling me."

Lobo barked and sat beside her, waiting on his morning piece of toast.

"In a moment, Lobo. You're spoiled, too."

Woof.

"You deserve it." Poppi sat beside William and gave him a broad smile. "Besides, he's been spoiling me for years now. It's your turn."

William said, "Poppi and I have decided that you and Sarah should stay here. At least for a few months, until you decide what you're going to do."

"Thank you, William." She hadn't considered what she was to do next. Perhaps return to Mexico to find Pappa. Perhaps wait and see if Trane had more luck. "I can't do that, though. Sarah and I will return to Queens."

Poppi eyed her. "Really?"

"Yes." She shrugged. "I still have a little money from my trust. But I'll find a job and take good care of Sarah and you."

Bonnie returned with a plate of steak and eggs for Ana, placed it in front of her, and set a fork and steak knife down beside the plate. She refilled Ana's coffee cup and withdrew, leaving the porcelain carafe of coffee on the table.

"The house is yours," Poppi said. "I'm moving in here."

"What?" Ana eyed her, then William. "Making it official?"

"Yes, very soon," William said, taking Poppi's hand. "After all that's happened, we realized time is too valuable to waste. We'll be formally engaged next week at a grand party being held right here."

"I'm so happy for you." Ana stood and went around the table to give Poppi a warm embrace and a kiss on the cheek. She repeated it for William before returning to her chair.

As Ana started to sit, Lobo jumped to his feet and turned toward the house, growling ferociously. "Lobo, what's wrong?"

"Si, Lobo, what could be wrong?" A voice said from behind them. "You see an old friend, perhaps?"

Even before Ana spun to see the large, robust man standing in the house entrance, the voice sent shockwaves through her and awakened needles stabbed every inch of her scars.

Colonel Luis Vergara faced them, holding a pistol aimed directly at her.

"No, this can't be." She stood and held up her hands, pushing nothing away from her. "You're dead. McLaren said—"

"McLaren?" Vergara laughed raucously. "I see you are very confused, Ana Montilla. As you should be."

"How?" she said.

"Lobo, no." Poppi reached down and grabbed Lobo's collar as he started to lunge at Vergara. She sat back down and pulled the dog to her legs to hold him. "Lobo, stay here. Quiet."

The dog snarled and tried relentlessly to pull free but couldn't.

"What is this?" William stood. "What are you doing here?"

"Shut up." Vergara strode to the table, picked up Ana's coffee cup and finished it in one long, deep swallow. He dropped the porcelain cup on the stone patio where it shattered, and gestured with his gun for Ana to back away from the table. "Where is Catalina Reyes and the boy?"

It was still all about Hemingway. Cat had been right. Havana would not let this go. They would not rest until she and Mateo were back in their clutches. If not for propaganda, for revenge.

"She escaped," Ana said. "The CIA is looking for her now. I don't know..."

"Liar. I want Reyes. I want the boy." Vergara stepped forward and cracked his pistol across her cheek, splitting her lip and knocking her to the ground. William lurched around the table, but Vergara's pistol swiveled at him and stopped him cold. "Do not, William. You will not get another step."

William? Vergara knows your name? The only way that could be is...

"William, you bastard." Ana got to her feet and spat a mouthful of blood at him. "You've gotten rich from men like him. I should have guessed you would buy and sell me as well. How much did I make you?"

William wiped the spittle from his shirt with his hand. His face was flush and angry. His eyes searched her, then Poppi, and finally rested on Vergara.

"Leave this house. Now." Poppi's face was ashen and her voice was unsteady as she confronted Vergara. "You have no right to be here."

"I have every right," Vergara snarled and kicked the table violently against her. "Shut up and stay quiet, woman. I won't warn you again."

Ana squared off on Vergara. "You are supposed to be dead."

"Yes, I know."

Vergara, for all his faults, was not a shy man. He told them everything, bragging about his prowess playing the vice president's office. Bragging about how he'd played everyone. When this mission was done, he'd be a rich man for the profits he was promised. Perhaps then he'd retire in Manhattan. Perhaps Havana would give him the brownstone as a gift. All he needed now was Catalina Reyes and her son, Mateo.

"I want them. If I don't get her, then you will die slowly, Ana Montilla."

Something behind Vergara caught Ana's attention that sent horror through her.

Sarah stood in the house doorway, rubbing her eyes and holding her favorite stuffed dog.

"Aunty Ana. Is it breakfast time? I'm—"

"Sarah, run!"

"Go, Sarah," Poppi yelled. "Get back inside."

Too late. Vergara spun, grabbed Sarah by the arm and pulled her to him, resting the pistol against her head. "Now, Ana Montilla, where is Reyes and the boy? Where? Make the right choice, Ana. I think you know what I will do for that information."

68

June 26, Morning–William Tillson's Estate, Western New Jersey

"Don't hurt the little one," Ana warned, preparing herself. "It's me you want. I'll go with you to find Reyes. Let Sarah go."

"No. She'll ensure you do as I require. I want Reyes and the boy. It is not too late to salvage their secrets. And there is, of course, punishment due them."

"Release Sarah," Ana demanded. "Do that and we can talk."

"There is no more talking." Vergara shook Sarah and made her cry out. "Stop, brat."

William started to move forward but Poppi grabbed his arm, momentarily releasing Lobo. "No, William."

Free now, Lobo lunged at Vergara. He grabbed Vergara's arm and savagely tore into his flesh, viciously biting and thrashing to force Sarah's release. When Vergara let go of her, the dog repositioned his bite onto his open hand, shaking and twisting—a death grip he wouldn't release.

Vergara screamed hideously.

Now, Ana Montilla, fight.

Ana morphed. She kicked a wrought iron chair set in front of her into Vergara's knees and smashed the porcelain carafe of coffee onto his face. She spun sideways, away from his line of fire, pushed Sarah away and onto the ground. Still moving, spiraling in a violent dance, she whipped her left leg around and kicked Vergara's legs out from under him.

He went down, backward, and hard. His breath exploded and he lay stunned.

Lobo was on him. The frenetic dog engulfed his hand, receiving a maniacal scream for his trouble. He thrashed, tearing into the villain's flesh, whipping himself into a protective rage.

Poppi was on her feet, clinging to William—half holding him back and half using him as a shield. "Stop all this. Stop now. Lobo, no."

Ana pounced. She drove her instep into Vergara's groin where he lay, pivoted sideways, and smashed a heel into his throat. As he writhed and tried to bring his pistol up, she kicked it from his feeble grasp. Lunging onto him, she clutched his throat in a death grip, just a few pounds of pressure away from crushing his windpipe.

Think, Ana. If you kill this man, you will be Ana Montilla forever. Show mercy and he could come for you again. Choose, Ana. Choose carefully.

In one smooth, tornadic move, she spun, grabbed the steak knife from the table, dropped to her knees, and plunged it into Vergara's shoulder.

His scream was excruciating.

"I won't kill you." She twisted the knife to ensure his surrender. "Not this time."

Vergara's face was a mask of pain—eyes wide, mouth open for a scream that curdled the air. His hands snapped up to pull the knife from his flesh but she extracted it, rolled away, and picked up his fallen pistol. Still, he struggled to a knee to fight back, but she cracked the pistol across his temple and knocked him onto the patio floor again, unconscious.

"No one move." Trane charged from the house onto the patio with his weapon drawn. "Ana, are you all right?"

"Trane?" she said, confused. "What are you doing here?"

"It's complicated." He knelt to examine Vergara. "Are you and

Sarah okay?"

"I think so." She scooped Sarah up and hugged her tightly. "Are you okay, little one?"

"Uh-huh, Aunty." Sarah was shaking, her eyes big and round, and she buried her face in Ana's embrace. "That man was going to hurt me."

"No. I would never let him do that," Ana said. "You're fine, Sarah. It's time to be tough like before—like in Cabrera. Can you do that?"

"Yes, she can." Poppi stepped away from William and held her hands out to take Sarah. "Come here, Sarah. It is all right now."

Ana held tight to Sarah, ignoring Poppi's outstretched hands. She whispered to the child, "Can you be tough? You are, aren't you?"

"I think so. I'll try." Sarah sniffled a couple of times and wiped her eyes. Then she looked closer at Trane as a big, wide smile blossomed. "You're the man who found us." She twisted around and pointed at Vergara on the ground. "When this bad man hurt Aunty Ana. Did you come to save us again?"

"Hello, Sarah. Yes, I'm that man." Trane touched Sarah's cheek and wiped a trail of tears away. "But Sarah, I didn't need to save you this time. Your aunty saved you just like always."

"I know." Sarah hugged Ana again. "She's tough."

William moved closer to Poppi again. "Who is this man, Ana? What is this really about?"

"It's about me, William," Ana said in a quiet voice. "It's about Mamá and Pappa, too."

Poppi's face fell. "Yes, of course it is."

Ana faced Trane. "What are you doing here, Trane? I don't understand…about Vergara?"

"Neither do I. But I'm working on that." He slipped a cell phone out of his pocket and held it up for her to see. "This is the phone you took off Tomãs at your house. We just checked it."

She shrugged. "Okay."

"We found something." Trane moved to the patio table and faced William and Poppi. "We recovered its calling history. It was one of Vergara's burner-phones from the brownstone. It looks like they only used it when they came to the States. Just like they did a couple months back."

Poppi and William exchanged uneasy glances.

"We reconstructed all the calls for the past year." Trane still had his pistol out and held low against his side. "Several of the calls made to this phone were from here, Ana."

Here? Yes, of course…William.

"Do you understand?" Trane asked.

"Yes, I understand." Ana sat Sarah in an empty chair beside her and thrust a finger at William. "What have you done?"

William's face blanched. "No. No. That's not right."

Trane went on. "There's several from about three months ago and then several from this month alone."

"William?" She slammed a palm onto the patio table. "I want to hear you say it. You betrayed me to Vergara."

"No, Ana," Trane said, "the calls were with your grandmother's cell phone."

What? Yiayia? No. Not her. That has *to be wrong.*

For a moment, Ana and Poppi's eyes locked together. Ana's demanding an explanation. Poppi's seeking an escape.

"Yiayia?"

Poppi clung to William's hand. Then, she stood, looking from Ana to William and back. "You don't understand, Ana."

"Understand what?"

"Any of it." Poppi's eyes poured. "I had no choice."

"No choice? How did you have no choice but to betray me?"

"It was your father, Ana." Poppi eased around William and tried to approach Ana, but stopped when she lifted Vergara's pistol. She stared at the gun, but Ana refused to lower it. "It was because of him. That bastard caused all this."

"Pappa is no bastard, Poppi. The evil one was Mamá."

"Listen to me," Poppi pleaded. "Colonel Vergara contacted me a couple months ago. They captured Irena in the jungle while looking for your father. They didn't want her. They wanted Manuel. They wanted him to help find that Hemingway person. If I helped find your father, then they would release Irena. That's all they wanted. Trade Irena for Hemingway."

"Lies. All lies." Ana's heart nearly stopped. "You told Vergara where I was in Colombia. That is how he knew I was in Cabrera. It was you who nearly got me killed."

"It wasn't like that. Can't you see?" Poppi said. "I was trying to save my Irena. She called me and begged me to help or they'd kill her."

"Mamá was no hostage. She was one of them. She tried to kill me herself."

"I don't believe that. My Irena would never—"

"First, she had me kidnapped in Mexico. Then, she tried to trick me into betraying Pappa to the Cubans. When that failed, she left me with them—left me for dead...*twice*."

Ana's eyes were a collage of sadness and rage as she recounted finding her mother in Nuevo Laredo—a story she hadn't yet shared with anyone but Trane—and of the last moments along Highway 1, when Irena tried to kill her. It was a difficult, pointed tale, but it left Poppi sobbing and William wide-eyed and astounded.

"It wasn't her fault." Poppi's face was twisted and defiant. "She only did it because of your father, Ana, he—"

"It was Mamá. It was always Mamá. She was the FARC guerrilla. Not Pappa. She was the Cuban agent. Not Pappa. She was the one who demanded I return each year. She demanded I become a fighter. It was her—your daughter—who was the terrorist. Pappa wanted me out of the camps, away from FARC, and back here. It was always her, Poppi. She tried to kill me—to destroy me a second time."

Poppi's face fell with despair. "It cannot be. Not my Irena."

***

October 2, 2009, Late Evening–A Small Village, Antioquia Department, Colombia

"*She cannot stay here, Irena.*" Pappa's voice was stern and unwavering. "*She's a young woman and needs an education. These camps are not for her. She needs a life. She is better than all this.*"

Mamá wasn't having it. "She will get all the education she needs here. If you want, send her to Havana for more. But she won't learn anything with her grandmother except distaste for us and what we do."

Ana looked down the desolate street, hoping the bus to Bogota would arrive soon and defuse the argument. "Mamá, I want to go. I'll come back. I promise."

"No, Ana," Pappa said, "never come back. Stay away from this place."

"Shut up, Manuel," Mamá snapped, pushing him away. "She is weak, like you."

"Irena, listen to her." Pappa held his arm tightly around her. "You of all people should understand she needs to return home, Irena. Look what you've become. I came to treat the sick. I have lost the taste for the other—the fighting and the blood. You…you seem to thrive on it."

"Stick to your patients, Manuel. I'll stick to my beliefs."

Ana reached for her mother's hand, but Irena pulled away. "Mamá, I'll come back after school. I promise. I'll come back to visit."

"No." Irena turned away. "If you go, Ana. You stay away. There won't be a place for you here again. You have disappointed me."

"Mamá," Ana cried. "It's just a couple of years. I only want—"

"This is because of him, isn't it? Because of Tommy?"

Ana's eyes filled with loss. "Tommy? Why would you say that?"

"Do you think I didn't know about you two? Do you think I didn't know about the letters and your secret trysts? I sent you to that school for information, not to be his whore."

Ana was horrified. "Don't talk about him…."

"I knew this would happen. I knew he filled your head with rubbish to take you away. You are a disappointment, Ana. Go. Don't look back. Don't come back. You're my daughter no more. I knew that bastard Tommy would ruin you. I should have killed him sooner."

***

Present Day, William Tillson's Estate, Western New Jersey

"Mamá told you the lie that she knew you'd believe: Pappa was evil and she was the victim." Ana took Sarah's hand as the child slid from the chair. "For that lie, I was nearly killed. Sarah was nearly killed, too."

The recognizing of truth slowly spread across Poppi's face. "Dear God, what have I done? They promised me—promised that if I helped find your father…. All I did was—"

"Betray me." Ana's thoughts reeled as she backed from the table, clutching Sarah. "You have broken my heart, Poppi."

Vergara moaned behind them and Trane returned to him, calling on his phone for assistance from his nearby operatives. "Take it easy, Colonel. You and I have a lot of talking to do. Save your strength."

"Trane?" Ana turned to him. "I must leave here."

"I came to get you both," he said softly. "I've made arrangements. There's a car out front, Ana. Get your things."

"Thank you."

William held up a hand. "Ana, I assure you that I had nothing to do with this. I—"

"No, William," Ana snapped. "I cannot be sure of you. Never again."

William took a step toward her but Trane blocked him. "Save it, William. She's going with me."

"Ana, please don't go." Poppi reached for Sarah, but Ana lifted her pistol and stopped her. "Really, Ana? You raise a gun to me over your father? You could kill me…"

"No, Poppi." Ana backed toward the house with Sarah beside her. "Because to me—and to my Sarah—you're already dead."

69

June 29, Dawn–Undisclosed Safe House in Eastern Pennsylvania

Trane watched the three black SUVs driving toward him along the long, dirt road. A cloud of dust swirled around them that he'd seen even before the vehicles had come into view. When they were still several hundred yards away, he lazily poured his cup of coffee over the stone house's porch railing and sat back in the rocking chair, like a farmer watching the sunrise. Beside him, resting against a stack of firewood, was an M4 rifle with a fresh thirty-round magazine inserted; a round was chambered and readied.

Trane did not suffer fools intentionally.

The first SUV drove off the road and circled around behind the house. The second waited at the end of his private drive—a short gravel entrance to the historic Dutch home. The third pulled to a stop, facing him.

On cue, twelve doors opened and as many armed commandos rolled out and surrounded the house.

Trane stood and waved at McLaren who climbed out of the closest SUV and walked toward him. Then, he casually picked up the M4 and slung it over his head, resting it across his chest.

He called out, "I didn't think you were such a morning person, McLaren."

"There's a lot you don't know about me, Trane."

Trane smirked. "Not anymore."

McLaren gestured to Trane's rifle and stopped ten feet away. "Why don't you put that down. All is well."

"You must have gotten up pretty early to drive all the way here."

"I had to hunt for this place, Trane." McLaren waved in the air and two of his commandos moved up and flanked Trane, facing him. "You violated protocol by not reporting this safe house. But I'll overlook that."

"Did I? It was an oversight. Sort of like Colonel Vergara not dying at the Caverns was an oversight."

"That part of the operation was classified over your head."

"Uh-huh. Right."

"Where's Reyes and Karras and the kids?" McLaren asked.

"Somewhere else." Trane made eye contact with the six commandos, one at a time, before turning back to McLaren. "I decided we should talk first."

"You decided? They're here. Get them, Trane. I'm taking them in for debriefing." McLaren gestured to the man closest to Trane. "Robertson, search the house."

Robertson, the team leader, started forward.

"No." Trane let the M4 rise a few inches without bringing it to a shooting position. "No one goes in. Especially you, Robertson. You stay right where you are. You need to hear all this anyway."

Robertson stopped and turned to McLaren for orders.

"What are you doing, Trane?" McLaren demanded. "Get out of the way. You work for me."

Trane lifted the rifle another inch and Robertson stepped back.

"Sweet Jesus, Trane," McLaren blustered. "It's only for debriefing. Trust me."

"Trust you? You're going to debrief a seven-year-old? About what, Scooby and the gang?"

"You're pushing things too far. I want them now. I let you have your way with Cannon and Danny. That doesn't mean—"

"You're going to execute them, McLaren. We all know that." He glanced at the semi-circle of commandos watching him. "You guys in on this? You're going to kill a little girl and her mother? A little boy and his mother? Follow those orders and your families might be next—just to keep you quiet, too. Where does it end?"

Robertson looked at his men. Some subliminal discussion ensued between them before he turned to McLaren, shook his head, and retreated back in line with the others.

"Look, Trane. Orders are orders. You were told to clean this up and you didn't." McLaren stepped closer. "So, I am. It's not your responsibility any longer. Move the hell out of the way and I'll finish this."

He shook his head.

"Take him," McLaren ordered.

None of the commandos moved.

"Loyalty is a funny thing, McLaren. It tends not to follow betrayal." Trane slipped his cell phone out and speed dialed a number. "Transfer."

McLaren watched him, seething. "I'm going to have your ass."

A few seconds later, a text message pinged onto Trane's phone: *Transfer complete, minus my fee. He only had 23-mill left from Afghanistan until someone deposited a nice little bundle ten days ago—untraceable. I tried. He's up 23.5 mill. He'll be hearing shortly, XXOO, Rodin.*

On cue, McLaren's cell vibrated. He took it out, read a text message from his Cayman Island bank, and frantically tapped a reply. A few seconds later, the next reply he received sent him ranting.

"Trane, you bastard. What do you think you're doing?"

"Taking out a little insurance policy, *Alex.*" He grinned. "I just made a twenty-three-million-dollar premium payment. Well, minus banking fees, of course. You spent two million already? Damn, you've been having fun with that Afghan loot, haven't you?"

"This won't solve anything." McLaren started toward him but Trane's finger slipped inside his rifle's trigger guard and stopped him cold. "So what? You have twenty-three million—"

"Actually, twenty-three-point-five; minus thirty thousand in fees. The Cubans pay pretty good for turning the other cheek."

"Screw you. You have a pile of money. It means nothing," McLaren scoffed. "Keep it. And if you won't handle Reyes and Karras, I'll get someone else to do it. Then, you can explain to Langley why you have twenty-three million. Who do you think they'll believe?"

"You're not really getting this, are you?" Trane laughed. "I transferred the money to Langley. Well, most of it anyway."

"Bullshit."

"Believe it. I had a meeting with the DDO at Langley last night via satellite. He was most interested in my report. And he was very agreeable to my minor withdrawals on the money for Ana and Cat's operating expenses, too. I promised him the balance of funds this morning after I proved my last point about you."

"Your last point?" McLaren's teeth ground. "What's that mean?"

Trane narrowed his eyes on him. "That you were gonna cover your Cuban connections and make Ana, Cat, and their two kids disappear. And by disappear, I mean kill. He gave me some slack with you and…here you are. All wrapped up in a bow. You tied the knot yourself."

"You're a liar."

Trane grinned.

"You'll go down, too, Trane. The way you handled the vice president. A heart attack? Sending our team into Nuevo Laredo for a busload of illegals? You'll be—"

"I'll be nothing." Trane moved closer to McLaren, jammed his finger into his chest, and pushed him backward. "The Deputy Director was very keen on the paper trail Rodin found on your bank account. I'm just waiting for his next order."

McLaren stared. His face paled as panic set in. "What next order? Do you really think he's got the guts to order you to kill me? I'll be in his office with a totally different spin on this by lunch."

"I wouldn't plan on that, McLaren."

Trane's phone vibrated and he lifted it, read the message, and walked over to Robertson. "Call up Langley Command on the SAT phone. So you know, I have my instructions as to what to do with you if you even hesitate."

Robertson considered him. "What's going on, Trane?"

"Call Langley."

Robertson walked to the lead SUV and slipped inside. He was gone only a moment. When he returned, he was listening intently to his earbud satellite communications link. "Yes, sir. Understood."

Robertson walked over to two of his men for a quiet, private conversation.

"What's going on?" McLaren demanded, but when Robertson didn't respond, he added, "Think carefully, Robertson, about what side you're on."

"There's only one, sir," Robertson said, and gestured to the two other commandos. "Take him into custody."

"Wait, what?" McLaren's face reddened as the two commandos grabbed his arms and quickly flex-tied them behind his back. "Trane, this is gonna cost you more than you know."

"Bill me." Trane forced a laugh. As Robertson's men stuffed McLaren into the back seat of the lead SUV, Trane said, "Robertson, you'll be under UAV surveillance all the way back to DC. I'd get going. Oh, and don't do anything stupid. No pee-stops, either."

"Yes, sir," Robertson said. He waved his men back toward the SUVs. "No worries, Trane. You can trust me."

"No, I can't."

The commandos hesitated, looked to Trane for approval, and after his nod, all retreated. A moment later, all three vehicles drove around the house, like Indians circling a wagon train, slowed at the drive entrance, then headed back down the road and out of sight.

Trane took a long breath. "Damn, that went better than I expected."

70

June 29, Early Evening–Rough and Ready, Pennsylvania

Ana stood with Trane beside the Suburban. They were parked along the lonely, dusty road that hadn't seen tractors or farmers for decades. Ahead, a new Jeep waited with its engine running and lights off. Behind it, a large trailer in tow.

She was terrified and happy at the same time.

"You know how to reach me?" Trane asked. "You understand the check-ins and contact instructions?"

"Of course." Ana smiled. "What about you, Mr. Trane?"

"It's just Trane."

"Not Choo Choo?" She giggled, a sound she hadn't made in a long time. "What will happen to you? What about McLaren?"

"Don't worry about him," Trane assured her. "He'll leave you alone."

"Are you sure?"

"Yeah, he's got his own problems."

"Oh?" She glanced back at the Jeep waiting for her. "He's dangerous, isn't he?"

"Not anymore." He went to the rear of the Suburban, opened the hatch, and pulled out her heavy, black canvas duffel. He handed it to her. "Here's a little going-away gift. A half-mill from Colonel

Vergara and a half-mill from McLaren. This ought to get you and your new family settled."

"A million dollars?" She considered the duffel. "What about the Cubans? They'll want their money back. I can't—"

"The Cubans won't want it from you. I dangled a message for them to find via my guy, Rodin. It will lead them to believe Vergara defected with their loot. Havana will not be very happy."

"I don't know what to say." She smiled and subconsciously touched the scar on her neck. She looked away and frowned.

"Ana? Is there something else?"

"I should have killed Vergara. He'll hunt me again."

"No, he won't. We've got him now—for good. He's talking a blue streak."

"I see." She looked back at him with doubt filling her eyes. "I don't want to be Ana Montilla ever again. Is that possible?"

"That's up to you." He grinned. "But I think she's pretty handy to have around now and then. Don't you?"

Yes, she is. "What of Catalina and Mateo? Are they…"

"They're fine. I have them somewhere safe; trust me."

"I do." She hesitated a moment, then added, "In the end, we became close, you know. I'd like to stay in touch, if that's possible."

"Somehow, I thought you would." Trane grinned. "I've set up a secure email exchange. Only for you two." He gave her the instructions and had her repeat them back. "It's untraceable and safe. There are rules, Ana, and it'll be monitored for security reasons. No disclosing your locations or discussing what's happened these past weeks. Ever. Got that?"

She nodded. "I understand. I do. Thank you."

"You're welcome." His grin widened. "Like I said, McLaren used to have a lot of money. They'll be well taken care of."

"Good to know."

"Oh, and you should know something else. I've checked out William Tillson. I didn't find any links between him and the Cubans—nothing. I think he was in the dark about all this."

"Perhaps." Ana hung her head for a moment. "If he was, then he's not a very good intelligence man, is he?"

"No, I guess not." Trane gestured to the duffel. "Those papers you wanted are all in there. Everything."

"And my father?"

Trane shrugged. "We're looking. But in Mexico, it's tough."

"If you find him, please bring him safely to me."

"And your mother?" He hesitated, then said, "The Mexican government got to the wreckage first. We let it lie. There's no telling…."

"Irena Montilla is dead."

"You don't know that."

Indeed, she didn't know for sure. Irena Montilla had committed the ultimate betrayal. She had tried to leave her to die in Oso's compound and then tried to kill her on the highway. Never would she have imagined such animus from her—not even as a Cuban agent or FARC guerrilla. Never.

"Either way, Trane, perhaps it's better if you simply don't find her."

Trane touched her arm. "All right, Ana. I'll deal with it. Check your messages every day, okay? And stay away, Ana. Canon's death is being questioned—quietly, but still questioned. Don't take any chances. Stay far away."

"I will." Ana hefted the canvas bag, leaned into him, and kissed his cheek. "You're a good man, Trane."

"Sometimes."

As Trane turned to leave, Ana walked quickly to him. "Wait."

A surprise flashed in her eyes as she took something out of her jeans pocket and handed it to him. It was a child's plastic coin purse and inside were two aspirin sized pills. He weighed them in his hand and studied her, embarrassed.

"Damn, Ana. You didn't do it. I was sure…"

"I know." She kissed his cheek again. "You didn't turn me in. You didn't double-cross me. I wanted to know if I could trust you. I can."

"Yes, you can." He touched her cheek, waved at the Jeep, and climbed into his SUV. A moment later he was gone.

Ana walked to the Jeep as the rear driver's side door popped open and Sarah climbed out. She ran to her and flung herself into Ana's free arm.

"Aunty Ana, I—"

"I am not Aunty Ana, Sarah." Ana set her back on her feet and put a finger on Sarah's nose. "I'm your Mommy."

"Mommy?" Sarah's eyes glistened. "Did Mr. Tranc say it was okay?"

"Yes, and others did, too." She took Sarah's hand. "And you are now an official American citizen; I have a birth certificate to prove it. You are my daughter and I am your mommy. We're a family."

The driver's window rolled down and Brennan leaned out. "What about me?"

"What about you?" Ana eyed him. "What am I to do with a policeman?"

"Former policeman." He struggled to keep Lobo from escaping over him through the open window to reach Sarah. "Saving you got me fired, remember? I'm unemployed and destitute—well…kinda destitute. Somebody has to take care of me. I'm too good looking to be homeless."

"What do you think, Sarah?" Ana asked. "Should we take care of this strange man?"

"Mr. Luke?" Sarah grinned ear-to-ear. "Sure, Mommy. He makes me laugh. And he makes pancakes that look like a mouse."

"I guess we'll keep you, Luke from *Star Wars*." Ana gently grasped Brennan's arm resting on the open window, turned, and looked after Trane just driving out of sight. "You two are the only family I have left."

*

ACKNOWLEDGMENTS

This is my first book with Suspense Publishing and one of the best experiences I've had so far. Thank you so much to Shannon and John—and of course, Kimberley C—for making this happen. I'm honored to be in your company. Truly.

As always there are a few special friends who helped me along the way—and encouraged me when I needed it most: Jean and Rail for always kicking me in the butt to keep writing (and making dinner); Nicci for editing and listening to my constant story plots and "I wonder if's;" Terri B and Stephanie F for edits and reviews; Laurie for giving me the time to write and constant edits and of course, for encouragement to make dinner in between; and for those who will understand, for Toby—my gone-but-not-forgotten Lab companion—who was forever under my desk keeping me company and willing to be paid in cookies.

There are a few new ones this book around, too: Mike P. for suggestions and plot points on the real stuff; Scott S. for a little aviation info early on; Mike F. for his spin on trains, planes, and Cuba; Kelly D. for the translations and geography help; Robert T. for being a fan, marketeer, friend, and generally being there when I needed (and I don't think he knows that).

For Greg O—for letting Jan be my friend, critic, and stepmom. Your loss is my loss. Different. The same. Hang tough, brother. Jan, you're missed.

ABOUT THE AUTHOR

Tj O'Connor is the author of *The Hemingway Deception*, *Dying with a Secret* (pending publication), *The Consultant* from Oceanview Publishing, and four paranormal mysteries from Midnight Ink and Black Opal Books.

Tj is an international security consultant specializing in anti-terrorism, investigations, and threat analysis—life experiences that drive his novels. With his former life as a government agent and years as a consultant, he has lived and worked around the world in places like Greece, Turkey, Italy, Germany, the United Kingdom, and throughout the Americas—among others. He was raised in New York's Hudson Valley and lives with his wife and Labrador companions in Virginia where they raised five children.

Learn more at: www.tjoconnor.com.

n the USA
nformation can be obtained
CGtesting.com
20832091223
3LV00065B/1205

9 798218 103323